More praise for *Sally Hemings*

"An act of great daring ... Deeply moving."
—*Chicago Sun-Times*

"We believe in Sally Hemings from the moment we first [meet] her. ... We believe in her elegant instincts, her well-turned speech, her continuing beauty."
—*The New York Times*

"*Sally Hemings* is noble and mysterious—a female cult object."
—Mary McCarthy

"*Sally Hemings* is an achievement, that rare novel that takes us far beyond mundane levels of reality and fabrication to a new vision of a much-repressed part of our history ... Beautifully written."
—*The Washington Star*

Sally Hemings

A NOVEL

Barbara Chase-Riboud

Ballantine Books • New York

ISBN: 0-345-38971-9

Cover design by Richard Hasselberger
Cover illustration by Stanislaw Fernandes

Manufactured in the United States of America

First Ballantine Books Edition: October 1994

To the enigma of the historical Sally Hemings
and to Thenia Hemings (1799–1802)

That God forbid that made me first your slave,
I should in thought control your times of pleasure,
Or at your hand the account of hours to crave . . .
                              WILLIAM SHAKESPEARE

Records are destroyed. Histories are annihilated, or interpolated, or prohibited. Sometimes by popes, sometimes by emperors,
sometimes by aristocratic and sometimes by
democratic assemblies, . . . such had been
and such is the world we live in. . . .
                              JOHN ADAMS

Contents

AUTHOR'S NOTE

There are documents included in this novel which are not only authentic, they are central to the story of Sally Hemings and Thomas Jefferson. These documents are like the sea on which their small and private boat sailed.

BCR

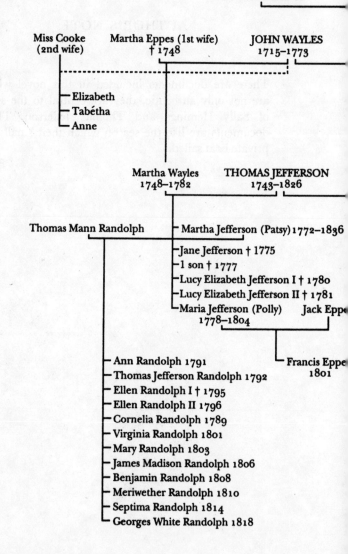

White Family

CAPTAIN HEMINGS

Miss Cooke (2nd wife)   Martha Eppes (1st wife) † 1748   JOHN WAYLES 1715–1773

- Elizabeth
- Tabétha
- Anne

Martha Wayles 1748–1782   THOMAS JEFFERSON 1743–1826

Thomas Mann Randolph   ⌐ Martha Jefferson (Patsy) 1772–1836

- Jane Jefferson † 1775
- 1 son † 1777
- Lucy Elizabeth Jefferson I † 1780
- Lucy Elizabeth Jefferson II † 1781
- Maria Jefferson (Polly) 1778–1804   Jack Epp

- Francis Eppe 1801

- Ann Randolph 1791
- Thomas Jefferson Randolph 1792
- Ellen Randolph I † 1795
- Ellen Randolph II 1796
- Cornelia Randolph 1789
- Virginia Randolph 1801
- Mary Randolph 1803
- James Madison Randolph 1806
- Benjamin Randolph 1808
- Meriwether Randolph 1810
- Septima Randolph 1814
- Georges White Randolph 1818

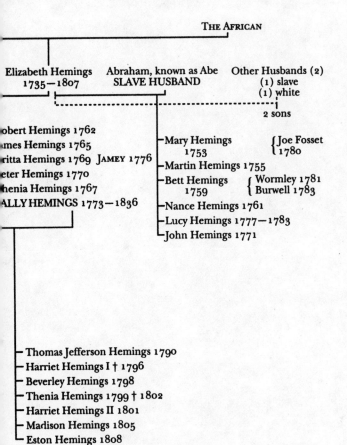

Black Family

THE AFRICAN

Elizabeth Hemings
1735—1807

Abraham, known as Abe
SLAVE HUSBAND

Other Husbands (2)
(1) slave
(1) white
2 sons

obert Hemings 1762
mes Hemings 1765
ritta Hemings 1769 JAMEY 1776
eter Hemings 1770
henia Hemings 1767
ALLY HEMINGS 1773—1836

Mary Hemings
1753
Martin Hemings 1755
Bett Hemings
1759
Nance Hemings 1761
Lucy Hemings 1777—1783
John Hemings 1771

{ Joe Fosset
  1780

{ Wormley 1781
  Burwell 1783

Thomas Jefferson Hemings 1790
Harriet Hemings I † 1796
Beverley Hemings 1798
Thenia Hemings 1799 † 1802
Harriet Hemings II 1801
Madison Hemings 1805
Eston Hemings 1808

PART I

1830
Albemarle
County

ALBEMARLE COUNTY, 1830

It is difficult to determine on the standard by which the manners of a nation may be tried, whether *catholic*, or *particular*. It is more difficult for a native to bring to that standard the manners of his own nation, familiarized to him by habit. There must doubtless be an unhappy influence on the manners of our people produced by the existence of slavery among us.

THOMAS JEFFERSON, *Notes on the State of Virginia*, 1790

THERE WAS a white man coming up her road, as if God had ordained it and as if he owned the road.

The woman standing in the dark square of the cabin doorway knew that this was the way white men arrived. Anyway, no slave would be driving a carriage unaccompanied. And the only freedmen for miles around were her sons, Madison and Eston. She never thought of herself as free, and now, at fifty-six, with her sons waiting politely for her to die so that they could move West (why was she so stubborn about it?), she was fixed in another time and space, belonging to another epoch, an epoch which had ended for her on the Fourth of July, 1826, four years gone.

The cabin in which she stood was the most beggarly habitation for miles around. The land surrounding it was cotton-exhausted and impossible to work. Yet they worked it, her sons, with a furor and a wrenching desperation, although it was not even theirs. Freed slaves could not own land in Virginia. It was rented; expensive and worthless—eroded, hilly, evil. The cabin leaned into its own decay. Backed as it was against the boundaries of the once-famous plantation of Monticello, it too now strangled in its own undergrowth.

The carriage was approaching, the iron wheels grinding against the deep ruts of the ill-kept road. She could see that it was not really a carriage but a buckboard. And what she had thought to be horses were really a very pretty pair of matched beige-and-brown mules, fat and glossy. Her eyes followed the advance of the little buckboard without surprise, as if the event that was to take place had already been explained to her, as if she knew who would be arriving in such splendor at an ex-slave's cabin door.

Actually her eyes were never surprised. They were eyes of a deep amber yellow, mark of a quadroon, which gave her whole face an illusion of transparency. Eyes that were liquid gold in an ivory mask; windows onto banked and mysterious fires that burned day and night, absorbing everything and returning nothing to the surface. The skin was drawn, but smooth. There was no way to tell her age; neither in the lines of her face nor the contours of her body—which was small and low, compact and strong, with that wiry vivacity of congenital thinness. Her head was bound in a white cloth that darkened the skin and set off the pale and beautiful mouth with its two deep dimples on either side. In her ears dangled small ruby earrings, like tiny drops of blood, incongruous next to the faded rough black-linen dress and its black apron. She was still in mourning. Her hands, which were hidden in the folds of her apron, were small, soft, and slender, unmarked by hard labor.

The buckboard had stopped at the bottom of the orchard. The man had gotten out and was making his way up the steep path to her door. As she watched the approaching stranger, her expression changed swiftly from curiosity to anger to apprehension. There were only two reasons for a white man to be coming to the cabin: either he was the census taker from the Albemarle County Courthouse or the sheriff with an eviction notice. Either would ask the same questions: her name, her age, and if she were slave or free. Well, everybody in Albemarle County, every Tidewater family for fifty miles around, knew her name; how many children she had, and by whom; knew too that as a manumitted slave she had no right by law to remain in Virginia—unless she had been granted a special dispensation from the Virginia legislature.

If the census taker, if that's who he was, had any sense at all, he wouldn't have had to come all the way up here in the afternoon heat to ask her what he undoubtedly already knew: if she was Sally Hemings of Monticello.

The slave mistress of Thomas Jefferson had been famous in Albemarle County for as long as he could remember. At least her name was famous. Few people had actually seen her and that was one of the reasons he was making his way slowly up this wretched road: to meet Sally Hemings face to face.

4

Not one person in a hundred would recognize "Dusky Sally" if they saw her, he concluded. She had seldom left Monticello in all her fifty years there, yet it seemed he had always heard her name. His father had known both her masters, John Wayles, the father, and Thomas Jefferson, the lover. Nathan Langdon, who was indeed the census taker for Albemarle County, smiled grimly. He was home. He was home in Virginia, with its passions, its blood feuds, its pride, its duels, its Southern honor. And glad of it. Even in the few weeks he had been back, the energy and efficiency of his affected Northern manner had disappeared like a lizard's skin. The heat, the languid pace of the tidy, beautiful mules, the lurch of the old-fashioned but elegant buggy, the reins softly caressing the palms of his hands, all gently contributed to make him feel at home. He settled his large frame into the cracked leather of the seat and raised his eyes to the little cabin sitting on the boundary between the wilderness of a ragged pine forest and the southernmost acres of Monticello. As he did he saw a childlike figure standing in the lopsided doorway. A woman. Sally Hemings. It must be. There were no other women out this way.

The shadowed figure in the doorway stood stock-still. Why was it that she could never control the dread and panic she felt at the approach of a white man? Any white man. A familiar uneasiness settled in her stomach. There had been only one white man she had ever welcomed. And he was dead and buried behind this cabin on his little mountain.

At least Madison and Eston were not home. If there was trouble, she preferred to face it alone. Facing down an angry white man was a black woman's job, not a black man's unless he was prepared to die. But then this man just might be the census taker Madison had spoken about the other day.

She felt a strange calm. The sheriff would have an eviction notice, if he had anything, and a writ to run them out of the State of Virginia— which would suit her sons just fine, if they could leave peaceably.

Sally Hemings knew her presence in Virginia and that of her sons depended on the will and whim of her niece, Martha Jefferson Randolph. It was Martha who had manumitted her, and it was Martha who had persuaded her friends in the legislature to allow her to stay. Her life here depended on Martha, and Martha depended on her silence. Both had their reasons. So be it. They both had reasons to keep silent— reasons that would die with them. It was against the law for a freed slave

5

to remain in Virginia more than a year and a day from the date of emancipation. The slave risked being sold back into slavery.

But she would die in Virginia, at Monticello, God willing, and not in some desert scalped by wild Indians. Madison and Eston were young and healthy. The West was their only chance; but she would finish her days here. Her sons would simply have to wait. It wouldn't be all that long.

The white man was approaching on foot. Weaving in and out of her apple orchards, the sun to his back. The pretty mules, shimmering in the heat, were stopped quietly at the bottom of the pathway. Sally Hemings heard the flutter of her chickens at roost in their pen, and felt the sun on her eyelids as she closed them against the glare.

Nathan Langdon had practically forgotten his fascination with Sally Hemings as he made his way toward the cabin. The strange destiny of Sally Hemings seemed less urgent to ponder than his own future, now that he was back.

His job as census taker would last only through the summer. He had to do it while helping to run Broadhurst. He was the heir now; his older brother, his father's favorite, was dead, a hole blown through him at point-blank range. His father was grief-stricken, unable to take even the most meager duties on his shoulders.

There had been relief and gratitude when he had announced that he would stay at home and marry. Esmeralda Wilks was rich and temperamental, and she had let him know in no uncertain terms that she was tired of waiting. It was her family who had gotten him his temporary job as census taker until he could finish his studies and pass his bar examinations. He had thought about politics as well; but not only was he too "radical" for this county, he would also be in competition with his brothers and brothers-in-law. Still, he could consider this appointment as a first "political" step to bigger and better things. He would apprentice himself to Judge Miner in Charlottesville, see more of Esmeralda, comfort his father, and run Broadhurst. At least he was rid of the necessity of forever explaining himself, his family, and his state—to say nothing of the entire South—to Northern friends, acquaintances, and reformers. One thing he never wanted to explain again was the Institution of Slavery. He could give a lecture, in his sleep, on this subject. He never again intended to endure Northerners and their impertinent questions, the sententiousness of their comments, the insulting familiarity of the exchanges.

He had managed, after years of arguments, to convince his closest Northern friends that a Virginian did not automatically own "thousands of slaves," and that he did not starve and beat the ones he had; that Negroes bred in nine months like everybody else, and that neither he nor his servants had tails, two heads, indolent or oversexed dispositions.

He always felt a general outrage that these ignoramuses could so presume on his private life and that of his kin and his native territory. Sooner or later their curiosity would get the better of their manners, and they apparently found it quite natural to ask the most unwarranted and intimate questions of a total stranger, one they considered the "expert" Southerner. They would never dream of asking such questions of their own family or class. Owning Negroes seemed to them to be a license for all kinds of forwardness.

What's more, they never seemed to be satisfied. There had always been "just one thing more I wanted to ask you." And these Northerners, he thought furiously, had been his friends. The well-bred and aristocratic sons of gentlemen and capitalists. Yet their greed for information about the South, and their fascination with slavery, knew no bounds. What had fascinated them most, especially the ladies, was not the economics, the humanity, or the Christianity of the Institution, but sex. Langdon's mouth tightened in exasperation. The only thing they really wanted to know about was the sex life of the Southern aristocrat and his slaves. They had all heard of the thousands of New Orleans octoroons, the dashing Washington mulattoes, the plantation quadroons, sometimes sired by the sons' fathers, and overseers of slave-owning families. Cross-breeding was something one didn't discuss in polite society. One didn't discuss it at all, even in the intimacy of one's private journal. It was something one relegated to that corner of the mind reserved for incest, insanity, epilepsy, suicide, and sodomy; it was sordid and unthinkable. He had never been able to explain to these morose Northerners the particular combination of cruelty and affection, detachment and possessiveness that made up the relationship between master and servant, a relationship all the more complex and intense if they were blood kin. How could he ever explain it to them? True, white men had begot and freed sons, even daughters, but the basic rule of this charged and intimate correspondence was that there

7

was a superior and an inferior race, and to intermingle them was an error against God, Nature, and Society. No matter how many mulattoes, quadroons, octoroons, métis issued from lust or passion. He also knew that freed slaves were not allowed to remain in Virginia. Why were the Hemingses so privileged? Who had petitioned the Virginia Legislature for special permission for them to stay? And why? Or did they remain without official permission? How was it possible that, at the pinnacle of his power, Thomas Jefferson had chosen a slave when he could have chosen any white woman alive!

His heavy shoulders moved uncomfortably in the loose woolen jacket. He was not dressed for the heat. His thoughts had taken him far away, so that he was startled to find himself looking at the most beautiful woman he had ever seen, a woman old enough and fair enough to be his mother. It can't be, he thought wildly, unnerved by her physical beauty.

The woman was indeed beautiful. The face was unlined, the gaze fragile but unyielding. The eyes were almost emerald in the bluish shadow. The mouth was soft and childish in its contours, and vain. The body was well proportioned. She had removed the white cloth and her hair seemed to glow like a silk cap, the braid coiled around her head breaking into planes of light.

No sound came from the dark recess, and Nathan Langdon struggled to find a way of addressing this woman. How did one address a creature who did not exist, who was the negation of everything he had been taught to believe? There were no white slaves. There could be no white ex-slaves. There were no women who looked like this, who lived in a Negro cabin at the end of a dusty, weed-choked footpath out of time and memory, who had been loved by a great man who had never freed her. The smell of poverty and cooking hung in the interior. The woman's dress and apron were of poor-quality black linen, faded to gray and without trimmings. A window in the room let in the afternoon light, silhouetting this figure who neither moved nor spoke.

Finally, he said, "You are? . . ."

"Sally Hemings." The voice was crisp and clear. "Are you the census taker for the county my son spoke of?"

"Yes, Ma'am. Nathan Langdon, at your service."

The simplest words seemed to explode into the atmosphere. Langdon caught his breath as the woman emerged gently from the shadow of the room into the light. In the brightness, her eyes assumed their true color, fringed with thick black lashes and by heavy eyebrows. The nose was slightly flared, the cheekbones abnormally high, the eyes wide-spaced. There were streaks of gray in the fine black hair, which, if loosened, would doubtless have reached her waist.

"You live here with your sons Eston and Madison?"

"Yes."

"Ages?"

"Mine?"

"Yours first, Ma'am, then your sons'."

"Fifty-six. My son Eston is twenty-two and Madison is twenty-five."

"All born in Albemarle County?"

"At Monticello."

"You are manumitted slaves, are you not? Do you have a special dispensation to remain in Virginia?"

"Yes."

"Former slaves of Martha Jefferson Randolph?"

"Of Thomas Jefferson. My sons were freed by his will in 1826."

"And you?"

"The same year."

"This cabin and land, the property of?"

"Cornelius Stooker of Charlottesville."

"Land?"

"Twelve acres."

"Yearly rent?"

"Two bales of cotton and seven bushels of corn."

"The professions of your sons?"

"Musicians . . ."

Nathan Langdon raised his eyebrows. "They farm the land as well?"

"Yes."

"No other adults living here?"

"No."

"Total?"

"Total?"

"That is, there are three adults and no children in residence, am I correct?"

"Yes, that's right."

"Other members of your family not living at home?"

"What?"

"You have other children, do you not?"

9

"They are listed as runaways in the Monticello Farm Book."

"How many?"

"Two—three."

"Three runaways?"

"Three."

"Five children in all?"

"Seven."

"Two deceased?"

"Yes."

"Are your sons at home?"

Sally Hemings hesitated. She was alone in the house and unprotected.

"They will be coming home shortly."

"Where are they?"

"At the university."

"Can they read?"

"Yes."

"Can you read?"

"Yes."

"Vote?" The question had come automatically to his lips. Now there was an embarrassed silence. Of course they couldn't vote. They weren't even supposed to know how to read and write. It was against the law. But then they were freed now, and there was no law saying freed slaves could not read and write. Or was there? He covered himself as best he could.

"Uh . . . property?" He flushed deeply. He was questioning her as if she were white. As if her sons were white farmers and musicians.

"Would you like a drink?" she asked suddenly. "Ginger beer, perhaps?"

"Thank you, Ma'am."

"Wait here. No. Come inside out of the sun. You have no hat on. It is finished, no?"

The strange involution of the sentence startled him. There was something foreign about her speech, as if she were thinking in a different language. It had no tremor of old age, but was delicious and young.

Nathan Langdon had to stoop to enter the somber cabin; quickly he took in the room. It was the most disconcerting interior he had ever seen. He had been in many slave and ex-slave cabins in the past weeks, so that he was not surprised by the simple handmade benches and tables, the rough plank floor, the whitewashed clay walls, the bits and pieces of hand-me-downs, broken, and repaired finery from the Big House, but as his stunned gaze took in the delicate cherrywood piano-forte, an exquisite onyx-and-bronze pendulum clock ticking away over the finely carved wooden chimney, the elegant dark-green leather chest with its brass fitting gleaming dully in the gloom, the French armchair, a huge ornate and gilded mirror, and, strangest of all, a French flag, a musket on which hung what looked like a small effigy or doll. He felt he had walked into the inner sanctum of some desperate and over-whelming mystery.

There was a large bouquet of fresh flowers, and on the floor lay a piece of black cloth, crumpled, as if discarded. In this incongruous setting, the light silhouetted the woman, and the effect was so intimate, so seductive, that Nathan Langdon instinctively took a step backward. As he did, his head almost hit the low doorframe, and Sally Hemings, in an unconscious, protective gesture, stepped forward.

"Please sit down."

"Thank you, Ma'am."

Even this invitation, so noncommittal, made Nathan blush.

"Your mules need water?"

"Why, I'd be much obliged." Langdon fell into the Southern formula for politeness. He had hardly used that term since his return. As Sally Hemings turned away from him, Langdon had the distinct impression that he recognized her; he knew he had seen this woman turn in that same way before. But where? He had lived four years in Massachusetts. It was five years since he had been in Charlottesville.

"But don't bother. . . . They'll be heading home now . . . this is my last visit."

Langdon had risen from his chair and followed her to the door, but she had already turned and was out of the cabin to fetch the water. Again, the same acute sense of recognition came back to him as the slender back disappeared into a shaded area not far from the house, where he supposed there was a well or a spring.

When she returned, she was carrying two buckets of water.

"You can take these down to those pretty mules of yours. If you'll be so kind as to leave the pails at the bend, my son Eston will see them and pick them up when he returns from work."

"I'm much obliged. Thank you. I'm sorry I missed seeing your sons, Ma'am."

"You must know them by sight. Pretty much everybody in town knows who they are. They work around the university."

"It's been a long time since I've been home. You see, I just arrived from the North not too long ago. I don't know much of what has been going on for the past four or five years . . . but now I'm staying to help my family."

"Oh, you a lawyer? You look like one."

"Not exactly yet, but shortly. I intend to finish my studies this year at the university. I've already spent four years studying up at Harvard."

"Many of those brick buildings—and the carpentry and windows and metal work—they were done by my brothers, Robert Hemings and John Hemings, for Master Jefferson when he started to build his school. Now Madison and Eston do a lot of repairing and additions, since they are the most familiar with the original work. You see . . ."

Her voice floated like silk scarves, sweeping and billowing the simple everyday language into a honeyed intimacy. He wondered whether she was, by nature, a talkative woman. Certainly many of his visits to the isolated farmhouses in Albemarle County had ended in long bouts of conversations with lonely farm women. Yes, he sensed a loneliness, a sadness here. Charmed, Langdon kept her talking, adding little bits of gossip he had picked up in town, explaining himself and his family to her (something he had done so often at Harvard it was by now second nature). He realized she knew a great deal about what went on in Tidewater. He had always remarked that the Negroes had a wonderful art of communicating among themselves. Information and gossip would run several hundred miles in a week; but where had she learned the art of conversation that would do justice to a lady in these backwoods?

They spoke late into the afternoon, the fair, blue-eyed youth and his mysterious hostess. He, with his feet planted solidly on the floor, hunched forward in his seat, elbows on knees, his large hands folded loosely in front of him. She, also leaning away from her chair, swayed slightly with the conversation, or suddenly propelled herself backward as her girlish laughter responded to some amusing tidbit of gossip. She knew everything and everybody, despite the fact she hadn't been near the town in years.

The lovely face glowed with the pleasure of unaccustomed male company. The pretty hands gesticulated, folded and unfolded, or moved to fondle a large oval locket that hung on a velvet ribbon around her neck—her only adornment except for the ruby earrings—but obviously a valuable and beautifully executed jewel.

Surely I'll have leave to come again after such a long conversation, thought Langdon. He tried to find more anecdotes and gossip to please her. Never in all his drawing-room experiences had he striven so hard to entertain a woman. When she laughed he was hopelessly flattered. Would her sons appear? Langdon wondered. He wanted to see what they looked like. Madison and Eston Hemings. Their names brought the reality of the outside world back to him. The pails of water stood like sentinels on each side of the door, unattended.

Piedmont, like the rest of Virginia, was caught up in the political and racial torment of the times, Nathan mused. Already, the distant thunder of the coming conflict could be heard if one cared to listen. Virginia had tightened its slave laws the past years, measures which invariably affected the freedmen as well. The large cities in the South, including Charlottesville and Richmond, were armed camps. There was the scent of violence in the air, and families were already divided on the slave issue. Tensions were high, and repressions against the black population had increased tenfold. It had been deemed a crime since 1814 to teach a slave to read. There were curfews as well as passports and grade-shotted cannon for those who didn't respect it. There were kidnappings and lynchings, and daily public whippings for even accidental infractions.

In this year alone more than seventeen resolutions concerning slavery had been introduced and debated in the House of Burgesses. The spread of slavery was fiercely fought state by state, territory by territory. A sinister stillness had taken hold of the soft, low-lying countryside from Williamsburg to Richmond. Wrapped in an unnatural suffocating calm, the elements seemed to be waiting for some sign.

Langdon finally gave up waiting for Eston and Madison. As the shadows lengthened, Sally Hemings gracefully brought the conversation to an end, and, before he knew it, he was out of the cabin and on his way down the footpath toward his buckboard and thirsty mules.

The census taker had spent all afternoon in her cabin. How strange, she thought, he had spoken to her as if she had been a white woman. She watched him disappear and reappear among her apple trees as he made his way toward his buggy carrying the two pails of water. She saw the tall figure emerge at the bend beyond the orchard, approach his mule team, and water them. Then he set down the pails and got into his buggy. She expected him to drive away, but he sat there for a long while. She watched him as the sun got lower in the sky and the silence broke with the beginnings of night sounds. Still he did not move. Maybe he's waiting for the boys. Maybe he has questions to ask Eston as the head of the family. But what could they be? Nobody was interested in their lives. A few dates in a Farm Book, a price in an account book, a bill of sale, a number in the ledgers of a census taker. No more. At least no more than she was telling.

Her silence was what had kept her alive and sane in this world where everything had been taken from her except these last two sons. And even they knew little about her life. Slaves revealed as little as possible about their origin and background to their children. It was an old trick. Not to speak was not to put into words the hopelessness of having no future and no past. But now, her sons had that future. It was only she who had none. And the past . . . what did she really feel about the past?

Sally Hemings continued to watch the census taker as he sat motionless in his wagon. Why could he not bring himself to drive away?

Nathan Langdon had descended the steep footpath leading away from the Hemings' cabin. He had felt the woman's eyes on him, felt the backward pull of her silence and her peculiar sadness. He could not rid himself of the feeling that once, before today, somewhere, he had seen her. He acknowledged an eerie recognition in their meeting. He smiled. Fate? Reincarnation? How many nights at Harvard had he spent discussing just such nonsense. He was an atheist, like Jefferson. No God could have a hand in anyone's affairs on this earth, for if He did, how could He make such a mess of things?

Monticello, he thought. It had to be Monticello. He had been in the mansion only once in his life, as a student when Jefferson was already a very old man. It must have been in '25, before he had left for Boston. A cousin of his had invited him to sit in the presence of the great man at dinner.

The memory was still vivid. The straight, thin, enormously tall man with the burning eyes and thick white hair, was pale and still freckled, though age had given his face a delicate transparency, and the famous voice had turned edgy and slightly petulant. Thomas Jefferson had dominated the dinner and the company of younger men with vast and brilliant monologues, virtuoso pieces almost like music, which were occasionally interrupted by sullen and inexplicable silences when his thoughts seemed to be elsewhere. But his rejoinders were always precise and to the point. He dearly loved a metaphor, an elegantly turned phrase, and had a genius for storytelling. People around the table spoke a little louder than normal, as is often the case with old people, but, so far as he knew, there had been nothing wrong with Jefferson's hearing or any of his faculties. Even then, at eighty, Thomas Jefferson was known to ride twenty or thirty miles a day. He, Langdon, had sat awed and silent while the conversation had ranged from the tobacco crop to Italian and French wines; the annexation of Cuba; the Monroe Doctrine; the Second Missouri Compromise; and the raging political struggle over the extension of slavery in Illinois.

At the end of the meal, over which his daughter Martha Randolph had presided, Jefferson had been taken with malaise, Langdon remembered. He had floundered in midsentence, gagged, and turned pale, then abruptly pushed back his chair, almost tipping it over. His daughter had quickly taken charge, and, with the help of one of the guests had led the old man from the table. As the company milled around the dining room, Langdon had glimpsed Jefferson being handed over to another woman, who had led him away. Sally Hemings? The small figure had been dwarfed by him; the small sleek head had not reached the stooped shoulders of the fainting man. He remembered, too, a fleeting glimpse of a coiled braid.

The picture was so sharp; it startled Langdon out of his reverie. He leaned down and absently stroked the warm living flesh of his mules, as if to bring himself back to the present. Then he got out his ledgers. He "knew" everyone in Albemarle County—by sex, age, religion, and occupation; by property, political party, race, and condition of servitude. But the two people he thought about at the moment didn't figure on his list.

One had been rich, famous, powerful, covered with honors, and years in the greatest office of the land, respected and loved. He was dead and buried. A permanent fixture in American history. The other had been a slave. A woman despised for her color and her caste; and yet still alive, and so had to be counted.

He opened to a new page in his ledger. If Sally Hemings was who and what people said she was, then Thomas Jefferson had broken the law of Virginia. A law punishable by fine and imprisonment. And he, Langdon, was an official of the United States government and a Virginian. He hesitated for a moment and then wrote:

Eston Hemings, Male, 22. Head of Family. Occupation: Musi-
cian. Race: White

Madison Hemings, Male 25. Occupation: Carpenter. Race:
White.

Sally Hemings, Female, between 50 and 60. Without occupation.
Race: White.

Whatever he thought of Thomas Jefferson, author of the Declaration
of Independence, third president of the United States, there was one
thing he, Nathan Langdon, was determined that Thomas Jefferson
would not be guilty of: the crime of miscegenation.

CHAPTER 2

MONTICELLO, 1815

The whole commerce between master and slave is a perpetual exercise of the most boisterous passions, the most unremitting despotism on the one part, and degrading submissions on the other. Our children see this, and learn to imitate it; for man is an imitative animal. This quality is the germ of all education in him. From his cradle to his grave he is learning to do what he sees others do. If a parent could find no motive either in his philanthropy or his self-love, for restraining the intemperance of passion towards his slave, it should always be a sufficient one that his child is present.

THOMAS JEFFERSON, *Notes on the State of Virginia*, 1790

MR. FRANCIS C. GRAY

March 4, 1815   *Monticello*

Sir,

You asked me in conversation, what constituted a mulatto by our law. And I believe I told you four crossings with the whites. I looked afterwards into our law, and found it to be in these words: "Every person, other than a Negro of whose grandfathers or grandmothers anyone shall have been a Negro, shall be deemed a mulatto, and so every such person who shall have one-fourth part or more of Negro blood, shall like manner be deemed a mulatto"; L. Virga 1792, December 17: the case put in the first member of this paragraph of the law is *exempli gratia*. The latter contains the true canon, which is that one-fourth of Negro blood, mixed with any portion of white, constitutes the mulatto. As the issue has one-half of the blood of each parent, and the blood of each of these may be made up of a variety of fractional mixtures, the estimate of their compound in some cases may be intricate, it becomes a mathematical problem of the same class with those of the mixtures of different liquors or different metals; as in these, therefore, the algebraical notation is the most convenient and intelligible. Let us express the pure blood of the white in capital letters of the printed alphabet, the pure blood of the negro in the small letters of the printed alphabet, and any given mixture of either, by way of abridgment in MS. letters.

Let the first crossing be of a, pure negro, with A, pure white. The unit of blood of the issue being composed of the half of that of each parent, will be $\frac{a}{2} + \frac{A}{2}$. Call it, for abbreviation, h (half blood).

Let the second crossing be of h and B, the blood of the issue will be $\frac{h}{2} + \frac{B}{2}$, or substituting for $\frac{h}{2}$ its equivalent, it will be $\frac{a}{4} + \frac{A}{4} + \frac{B}{2}$, call it q (quarteroon) being $\frac{1}{4}$ negro blood.

Let the third crossing be of q and C, their offspring will be $\frac{q}{2} + \frac{C}{2} = \frac{a}{8} + \frac{A}{8} + \frac{B}{8} + \frac{C}{4}$, call this e (eighth), who having less than $\frac{1}{4}$ of a, or of pure negro blood, to wit $\frac{1}{8}$ only, is no longer a mulatto, so that a third cross clears the blood.

From these elements let us examine their compounds. For example, let h and q cohabit, their issue will be $\frac{h}{2} + \frac{q}{2} = \frac{a}{4} + \frac{a}{8} + \frac{A}{8} + \frac{B}{4} = \frac{3a}{8} + \frac{3A}{8} + \frac{B}{4}$, wherein we find $\frac{3}{8}$ of a, or negro blood.

Let h and e cohabit, their issue will be $\frac{h}{2} + \frac{e}{2} = \frac{a}{4} + \frac{A}{4} + \frac{a}{16} + \frac{A}{16} + \frac{B}{8} + \frac{c}{4} = \frac{5a}{16} + \frac{5A}{16} + \frac{B}{8} + \frac{c}{4}$, wherein $\frac{5}{16}$ a makes still a mulatto.

Let q and e cohabit, the half of the blood of each will be $\frac{q}{2} + \frac{e}{2} = \frac{a}{8} + \frac{A}{8} + \frac{B}{4} + \frac{a}{16} + \frac{A}{16} + \frac{B}{8} - \frac{C}{4} = \frac{3a}{16} + \frac{3A}{16} + \frac{3B}{8} + \frac{C}{4}$, wherein $\frac{3}{16}$ of a is no longer a mulatto, and thus may every compound be noted and summed, the sum of the fractions composing the blood of the issue being always equal to unit. It is understood in natural history that a fourth cross of one race of animals with another gives an issue equivalent for all sensible purposes to the original blood. Thus a Merino ram being crossed, first with a country ewe, second with his daughter, third with his granddaughter, and fourth with the great-granddaughter, the last issue is deemed pure Merino, having in fact but $\frac{1}{16}$ of the country blood. Our canon considers two crosses with the pure white and a third with any degree of mixturé, however small, as clearing the issue of the negro blood. But observe, that this does not re-establish freedom, which depends on the condition of the mother, the principle of the civil law, *partus sequitur ventrem*, being adopted here.

But if e emancipated, he becomes a free white man, and a citizen of the United States to all intents and purposes. So much for this trifle by way of correction.

His long legs under the full-length gray frockcoat shifted position, itching for the feel of his horse Eagle between them. He was seventy-two years old. His presidency was six years behind him and those six years had been spent here at home, in retirement, surrounded by those he loved most in the world: his women, his children, his grandchildren, his slaves, his neighbors, his kin. Restless, he rose from his writing table to his full height, the face ascetic and serene in the bright light. He sat down again, and his left hand took up his pen, and as it did, the copying machine he had invented by which a letter written manually with one pen was simultaneously traced with another by a series of connected levers, called a polygraph, followed the movements of his hand. This would be the last letter of the morning.

He looked out of his study windows: it was a view in which nothing mean or small could exist, he thought. That was why he had chosen the site, which commanded the Blue Ridge Mountains: it was one of the boldest and most beautiful horizons in the world. His house, which he called Monticello, giving it the soft Italian pronunciation, stood upon a plain formed by cutting off the top of the mountain.

The light this morning is so pure and delineating, he thought, touched with the soft promise of spring that turns the mountains their deepest blue.

He stared for a moment more at the west lawn, noting several figures gamboling on it—children, he supposed. He smiled. Whoever they were, black or white, they belonged to Monticello. And to him.

He turned his eyes away and picked up his pen. Absently, he massaged his wrist before signing: *Thomas Jefferson.*

CHAPTER 3

ALBEMARLE COUNTY, 1830

> But generally it is not sufficient. The parent storms, the child looks on, catches the lineaments of wrath, puts on the same airs in the circle of smaller slaves, gives a loose to his worst of passions, and thus nursed, educated, and daily exercised in tyranny, cannot but be stamped by it with odious peculiarities. The man must be a prodigy who can retain his manners and morals undepraved by such circumstances.
>
> THOMAS JEFFERSON, *Notes on the State of Virginia*, 1790

"MAMA, what did you talk about all that time?"

"I don't know, Eston, different things, gossip mostly."

"You mean a white gentleman traveled all the way from Charlottesville to come up here and gossip with you? What did he want? What kind of information? And how do you know he weren't one of those journalists?"

This was Madison Hemings speaking. His voice had a perpetual edge of violence and irritation.

The question sent a flush of surprise up the back of Sally Hemings' neck. As a matter of fact, she had no idea at all if he was a journalist or not. He didn't seem or speak like one, or at least her idea of one, since she had never met a journalist in her entire life. Therefore, she wasn't sure. Besides it was evident from his knowledge of local families and his accent that he was from these parts.

"I told you, Madison, I was afraid it might have been the sheriff and when I saw that it wasn't, well, I was just so relieved I guess I just believed anything. He had to be one or the other, and if he was white and wasn't the sheriff, then he had to be the census taker. He said he was the census taker, and didn't you tell me the census man would be coming round these days? I just assumed he was telling the truth."

"Mama, you believe everything a nice white gentleman tells you! You had no business letting a strange man, white or black, into my house!"

"Our house, Madison," Eston said. "And leave Mama alone. You just scared it might have been the sheriff. I told you Martha Jefferson Randolph is not to be trusted. She hates all of us, and always has."

"Leave Martha out of it, Eston," Madison said. "She had her reasons for helping us—if you can call this run-down, no-dirt farm 'help.' She's no better off herself, living down there in Pottsville, in that dinky house with all her children, and Thomas Mann Randolph, dead as crazy and drunk as a loon. I'm not shedding any tears for Martha Randolph! She didn't have to marry that bastard!"

Of all her children, she thought, Madison was the most difficult, and because he was the one who reminded her of her brother James, she favored him in a way. He, of all her children, was in the most danger. Eston, with his placid nature and good looks, would always get by as a black man or as a white one.

"Mama, admit you were wrong to let him in! He could be a journalist pretending to be the census taker just nosing around for dirt to print," Madison went on.

"You can surely find out if he is the real census taker," his mother answered. "Just ask in town. He said his name was Nathan Langdon and he was born at Broadhurst. He has six brothers and sisters, and his father is old Samuel Langdon and his Uncle John was a friend of Thomas Jefferson. He is fair with a dark beard and about six feet tall, light for a young man, about twenty-seven or eight. He is going to marry a Wilks girl from Norfolk by the name of Esmeralda, and he just came back from Boston and Harvard, cause his pa is sick and his fiancée upset about his taking so long to come back. Then too, his brother . . . killed in a duel . . ."

"Mama, you found all that out!"

"I was the last count to be made for the day and he was hot and tired. I guess he just stayed on longer than he intended."

"Was he waiting for us to come home?"

"Not really. He asked about you both; and wanted to know how he could reach you for some work his father needs done at the plantation. I told him he could find you after curfew if he needed to."

"You mean you invited him back?"

"Well, that was the least I could do, he's—"

"White, Mama! I don't want him in the house. Any business he has with me, he can find me at the university. Any business with anybody can be conducted at the front door. And you were alone. . . . What if—"

"Madison, for heaven sakes. Not all white men are rapists!"

"No? Just remember Stokes's wife, stuck out there past the Channing place. . . . Didn't happen less than two months ago. A free colored man's wife, free colored man's property doesn't mean anything in this county. They don't want free coloreds in Virginia. They've made that pretty clear. One false step—even one—and you are in a chain gang heading for Georgia or South Carolina, papers or no papers. Just sudden like that. Nobody ever found out what happened to Willy Dubois. Where'd he go? In the dead of night? After curfew. Just disappeared, leaving hearth and home, wife, mother, and five children. Now just where did he go? I don't want any strange men in this house, Mama, black or white. You hear me, Eston?"

"I hear you," Eston said, moving over protectively to his mother.

Eston Hemings was a beautiful man. He was huge, over six feet four, with bright red hair and a continent of pale freckles on a clear milky skin that showed no trace of a beard. He had enormous hands that could carve the most delicate designs—flowers, scrolls, fruit—in any wood that grew, and could wrench the most beautiful notes out of his instruments—the pianoforte and the Italian violin. His features were regular and delicate, like his mother's, with a high wide rather long nose and a generous sensual mouth. Already there were laugh marks around his pale-blue eyes. He was broad of shoulder with a surprisingly long and girl-like neck.

Eston knew that when Madison was like this, something bad had happened to him in town. Maybe he would tell them, and maybe he wouldn't. Madison had a damned irritating way of doing everything. He was the darkest in the family, and his cool slender grace, his animal vitality and cockiness, seemed an affront to both races. He was always getting into trouble: rows with shopkeepers over bills, with foremen over plans, with masons over blueprints, with other carpenters over techniques, with the landlord, with the bank, with the tax collector. With everybody, nigh on. Madison should leave for the Territories, thought Eston. Now. Before he really got into some scrape he wouldn't be able to get out of. Eston knew why Mama would never leave here. He could take care of Mama alone. He wasn't in love. He wasn't trying to prove to some freeborn girl how great a man he was.

Madison Hemings felt the gentle but firm pressure of his brother's rough hand steering him toward the back door of the cabin and the cool fragrant night air. The gentle, insistent pressure calmed and soothed him. He clamped shut his jaw in an effort to stop tears of rage.

Why was he so upset? Why had he yelled at his mother? The real reason, he knew, was fear. . . . He was scared to death that something was going to happen to ruin their fragile existence, before they even got a chance to live it. He didn't want to tell anyone about what had happened to him today in town. Not even Eston. Eston could feel his brother's neck muscles tense, but he said nothing.

Outside, they faced the dying red sun sinking below the delicate line of the peach trees they had planted more than a year ago. Beyond that lay the boundaries of Monticello. Normally a thick whitewashed birch fence cut across the dark green of the pine woods, marking the end of the plantation on the southwest side. But the fences were now mostly down, and those standing were a dirty disinherited gray. The crossbeams lay on the nettle-packed ground where they had fallen.

Madison stared at this unkempt frontier. It seemed to be the line between his former life and this one. He would never understand why his mother refused to leave this place; why she deliberately chose a rented house so close to Monticello. Was it that she wanted to be reminded, every minute of every day, of her former servitude, of her concubinage?

His mother had never told him anything of his origins. He knew that slave women never told their offspring anything. So slave children learned what they could when they could, in bits and pieces from older slaves, mammies, white people's conversations, and the bitterness of what they learned was all the more wounding. It intensified the shame without alleviating the burden. He remembered the shock of learning from some old crone that he was the son of the master. Even his grandmother hadn't told him! He was their son; yet neither father nor mother seemed to love him for it! He had tried to understand. He had stood for hours looking at his pale-yellow face in the polished silver mirrors of the Big House. He would run down to this very frontier, far from the Big House, and butt his head against the white-birch fencing until the blood came, because he couldn't understand why his father didn't love him. Madison stared at the fence posts now, as if he expected to see the stains of his childish blood still on them.

Madison looked up. He and Eston watched their mother slip under the high gray railings of the frontier of Monticello. Gathering her skirts as she went, she was walking up the mountains toward the cemeteries.

When she was upset or angry she could usually be found either by the grave of Thomas Jefferson or that of her mother, Elizabeth Hemings. They divided her loyalties in death as they had in life. When her sons saw her turn eastward, they knew she was heading toward the slave cemetery and their grandmother.

CHAPTER 4

ALBEMARLE COUNTY, 1830

And with what execration should the statesman be loaded, who permitting one half the citizens thus to trample on the rights of the other, transforms those into despots, and these into enemies, destroys the morals of the one part, and the amor patriae of the other. For if a slave can have a country in this world, it must be any other in preference to that in which he is born to live and labour for another: in which he must lock up the faculties of his nature, contribute as far as depends on his individual endeavours to the evanishment of the human race, or entail his own miserable condition on the endless generations proceeding from him.

THOMAS JEFFERSON, *Notes on the State of Virginia*, 1790

SALLY HEMINGS closed her eyes and sank down at the foot of the neat rectangle marked off by smooth stones and planted with primroses. Fresh grass was growing within its boundaries. A wooden cross that had been lovingly carved by Eston Hemings had replaced the original tombstone. It didn't seem possible that twenty-three years had passed since one of the two pillars of her life had crumbled. Elizabeth Hemings had died on August 22, 1807, at the age of seventy-two. She had outlived her daughter's father, John Wayles, by over fifty years. It had not been an easy death. It had taken the whole, humid fever-infested month of August to kill her. Two months before she had died, she had stopped eating and had taken to her bed. But even starvation had been slow to weaken the fabulous constitution that had survived almost three-quarters of a century of slavery and the birth of fourteen children. Resistant to all the infections that killed childbearing women in their forties; immune to all the malarial fevers, the typhoid and yellow fevers that struck eighteenth-century Virginians in their swampy, unhealthy climate; untouched by the periodic outbreaks of cholera; without physical blemish or congenital weakness, she had survived everything, including her own biography.

Against her closed eyelids Sally Hemings could still see the oppressive, insect-filled interior of that slave cabin where she and Martha Randolph had watched her mother strain toward death with the same prodigious will that had sustained her in life. In the sweltering heat of that room she and Martha had sat in a strange and southern circle of complicity: the concubine, daughter, the mistress and the slave; the aunt and the niece. All three women were reflecting, each in her separate way, on the intricacies of their blood ties and relationships. There had been love, servitude, hate, womanhood. It was all flowing together that day when Elizabeth Hemings, struggling, frantically seeking an exit from the life she had endured, had whispered, "Put your hand on my chest and push down; my heart won't stop beating."

Monticello, August 22, 1807

"I never knew of but one white man who bore the name of Hemings. He was an Englishman and my father. My mother was a full-blooded African and a native of that country. My father was a Captain of an English sailing vessel. Captain Hemings, my mama told me, was a hunter of beasts like her father, except that he hunted in the sea and his prey was the whale.

"He sailed between England and Williamsburg, then a great port. When the Captain heard of my birth, he determined to buy me and my mother, who belonged to John Wayles. He approached Master Wayles with an extraordinary high offer for us, but amalgamation was just beginning and Master Wayles wanted to see how I would turn out. He refused my father's offer. Captain Hemings begged, pleaded, threatened, and finally they had words. All to no avail; my master refused to sell. My father, thwarted in the purchase but determined to own his own flesh and blood, then resolved to take us by stealth. His ship was sailing; everything was in readiness. But we were betrayed by fellow slaves, and John Wayles took us up to the Big House and locked us in. Captain Hemings' ship sailed without us.

"We were kept at the Big House, but my mother never recovered. She kept running away. I must have run away six times before I could walk! Her master warned her that the next time she did it she would be punished not by the regular beating she got every time they sent her back, but by the legal punishment for runaways: branding of an 'R,' for runaway, on the cheek.

"She ran away again, and John Wayles ordered the punishment. It was the overseer that was to do it. My mama screamed and hollered and fought. She was a strong woman, my mother, and it took four men to hold her. But when the brand approached her skin, John Wayles's hand shot out against that iron. He had meant to knock it from the hand of the overseer, but the blow only spoiled his aim, and the brand came down on mama's right breast instead of her face. The slaves witnessing the punishment thought Master Wayles was going to kill that overseer.

"My mother never ran away again. There is something about a brand in the flesh that will stay with you until death. You never forget. Beatings you can forget. But not the scar. Especially a woman. My mother went to the fields, and I was kept at the Big House.

"Then one day when I was about fourteen going on fifteen, my mistress took me by the hair. I mean she just took a whole handful of my hair and half dragged me down to the tobacco fields. And there she left me, just left me. I never saw her face again, for when I returned to the Big House, she was long dead. I stayed in the fields. I was given to a slave named Abe for Abraham, and bore him six children.

"Twelve years later, John Wayles took me as his slave mistress, despite the fact I had already bore six children for Abe, who went and died on me. John Wayles had seen three wives die. The first, Martha Eppes Wayles, died within three weeks of her daughter Martha's birth. The second wife, a Miss Cocke, bore four daughters, three of whom—Elizabeth, Tabitha, and Anne—grew to maturity. After she died, he married Elizabeth Lomax, who survived only eleven months. When that last one died, he took me into the Big House as concubine. I had grown up in the Big House, and now I came back as housekeeper. I was twenty-six-years old, the year was 1762, and Martha Wayles was thirteen. In 1772, John Wayles was still dealing in slaves, buying, selling, and breeding them. By that time I had borne him four children: Robert, James, Peter, and Critta. In 1767, when Martha was eighteen, she married her cousin and left Bermuda Hundred, only to return less than two years later a widow. She stayed at home until she married Thomas Jefferson three years later on a snowy January first. I served the passions of John Wayles and ran his household for eleven years, from the time I was twenty-six until he died in 1773, three months after the birth of his last child, Sally. My life was connected with his white children, especially Martha, as well as my own children by him. I loved them all.

"I cared for them all. Like they were mine. The younger girls didn't remember, but Martha always remembered. Of all the white children, I loved her most. I followed her to Monticello; I nursed her in her illnesses and saw her die a little after every birth, trying for a son for

Thomas Jefferson. For her darling. And he let her try and let her kill herself trying, then mourned her—monstrous—as did I.

"Somehow, I could never forgive him when he knew he was killing her; when he knew after the first child she had no business trying again. Her body going give out. But he was hit even harder than me. We struggled, we did, both of us to gain our equilibrium. I cried and he burned. Burned all her things. All her letters. Her portraits. Her diary. Her clothes. Everything. Weren't right to destroy what was hers like that. That was rage. Rage against God, and rage against God is blasphemous. He could get angrier than any man I knew. For a while, I thought he was going to get so mad he was going to kill himself.

"But I couldn't think about self-murder 'cause I had all those children. I had ten of my twelve children with me when I went to Martha. John Wayles died not freeing me, nor any of my children. I told all my daughters, beautiful things all of you, don't love no masta if he don't promise in writing to free your children. Don't do it. Get killed first, get beaten first. The best is not to love them in the first place. Love your own color. That brings pain enough. Love your own color if you can, and if you're chosen, get that freedom for your children. I didn't get mine, nor for my children. I can't say he promised it to me, so I can't say he didn't keep his promise. He never promised and I never asked. I just expected. A terrible thing for a slave to do. Expect.

"Found myself at Monticello, property of Thomas Jefferson. I just said to myself I weren't going to die of it. I'd just get on with caring for Martha and my children and hers. I couldn't let go, you see, I just had too many heads to hold. My last two children were born at Monticello. One by a slave husband Smith. The other, I don't like to speak about. Got raped is what happened. And not just once. Nothing to do about it. He was a white carpenter named John Nelson. Nothing to do but to have the child and to love it. It wasn't his fault how he got here. He was my last. My baby. When I was almost fifty.

"Despite all the misery, and the bondage and the hard work, I loved life. The idea, you see, was to survive. Not go under with grief: the game was to last out the day and the night and garner enough strength for the next. And, Lord, I needed that strength. First, I had Bermuda Hundred to run, that huge sprawling house and all them slaves. Then I had Monticello. The house was smaller, but Thomas Jefferson was always tearing it up, rebuilding, so I could never get that plantation running like I wanted. Every time things would quiet down and I would get the house and the servants all orderly, why he would come back from

Philadelphia or New York and we would be in the brick and plaster again. Reduce me to tears, it did. Poor Martha never did see her house finished. She was poorly a lot of the time and she hated when he was away. She hated that politics anyway. But she loved the man. She loved him. I kept telling her to hold on. To try and garner her strength. Not to try to keep up with him, because Thomas Jefferson would live to be a hundred. Strongest man I ever did see. Twenty, thirty miles on horseback every day. He was like me in temperament, except he sometimes got his moods or his 'depressions,' as Martha would call them. He liked his privacy, too. Didn't want Martha sticking her head out too much either. He was a jealous and possessive man. And he had a temper—oh, he was sweetness and light—but I saw it. He had a monumental temper when he was riled. Even when it didn't come out. He thought it weren't dignified . . . but he had it. I could sometimes smell that brimstone inside him. Sometimes he would just look at me smelling it, and laugh. He stayed out of my way. He stayed out of my household affairs, so we got on. I liked him, I did. And I guess he did love my Martha in his way. But he never did understand women, really.

"When his mother died in 1776, why he did the same thing he did later with his wife's belongings when *she* died; he burned everything—letters, portraits, mementos—everything. He didn't want anyone to know him, yet I never saw a man who so much needed to be known and loved. Well, Martha Wayles loved him, and so do you Sally. I can pass down to you what I knowed about Thomas Jefferson, which ain't much. But nobody can teach you how not to be hurt when you love a white man.

"I say 'love' if that's what can pass between a slave and a free white man, or a slave and free white woman. I loved Martha like a mother, and I loved Wayles like a wife. Trouble was I didn't ask for nothing, and nothing's what I got in the end. When I realized who I was or what I was, I made up my mind I might be called a slave, but I wasn't going to live no slavish life. I wasn't going to go out of my way to be no slave. I tried to pass that on to all my children. One thing I always insisted was that we had a family name—Hemings. Hemings. And I wanted all my children to be addressed by it. Made them remember they had a surname! I tried to get them interested in life. In seeing what was going to happen next. Even slaves have things happen to them. Even in a slave's world, something got to be happening all the time. I believe in life-preserving and love.

"I believe in having a secret life with secret plans and secret dreams.

Just like having a little vegetable garden to yourself out back of your cabin like mine. You got to work it at night or real early in the morning, but it's yours. Same with dreams. Maybe you got to work them late at night or real early in the morning, but nobody can take them out of your head lest they kill you and if you work ain't nobody going to kill you, cause you too valuable. Lord, God, I would fight the suicides."

All through the sweltering summer afternoons, Elizabeth Hemings ran out her life with words. They flowed on until dusk and until she was too exhausted to speak. Many of the stories, Sally Hemings and Martha Randolph had heard a dozen times, yet they clung to Elizabeth Hemings as to a floating log in a rapid. And Elizabeth Hemings carried them faster and faster down her particular river of memory. Rivulets of incidents, old family jokes, intrigues, feuds, births, and deaths, trickled through the ramblings of each afternoon.

She reached back further and further, her hands hovering over the quilts as if she were choosing the bits and pieces of a mosaic in colored glass, each cut glass reflecting other past events which brought on still other images of her life. Sally Hemings thought that she would never be able to remember her own life so well, and Martha Randolph too was amazed at the richness of this slave's recollections. For the two women tending her, there had never been a time when there was not an Elizabeth Hemings.

"After John Wayles's death, all of us slaves were divided up amongst the inheritance of the four living daughters, Martha and her three half sisters. Martha took me and ten of my children. The other two went with Tibby. I didn't come here to Monticello until after your birth, Patsy. Came with Sally, who was two years old, and the baby Thenia.

"Thomas Jefferson was a rich man in those days. Yea, rich. He inherited one hundred thirty-five slaves from John Wayles, including us Hemingses, and eleven thousand acres. He had four plantations: Monticello, which wasn't much to begin with, but with all his building, became the most beautiful; Poplar Forest, where we all went after them British came 'round for us; Elk Island; and Elkhill. Life was sweet for Martha up until all the trouble about the independency came along. First thing, Thomas Jefferson out defending a mulatto who claimed freedom because his great-grandmother was a white woman who had him by a black slave father. Masta Jefferson saying the sins of the father shouldn't be visited on the third generation, or generations without end, and that that boy was free because he was the great-grandson of a free white woman, and it is the mother who determines slavery in Virginia. He lost. Didn't no Virginian wants to hear nothing about no white lady having no black children. Used to sell any white woman and her child into slavery for it: five or ten years for the mother, and thirty for the child. They used to believe, back in those days, a white lady have one black baby, all her babies coming black. Now, if that were so, why didn't it apply just as well to us? Then came this Stamp Act. I heard all about that. This ruckus up in Boston with white men disguised as black folks and Indians throwing tea into the water, and first thing, Thomas Jefferson finds this thrilling and writes a 'revolutionary document,' as Martha called it. Telling the English where they could go and what they could do, which made him a traitor to the Crown and liable to get himself hung and quartered. Poor Martha was fit to be tied. She told me all the terrible dangerous things her husband was doing, running risks of losing his fortune, his name, and his head.

"But Masta Jefferson was right happy. He racing around feeling good, smiling, writing, speechifying. Then he got one of them headaches like he got after his mama died. Headaches and dysentery were his two ailments. All coming from his nerves and that hot temper. Then he left home with my son Robert for Philadelphia. He went to the Continental Congress with all them famous men of those revolutionary times. His little girl died at eighteen months, and Masta came racing home, but it was too late then. Martha grieved something terrible and Masta Jefferson begged her to come back with him to Philadelphia, but she wouldn't go. Masta Jefferson went on back to Philadelphia and wrote his Declaration of Independency which made him the most famous man in Virginia, maybe in all the colonies. Martha didn't care. She didn't want no revolution, but she didn't say nothing to her husband but once.

"Only that Christmas in '75 she pleaded with him to give up politics. There was the death of little Jane still grieving her, and she pleaded with him to give up politics, to give up making war on England. Of course by this time it was too late; I could have told her that. Masta Jefferson was not going to give up his politicking for no mortal. She mostly couldn't stand the separations. She said she wasn't like Abigail Adams, who loved politics and who pushed her husband. Yet she wouldn't go to Philadelphia with him even when she was well. She fought and pleaded, but he struggled. It was a hard thing to ask an ambitious man like him to give up his life's work. Well, England was getting riled up and sending troops and commanders and generals, and landed them mostly where they liked. It got around amongst the slaves that the English was taking slaves into their army and offering them their freedom and giving them uniforms. It seems they had three hundred in the army in Maryland with 'Liberty to Slaves' on their breasts. I sure would have liked to have seen that. Black men in uniform with rifles, and before you known it, we was at war.

"The second year of the war, Martha finally bore a son for her husband. He lived only until June fourteenth, and we buried him without a name. Only Patsy lived now, and I thought Martha was going to lose her mind. She had lost three children, counting her son by her first marriage. I had seen women lose five, seven, ten children before they was two years old. There's nothing in this life harder than burying your own children. I thank God it never happened to me. Oh, I've buried two now, but they were full-grown men.

"Martha got with child again as soon as she could, and the next year she had Polly, who was blessed to live. At least she lived long enough to marry. But Martha was slow coming back this time. She was scared of dying, scared of losing Polly, scared of losing another child, and scared of having another.

"Masta Jefferson started in rebuilding again Monticello. Things weren't going too well for him. It seems we were losing this war he started. He was governor of Virginia now, with his seat of government in Williamsburg, but he weren't made to be no war general. The generals and officers that did come to Monticello during those times was mostly German and English, prisoners of war, at least that's what they was called. But, they was treated like guests. Many a musical evening and dinner took place for foreign gentlemen fighting against us. One German lady, wife of a general, followed her husband clean to our shores and was lodged at Monticello along with him. Twenty-two slaves run away from Monticello to join the English army, eleven of them women. Lord, then come the day British dragoons come looking for Governor Jefferson, saying they wanted to put a pair of silver handcuffs on him. Searched the house they did from top to bottom and took off poor Isaac to the army, with his mother there screaming and crying. I guess this decided Martha to move to Williamsburg with the masta and then to Richmond, where she again got pregnant. This left the plantation for me and my son Martin to run alone. Never knowing when the soldiers would show up or nothing. Coping with slaves running to join the English right and left, and taking everything they could eat and anything that weren't nailed down. In November eighty, Martha come home and Lucy Elizabeth, the first, was born."

"Lord, here come the British again. They showed up again in June eighty-one. Jack Jouett rode all night to reach Monticello with the news that the British general, Tarlton as I recall, was coming to capture Thomas Jefferson. Jouett was all cut up from the thickets. He carried them scars on him to his grave. He was in a *state* that morning. I cleaned him up and got something to eat in him and then off he rode. Masta Jefferson sent off Martha and Patsy and Polly and all the white people to Poplar Forest. You remember that, Patsy? Sally, you stayed with me. You was scared and trembling something terrible. Thomas Jefferson sat and had his breakfast at his leisure and then when he saw through his telescope that the English was coming up the mountain, he got his horse saddled and rode off toward Carter's mountain. I was the one who met the English at the door. But I made Martin open it for me. But before that we was running around getting the silver together for Caesar, who was hiding it under the floorboards. The English was banging on the door and Martin, he let the plank drop on poor Caesar, leaving him under the house, trapped underneath the floorboards. He told me later that he could hear them boards groaning and creaking under them dragoons' feet. One of the soldiers put a gun to Martin's chest and said he'd fire if Martin didn't tell him in what direction Masta Jefferson had rode out. Martin said 'Fire away then!' And poor little Sally thought she was about to see her half brother shot dead, and she started screaming, but they didn't shoot anybody. They rode out the next day just as nice as you please, not taking anything and leaving me and Martin in charge. If I had thought, we could have hid Thomas Jefferson in Caesar's place! I've often laughed with the masta about that.

"Masta Jefferson, he didn't have no more heart for governing after that. Them militia weren't fighting properly, breaking and running and deserting, and half of them couldn't shoot straight no-how. Wouldn't let the slaves fight, those Virginians, although slaves was fighting on both sides in Maryland and Pennsylvania and Carolina. But those militia boys, they was just farmers and yeomen and backwoodsmen. They didn't know anything about fighting a real army with real uniforms and all. It was just a mess. Then to top it all off, Masta Jefferson fell off Caractacus and was laid up for six weeks. He's had six horses in his life.

He loves them bay horses, especially that tall horse with white hind feet.
Well, anyway, he was a changed man after the British raided the
capital. Martha, she was in heaven and hell—that is she was with child
again, even after all the troubles we had after Lucy Elizabeth. This here
was her seventh pregnancy. I didn't leave her for the whole nine, and
Masta Jefferson neither.

"He put his office up in the little room next to hers at Monticello to
wait it out. Started writing a new book on Virginia. Heard it said he
didn't care much for black folks mixing with white folks. Anyway, about
that time Masta Jefferson sent Martin out after that slave boy Custer,
who had run off to Williamsburg—never did catch him. In May of
eighty-two, Martha gave birth to another girl child and named it after
the one she had lost, Lucy Elizabeth. I didn't say nothing, but I didn't
want that name for that child. It seemed to be a bad omen, and I was
right. Lucy survived until the age of four, but Martha didn't live to see
her face but for another seventeen months. Martha knew she was dying,
and I knew it, and Masta Jefferson, he knew it, but nobody said nothing
until the end. Lord, when he see her die . . . And she not yet thirty-
four."

Elizabeth Hemings gazed from under the half-closed eyelids at the
two women watching her die. Martha was stubborn about coming to sit
with her. It was her duty as mistress of the house to attend to dying
slaves.

Those two sat there like they were made of wood, Elizabeth Hemings
thought. They had always had a talent for stillness. She had never been
able to sit still. She was doing her best to die, before they murdered
her, but she was dying hard. She always knew she would have a hard
time dying. There they sat, and she lay, the three of them, waiting for
death. They had all lived their lives according to the rules: the rules of
master and slave, man and woman, husband and wife, lover and mistress. The one who had called the rules and who had made the game
was gone riding, loath to associate himself with all this women business of dying and watching other people die. She knew these two would
mourn him when his time came, more than they would ever mourn
her, and could she blame them? They had been birth'd and trained for
that. She herself had trained her own daughter, her favorite child, to
the triple bondage of slave, woman, and concubine, as one trains a
blooded horse to its rider, never questioning the rights of the rider. If

she hadn't done that, her daughter would never have come home from Paris.

Lordy, yes. She had procured for her master. She had made him a present of what she had loved most in the world. How could she have known that her vision of the perfect slave would coincide with his vision of the perfect woman. And Sally Hemings loved Thomas Jefferson. That was the tragedy. Love, not slavery. And God knew how much slavery there was in love . . .

Oh, the small degree of love she had felt for John Wayles had given her some measure of privilege, of barter, of freedom, of pride, of comfort. . . . No, her daughter's was a love of which she had had only an inkling. Sally had no worldly pride, no independence, no idea of justice. She was still childish, rancorless, detached, except for that which concerned what she loved. Sally was not even conscious of injuries inflicted upon her, and of the self-possession it took to forgive, she had not one grain of that.

The old woman continued to examine the placid and unlined face of her favorite daughter. She wanted to scream at her to run away. But it was too late. Much too late. Nothing could change now. If only she had understood in the beginning that her daughter had been constituted for love the way some women are constituted for breeding. Her life had left no trace on her body or her spirit. She could absorb everything. Not like poor tormented Martha Randolph with her twelve children by her insane and drunken husband, and her passion for a father she could never quite please. Martha with her awkward body, and her plain looks, and her quick temper hidden under migraine headaches, like her father.

Elizabeth Hemings felt a sudden mixture of love and contempt for them both. She turned her head away from them and fell silent.

The pause seemed longer than necessary, and Sally Hemings automatically continued: "I was forty-seven and Sally was thirteen, Martha she was twelve," and waited for the discourse to continue. But Elizabeth Hemings did not pick up the thread of her tale.

"Mama?"

"She's dead, Sally." Martha's voice was like a rock under her.

Martha tried to rise, fell back, and then, with a moan, threw herself over Elizabeth Hemings' still body.

Sally Hemings remained seated, staring at Martha as if she had gone mad. Her mother couldn't be dead. Her mother had something eminently important to tell her. She had waited all these weeks to hear it.

don imagined their separate worlds coming together. He was filled with a sense of intimacy.

"What is it?" asked Sally, eyeing the package he was offering her.

"New poems by Lord Byron. Straight off the ship from London!"

"I have never read much poetry. . . . A little in French when I was in Paris. My teacher used to give us lines to memorize. . . ."

"Byron is the most famous English poet living."

"Thank you, Nathan. How I envy those who can express themselves with words."

"Most people express themselves with too many words . . . such as Southern lawyers. Verbosity is not lacking in any Virginian. And what they can't talk about, they write in their journals. Even I have succumbed to it."

"You keep a journal, Nathan?"

"Since I went North. I felt it was my duty to record the horrors of the North as seen by a true Virginian for my compatriots who didn't dare cross the boundaries between Heaven and Hell. . . . I called it 'Reflections of a Virginia Gentleman on the Manners and Morals of Boston Society.' I fancied myself a Southern de Tocqueville. . . .

"During your stay in France, didn't you keep a journal?"

"I?" Sally Hemings smiled. "I was fifteen and though I spent most of my time inside the ministry, I did see a great deal that I felt I wanted to record. I was also there during the storming of the Bastille in 1789. My brother James saw much more than I did. He ventured outside and mixed with the crowds. It was like being in the middle of a rapid, he said. I will never forget that day."

"And you kept a record of it?"

"A childish record, but a record nevertheless."

"It should be a precious document."

"My diary, a precious document? For me, perhaps. Maria gave it to me on the boat sailing to France. I could hardly write at the time. . . . I have since copied those first attempts over. . . ." Sally Hemings stopped talking. She wanted to change the subject. Did he think she could be persuaded to share her most private possession?

She frowned. When she had decided to receive the census taker as a "caller" rather than as a representative of the class and power that governed her life, she had done so impulsively, responding to a strength and warmth she sensed in him. He had never asked to visit, nor had he been invited; yet week after week, he appeared at the cabin. Why she continued a relationship which she knew to be dangerous to her sons, she didn't know. And now she felt trapped. What was it that made her look forward to his visits? Vanity? Yes, she enjoyed the attentions of a young man, his strivings to please her. Loneliness? Perhaps. Langdon seemed to infuse a confidence in her she had never known before.

In the long afternoons of recounting her past, she had discovered that she had indeed had a life: a life full of deep and complex feelings. When he had questioned her, she had answered him in the only manner she was capable of: truthfully. Searching for the right tone, the exact phrase evoking as accurately as she could what she remembered. A sort of conspiracy had developed between them. There were times she didn't even feel like mentioning his visits to Eston and Madison. After all these years, she thought, how could she again be anticipating a man's visit? She found herself careful of her clothes, of her hair.

The secretive nature of their relationship seemed almost fitting. Had it not always been thus with her? Always the forbidden? It would have been more fitting, she thought, if, instead of exchanging thoughts, they exchanged pleasures. This would have been much more acceptable than what they were doing; for thoughts, feelings, and memories were all a slave, or an ex-slave, had to call her own. Even Thomas Jefferson had bowed to that rule. He had loved her as a woman and owned her as a slave, but her thoughts had always remained beyond his or anyone's control.

Nathan Langdon realized he had crossed the invisible barrier Sally Hemings had put between them and she smiled back at him.

"My writing upsets me. It reminds me that so many years have elapsed since anything has happened in my life."

"Do you know of the famous poetess who lived in Boston, named Phillis Wheatley? She was an ex-slave and highly praised for her poetry."

"No, I have never heard of her."

"I hear the abolitionists publish her widely."

"Even in the South?"

"Oh, publications slip in. Many people read and like her poetry and don't know that she was black and an ex-slave."

"You should say 'freedwoman,' not ex-slave, Nathan. You make it sound like a punishment instead of a liberty."

Nathan Langdon stared at the small face gazing intently into his. He wondered how these conversations would sound to an eavesdropper of his own color. In the beginning, he had posed simple questions, staying away from the subject of slavery. Yet as this had been the central element of her life, it was impossible not to touch on it in a thousand ways. As Sally Hemings' life story was unfolding, both the narrator and the listener had been overwhelmed by the weight and breadth of it. Langdon was awed at the intricacy of the information he was receiving. He was also well aware that it was compromising him both politically and emotionally. He had by now become hopelessly attached to this woman. More than that he had become involved with her.

He was spellbound by the fading echoes of her existence as bits and pieces came to him.

Sally Hemings regretted her confidences to Nathan, yet on the days that he didn't come she was disappointed. She still prepared for his visits carefully, reaching in her memory for incidents or names that would impress or amuse him. Despite herself, she spoke more and more openly. She opened drawer after drawer of memories, which she re-arranged, changed, aired, discussed, and counted, like linen. Her volatile performances, for that was what they were now, excited and fascinated Langdon.

"They were just men," she would say with a smile when she spoke of those heroes already carved in marble (all except the dubious Aaron Burr). She and her sisters and her uncles and her mother and her mother before her had all been an unseen army, treated as if they could not see, hear, or feel.

Clinging to her words, Nathan followed the complicated plots and the many famous characters, slave and free, devotedly. Now, Langdon hardly asked a question. There was no need. Words followed in an unending stream. Sally Hemings spoke with a kind of desperation, willing him to understand. Sometimes she would take on the accent of the person she was describing. She was a talented mime. She didn't realize that while she was merely recounting her past to Nathan Lang-don, she was in fact uncovering a person she had never known from a life she had had no sense of. From these afternoons emerged a new Sally Hemings.

CHAPTER 6

ALBEMARLE COUNTY, 1831

Indeed I tremble for my country when I reflect that God is just: that his justice cannot sleep for ever: that considering numbers, nature and natural means only, a revolution of the wheel of fortune, an exchange of situation, is among possible events: that it may become probable by interference!

THOMAS JEFFERSON, *Notes on the State of Virginia*, 1790

NATHAN LANGDON had run into the close-mouthed, protective silence of Tidewater society concerning the Hemings affair, as well as the "official" family denial by the Randolphs. But everyone knew the reason the Hemingses were left in peace; the reason Sally Hemings would not budge from the frontier of Monticello. For Nathan Langdon, the Hemings affair was a parenthesis in the Institution; it neither condemned nor knighted it. He felt that there was something sinister in this blatant misuse of a master's absolute power. But then, did one have absolute power when one was in love? That Sally Hemings was a victim was certain. Her submissiveness was what had made her the perfect slave, but, to his mind, the perfect woman as well. To misuse his moral or physical power over a woman, however, was abhorrent to him. A man's power over a woman was like the master's power over a slave. It came from an innate superiority.

"You would think my life depended on my telling you everything, Nathan." She paused. Perhaps it did, she thought. She stared at the man she had just addressed. Langdon returned her quizzical glance with one of such tenderness that Sally Hemings was forced to lower her eyes, but not before returning the look in a way that told Langdon he was not the first to have fallen in love with Sally Hemings. He had the impression that this woman had never really used her beauty to manipulate men. Was it because, as a slave, she had had no concept of power? Or was it because, as a slave, her beauty simply had held no threat and was thus neutral both to herself and others? Had she used this power in Paris? Over Jefferson? He flushed. He would soon be a married man, he thought ruefully, and instead of concentrating on Esmeralda, he was obsessed with a slave and her strange reclusive life and its secrets.

Langdon had been well aware for some time now of his physical attraction to this woman.

It was almost ritualistic by now to admire the slick black hair she never unwound, and to imagine it racing in one thick coil, like a black wave down her back. Now he was admiring the tender curve of her neck bending toward the pages of the book. The quiet folds of that indentation between her thighs, the sheen of old silk, filled him with a kind of fainting sickness. Would he ever dare to lay his head on those folds? Shocked as he was by his own thoughts, he tried to face them honestly. How many other Southern white men had dreamed similar dreams? He felt foolish and giddy. This pale, almost white woman was connected with darkness, with dark recesses, with dark flesh. Those first memories of comfort and warmth that all white Southerners share.

There had been a long pause in their conversation, and Langdon looked up to find Sally Hemings staring at him in a strange, intense way.

She seemed distracted as she rose and came toward him.

Sally Hemings, trained since birth in obedience, had heard the silent command of Nathan's mind and body and had obeyed. In her loneliness and weariness she had failed to remember the first lesson of black womanhood: never touch a white man.

She knew that in Virginia, her color alone was a provocation to any white man. An invitation. Yet any gesture or familiarity on the part of the slave woman, no matter how maternal, how pure, was inviting disaster. She knew this, but she forgot. A mistake that was to cost her dearly.

She took one of his hands in hers, and with the other she pressed his face into the folds of her dress. It was the first and last time Nathan Langdon would experience such a feeling of pure happiness. Sally Hemings' blunder, as offhand and unconscious as it was, awoke in Langdon an unbearable jealousy of a dead man.

"I begin to be jealous."
"Of a dead man?"

"Jefferson lives. Didn't you know that? That is the chorus of a new patriotic song."

"He lives for me."

"How do you think Langdon got so well into the good graces of Mama, knowing how particular she is?"

"I don't know how he did it, Mad, but he's here and it don't look like he's going to budge any time soon."

Eston hoped Madison was not going to make a scene. His mother was happy.

"What I don't understand, Eston, is why the hell he comes up here all the time. What does he stand to gain? We ain't got nothing worth stealing! Or do we?"

"Our mama!" Eston laughed.

"Eston!" Madison was shocked.

"Oh Mad, I didn't mean he would try anything! And I don't think he's out to *get* anything. I just mean she's fond of him. I think she's kind of taken him under her wing, like . . . like a son. . . ."

Eston wished that last word had not come out of his mouth.

"A son!" exploded Madison. "She's GOT two white sons who haven't even seen fit to let us know if they're living or dead! That's not two white sons too many?"

"I think Mama knows where they are, and how they are. She just doesn't want to talk about it."

"Well, Nathan Langdon is hardly some poor ex-darky, passing for white, that Mama has to protect, you know. He's Tidewater, and even if his family ain't rich anymore, they still got their place in society. . . . What's he doing up here? He's got a fiancée; he's passed his law examinations; and he has started out on his own. And you saying he needs our mama for a friend? That he can't do without Sally Hemings? He's picked up some strange ideas up North!"

"I know it's strange, Mad, but I really think he can't do without her."

"Eston, sometimes you haven't got the common sense of a jackrabbit. He's using Mama. Nathan Langdon is eaten up with curiosity about Thomas Jefferson, that's all. It's fascination with our *father*, not with Sally Hemings!"

"He also has political ambitions, Mad. He wouldn't risk any kind of compromise over Mama."

"Love is always at another's expense."

"Love is doing something for that person. Changing things."

"But there is nothing you can do for me. You can't change the past."

"I can change myself."

"But don't you see; that's the danger. You change yourself, and first thing you want is to change me, then those around you—your family, your life, the South, everything. There is danger when you contradict your roots, what is considered 'right,' what is accepted."

"I said you were a dangerous lady, and you laughed," Langdon said.

"I just don't want to see you hurt. Not by others and not by me. All these months, there have been remarks about us."

"I know that."

"And there are Eston and Madison to consider."

Langdon suddenly sensed Sally Hemings slipping out of his grasp. Several times in the past he had had this sensation of panic.

"Damn Eston and Madison!" he said. "What about you? What do you want?"

"I've never had what I wanted, Nathan. Never."

"Why?" he asked, like a stubborn child.

"Because . . ."

Sally Hemings did not continue, and she smiled at this childish exchange. There was something naïve and touching about Nathan. Some basic innocence white men seemed to take in, she would have said, "With their mother's milk," had it not been for the fact that that "milk" had been black. There were times she believed that white skin was just a protective covering—nothing ever really seemed to penetrate it.

"This time you will," Nathan said.

The violent temper Sally Hemings had striven all her life to conceal flashed to the surface; she suddenly wanted to slap his face hard, to bury herself in his chest, and scream curses at him.

"No, I won't," she answered vehemently. She wanted to hurt him. "It will end, Nathan . . . and I shall miss you."

"There is no reason on earth why it should end."

There was every reason on earth, she thought.

"Let's not talk about it," she said.

They both looked away at this. To put the possibility of an ending in words was tempting fate with their fragile happiness. The same fate that had brought the lonely woman and the lonely young man together in the first place. Langdon knew he must break the tension.

"Besides," he said lightly, "if I stopped coming to see you, where would you get your weekly gossip and slander? Madison has no imagination, and Eston has no malice."

They both smiled at this. Eston's good nature and Madison's bad temper had become a private joke between them. Nathan Langdon felt a rush of affection: everything was all right again.

He smiled and rose.

"You're leaving?"

"I must. I only stopped for a minute." He looked at his watch. "I am going to miss the post."

"Oh, Nathan, I've kept you again."

"No," he said sharply. "I wanted to come. I hadn't seen you in more than a week. But I haven't had any time since this new lawsuit started."

"How is it progressing?"

"Badly. I'm up against one of the slickest, most outrageous liars I've ever had the misfortune to represent. He changes his story every day. At least I can say that the adversary is consistent—consistently lying. . . ."

"Nathan, how are you supposed to defend someone who lies?"

"It can be done. Liars can be defended brilliantly and honest men can be destroyed. You should know that—you've seen many an honest man lose . . . especially in politics."

"Promise me." Sally Hemings suddenly reached out and touched Nathan's sleeve. A flicker of memory, like a grain of sand, made her blink.

"Yes?" he said, his voice low.

"Promise me you'll bring the latest ending to the Randolph saga of the 'look-alike chickens coming home to roost'!"

The young man burst into laughter. Then he said softly, "I promise."

"No excuses. . . ."

"Please, Ma'am, am I the kind of gentleman who would bring excuses when I could bring mayhem and scandal? By the way, the latest Andrew Jackson joke is that when he puts on his reading spectacles, he turns out all the lights!"

With that he was already out the door. She watched him descend the steep pathway to where his horse waited, waited until she could see him no more.

CHAPTER 7

ALBEMARLE COUNTY, AUGUST 1831

The Almighty has no attribute which can take sides with us in such a contest.—But it is impossible to be temperate and to pursue this subject through the various considerations of policy, of morals, of history natural and civil. We must be contented to hope they will force their way into every one's mind. I think a change already perceptible, since the origin of the present revolution.

THOMAS JEFFERSON, *Notes on the State of Virginia*, 1790

THE SUMMER was passing and Sally Hemings' thoughts were enclosed in a soft, weary happiness. Slowly, out of an almost invisible but very deep wound, in an unceasing stream, thoughts and feelings welled up and spilled out. She felt herself floating, felt an odd excitement in answering Nathan Langdon's questions, and even while speaking was divided between pleasure and torment. She had lived a life; she was startled to perceive that life. As if it had been kept in a long underground passage which ascended now and again into the midst of tremendous events called History. History, which had left her alone in a vast, unfamiliar, unwanted wasteland.

Furtively, she looked across at Nathan Langdon. He really was quite an ordinary man, yet it was only with him that she felt this new sense of her existence. Had he given her that, or had she taken it herself? It was so hard to know.

"What are you thinking?" he said from the shadows.

"My own thoughts," she answered.

Nathan sensed a resistance, even an irritation. He knew the mood. Since summer he had treaded softly with Sally Hemings. He remained silent and let the moment pass. There would be other moments, a long series of moments in which to unravel the mystery of Sally Hemings. He would bide his time.

Nathan Langdon sighed in the stillness. It was an afternoon like many he had spent with this ex-slave. He felt himself sliding deeper

and deeper into compromise with his race and his class and less and less
inclined to shake himself out of a numbing lethargy, an insidious guilt
that kept him peering into the faces of his slaves, his servants, his
mother, his brothers, his fiancée. For what? He didn't know. He really
didn't know anymore why he had returned to Charlottesville. He had
certainly begun to question his earthly destiny. When Esmeralda and
his mother had begged him to come, it had been with relief that he had
returned South to take up the responsibilities of his family. He had
made little headway in Boston. The possibility of success in the North
for a Southerner, without means or influential friends, was dubious. He
also knew that he was wanting in the bitter, energetic ambitions of most
of his Northern schoolmates, but he had blamed this on his "Southernness." Yet his luck had been no better here in Charlottesville, where he
could hardly call himself a stranger. He found it difficult to slip back
into "Virginian" ways. He had acquired sharper edges in the North. At
least he liked to think so. The coying slickness of Southern manners now
stuck in his gullet. The only thing he had accomplished in the past year
had been his job as census taker. That had ended now, he thought, and
he hadn't succeeded in extending his connections or his business. He
had tried to form a partnership which had not worked out well. His
clerkship with Judge Miner was over and he had not been invited to
stay on. He had always had a desire for public life; to shape national
conduct seemed to him the highest form of achievement, he mused, but
he had no money and what influence there was had to be shared with his
two brothers, who also had political ambitions. There was little that
was public in his solitary room, or his solitary office, or his solitary visits
to Sally Hemings. He didn't think consciously of his unhappiness, or of
what Sally Hemings might have to do with it. If he had, he might have
prevented what happened that peaceful August afternoon.

It was several days after the much-awaited eclipse of the sun.

It was the same August 31, 1831, that the slave Nat Turner, property
of Putnam Moore and born the property of Benjamin Turner, and his
aide-de-camp, the slave Will Francis, born the property of Nathaniel
Francis, were, with a small army of sixty or seventy men and one
woman, all born slaves, sweeping through the County of Southampton,
Virginia, and in two days and one night, murdering every white man,
woman, and child that had crossed their path, systematically burning
everything as they killed. Fifty-five men, women, and children would

perish this day because of the one favor of God they held highest and in common: being white. Turner's goal was the arsenal in Richmond where, he, hoping to have gathered around him an army of hundreds of runaway slaves, had planned to organize an uprising of all the slaves of Virginia, in the name of the Father, the Son, and the Holy Ghost. He would fail.

"If your brother doesn't want it, why don't you take on the case, Nathan?"

Langdon shifted nervously in his chair. He hadn't come to see Sally Hemings today to be challenged. Confronted with a difficult decision. One that basically went against his grain. The Hemingses were one thing. Mulattoes were another.

"He didn't say he didn't want it. He said it couldn't be won in a Virginia court of law."

"I know the atmosphere, with all these new laws, is tense, Nathan, but perhaps you . . ."

Who did she think he was, thought Langdon, Thomas Jefferson?

"The case, as I said, is un-winnable. It will be one of those trials that is decided even before it begins."

"As are all trials concerning mulattoes in Virginia," said Sally Hemings. She had almost forgotten. If Virginia courts condoned murder, they wouldn't blink an eye at fraud.

"Yes, most."

"And you can't help him?"

"I would, if I could."

"Jefferson once tried to defend a mulatto when he was young. . . ."

"And he lost." Nathan Langdon said this not without pleasure.

"He lost, to be sure, but he tried." Sally Hemings was trembling. She rarely asked for anything. She hadn't realized how difficult it was. "It took courage at the time," she said, and looked intently at Langdon. It had been the wrong thing to say.

"Courage or foolhardiness? You must know that with the situation as it is now, any mulatto who sets foot in a court is going to lose just for having the temerity to do so."

Sally Hemings was still looking at Nathan Langdon. There was something in her gaze that profoundly irritated Langdon. Something childish and stubborn. Or was it only his anger and terror at being compared with the great Jefferson, the constant references to him as if he were a touchstone, a holy relic? . . .

"But this case is different, Nathan. This man was never a slave. He

49

was freeborn to begin with. You see, Master . . . Jefferson's case was one of a slave who sued for freedom on the grounds that his mother was white, and a child by Virginia law inherits the condition of his mother. But this man was born free because his mother was freed before he was born and left the state. His father recognized him in court in Philadelphia, and he should have the same rights as any citizen of the United States, being born outside Virginia, to inherit property. In this instance, his property is his own slave kin! Brothers and sisters and uncles!"

"He is still legally a mulatto, therefore he cannot testify against his white cousins in the case. It is no longer a question of slavery but that of a black man testifying against a white man."

Sally Hemings was silent. Nathan Langdon felt the gall rise in his throat. Women. She still wanted a hero. The heroic age was over. Didn't she know that? Ended with James Madison. This was the age of mediocrity, small-mindedness, caution, calculation, money-grubbing. The age of the common man. An age that deserved what it got: Jackson, not Jefferson. Then he heard her say:

"Think if it were Madison or Eston."

"It could never be Madison or Eston."

"Why not?"

"Madison and Eston," Langdon said very deliberately, "are white. I made them white. Legally. They can testify against anybody on earth."

"White?"

"In the census. I listed them and you as white."

There was a stunned silence. Outside, only the sounds summer makes. "It takes more than a census taker to turn black into white." Her voice had an ominous quality to it: a sudden chill that should have warned him.

"After all, by Thomas Jefferson's definition, you are white."

"By Thomas Jefferson's life, I'm a slave."

"Think how much easier it is for you now, staying in Virginia with all that's going on . . . not to have that sword of expulsion hanging over your head! I . . . decided."

"*You* decided." He couldn't tell whether she was going to laugh or scream. "*You* decided! For fifty-four years I've been Thomas Jefferson's creature, and now . . . now *you* decide it's time for me to be yours. *Yours!*" She began to laugh. "It's Judgment Day! Instead of being black and a slave, I'm now free and *white*."

Her eyes showed something of that lurid yellow that had frightened him on his first visit.

If he had been a good lawyer, or even a competent one, Langdon would at this point before it was too late have laughed and tried to turn the whole thing into a joke. Or he would have lied by saying she had completely misunderstood. But Nathan Langdon was not a good lawyer. He blundered on, insisting, explaining. Perspiration was forming on his high forehead. There were undertones, nuances, secrets he hadn't calculated and that he had no way of gauging.

Her laughter had shattered what composure he had left. Instead of reading her face, in which was reflected shock, disbelief, horror, as well as a plea for rectification, he went on pleading his already lost cause, repeating himself with a kind of childish despair. Surely she knew he had meant well. That he had done it for her!

The shrillness of her laughter had given it a loud, raucous, almost drunken quality. Then suddenly it stopped.

"Why did you have to tell me? Why couldn't you have kept quiet? What did you think you were doing—playing God?"

"I did it for you and your sons."

"Don't be a fool, Nathan. You didn't do it for me. You didn't even know me. You did it for him. To make him not guilty. To shield him . . . so that he wouldn't have a slave wife!"

Her eyes had turned darker. A strand of black hair had escaped from its knot. He wanted to go down on his knees and hide himself in the folds of that skirt again. Surely, it was going to be all right. Surely, he wasn't going to lose her over this.

"Forgive me, I didn't realize . . ."

"Forgive you because you didn't realize . . . That's what black folks are here for. To forgive white folks because they didn't realize. Forgive me. Forgive me. My father said it. My lover said it. My white sons will say it. Yes, I forgive you. All of you, and your insufferable arrogance. But I never want to see you again."

"Please . . ."

"You are not welcome here anymore."

"I beg you . . ."

"If you come back, Nathan, I'll have Madison throw you out." She went on before he could cut in again. "I'm tired, Nathan. I'm tired of white men playing God with my flesh and my spirit and my children and my life, which is running out. I thought you understood that.

51

You've left me nothing of my own. Not even my color! I've been asked to give, and give, and give, and now I can't give any more. I can't forgive another man, Nathan. I'm sorry."

He had made one of those blunders of enormous consequence that only a fool or the very young makes. One that afterward plays again and again in the mind like a set piece in a game of chess long after the match has been lost. It would seem to him incredible, later, that such a small miscalculation, flung so nonchalantly on the board, would have cost the game.

"Oh, God." He groaned. "Tell me what to do. I'll do anything. Pay any price."

"That's what all white men say." There was dullness and pity and contempt in her voice. "You are just like all the rest. You haven't understood anything of what I've told you all these months. You still think I exist by your leave. You always will."

The bitterness shocked him. She meant what she said. He had not understood.

"Please, I love you."

"That's what all men say. That's what he said. That's what he said!"

Suddenly, there was no Sally Hemings. No Nathan Langdon. There was only unfathomable, uncontrolled black rage. A rage that went far beyond the terrified young man who skimmed and rocked on its surface like a storm-tossed skiff.

Sally Hemings rose like some outraged goddess in her sanctuary, now defiled. Like pure crystal light, her rage, he felt, could maim or kill at will. There was something diabolical and possessed in the scream that echoed after Nathan Langdon as he fled from her.

That sound would remain for him one of the bitterest and cruelest memories of his life.

For a long time, Sally Hemings stared at the receding figure of Nathan Langdon. Then her head snapped back. There was a pressure in her head that seemed to push her neck forward and made her want to lower it.

When she looked down, there were spots of blood on her apron. Blood. Her nose was bleeding. She lifted the white apron and buried her face in it. Blindly she whirled and entered the darkness. She let her apron drop.

She owned nothing, except the past. And now, even that had been taken from her. She had been raped of the only thing a slave possessed:

her mind, her thoughts, her feelings, her history. Among all the decisions of her life, she realized, not one was ever meant for herself.

Sally Hemings was trembling. She went to her dark-green chest. This moment she knew had been coming ever since that April day the census taker had arrived at her door, interrupting her solitude, disturbing her memories, changing her color. She took out a small linen portfolio, opened it, and stared at the yellowing, unframed sheet within. It was a pencil drawing, a portrait of her as a girl in Paris. She had never shown this drawing to anyone—not to her sons, not to Nathan Langdon, not to Thomas Jefferson. She had never reasoned why. Except that somehow, on this small scrap of paper, John Trumbull seemed to have captured something that made her see herself for the first time. This one was the sole image of herself that belonged only to her.

For a long time she studied the delicate lines on the aging paper. Had she ever been this young? Could she ever believe, invisible as she was, betrayed, and drowning in this sea of loneliness, the generations passed from her, that she had loved? . . . *Had loved the enemy.* . . .

She turned and strode to the fire. Sacrifice. For one instant of pain, she hesitated, and then she threw her image into the fire. Blood. A blood sacrifice.

For one moment her eyes went to the small bundle of cloth and clay on the mantle. What more did the gods want? She strode again to the chest and stared down at the yellowing diaries.

"In order to burn them I would have to forget you."

There was a slight smile on her lips as she began to burn paper. She burned through the afternoon. The last to go were her diaries. As she knelt, tearing the pages one by one, her eyes shone like a cat's in the light of the fire, her face was streaked with tears. George . . . George. Like George. A human sacrifice. She destroyed all but the last diary. There was still one more thing she had to do. She tried to rise. Her long black hair had loosened and fell like a nun's chaplet over her shoulders to her knees. She no longer had the strength to pull herself up, so she continued kneeling in an attitude of prayer, her diary open to the last page on her bloody apron. There, before her, in small neat script, was the account of hours: every visit with its date and length of stay Thomas Jefferson had made to Monticello from the time she had returned to Virginia with him. Re-enslaving herself. Thirty-eight years. Thirty-eight years of minutes, hours, months. A certainty that her fate was something more than a personal one overtook her.

Like an abbess at her devotions, she repeated each date. The last inscription was not the date of his death, but the date of his last return to Monticello, twenty-six years before.

She would make this act her very own, she thought: neither black nor white, neither slave nor free, neither loved nor loving.

She burned it. She felt a deep calm. She no longer feared anything; not death itself. She had crossed that line. Even if they hanged her.

As for Nathan Langdon, he had helped her leave her life. She never intended to see him again.

CHAPTER 8

JERUSALEM, 1831

> The spirit of the master is abating, that of the slave rising from the
> dust, his condition mollifying, the way I hope preparing, under the
> auspices of heaven, for a total emancipation. . . .
>
> THOMAS JEFFERSON, *Notes on the State of Virginia*, 1790

THERE WAS not one black person to be seen as Sally Hemings stood in
the white mob disguised by her color, shoulder to shoulder with other
tense women and men who had come to Jerusalem. It had taken her and
Eston one week to get to this place; yet she had felt compelled to be here
in the chill of this November day, a long, once elegant cloak covering her
from head to foot.

. The remnants of Nat Turner's army, twenty-eight in all, had been
destroyed or apprehended, and thirteen of them, including the woman,
had been executed—all without confessing. There remained only Nat
Turner; only Nat Turner had confessed, and this was his trial. As
reports and rumors of Turner's revolt had spread through Virginia,
Sally Hemings had been so affected by it that she, who for almost thirty
years, had never ventured outside the boundaries of Monticello, now
stood in this place, in awful danger, against the will of her sons.

It was as if Nat Turner's giant hand (for she thought of him as being
immense) had pushed her into this heaving crowd that seemed to rest in
the hollow of some enormous bloody bosom, now calmed and stroked
by the awe of true massacre.

She felt as if this man had taken her hand and lifted her out of the
loneliness after Nathan Langdon, after the destruction of her diaries.
Now, alone, she faced the truth of her life: she had loved the enemy. She
had denied and denied and denied the mesmerizing violence of Turner
and his avengers that had been around her and in front of her and a part
of her, always. Nat Turner, the nullifier of her life.

The silence was deep and sensual; she felt the fear and hatred and dread of her blackness like twin asps at her bosom. She had begged and pleaded and finally forced Eston to bring her here without being able to give a reason, but now she knew there was one: to force back invisibility forever, to confront her life. The danger was immense. Blacks, slave or free, all over Virginia, were hidden, crouched behind locked doors or plantation masters. Reprisals had been heavy, sweeping through counties as far away as Alberdale, as far south as North Carolina. Already more than a hundred blacks had been killed in the orgy of revenge that followed the two-day insurrection. Fifty-five whites had been killed. The number glowed before her. Blacks had perished because of the color of their skin, but for whites to perish for the same reason was revolution!

They were not invincible!

It was like the day she had stood in the yellow salon in Paris and listened to her brother James describe what was going on in the streets of the city. Blue blood had proved as red as peasant. White blood would flow as easily as black. Virginia had begun to bleed. This day's wound was staunched for the moment, but, like some royal disease, it would result in a never-ending hemorrhaging. Invincibility, Sally Hemings knew better than most, was in the mind. Her head whirled. She saw now the contradiction of her life. The weight of every moment of it. The weight of power was being exchanged. Just as, for two delirious days, the power of life and death had passed from white hands to black, so the power over her life and death passed at last from her master's hand to her own.

The thought rocked her back on her heels. She swayed slightly, and as she did the crowd stirred with her as the courthouse door opened. Sally Hemings clutched her son's arm with both hands as Turner stepped, stumbled, and was half-dragged into the dappled sunlight.

Eston's arm trembled under her clutching hands. They were without doubt the only black witnesses to this awful moment.

The pale woman standing beside her bastard son had thought she knew all about real power. Sally Hemings had spent forty years of her life in daily contact with one of the most powerful men in America. She had seen his friends and his enemies sweep in and out of their mansion in quest of power or in homage of it. She had never understood until now, however, why men lusted after it with such ferocity; why they fought, killed, slandered, flattered, begged, worshipped, begot sons in its name. All the Burrs, the Hamiltons, and the Washingtons that she had seen come and go had never been able to convey the meaning of it as well as this black man about to have terrible things done to him. He was now being dragged, spit upon, and kicked. He seemed half-crazy; wounded, a hunted animal, caught. Yes, this man's dignity had become real power to her. There was something almost obscene about seeing it here, so naked. This man had killed her enemies. For her! He had taken them on and fought them to his last breath. For her! He had stood while she had done nothing for herself all these years except submit. She wanted to cover the convicted man with her cloak. To blot out a vision of herself more terrible than she had ever imagined. She felt herself sinking into this white world as into a watery grave.

She raised a hand above her head as one does in drowning, but it was really to signal Nat Turner that he was not alone. Her hand was dragged down by her distraught son, in whose blue eyes she saw tears of fear and loathing.

Nathan Langdon made his way through the restless ugly crowd. He had ridden two days from Washington City to get here. He was haggard and uncoordinated in his movements; his face showed the same savage and perpetual bewilderment that had clouded his features since his precipitous departure from the Hemingses' cabin three months ago.

He shoved and pushed at random, but it was like trying to move some great mountain of flesh. People felt neither pressure nor pain. Shoulders and elbows knocked and prodded into tissue without the least response from the victim. Langdon even found he was shoving women in his frenzy to reach the courthouse before it adjourned and spewed out the criminals.

It was a nasty day, with sudden bursts of occasional sunlight. It seemed the right climate for the drama of the trial.

He too had been compelled to this place for reasons he only dimly perceived. He knew they had something to do with Sally Hemings. He was here to find out something about her, but also about himself; about Virginia, about slaves and insurrection and murder. People from all over the Tidewater region were calling Turner's rebellion an aberration, yet all Langdon's instincts told him this was not so. This event was logical and inevitable. There was no mayhem here. Here was systemized homicide as the perfect and indelible equation to slavery.

There had been talk of slave armies, thousands of men marching on Jerusalem, killing and raping and burning by the hundreds. The governor of Virginia had even begun to muster an army to meet the insurgents, and there had been talk of the federal army marching from Fort Lauredale in Maryland. Panic had seized the capital, yet Turner had been captured less than fourteen miles from where he had started his crusade.

The race from Washington City to arrive in time for Nat Turner's condemnation—one couldn't call it a trial, since he had confessed beforehand—had also been a sudden decision. Sally Hemings' words had echoed in his head like the rhythm of his horse galloping toward Jerusalem: "You haven't understood anything! You haven't understood anything!" He smelled the restless, straining crowd, the odor of death like singed hair, the overexcited bodies swaying in some kind of primitive dance of retribution. . . .

Turner was mad! Of course he was. Being an atheist, Langdon had only contempt for religious fanatics. It was Will Francis, Turner's aide-de-camp, who fascinated him, for here was pure, unadulterated logic, unclouded by biblical hysterics. My God! What was he thinking? How could he be rationalizing insurrection? What had become of him? His eyes narrowed against the brief glare of the sun, but soon the ray disappeared behind the clouds.

But Francis, ah, Francis . . . Francis had killed more than twenty-five of the fifty-five people murdered.

Langdon was sweating under his greatcoat as he burrowed his way toward the red brick courthouse. He now had no hope of reaching the courtroom or getting inside, although he had used what little influence he had to get a seat.

He had to see Nat Turner and Will Francis with his own eyes. His very life depended on it. If Nat Turner existed, then all he had been taught to believe was false.

Nat Turner, the nullifier of his life! Nathan's personal bewilderment seemed to flow into the larger drama.

Nathan Langdon had thought of Nat Turner as gigantic and black. But the man who was dragged into sight was of medium size, not more than five feet eight, slender, and a light-brown color. This visionary had made a full confession of his crimes. Crimes committed in the name of justice. God knows how many innocents in Virginia would pay, thought

Nathan. He had to urge the Hemingses to leave Virginia with their mother. She was no longer safe here.

Nathan passed so close to Sally Hemings that day he could have touched her cloak. Not in his wildest speculations would he have imagined, however, that the delicate recluse would be in this heaving, bloodthirsty mob. He had been promised that this could never happen, and that was what he had intended to tell his sons. Now he wouldn't be able. He stared intently at the dark figure being dragged through the crowd. Women and men were spitting, screaming, and cursing—especially the women. The man seemed but a sack of flesh; all spirit had fled him.

Later, Nathan learned that Nat Turner's body had been skinned; grease made of the fat, and souvenir money pouches made of the skin.

Eston Hemings knew his mother was in a near-hysterical state by now, and looked around wildly to find a way out of the crowd. They were jammed tight into this solid block of humanity. There was no escape. His mother was screaming that Turner was accusing her of something, but that she was not guilty. He could not make out what it was she was saying over the din of people. He bit his lip in exasperation. He was terrified. His bowels were gripped with spasms as if he were about to be seized and herded with the insurgents.

He knew in his heart he was as guilty as Turner. They were all guilty. Every slave or ex-slave had as much murder in his heart. His terror broke loose and spread out over the crowd, mixing with the miasma of stagnant hate that rose from the packed bodies. Nausea overcame him. His mother—he must get her away from here. He must get himself away. Not only away from here, but out of Virginia, out of the slave states. Madison was right. As long as there were slaves, there would be murder, and as long as there was murder, retaliation could fall on anything and anyone who was exposed. That included all Hemingses.

Eston turned his back on the courthouse and Nat Turner, placing himself in front of his mother to protect her. He put both his arms around her and leaned back using all the muscles at his command to secure a little breathing space around her head. Her pale face was transfixed; small beads of perspiration stood out on her forehead; she drew her cloak around her. Her mouth was slightly open, and her eyes glinted.

Eston understood now why she had made the long and dangerous journey to Jerusalem. Her obsession with Turner's rebellion, his trial, his execution—all that made sense to him. With the same intensity that had made her refuse to see Nathan Langdon, she had devoured every scrap of information she could obtain about Nat Turner. If Nathan Langdon had given a meaning to his mother's life, then Nat Turner had taken it away. He doubted if Langdon would even recognize her now. He had seen his mother change from a young woman to an old one, the amber eyes turn a dull brown, the jet-black hair streak with gray, almost overnight, the slender body dehydrate and fold like parchment. The glow of continual fever gave her an iridescent glow like that of a religious fanatic. But to what or to whom?

She sat for hours now staring into space. She would either talk to herself or fall silent for days. Sally Hemings had agreed to leave Monticello. But Eston worried that she would not survive the hardship of the journey West. He saw life running out of this proud, passionate, and secret woman.

Eston continued to fight to give his mother breathing space, but she seemed transplanted to another space, another time.

"O God," she whispered, "now forgive me for ever loving him." And Eston wondered which man she meant.

CHAPTER 9

ABOARD THE *GREENHELM*, JUNE 1787

> I am more and more convinced that Man is a dangerous creature,
> and that power whether vested in many or few is ever grasping, and
> like the grave cries give, give.
>
> ABIGAIL ADAMS

> I never hoped for mercy . . . for more than fifty years I have lived in
> an enemy country.
>
> JOHN ADAMS

I BELIEVED myself to be happy. As a child I *was* happy. I was brought up around the Big House at Monticello, and I loved those around me: my mother and uncles, Martha, Maria, Master Jefferson. Like all slaves, I was told nothing of my origins, which little by little I pieced together. Once, when I was eight or nine, my brother James and Martha went off to play and left me behind. I don't remember the reason, only that I felt abandoned and was crying.

Master Jefferson came upon me and tried to comfort me. He said being sad was a waste of time and the best thing to do when you were sad was to write down everything you saw about yourself, even the tiniest detail, and then to think about them one by one. By the time you had got halfway through the list, he said, you wouldn't remember the origin of your misery anymore. He left then and returned with a smooth pine board and some charcoal. He sat beside me and we made a list of all the plants, flowers, trees, and vegetables we could see in the kitchen garden and beyond; all the fish we could imagine in the little river by the northwest boundary; all the animals we could imagine living in the pines of the southwest boundary. It was my earliest recollection of him, and, that moment knowing neither past nor future, I felt only an immense calm and safety in his presence that rested on my shoulders like a warm cloak.

When Martha and James came back and found us together, Martha flew into a rage of jealousy, took off her boot, and started to hit me with it. The heel of Martha's boot came down above my temple and raked the skin and broke it. More blood than was warranted by the wound streamed down my cheek. It mingled with my tears of confusion and grief.

Out of desolation, I ground my teeth to keep from crying and brought my petticoat up to my ear to stem the flow of blood. But he was there before me. He held my head and pressed his handkerchief to the wound. Then he picked up Martha in his arms to keep her from hitting me again.

I remember her bright head meeting level with his great height in a blaze of red. He had flung her over his shoulder, but his eyes met mine in an attempt to console me, too. I despised Martha for being jealous of those few minutes I had had, when she had him as a father forever. . . . That day made me a list-maker. And a diary-keeper. I would continue all my life.

The *Greenhelm*, June 17, 1787

It was June seventeenth. I remember that day we were five weeks out of Norfolk, and we were, as Captain Ramsay would have said, "becalmed." There was not a sniff of wind; all the great square sails were furled and bound. The sun was hot on my head, and even now, if I close my eyes, I can still see the reflection of the sun on that smooth sea, like the field of white clover that runs down the back toward the river boundary of Monticello. I had found a wonderful hiding place, and intended to keep it for myself. It was high up on the forward mast, well, not so high up, but it was quite a dangerous climb. There was a little niche where I could watch what was going on below without anyone seeing me. I used to go up there and take off my bonnet. I can still hear little Polly screaming not to take her bonnet off, for if she got freckles in the sun, her father had written, he wouldn't love her anymore. Well, I would take my bonnet off and let my hair down and feel it curl round my waist. At home I was made to wear it tied up. My charge, Maria Jefferson, known as Polly, had done nothing but cry and cuff me for the past ten days. We, that is, her cousin Jack Eppes, Mistress Eppes, and myself, had lured her on the ship by deceiving her, and she still wasn't over it. She hadn't wanted to leave her Aunt Eppes to go to her father. Now she found herself on a strange ship with me, on her way to a foreign country to see a father she didn't remember, who said he wouldn't love her if she got freckles! From the time she had awakened, hours out of the port, she never stopped screaming about being shanghaied. I was just fourteen and Polly was nine. On the ship she had been left with me, who was as scared as she, and who felt just as abandoned. We were on our way to Paris, France, and her father, Thomas Jefferson, the minister to that kingdom. But by then, the worst was over. She had liked the captain, Mr. Ramsay, who had taken charge of her. She clung to him.

We were the only females on the ship and were made much of by the five other male passengers and the captain. For me, it was the beginning of my real history. From the moment I stepped onto that ship as nurse for Polly, everything that had happened to me before seemed to recede and grow smaller, until nothing remained except the sweep of the sea and the vastness of the sky and those unexpected days of peace and freedom.

I was still quite childish at fourteen, although I looked older than my age. My childhood days at Monticello—the little school, run for the white children and the house servants, taught by Mrs. Carr; old Cook's underground kitchens with all their intrigues and noise and heat—faded away in the bright sea-sun. I missed my mother. I thought for a while she was going to take Polly to Paris herself, but finally my mother had decided on me. It had been a queer choice.

It was Mammy Isabel who was supposed to have gone with Polly. When Mistress Eppes arrived to fetch her to Norfolk, it became known that Mammy Isabel was well gone with her eighth child and wasn't fit to travel. Mistress Eppes, who was altogether distracted anyway about losing Polly and sending her so far away against her will, was beside herself. First, because Polly really didn't want to go; and second, because there was no one to take her.

My mother had suddenly turned and looked at me and said, "Sally will go. She'll have James to look out for her." And before Mrs. Eppes could get her breath to ask if I had had my smallpox, or how old I was, Mama swept me out of the parlor, down the hall, and out through the kitchens, leaving Cook with her mouth wide open, ready, but unable to get her two cents in. I was breathless and scared. I had never been a nurse or a lady's maid or anything. Most I had been before then was a child! But Mama, she kept right on going, I can remember her skirts whistling, up the back stairs, into the linen room in the back, out with a straw trunk and three cases, then back to her own chests of linen to find chemises and petticoats and stockings and bolts of cloth for dresses.

Nothing Isabel had for the voyage fit me, even the underwear, so, in less than a week, everything had to be made new.

I was going and we couldn't miss the ship that was waiting in Norfolk. Master Jefferson was not going to tolerate any more delays. I suppose my mother could have found someone to fit into Isabel's things. After all, there were some three hundred and sixty-four slaves she could pick from, at least half were female and grown. But something pressed her to send me. To this day I don't know why. If it was fate, then she had a hand in it.

"It will be Sally, then. I can't think anymore," Mistress Eppes had said, finally and belatedly, for her voice was lost in the preparations of my departure.

I was leaving Monticello, the only home I knew, for a strange country.

Monticello, the most beautiful place in the world. The grass was greener, the scent of flowers keener, the blossoms bigger, the air clearer, the animals more healthy, the rigs more elegant, the cooking better, the slaves happier, the master—whom I had not seen since I was ten— better than any other place. Of course, I had never been outside the boundaries of Monticello. I was born at Bermuda Hundred, the planta- tion of my father, but he died three months after I was born, and the next year I came with my mother to live at Monticello, perched on its mountain, looking onto the Blue Ridge Mountains. My mother loved it more than I. It was always cool, with a breeze even in the hottest summer, and had a great hall that carried the freshness through the house. With horse and carriage, it took almost one hour to reach the main gate from the road.

Master Jefferson spent much of his time away from the plantation, in Philadelphia or New York, but every time he came home he would tear something down or build something new or rebuild something. He always arrived with his plans, and he would summon my brothers James and Robert and the white workmen, and they would start to work.

The slave cabins dotted the hillside in back of the Big House; they climbed up the hill like white morning glories gone wild with the smoke drifting out of the chimney fires. Along the back of the main house was a long covered walk, looking onto the kitchens, the meat house, smoke- house, icehouse, laundries, storehouses, and servants' quarters. This was my mother's domain. She oversaw twenty-five or more house servants.

We never had the number of servants a big plantation had. Master Jefferson didn't want it, and as Mistress Jefferson was frequently ill, she couldn't have managed to run them. My mother could have, of course, but there didn't seem to be much point in having a footman behind every chair and no mistress.

And, of course, there were always everybody's children, black and white, running everywhere. Once Master Eppes came rushing in to find Master Jefferson, tripped over a baby in the hallway, and slid seven feet on the parquet that had just been waxed for the fourth time that day. Fractured his rib, I remember. My mother usually kept everybody in the back and made do with Martin and Big George when the master was home.

My mother was beautiful. She was not very tall, but well formed and light mahogany in color. Her skin changed colors on different days; sometimes there was a rose tint and sometimes a yellow tint. She had her "dark" days and her "light" days. She used to say that my father would always remark on her color every morning. Once I surprised her in the fields just standing perfectly still like a statue among the tall wheat; her skin had taken on the same color, her eyes were blazing, and there were two tears running down her cheeks, but there had been no sounds of weeping.

A great calm had settled on our ship. Another day and still there was no wind, so we lingered, sitting on the tranquil sea, like a turtle in its shell. Sailors and passengers alike were lulled by the silence, the absence of movement. Games were organized and promenades. We made friends with the sailors who would make us gifts of little soft animals, creatures made out of rope and hemp. Polly and I used to "fish" over the side of the ship, which amused the sailors, who would ask us if we had caught any "catfish." One fat, red little sailor with a blond beard and green eyes made me the figure of a little dog in the image of a certain race they had in France. He made it out of hemp, and around the neck, tail, and legs was a mass of curls shaped like shrubbery. I later learned this race of dog was called *"caniche"* and was in fashion with the Paris gentry. I tied a ribbon on mine and called him George Washington. I would climb up to my hiding place, my "Monticello," with Washington, and there I would sit, making lists in my loneliness, to pass the time.

Blue. Sky. Water without wind. No clouds. Sixteen sails. Three flags. Birds. Seven Masts. Sun. A long railing of polished brass. God. Silver on blue. 85 spokes in the railing. 48 sailors on the ship. 3 cooks. 1 surgeon. 2 mates. 1 adjunct. 4 officers. 1 Captain. Captain Ramsay. The cargo; sugar. tobacco. rice. barley. molasses. peanuts.

Partial inventory of Polly's trunks: 1 stiffened coat of silk; 2 silk dresses, 1 cloak, 8 petticoats; 8 pairs of kid mittens; 4 pairs of gloves; 4 pairs of calamanco shoes; 8 pairs leather pumps; 6 pairs fine thread stockings; 4 pairs fine worsted stockings; 2 fans; 2 masks; 4 pairs of ruffles; 7 girdles consisting of 2 white, 2 dark blue, 1 rose, 1 yellow, 1 black; 6 linen drawers; 6 silk drawers; 13 chemises; 1 silver mirror; 16 dolls; 1 flute. . . .

Inventory of my trunk: 2 cotton petticoats; 1 quilted petticoat; 6 dresses, 1 pair worsted stockings; 4 linen aprons; 2 girdles; 12 chemises; 1 pair of shoes; 2 nightshirts; 1 wooden crucifix carved by John; 1 woolen shawl; 1 flute.

We got under way again. It had been still the whole day, when suddenly a breeze whipped the ribbons of our bonnets as Polly and I strolled on deck. There were sailors everywhere, running and leaping in a noisy slippery dance. The sails swelled before our eyes and the ship shuddered, rolling under us like one of my master's galloping bay horses. In about an hour we had begun to take on speed, and what a beautiful sight were the waves we made, frothing in the setting sun, the last streaks of light quarreling with the dark that finally came, dropping like a black cloth. From then on we made good time. I started looking forward to the future instead of being homesick for the past. That night we celebrated the trade winds.

Everyone dressed for dinner, and Captain Ramsay put on his dress uniform and fairly took our breath away. It was of a bright- but deep-blue hue, a velvet jacket with golden tassels on the shoulders hung with golden cords. The lapels were red satin, with a matching waistcoat. His cravat and shirt were a snowy white, with lace at the cuffs, and his small cloths were also white with blue stockings. His hair was powdered and tied with a blue ribbon, and his shoes were black patent-leather, with silver buckles. His buttons were of silver and he had a silver watch and a great sword in a silver harness and a blue sapphire on his hand. I will never forget the splendor of Captain Ramsay. Little Polly had found her first love. Oh, he was a splendid man, Captain Ramsay, and Polly did adore him! I think it was because she missed her father.

I remembered her father well, but Polly had been only four when he had left, and she had no recollection of him at all. All that she had known, as love and family, she had left in Norfolk with her aunt's family. I felt sorry for Polly. I loved her in a way I never loved her sister Martha. Martha was one year older than I, yet I was her aunt, just as I was Polly's. We had grown up together at Monticello, fought, played, rode, and laughed together. I was with her when Mistress Jefferson, my half sister, died. A long, pale, hot afternoon, stinking and mosquito-filled. We had tried to keep the bugs off her, taking turns fanning her. The doctor came at the end, but Master Jefferson wouldn't let him bleed her. My mother had dropped all her household duties to nurse her mistress. Master Jefferson had moved his study next to her bedroom and had not left her for the whole time it took her to die. Monticello, which had always been a house full of people, babies, guests, kin, and animals, seemed to empty out, and there was just my mother, Master Jefferson, Martha, Polly, and me, and the rest of the servants. At the end, my master had fainted dead away. He remained unconscious for so long his family thought he had died with her. The last thing she had made him promise was not to marry again.

It was my mother who had bathed her and laid her out and wept over her. The mistress had been like a daughter to my mother, even though they had been, like Martha and me, almost contemporaries. Whatever accommodations they had had to make in their lives because of my mother's concubinage, they seemed to have made long ago, because they genuinely loved each other. Mama combed her long hair out onto the pillow. Mama wept and wept and cleaned her and put on her jewels, draped the room and filled it with fresh flowers, and wept. She wouldn't let anyone else touch the body. She had tended Master Jefferson as well, who seemed to have lost his senses and his will to live. She cooked his meals and practically fed them to him, nursed him until he was able to go out riding again. Then he had ridden like the wind for days and days until he was exhausted. Martha rode with him sometimes, but mostly he was alone. And mostly Martha was alone. She couldn't reach her father in his terrible grief, so she turned to me. Or rather we turned to each other. We didn't cry over Martha Jefferson's death, but then Master Jefferson and Elizabeth Hemings wept enough for all of us. Martha and I seemed to enter into some kind of covenant; tearlessness. We were shocked by the conduct of the grown-ups. Somehow it didn't seem dignified. One day Martha, who was called Patsy to differentiate her from her mother, held up a mirror to my face and said: "You look more like her than I do. I look like my father."

In seven more days we were to reach England. I was happier with every passing day. Everything in my former life grew smaller as we put more and more ocean between our ship and Virginia. Monticello became farther and farther away.

I felt myself breaking a barrier, leaving childhood for adulthood. I already knew that I looked much older than my age, and something happened on board which brought home to me the fact that I was no longer a child.

It was June nineteenth, and Polly was busy playing cards and learning curse words from Captain Ramsay. The sea was navy blue, with lacy frills of soft waves made by a gentle easterly wind. The sky was bright blue without a cloud. We had had nothing but good weather. When I told the captain that I too would have loved just one storm at sea, he had laughed and said beautiful girls shouldn't make wishes that beautiful girls might regret, as beautiful girls usually got what they wanted in life. Considering my place in life, I thought he was making fun of me, and my eyes filled with tears. I started to speak, but he had already turned away, occupied with his affairs.

Later that day, one of the five gentlemen passengers, Monsieur LaFaurie, a Frenchman, spoke to me for the first time. I was delighted, for on my own I could not have addressed him. I was anxious to ask him about Paris, the French people. We had often had French visitors at Monticello. My mother always took special care with the food on those occasions, since she said the French put great store in what they ate. And always Mistress Jefferson took special care with what she wore because, as with their food, she said, the French cared a great deal about what they put on their backs. This, I found out, was a contagious disease, for never was I so consumed with envy for clothes and despondent not to have them as in Paris.

It seemed to me too that the French were very careful about the way they spoke, for Monsieur LaFaurie hemmed and hawed for over an hour before he finally asked me: Why did people refer to me as being a Negro slave? Since obviously I was neither a Negro nor a slave. "Why, you are whiter than I," I remember him saying in astonishment.

I could have told him that I was a slave not because of my color, but because my mother was a slave and her mother before her. But I was, I found myself lying, a Spanish orphan from New Orleans (that sounded distant and foreign enough), engaged as a lady's maid for Miss Jefferson. I was on the seven seas, far from Monticello, and I let my imagination take me through a most convincing childhood. I had had much practice with Martha at home, making up imaginary childhoods.

But, of course, he asked Captain Ramsay later, who told him the truth, plus my age. He also gave me a scolding I would never forget. After the gentlemen had had their brandy and cigars, Captain Ramsay sent for me.

"Sally, I want to know why you deliberately lied and misled Monsieur LaFaurie this morning."

"Because he wouldn't have believed me if I had told the truth."

"I can't believe that a slave at Monticello has been brought up to lie. Your master would be shocked, and what an example to set for young Miss Jefferson!" He sighed and waited for me to say something. When I didn't, he continued. "You know it is very difficult to have two female passengers on this ship. Of course, Miss Jefferson is a child, but you are not, and you should be careful how you conduct yourself. I know that at home you have all kinds of freedom and license and that you are . . . are . . . are even encouraged . . . but you must remember in the close quarters of a ship, you cannot . . . I will not permit that you give . . . provocation to my gentleman passengers. You may look sixteen, but I know you are but fourteen, and you invite . . . something you are not prepared for, to be sure. . . . You are a child, and I might add a not very well-brought up slave and servant, and if you have not been taught as yet your place in life, then I will confine you to your cabin until we reach shore."

All my pretensions of womanhood dropped like so many petals. I had wanted to impress Monsieur LaFaurie because he hadn't treated me any differently for being "black." I supposed French people didn't know any better.

"I have not said anything to Miss Jefferson, nor do I intend to. Nor do I intend to punish you myself. That is, if you behave yourself. Am I understood?"

"Yes, Master."

"Now, another thing, Miss Hemings. You have the habit of sitting on the first platform of the forward mast. Sitting there, you may not be aware, but you are in *full view* of the sailors working beneath the upper deck. You cannot see them, but they can see you. You sit there for hours, and undo your hair and let it stream down your back, and this is dire provocation for the sailors who call you the 'siren.' I know you don't know what that means, but let me say, for a sailor, a siren ... is someone who makes ... who provokes."

"What's that?"

"Provocation ... flirting ... frolicking," he said.

I almost fainted with shame. Captain Ramsay, who had been getting redder and redder, paused, and I began to sob. I was suddenly lonely and miserable.

For the first time in my life I realized that I was truly alone. I had never had a father, and might never see my mother again. I had no rights before society, whatever Monsieur LaFaurie said. I had no rights even over my own body, which was changing and unnatural to me. I could be coveted or punished at the whim of any white man, not just my master. No kin of mine could protect me, for they had no rights either. This horrified, tobacco-smelling white man before me could beat me or confine me or take me to his bed and I had no redress: no man would step forward to protect me, and I had no right to protect myself if I could.

I was a slave. A female slave. I felt sick.

Poor Captain Ramsay was utterly undone. He sat me down. Then he stood me up again. He poured me a glass of some kind of spirits and made me drink it. But it did nothing against that great dark desolation that crouched in my soul that day.

We would get to Paris; Polly would find her father, but I would not find mine. I was a slave. Captain Ramsay sat with me in the dark cabin a long, long time. He said how sorry he was for having been so stern. He hadn't realized how innocent I was, how young. He tried to take me in his arms, but I let out a scream of terror. So we sat there like two stones, me with tears rolling down my cheeks. Finally, he let out a big tobacco-ish sigh and got up. He paced around for a while, lit a cigar, and stared out of the porthole, so that I saw only the broad blue of his back.

After a time he left, saying he was going to fetch Miss Jefferson. Polly finally came much later, bringing Washington with her, and she took me in her arms.

The next two days, Polly and I spent the afternoons listening to stories about Paris from Monsieur LaFaurie. It didn't seem possible that such a city could exist on the same planet with Charlottesville, Virginia. We never tired of hearing the descriptions of the ladies and their dresses, the coiffures, the gardens of the Tuileries and Versailles, the palaces of the king, the Royal Palace, Marly, Fontainebleau. I dreaded that I would be sent back to Virginia once Polly was safely delivered to London. Polly said she wouldn't allow it, but I had already learned not to put too much faith in the promises of mistresses.

Captain Ramsay announced that we would reach our destination the next day, the twenty-sixth of June, and little Polly understood that she would be separated from Captain Ramsay, to whom she had become so attached. She too made everybody laugh by announcing that she would not leave the ship until she had her storm at sea. That she felt cheated, after being practically kidnapped onto this ship, not to have had a real storm and waves *that* high. Captain Ramsay laughed and said he would ask the cook if he would "stir" up a storm for Polly that night.

The last night I dressed Polly in white muslin and put her hair up. I dressed myself in red with a dark blue girdle and I let my hair out and tied it with a red ribbon. The gentlemen seemed quite pleased. Captain Ramsay seemed relieved that I was myself again, and all the officers and gentlemen rose when we left the table.

The next morning we saw birds and smelled land. After a long voyage even the inexperienced can smell land. Everybody was up early so as not to miss the first glimpse of the shore and the famous Cliffs of Dover. We were to go up the Thames to London. We had spent six weeks on the sea. I had stored up those six weeks of freedom, of being at no one's beck and call, making lists in my diary and entries in my heart. I had read and I had written and I had dreamed. And I had grown up.

When land was sighted, a great cheer went up from everybody on deck, and Captain Ramsay appeared resplendent in still another new dress uniform. He was a vain and beautiful man! The sailors too had on their best tunics. The ship's orchestra started playing a very gay tune as the banks of the river closed in on us. We slipped along the narrow channel toward the port of London Town.

I had never seen such a place filled with more white people than I had ever imagined in one place. Not one black face anywhere. It was for me a strange and new sensation. There were no slaves. This was another world.

We had dressed in white that day. Polly was trembling in agitation, and clinging to Captain Ramsay as he led us down the gangplank toward a bright-yellow carriage with magnificent horses, in front of which stood a couple dressed in black. The couple was Abigail and John Adams. They had come to fetch us. They seemed a pretty couple as we approached them. They looked stern and straight in front of their pretty carriage, with a splendid liveried footman atop in scarlet. Abigail Adams was short but still slightly taller than her husband, slim and in black silk. Her husband, holding her arm, was short, round, and portly, with a large square head that seemed especially bald because of the abundance of his side-whiskers. His face was ruddy, his mouth stern, his eyes direct, and his expression happy.

I followed slightly behind Polly and Captain Ramsay, and stood apart while the greetings were exchanged. The Adams couple seemed to know Captain Ramsay and greeted him warmly. I could tell from the set of Polly's body that she was about to burst into tears. She was clinging to Captain Ramsay with both hands, as he and the handsome couple tried to coax her into the waiting vehicle. She called my name in terror and Abigail Adams, in one swift movement, turned her gaze toward me.

I got a good look at her, too. She had an oval face with a long regular nose, a pointed, almost fleshless chin, and a thin mouth. It was her eyes that made her face; they were tear-bright and sparkling, closely spaced and quick, like the eyes of a small animal. From beneath her bonnet sprang bright-red curls. Her eyebrows were arched high, giving her whole face a mischievous look. It was a face that had no age, although at the time she was middle-aged. Her color was high, as in people with that color hair, and, as she turned, there were two bright spots of exasperation on her cheeks.

"And who are you, Miss?"

"I am Mistress Polly's slave, Ma'am."

Several expressions passed quickly across her face, but the one that settled there was one I already knew well: that of a rich white lady eyeing a poor darky slave. She looked first at her astonished husband, then at Captain Ramsay, who still had hold of one of Polly's hands while I had taken the other in mine.

"What!" she said.

It was the first time, I am sure, Abigail Adams had ever seen or addressed a slave of her own country.

CHAPTER 10

LONDON, JULY 1787

I cannot feel but sorry that some of the most Manly Sentiments in the Declaration are Expunged from the printed copy. Perhaps wise reasons induced it. . . .

ABIGAIL ADAMS, 1776

I have had for a fortnight, a little daughter of Mr. Jefferson's, who arrived here with a young Negro girl, her servant from Virginia.

ABIGAIL ADAMS, JULY 1787

"A WHITE SLAVE!" Abigail Adams would never get over the shock of seeing the image of Thomas Jefferson's late wife descending the gangplank of Captain Ramsay's ship in the guise of a Negro slave.

"So it seems. Since we are hosts to one."

"I won't have a slave, black or white, under my roof. It's . . . abhorrent to me."

"I know, Abigail, but the child is here, and we cannot do much about it until we have further instructions. Now, if she had been middle-aged and black . . ."

"Oh, John. It's not that . . . or maybe it is that, I don't know. Her color only underlines the horror of her condition because it's our color. But, even more serious, I can't in good conscience entrust the care of a child to another child. The girl is a child, a beautiful one, but one with undoubtedly no training as a nurse or even a maid. Why, she needs more care than Polly herself!"

"She seems very sweet—clean and good-natured."

"I insist she go back to Virginia. She is of no use to me and I don't see how she could possibly be of any earthly use to Mr. Jefferson."

John Adams, shifted his rotund body in the stiff, uncomfortable, new English furniture they had ransomed their lives to buy, and looked at his wife. She was the very essence of his life and his good fortune. The long years of separation—first when he left for the Continental Congress in Philadelphia, then to Europe—were over now, forever. He

73

would never leave Abigail again. His life was comfortable, happy, and so well-run with her here in London. He wouldn't want anything to mar this perfect felicity. He knew Abigail could be stubborn in matters which she considered principles. She was a staunch abolitionist, as he was, but without any of his compromising instincts. God—the child did look like Jefferson's dead wife Martha, thought John Adams. Years later, they would learn that Sally Hemings was Thomas Jefferson's half-sister-in-law.

"Abigail, we can't do anything until we have instructions from Thomas Jefferson. Which, I should think, will be forthcoming."

"Mr. Jefferson! Where is he? Why isn't he here to fetch his daughter? I've already written him about Sally."

"Well, we'll have to wait for an answer then."

"Captain Ramsay's ship sails shortly. She ought to be on it."

Abigail was being particularly stubborn about this, thought John Adams. Why? The poor girl had just endured a long sea voyage.

"First of all, Abigail, if Sally leaves before Jefferson arrives, Polly will be stricken with grief. She is wholly attached to Sally, who is her only link with the loved ones she's left in Virginia. She's a sensitive child. She'll be upset. You don't want that, surely?"

"I would do anything for Polly's happiness. I have taken her to my heart, John—so gay, so fragile, so beautiful. Like Nabby as a child. But when Mr. Jefferson comes—"

"If he comes. Meanwhile, we can't deprive Polly of Sally. Besides, I don't like the idea of sending Sally back unescorted on another dangerous journey. We haven't the right. She is, after all, under our protection until her master comes. Jefferson himself may be expecting her. He may have sent for her, for all we know. We can't dispose of her. She is," Adams continued wryly, "his own property, and we have no legal right to tamper with his rights over her."

"Property!" Abigail Adams stifled an outraged cry. John was baiting her, to be sure, in his lawyerly way, but she couldn't help it, the word fled to the top of her head and burst there like a shell. It was the most iniquitous scheme God had ever invented! How she wished there wasn't a slave in the States! They had fought and won for themselves what they were daily robbing and plundering from those who had just as good a right to freedom as they did; who had set foot on the soil of their blessed nation at the same time their forebears had; who had fallen in battle against England first!

"You know, my dear," Adams continued, "if Sally does get to Paris with Polly, she is, by French law, free. Slavery has been abolished on French soil. By sending her back, we may be depriving her of her only chance for emancipation. She has only to claim it." John Adams knew this would clinch his argument and he had saved it until last. His wife had an acute sense of justice, which he cherished and admired, and slavery had a moral and physical repugnance for her. She felt, as he did, that it corrupted not only the fiber of the best class of the South but threatened the very existence of the nation.

"I didn't know that, John." Abigail was stunned by this news. Had it been fate, then, that had chosen Sally out of the hundreds of Monticello slaves for this potential blessing?

"It is true, Abigail. Think about it."

But Abigail was thinking about something else. She had a strange sense of foreboding, and the obvious origins and extraordinary beauty of Sally Hemings did nothing to dilute her alarm.

Those Southern white planters lived like the patriarchs of old. Even as she thought this, she realized that her own motives were not entirely pure. It was not only the presence of a slave in her household, however temporary, that was so upsetting.

Abigail Adams was nothing if not honest. It was an honesty so total and so dulcet it gave her whole person a kind of brilliant transparency that more than made up for her lack of physical beauty. The maid was a charming and docile child. But the maid was also an affront to white womanhood, she thought, a living and most visible proof of the double standard of white male conduct. The master-slave relationship appalled her not only because the dignity of both master and slave were destroyed but the exercise of total power over other human beings who lived in the closest possible intimacy with them provoked the kind of reciprocal sensuality Abigail Adams both feared in herself, recognized as part of human nature, and read in the face of Sally Hemings. This girl was both a provocation and a victim, she thought. In her still unformed personality there resided the innate arrogance of the totally possessed . . . an elusive disinterestedness that was both an insult and an invitation. How to explain these ambiguous feelings to a man? How to explain powerlessness to any man who had never experienced it? Abigail Adams bit her lip and finally looked up at her husband. "Why didn't you tell me before of this chance for her in France?"

"I hadn't thought of it, actually. There is something disloyal to Jefferson about it."

"I know. And I would sooner be disloyal to myself than to him. But . . . shouldn't we tell her?"

"We'll talk about it again, Abigail. We have nothing to decide just yet. We can decide later. Jefferson, at any rate, knows the law."

"No, I don't think we should discuss it again, John. Let fate decide."

John Adams knew from the tone of his wife's voice, and from her face, that he had won. It was the moment for concessions.

"Of course, you should do whatever you think best," he said. "This is your domain."

"She is devoted to Polly. If we can improve her lot in life, we have the duty to do so, now that I know what Paris might mean to her . . ." Abigail's voice trailed off. She knew her feelings about Sally Hemings. What she didn't know was Sally Hemings's feelings about her. She would have preferred outright hostility in a slave. A sense of injustice . . . of rebellion . . . but this mixture of abject love, indifference, and unquestioning, nay luxurious acceptance, disturbed the neatness of her soul. There was a feral self-satisfaction in the submissiveness of this adolescent, she thought, that was more than that of a servant. It was demeaning to a woman and addicting to a man.

"Besides," her husband's voice continued, "it is pleasant to hear an American accent among the servants."

John Adams liked Sally Hemings. He liked her reserve and the limpid good character he sensed in her. And her voice: he had never heard a more pleasing one—fresh, lovely, and melodious.

Abigail Adams said nothing. She had no desire, she thought to herself, to upset her domestic tranquility over so trivial a matter. Her nine years of separation from John Adams had marked in her a feverish desire for harmony. She had spent those years alone, running the farm and raising the children, six of those years separated from him by the Atlantic Ocean. After so long a wait, so deep a commitment to public service, so passionate an attachment of the heart, she thought, she looked forward only to peace and love in her middle years. Besides, she herself would discuss the problem with Jefferson when he arrived. They were old friends, weren't they? They understood each other, and her admiration for him knew no bounds. He was one of the choice of the earth. She remembered their happy days in Paris together, just after she had been reunited with John, and she remembered the awe of her son, seventeen-year-old John Quincy, who had come with them, for the great Thomas Jefferson.

The affection Abigail Adams lavished on Polly didn't extend to me, although I was also of a tender age and I too had left everything I loved behind me. She was kind to me, but with every effort I made I seemed to provoke more than please her.

Abigail Adams was a Yankee, the first I had ever met. She knew nothing about slavery. I doubt if she had seen a slave before. She knew only that she did not want "one" under her roof. When I came to understand that it was my origins she disliked and not my person, I began to respect and even like her, although I knew she was determined to send me back to Virginia.

Master Adams seemed to understand better. I know he was the one who argued against sending me back to Virginia. But Abigail Adams was adamant. Back to Virginia I would go. So I spent my days in the great house on Grosvenor Square under a cloud of apprehension. Captain Ramsay's ship was making ready to return to America, and Master Jefferson had not yet come for his daughter and me.

I had learned as a slave never to hope, never to anticipate, and never to resist, so I lived from day to day with the other servants, trying to please Mistress Adams—taking care of Polly and keeping as quiet as possible. I took every opportunity to get out of the house and see London, which appeared to me both terrifying and wonderful. Paris, I thought, could not be greater than this!

When we traveled on foot, the carriages and *porte-chaises* of the gentry would pass us as we made our way past the great town houses, which were palaces compared with the mansions I knew in Virginia. I had never seen such beautiful people, clothes, and carriages. The London ladies walked a great deal and very fast. I was used to long walks at Monticello, so I managed many miles a day through London. The sides of the streets were laid with flat stones, and the streets were filthy, but they were always crowded with people laughing and cursing.

Finally, the word came that Master Jefferson was not coming for Polly and me, but that he was sending his *valet de chambre*, Monsieur Petit. Abigail Adams was fit to be tied and Polly refused to leave. With Polly so upset, there was no longer any question of my returning to

Virginia. Why Master Jefferson did not come to fetch Polly, I learned later, but for Mistress Adams it was unforgivable.

Abigail Adams' thoughts were on Jefferson now. That his sex was naturally tyrannical was a truth so thoroughly established as to admit of no dispute, but men who wished to be happy, she muttered to herself, should be willing to give up the harsh title of "Master," and all such power of life and death over female souls.

Jefferson wasn't a cruel man, Abigail Adams thought, not by any measure. He was especially tender and gallant with the female sex. Why, then, this cavalier attitude and heartlessness toward his own small dear child, whom he hadn't seen since she was four. Why had he submitted her to the perils of a long sea voyage, uprooted her from those she loved and knew, only to insult her by sending a servant to fetch her! What could be holding Thomas Jefferson in Paris?

"I have written Thomas Jefferson and told him how deeply I regretted his not coming in person for his daughter." John Adams was also trying to calm the furor of his wife.

"I've endured all kinds of heartbreak because of long separations, John. The canceled visits, sickness in solitude away from my heart's partner, and other cruel infractions on my hopes and plans deemed necessary by duty or misfortune . . . have swallowed my grief in silence and self-abdication. But this I will not abide!"

"I'm afraid Adrien Petit is arriving to fetch her."

"Well, he'll have to leave without her if she doesn't want to go," said Abigail Adams stubbornly.

John Adams gazed at his wife in silence. There was something too excessive in her reaction to little Polly's plight. Mightn't she be overreacting, compensating for her own secret hurts all these years? Was she projecting onto this situation her own concealed rage at having been "abandoned" by him, John Adams, in the name of Public Duty and the fate of the newborn United States? He had left her alone so many years. . . . Had he seriously neglected his children in favor of his country? One thing was certain. He would never leave Abigail alone again.

True to her word, Mistress Adams made Monsieur Petit cool his heels for two weeks, while Polly refused to leave with a man "she couldn't understand." But no more messages came from Master Jefferson.

And Petit was unmovable. He would not leave without us; he had his orders. Finally, through the combined efforts of Mistress Nabby, Master Adams, and me, Polly Jefferson was finally detached from the skirts of Mistress Abigail Adams and bundled into the carriage that would take us on our road to Paris.

PART II

1787
Paris

CHAPTER II

PARIS, JULY 1787

I leave to time the unfolding of a drama. I leave to posterity to reflect
upon times past; and I leave them characters to contemplate.
ABIGAIL ADÀMS, 1801

THOMAS JEFFERSON stood in the tall rectangle of the French window
looking onto his gardens at the Hôtel de Langeac and guessed at the
hour. The tall frame stirred in the soft light and the nervous fingers of
Jefferson's left hand groped for his timepiece. Then, after a moment's
hesitation, he lowered his left hand and, with difficulty, raised his right
hand to his waistcoat and extracted his watch. For a brief second, he
pressed his right wrist against his breast as if in salutation and then he
brought the left hand up to cover the exposed wrist and hand which
were slightly twisted inward, the hand having an atrophied look. Slowly
his left hand caressed his injured right one, his pale eyes blinking away
the pain. A slight smile played at the corners of his fine mouth. As he
had guessed, it was almost five.

If Petit and Polly had started out early enough from London, they
would be in Dover by now. The thought of London made him pensive.
There was still no news of Maria's arrival. How long had he been
waiting for word from her? It seemed like years. He dared not move
from Paris lest he miss her. Jefferson turned and walked away from the
glowing windows and the multicolored flower beds framed by the
windows of his salon. A slender man, with a stiff air, accentuated now
by the way he now held his injured wrist, Jefferson's eyes were his finest
feature. A sapphire blue of dazzling clarity, they seemed to look out
upon the world like twin mountain peaks from his great height, frosted
and glacial, tinged with melancholy, with lashes the same color as his
red-gold hair. His complexion was fair, the fine skin almost transparent

under a rash of fine reddish-brown freckles that gave him a youthful, innocent look. The face was aristocratic and handsome with its long, slightly turned-up nose, sensual mouth, and firm, protruding, dimpled chin.

He did not consider himself vain, but he was quite pleased with the likeness the sculptor Houdon had begun of him. He had seen the plaster for the first time a few days before.

Entering his forty-fourth year, Thomas Jefferson had become, since he had been in Paris, almost dandyish in his manner of dressing, favoring creamy lace and sapphire-blue worsted. Even his injury had a certain romantic elegance. After his mysterious fall last year, which had deprived him of the use of his right hand, he had been forced to re-educate himself, and he now wrote almost as well with his left hand as he did with his right. But he was in pain at the moment. Both the wrist and the steady throbbing in his head had not abated since yesterday noon. He would force himself to work tonight. It did not seem possible that Petit and Polly could arrive before the day after next. He was very fond of his *valet de chambre*. He did feel slightly guilty that he had not sent James to London when he had learned that his sister Sally had been sent to accompany Polly from Virginia. He had hesitated, know-ing the Adamses' disposition toward Negro slaves; and knowing James's own temperament, he felt safer with Petit. Of course, he could have sent them both, but the extra cost, simply to please James, seemed excessive, especially now when the ministry and his expensive obliga-tions were taking all his official funds.

He stood absently in the middle of his magnificent oval salon with its painting of "Dawn" by Berthélemy on the ceiling, backlit by the late-afternoon sun, a figure in black with white linen and a blue waist-coat, the fair hair pulled back in a pigtail and lightly powdered.

When a servant in pale-yellow livery entered, he was startled. He had forgotten he had asked for the medicines and hot water to bathe his wrist at precisely five. Thomas Jefferson looked into the eyes of his slave James Hemings as if he were contemplating a mathematical equation.

James Hemings had not seen his sister in four years. She had been ten and he eighteen when he had left Monticello as body servant to Thomas Jefferson. He loved her more than any of his family and now that in two or three days she would be in Paris, the waiting was unbearable. She would bring the sweet breath of Monticello and all that it represented for him—family and the slavehood he had never forgotten.

He knew he could disclaim his bondage any time he wished on French soil. No one could hold him in slavery and now no one could hold her, either. What providence!

Thinking himself on the brink of freedom, he could even look on his master now with a certain affection. He did feel affection for Thomas Jefferson. His master had been more of a father to him than his real father, John Wayles, had ever been. When he and his brothers and sisters had not been freed, as Wayles had promised, and were sent to Monticello as part of his half-sister's inheritance, he had been nine years old. Old enough to work. Old enough to grasp the dream they had been deprived of. His mother, with all her wiles and cleverness, her airs of superiority and her concubinage, had failed. She had failed in the only way that matters to a slave concubine: she had not made his father love her enough to free his children by her.

When James entered the room, he found Thomas Jefferson standing, as if he had forgotten something. He had been in this mood for days now. He was, James knew, expecting word from London on the arrival of Lady Maria Cosway. The servant felt a wave of affection and pity for his master as he saw him there cradling his wounded wrist. Thomas Jefferson was not a happy man, thought James, despite all his fame and riches and celebrated friends. He was lonely. The death of his wife had made it impossible for him to believe again in happiness or good fortune. Moreover, his master missed his home more than he admitted.

Personally, James never intended to see Monticello again, nor Virginia for that matter, but he could understand pain and homesickness, especially since the sudden death of Jefferson's third daughter, Lucy. Now Thomas Jefferson's two remaining children would both be with him, and he, James, would be reunited with his beloved sister. As if they shared the same thought, Jefferson gave him a strange look, then smiled and squeezed his arm. Without a word, Jefferson sat in one of the armchairs and asked his servant to bathe and massage his wrist.

Two days later, a public coach drew up to the gates of the hôtel, and Petit, a little girl, and a very young woman stepped out. Polly Jefferson burst into tears at the sight of her father, whom she didn't recognize, while her maid paled at the sight of her brother. The two girls clung to each other, and finally the two of them embraced James Hemings, as Polly would not let go of her maid.

The joy of seeing the beauty and purity of his sister's face moved James deeply. She was well dressed, he thought, in new black silk that showed off her pale complexion and her dark hair, and she was fully formed. Her eyes were a pure liquid gold, a color he had not seen on anyone else. He took her in his arms and watched as, shyly, his master approached his daughter and pulled her away from her slave. James knew that the paleness of Jefferson's face was an indication of great emotion. Thomas Jefferson was intimidated by his own daughter. Later, he said he would not have known her if he had met her on the street, nor she him.

Polly Jefferson was to make him pay for those four lost years, and Thomas Jefferson paid gladly. He ruled his daughters, as he did everyone, with a fastidious tyranny. It fell hardest on Martha, who loved him most, but all of them were to feel the weight of that demand and its fetters of steel.

But that day they were a happy and reunited family. Martha, home from her convent, was dazzled by the beauty of her little sister and her maid. After much kissing and embracing, Thomas Jefferson and his two daughters went inside. Brother and sister remained behind in the sunshine.

Only Petit remained apart from this "family" celebration. How strange were the ways of Americans and their servants, he was thinking. James had explained to the Frenchman that they were literally the same family. This had shocked Petit, for he was the perfect servant: discreet in his service, correct, loyal in his protection of the ruling class and their privileges.

As they kissed and embraced, Adrien Petit saw more clearly than any of them the farce and the tragedy of that reunion.

Before the week was over, Polly Jefferson was in the Abbaye de Panthémont with her sister Martha. Sally Hemings was installed at the ministry and being taught by James's tutor, Mr. Perrault, and Petit began to teach her to be a ladies' maid.

Jefferson remembered everything and asked questions about everyone, white and black. Sally Hemings, through her mother, knew everything that had gone on in the intervening years. She delighted him with her stories, her reports on the crops and gardens. She took over from James the duties of nurse, and every day, her small but surprisingly strong hands would bathe and massage his wrist while she kept up a steady stream of conversation in her soft Virginia accent, a relief to his ears from the harsh beauty of the French he had become so accustomed to. Nothing seemed to be too trivial for him to ask about.

"Tell me everything," he begged. "Who has died, who has married, who has hanged himself because they cannot marry?"

The mansion where she would live now, explained James to his sister, was called the Hôtel de Langeac. James had moved there with his master about a year after they had arrived in Paris, where his master was minister plenipotentiary and ambassador to the French king, Louis XVI. The Hôtel de Langeac was situated halfway up the Champs-Elysées, one of the main thoroughfares leading out of the city. It went up to and then down the bridge leading to Neuilly and thence to Saint Germain-en-Laye, Marly, and the king's palace of Versailles. The hôtel (which James explained to her was the French name for a private mansion) adjoined the Grille de Chaillot, a large and beautiful wrought-iron and gilded-bronze gate that marked the limits of the city and was one of its exits and entrances at which the city tolls were levied.

The mansion itself was in creamy white stone with sculptured friezes. The main gate led into a spacious courtyard. To the right were the steps that led up to the front door. To the left of the reception hall was a sweeping pink marble staircase that led to the upper stories. On the ground floor was a circular room with a skylight, and adjoining it was an oval drawing room, one of the most beautiful of the mansion, from which steps led into the garden. It was the ceiling of this oval room which was decorated with the painting of Jean-Simon Berthélemy's "Dawn," the master's favorite.

James led his stunned sister through the elegant, beautiful rooms. On the second floor were the master apartments, with their spacious sun-filled bedrooms, each the size of the drawing room at Monticello, and each with its dressing room and bathroom attached with a hammered-copper and porcelain bathing tub. Then, with great excitement, James showed his sister the *"lieux anglais,"* or water closets, the latest invention and most modern installation imaginable. The young girl marveled at the painted ceilings and walls covered with silk. She looked out of the tall rectangular windows. And to think Virginians had the nerve to call what they lived in "mansions"! Monticello. She burst into laughter at what she had until now called with awe the "Big House."

CHAPTER 12

PARIS, DECEMBER 1787

"SLAVERY is outlawed in France. We are on French soil. That means we are emancipated. Free."

"I don't believe you," whispered Sally Hemings, as if they were being overheard in the empty pantry under the kitchens.

"It is true!"

"You make so many jokes, James, tell so many far-fetched stories...."

"Why don't you ask your master, if you won't take your brother's word? Ask a white man."

"Have you ever asked him?"

"I don't have to ask what I know to be true. There are white men in Paris and London and Boston who are working for the freedom of Negro slaves everywhere, but Thomas Jefferson isn't one of them."

"It seems so unbelievable."

"It's not, not if you have the courage to claim what is yours by right."

"It would hurt him to know we were talking like this. He is all we have."

"All we have!" James Hemings slapped his sister's face. It was an instinctive gesture, directed more against his own rage than at her disbelief. The effect on her was immediate. Her eyes welled tears and she stopped listening. The enormity of what her brother had said struck her with the same force as had his hand. She had never contemplated freedom. Freedom, to Sally Hemings, was a vague, glimmering place no one ever returned from to prove it really existed. Before she

89

realized it, she spoke her thought aloud. "What do 'free' people do?"

"They work for themselves and their families," James answered. "They get paid for their labor. They go where they want and do what they want according to the nature and demand of their trade. They vote. They hold property. No one can imprison them, brand them, beat them, kill them with impunity, and no one can sell them." James Hemings tried to control his anger and tried to explain as he would to a child, for he remembered that his sister was still a child.

"Free people marry and have children, who belong to them and for whom they are responsible and who in turn take care of them in old age. Free people do what they want without asking permission of any man. Many are like us, mulatto, métis, or quadroon, but there are black freedmen as well. In the French Indies, one can buy one's freedom by accumulating enough money to buy oneself back. A few slaves have even done it in America." James took a deep breath and continued. "Freedmen protect their home and hearth and children and wife. They congregate with their friends when and where they wish. They choose their holidays and travel without permission from anyone. They have rights and are protected before the law. Free people have family names that they pass from father to son. They have property, and they can learn to read and write."

"But we already know how to read and write, and we have a family name!" said Sally Hemings. She clung to the one thing she understood.

"Not our family name—a white man's family name, and what good does it do us to read and write? To read and write is to be able to rise in the world, not to amuse one's master or mistress by reciting like a trained monkey, or reading to them when they are too lazy to do it for themselves. We must refuse to go back to Virginia and prepare ourselves for the day we are commanded to do so."

"Stay in France?"

"Or Europe. There are other countries besides France."

"What would I do?"

"Let me worry about that."

"They have children that really belong to them? They cannot be sold? Explain it to me again. From the beginning."

"In the beginning . . ." James smiled. He smiled and lifted her up in his arms. "Little sister, you are going to learn; learn to walk, then learn to run! Then you will learn some other things as well. Your French is not bad. . . . And that voice!"

Sally Hemings smiled uncertainly. She found it difficult to follow

James's changes in mood. His ideas, which would spill out of him in a torrent of words, admonishments, curses, lessons, and silences, always frightened her. The catlike eyes would gleam with malice one minute and brim with adoration the next. Sometimes he would let loose such a cyclone of abuse that the air itself seemed to shrivel. He had done this at home as well, provoking gales of laughter from the gathered entourage. Her mother had been glad to see him leave with Master Jefferson; at least it was less likely he would end up swinging on the end of a rope in Paris than in Albemarle County. Her half brother Robert called James's swearing raunchy, pole-cat, ornery, low-life, filthy swearing, and the whole family would burst out laughing, since Robert would find himself swearing at swearing. Then someone would break down and plead for one of his imitations, for no one at Monticello possessed the art of mimicry better than James. He had the ability to make people laugh and make their blood run cold at the same time. He would choose his words carefully and would work himself up into a malicious frenzy. This was what he was doing now. He was taking her carefully through an insurrectionist garden, having her smell first this flower, then another, leading her gently toward the strong scents, the bolder colors, the mandrake, and the poison. Little by little, he led her where he wanted her to go, stopping to explain an idea. All these ideas were new to her, and James had to explain them to her over and over.

He made her study seriously, she read anything she could get hold of. They were already planning what to tell their master when the time came.

Sally Hemings acquiesced to everything. She was borne along on the tide of her brother's vision and excitement. After a long lesson, she would make her way to her room, lie on her narrow bed, and stare at the ceiling.

James Hemings knew that it was lonely for his sister in the ministry. There was no one her age, and she had no official duties besides that of bathing her master's injured wrist. Except for an occasional errand, or a visit to the convent, she spent most of her time strolling in the gardens, or reading.

She applied herself to learning everything she could, the rudiments of dressmaking, hairdressing, and clothes-cleaning. In a few months the backwater-country slave had learned to speak the language well. Brother and sister were now speaking French together. They would also at times combine their Virginia-slave English with French, inventing ther own secret language. But with Thomas Jefferson, Sally Hemings spoke only her soft Virginia-accented English. Thomas Jefferson sought his slave's company more and more. They seemed drawn to each other, master and slave, by mysterious threads that Sally Hemings did not completely understand. Thomas Jefferson indulged her as a child rather than as a servant, laughing when Petit remarked that it didn't matter if she was useless around the ministry; she was such a joy to be with and to look at. And often he would gaze at her, staring without realizing it, or without realizing that he was being watched.

Both James Hemings and Adrien Petit saw this affection develop. Petit, observing with the cynicism of his race and his caste, and James like a blind man; he had been away from Virginia and slavery too long.

"James?"

"Yes?"

"Do you remember our father at all?"

"Master Wayles? Sure I remember him, I was nearly ten when he died."

"What was he like? Was he kind to Mama?"

"I suppose you could call him kind. He never mistreated her and she had the run of the house, nay, the whole plantation. He was never there."

"What happened to her husband?"

"He died. At least I think he died. I never knew Mama to say anything about him."

"And her other children—those who didn't come with us to Monticello?"

"There were two who became the property of our half sister Tibby Wayles."

"And Mama's mother, our grandmother?"

"Knew her too at Bermuda Hundred. An Afric she was. The most beautiful woman on the plantation, and she was old when I saw her. She had run away many times. She had an 'R' for runaway branded on her chest—it should have marked her cheek, but at the last moment our father didn't have the heart to do it."

"Mama never speaks of her."

"I know."

"And on the other side, our father's mother?"

"He was an old man, our father. He died a few months after you were born. I never saw anybody who looked like his mother."

"So strange to have blood in your veins and not know where it comes from."

"Yes. Not like the Bible, where you can say he was the son of . . . who was the son of . . . who was the son of . . . That's what you mean?"

"Yes," she said, "yes, that's what I mean. If I could know that the son of the son of my son would have some knowledge of me, would have something . . . a portrait of me or a mother or grandmother who remembered me . . . if something of mine, some object or some memory could touch him years and years and years from now . . . That he would know who I am. Who I was. That it wouldn't all be silence."

There was so much fervor in Sally Hemings' voice that it stopped James from making a derogatory remark about ancestors. She was right in a way. Blood was magic. To be able to trace it back was the most precious thing they had lost. He thought about the plantation and the old people with their fetishes. They knew blood was magic, a link to the past, a curse or a blessing on its inheritors, a fearful potent magic. Even their mother, Elizabeth Hemings, was not completely free of ancestor worship. She knew a few spells herself. He smiled bitterly. If only she had used them at the right moment.

It was enough for white people to know that they were "sons of God" straight down from heaven. No intervening generations to cloud their divinity; their blood was "pure," yet they deigned to mix it with the blood of Africa, a blood laden with the responsibility of a million years.

The two young people looked at each other, their eyes meeting in frail comprehension.

"Yes," James said, "it is as if part of you is recovered if you claim ancestors and expect descendants."

"But if we don't know them—can't find them or their graves or anything?"

"Then it is very bad voodoo. Very bad spirits. The gods are angry and turn away from us."

"And if our gods are angry, can we go to their God?"

"It seems we started off wrong 'cause of somebody called Ham. And so we are damned to be waterbearers and woodchoppers and servants because, all of a sudden, we are back with blood curses. We arrive here in trouble. Everybody else starts out with a new soul, only we come here with the curse of Ham around our necks. No purity for us. Christ didn't get around to it."

"And the Afric gods say this, too?"

"Of course not. They haven't even heard of Jesus. He hasn't been around long enough to even make the acquaintance of those gods. Frankly, if people get the gods they deserve, then white people sure got theirs because He's the meanest God I ever heard of. And the more He loves you, the harder it's on you. So He must really love us!"

James threw back his head and let out a roar of laughter.

James Hemings had the narcissistic energy of a forest animal. Almost as tall as his master, he was lean and muscled. His body gave him a European rather than an American look: the coal-black wavy hair, the thin flared nose, even the dark-ivory color seemed less exotic here against the rich brocades and silks of French interiors than in the simpler trappings of Monticello. His face was a harder replica of his sister's. The shadow of his heavy beard and eyebrows shaded his face with a kind of violence entirely absent from hers. The generous mouth was almost always engaged in complaining and turned down in perpetual discontent. Yet, instead of giving his face a somber, even disagreeable aspect, his bad nature took on a melancholy and romantic tinge. Both black and white had always indulged him in this, and everyone said that he had a handsome, even noble face, despite its latent anger, which could be dispersed with one delicious smile. This had saved him from many a reprimand and several beatings.

His arrogance and adventurous nature stood him in good stead as a cook, and his long, beautiful hands had begun to shape masterly cakes and pastries. He was now in the midst of his third apprenticeship. The first had been with a *traiteur* named Combeaux. He was calm and patient in the kitchen. Meticulous and infinitely careful. Never did he lose his temper while cooking—the mark of a true chef. Adrien Petit recognized this, and although he was hazy on the dictates and protocol of American slavery, he had already indicated to "Jim-mi" that he would be welcomed in several French households when, as James put it, "the time came."

One day, six months after her arrival in Paris, Sally Hemings passed the gilded mirror in the entrance of the Hôtel de Langeac and caught a glimpse of herself. She was pleased with what she saw. She had completely recovered from her mild case of smallpox, an experience that

94

had terrified her and through which James and Petit and Master Jefferson had nursed and indulged her. She had had only a few eruptions on her face, but those had caused her untold misery. The doctor had been kind, and her ordeal had left her without a mark on face or body.

Her provincial air and homemade country clothes had disappeared with the fever and her new skills in dressmaking. The clear liquid gold of her eyes gazed serenely at her image in the polished silver. She was satisfied.

Her lips turned up in a smile and two dimples flashed for an instant on either side of her mouth. Abigail Adams had been right. It was more criminal to be out of fashion in Paris than to be seen naked. To which the Parisians were not averse, as Mistress Adams had noted . . .

The French ladies, she thought, as she looked at herself in the mirror, displayed such an art with powder, rouge, wigs, perfumes, and elaborate clothes that you couldn't be sure they weren't the famous dolls of Mademoiselle Bertin, dressmaker to the queen, that traveled from court to court all over Europe, dressed in the latest fashion.

The French ladies spent a great deal of time making themselves beautiful, she mused. The French ladies also possessed a most voluptuous room installed only for bathing, called a *salle de bain*. She repeated the expression out loud. The French ladies would even sometimes receive visitors there! They would empty a pint of milk into the water to cloud it, and called it a *bain de lait*. The French ladies . . .

The young girl repeated the new French expressions she was learning, savoring them each time anew. She laughed outright. She was happier than she had ever been in her life.

She was learning new and independent ways of thinking and behaving. Her eyes no longer slid off the glances of whites. She was able to look white people in the eye, even to address them in French or English without hesitation.

Humming to herself, she smoothed the folds of her new dress, pulled the hood of the soft woolen cloak she wore over her head, and stepped out into the crisp December air.

In December a young painter from Massachusetts named John Trumbull arrived at the mansion. I liked him from the beginning. He was to spend some time with us, sketching the French officers who had fought in our Revolution and doing a portrait of my master for the painting commemorating the Declaration of Independence. He was tall and thin, with dark round eyes that seemed to see everything and consume what they saw. Things, he told me, were lines and planes to him, light and shadow. I asked him if he saw me this way and he replied by making several sketches. He showed them to me.

"This cannot be me," I said to him.

"But it is. You have only to look in the mirror."

I tried to please everybody: my master, my brother, and the girls; but it was not always easy. James had always been demanding and quick of temper, and now he had taken on all the airs of the French servants. He took me in charge and rationed my contacts with the other servants. Polly had wanted me to accompany her to the convent, where the young ladies were allowed to keep their maids, but Master Jefferson was against it. He, too, was making more and more demands on my time and guarded me jealously from the outside world.

As consolation for my disappointment at not being allowed to stay at the convent—it was a calm, beautiful place, which I had liked at first sight—he had allowed me to study with Monsieur Perrault, James's tutor in French.

"You have a lovely voice, Sally. Married to the French language properly spoken, it will be extraordinary. Extraordinary." It was the first compliment I had ever received outside of my slave family and I had blushed. But Monsieur Perrault went on, without apparently noticing.

"It is not so much in the tone as in the timbre. Like a musical instrument. A pity you have had no musical training. I am sure you should sing. And you, 'Jim-mi,' at least you've learned how to swear in French to perfection. A notable necessity for a chef."

Monsieur Perrault had looked from me to James. I knew he was really very fond of "Jim-mi" despite his *"sottises"* and *"mauvais traitements."* James was horrible to his tutor, but diligent in his studies, preparing himself for his "future." He never said exactly what this future consisted of. It was a "secret," only to be revealed at the "right" moment.

There were only nine months between us, and Patsy and I were preoccupied with the changes taking place within ourselves. I was almost fifteen, she sixteen. Polly was still a child, but she had all the beauty and grace denied her sister. Martha had long resigned herself to not being beautiful but she was still unhappy about being in a country, and a society, that placed such importance on it. Because she was plain, several beautiful ladies befriended Martha, as she was no threat to them. She was the image of her father, and almost as tall as he. She towered over most of the men who were introduced to her. She had bright-red hair like her father, and freckles, which were her despair. Still she had a kind of touching grace, and she was an excellent horsewoman. She had her admirers, but she rarely went out in company. Sometimes she returned home for a special party or dinner, but during my first months in Paris, Master Jefferson was occupied with the mysterious Maria Cosway and rarely saw his daughters, except for Sunday dinner and an occasional tea at the Comtesse de Noailles. So, I would often visit Martha and Maria at the convent and bring the latest gossip, of which I got an earful from James and the other servants. Martha was annoyed by her father's infatuation with Maria Cosway and repeatedly told me so. Her jealousy was bitter, and I was later to feel its cruelty. I was just as envious of Maria Cosway—her exquisite manners, her magnificent gowns, and haughty condescending and languishing airs. She came to see Master Jefferson with a proprietary attitude that made James mimic her behind her back, and the servants raise their eyebrows. Only Petit knew the real story, and he was as close-mouthed about it as old Martin back at Monticello.

"I wish she would go back to her husband!" This seemed to explode from Martha's very soul, and I realized that Paris gossip didn't stop at the convent gates.

"She is very beautiful."

"But so old! She must be at least twenty-five!"

We sat in silence charged with malice. How could men be so anxious to pursue such decrepit creatures? I thought. They seemed to be made out of some soft, pudding-like material that had nothing to do with muscles and bones. What would they do if they had to run?

I remembered the joy I felt when, picking up my skirts, I would race as fast as I could down the Champs-Elysées, across the fields, toward the bridge of Neuilly, looking behind to make sure no one was watching. I would run until I had a stitch in my side and then pause, listening to the pumping of my heart, the pounding of my breath. . . .

We did not know that at that very moment Maria Cosway, the object of all our jealous envy, was already on her way back to her husband, having quit Paris that very day for good.

Martha then turned to me and whispered, "There was a gentleman a few days ago . . . you know, who killed himself because he thought his wife didn't love him. They had been married ten years. . . . I believe that if every husband in Paris was to do as much, there would be nothing but widows left." And then suddenly, with an emotion I didn't understand at the time, she said, "I wish with all my soul the poor Negroes were all freed. It grieves my heart!" And she reached over and embraced me.

CHAPTER 13

PARIS, MARCH 1788

PERHAPS I had always known that he would claim me. Had not the same happened to my mother and my sisters?

I watched him secretly to see if he knew, but I realized he would know only when the moment had arrived. I could hasten or delay that moment, but I felt powerless to prevent it.

Once I went with Martha and her father to Notre Dame Cathedral to hear a mass by Cardinal Beaugrave. Both Martha and I were so overwhelmed by the beauty of the cathedral and the mass that we burst into tears. When I accompanied James on his excursions to the city, he would speak of what our life would be together, once we had our freedom. He would speak wildly and with arrogance, as if what he dreamed could be had at the wave of a hand. Perhaps so, but I knew as sure as death that I belonged to Thomas Jefferson.

I hardly strayed from the mansion on the Champs-Elysées. My first nine months in Paris had been happy ones, and now I tried to prolong that happiness, plunging into my studies, grateful and hardly believing my good fortune, honing the knowledge I had acquired and forgetting the sword that hung over my head.

Everyone was homesick for Virginia as one gray, damp Parisian day followed the other in monotonous succession. Even the famous Paris rats had disappeared, frozen into the sewers under the Seine on which the nobility and bourgeois skated. There was fire after fire on the outskirts of the city as entire shantytowns went up in smoke. The men were bored, and an oppressiveness hung over the days as we roamed the mansion, each in our little orbit. I remember the silence of those short days when candles burned at noon.

In January, an unheard-of freeze took hold of the city and confined us to the mansion. We knew that the poor people of Paris had begun to die of the cold and of starvation.

Haughty French officers came and went; Trumbull sketched them for his painting of the Surrender of Cornwallis at Yorktown. James became more and more mysterious, speaking of "freedom" and "revolution" and "liberty." Each time he would speak in this way, I remained silent. A sense of fatality took hold of me. I was the center of a drama; yet no one else seemed to know it. Only the painter Trumbull, with his great black eyes, seemed to have a sense of what was happening.

"Do you like it?"

"Oh yes, Master. It is very fine."

I had come to serve his tea. He was finishing his study of my master for his painting of the Declaration of Independence. I gazed at the portrait. It showed a man of high countenance, young with a long and serious face, a high brow with soft curling red hair covering it and a wide unsmiling mouth that made him appear rather stern. It was a good resemblance.

I often sought John Trumbull's company. He was a gentle man. Sometimes I would be impatiently waved away. When, later, he had finished his work in Paris and was folding his easel in preparation for his departure, I felt more alone than ever. I could not confide my fears to James. I thought of Petit, who liked me, but he was devoted to his master, unlikely to thwart him in anything he desired. As for the other women in the house, I was afraid of them and realized they would have no sympathy with a so common and sought-after situation. Above all, I was separated from Polly and Patsy by their innocence. I was alone, in a strange world, as I waited for a sign.

Spring came.

The ice on the Seine cracked, and its black water seeped between the glistening white. The days became longer and the candles went out. The rats came back and the brilliant stones of Paris shone again in the pale sunlight, which had timidly reappeared.

I was fifteen years old.

"I'm going away, Sally. To Amsterdam with Mr. Adams and then to the Rhineland. I'll be gone for six weeks. I want you to study hard while I'm away."

"Yes, Master."

Away. I hadn't counted on that. More waiting.

"Don't look so sad, my Sally. It is only for a little while."

"Yes, Master."

"Your friend John Trumbull recommends the journey highly."

The tall somber image of Master Trumbull distracted my thoughts for a moment.

"When I leave, you will stay with Madame Dupré, near the convent on rue de Seine. You can visit Polly and Patsy, and I have arranged that you may spend Sundays at the convent. Mr. Perrault will come to give you your lessons during the week."

"Yes, Master."

"I'm giving all the staff a holiday. It is not proper that you stay here . . . alone."

"Yes, Master."

"I shall miss you, Sally."

"Yes, Master."

"Sally, is that all you have to say?"

"Yes, Master."

"Sally, I shall miss you. I promise . . ."

"Promise me!"

The words burst out of me, more a sob than an exclamation. I could bear the waiting no longer. I drew my head up and looked long into his eyes. Deep in the centers was a dark pinprick. My own reflection.

Yes, I thought, the time has come.

A thousand times a day fear would overwhelm me. Blood would rush to my head, and often I would clutch a velvet hanging or the back of a silk-covered *fauteuil*. I stopped seeing Polly and Patsy. I dared not leave the house lest he send for me. At night I fell asleep sitting upright on the side of my bed. My body would be turned away from the door, but my head and shoulders would be turned toward it. There was no lock, and I would not have dared turn the key had there been one. I would not face the door lest I invite its opening, yet I could not turn completely away. Thus I sat watch through the night.

Lord keep me from sinking down.

Lord keep me from sinking down.

Lord keep me from sinking down. I would repeat to myself. In the early hours of the morning, exhausted, I would sleep. The night before his departure, he sent for me, but he did not appear. I fell asleep in his room, and when I awoke an immense shadow blocked my vision.

I had no idea how long he had been standing there. Now that he had come, I felt no fear, only an overwhelming tenderness. His presence for me was command enough; I took control of him. I bent forward and pressed a kiss on the trembling hands that encompassed mine, and the contact of my lips with his flesh was so violent that I lost all memory of what came afterward. I felt around me an exploding flower, not just of passion, but of long deprivation, a hunger for things forbidden, for darkness and unreason, the passion of rage against the death of the other I so resembled. For in this moment I became one with her, and it was not my name that sprang from him but that of my half sister.

At once he left me, surveying me from above with the eyes of a man afraid of heights scanning a valley from a tower. Then his body tensed and rushed toward me as if he had found a way to break his fall.

Thus did Thomas Jefferson give himself into my keeping.

When I awoke the bed was empty beside me. I slipped from the abandoned bed and stared at the gray rectangles of light from the tall windows barred by the shadows of the balconies. In the strange, majestic room, I gathered my clothes from the four corners where they had been flung in the violence of the night. I stared at the sheet and then quickly, without thinking, covered the bed with its counterpane. The feeble groping for James's dream had been erased by the force of a man's body and a man's will.

I washed and dressed, and quickly left the house by the front door. The morning was cool, but the day would be fair. Frost was still on the trees and bushes of the garden, but tiny sparks of green had begun to appear.

I started to walk slowly toward the Pont de Neuilly. I had taken my brother's heavy cloak, yet I trembled uncontrollably either from shock or cold, I don't remember. To my surprise, I recognized ahead of me his solitary figure breaking pane after pane of silvery light. Even at this dawn hour, and for every dawn to come, Thomas Jefferson had risen before me and had chosen the cold bitter morning to walk abroad.

I was filled with confusion. Should I turn back? Hurry to greet him? Stay as I was now, fifty paces behind him? Call out to him? I followed for a long moment, dreading that he would, for some reason, turn around and see me, but he kept his eyes ahead. I fell farther and farther behind as his long legs strode through the Elysian fields spread out before him. The bottom of James's cloak, wet with dew, dragged behind me. I was seized with a terrible yearning. I thought of my mother and her mother before her. Nothing would ever be the same again. Nothing would ever free me of him. Nothing would erase those strange words of love which I had to believe in my weakness.

"Je t'aime," he had said.

In his terror, he had used that most potent of weapons, the ruler of the mighty as well as the helpless. And I had answered, without any other words passing between us.

"Merci, monsieur."

CHAPTER 14

SPRING 1788

JAMES DISCOVERED the concubinage of his sister that morning when he turned back the counterpane of his master's bed. He had waited, first outside the door of the bedroom and then in the gray shadows of the arc made by the curved marble stairway of the Hôtel de Langeac in the early dawn. He had seen Thomas Jefferson descend the grand staircase and carefully unlatch the front door and step out into the courtyard of the mansion. For one moment, the rosy light loomed against the blackness of the arch. Then the door had slammed shut. James had waited for a length of time he could not measure when Sally Hemings came down the same stairs. She had turned, almost facing him and wearing his heavy black cloak and had gone out the front door.

Sally Hemings' brother now stood in his master's empty room under the painted ceiling of "Night." He was twenty-three years old. Of those twenty-three years, fourteen had been spent serving, loving, and tending Thomas Jefferson. Like some demigod who descended from the heavens to mingle with mortals, he would ascend, leaving that which had to be cleaned up to his servants. His master had left Paris.

He was in throes of some powerful emotion, yet he couldn't sort out which emotion it was. James Hemings was a virgin. His master and his sister had gone beyond the pale of his existence. He gathered the stained sheets in his arms. The complexity of his new feelings paralyzed him. Violence, like an ague, shook him. What should he do? How should he conduct himself as a free man? Kill?

"Help me," whispered James. "God, help me."

He didn't—would never—have the courage to kill Thomas Jefferson.

From that day on, James dreamed of those spots of blood. The whole bed would turn red as he touched it, staining his own hands as if he had plunged them into the entrails of a living creature. He would struggle to take the sheets off the bed, but they would heave and swirl, and sickening sounds would come from them. Terrified, he would back away, but the sheets would pursue him, leaping at his throat like a wild animal, enveloping him in a slimy embrace. In the ensuing struggle, he would be hurled into the fire burning in the room's hearth. His hands and feet, still swaddled in the sticky sheets, would begin to burn. Then his arms and legs. Then his private parts. Finally, only his torso would remain with a blackened and charred head, the mouth opened in a horrible but soundless scream. The head would begin to spin itself in agony until it literally spun itself off the burning body and lay in the ashes which filled its mouth and eyes and nostrils, strangling and suffocating him.

That same dream would come back time and again, and would remain with him until the day he died. The first time he had awakened to find himself being shaken by a pale Petit, terrified by his screams.

"Jim-mi. There is nothing to be afraid of. *Réveille-toi, mon garçon.* It's only a nightmare. Wake up, son."

"No, not like that! Glide. GLIDE! You're not supposed to lift your feet from the floor!"

"I'm *not* lifting my feet from the floor!"

"You are too. You walk like a duck! Look at Sally. She does it perfectly; better than either of us."

"That's because I've watched the *frotteur* do it every day for a year now! Just think of waxing floors with your feet like he does and you'll have it."

"Waxing floors! Will you just imagine the queen of France waxing floors!"

"I'd never thought of it! Marie-Antoinette, '*La Frotteuse.*'"

The three girls dressed in their undergarments and perspiring, collapsed into loud laughter, falling onto the deep featherbed in Sally Hemings' room at Madame Dupré's boardinghouse.

Martha and Maria had doffed their crimson convent uniforms, which lay in a heap on the polished floors. Sally Hemings had been in her chemise, being fitted for a new dress, when the girls arrived. Martha and Maria had begun to visit their maid regularly in her comfortable and cozy rooms. There was absolutely no privacy for the girls in the convent, the fifty pensioners slept in two immense rooms without curtains, the other rooms being reserved for drawing rooms and classrooms. Sally Hemings was overjoyed and welcomed the company of her two playmates. Released from the oppressive Hôtel de Langeac, from the smoldering power of Jefferson's sensuality, and the bitterness of her brother James, she had found relief, joy, and affection in the adolescent company of Marie and Martha. Her initiation into womanhood forgotten, she basked in her temporary return to childhood.

Often she would leave her rooming house and walk the several blocks to the Abbaye de Panthémont, entering through the chapel on the rue de Grenelle and stepping into the courtyard filled with crimson-uniformed ladies of the gentry. As this was not only a school for girls, but a retreat for spinsters, abandoned wives, and ladies of the court in temporary seclusion, the ways and gossip of Versailles and the court found their way here with rapidity, and girls were playing a game now popular at the school: attempting to imitate the famous walk of the queen, Marie-Antoinette, the "most beautiful walk in France."

With the voluminous hoop skirts in fashion called *robes à paniers,* which completely hid the bottom half of a lady's body, the desired effect of moving oneself from one place to the other was that of floating disembodied along the galleries and antechambers of palaces like ships on water, rather than humans on legs and feet. The effect was obtained by never lifting the feet from the floor, but by gliding them forward and slightly outward along the surface of the floor in a skating movement, and keeping the tightly corseted upper part of the body erect and rigidly immobile. The walk was practiced by both the ladies and gentlemen at the court of Versailles, but no one in the kingdom achieved the desired effect with greater success than the stately, full-bosomed queen herself.

"One of the ladies at Panthémont said that she had never seen such a sight as the queen sailing along the gallery of mirrors. One could see nothing in the throng of courtiers but a forest of waving plumes a foot and a half taller than her ladies' heads," Martha said. She turned to Sally Hemings.

"Can you imagine such a thing, Sally? Oh, how I would love to see it just once, the court of Versailles. Papa has promised to take me to the public galleries when he returns. Anyone may enter, you know, and the gardens as well are public, and you may come across the queen herself walking with her ladies. Of course, we shall have an *entrée* in the person of the Comtesse de Tessé, who is a lady in waiting to the queen. I will find her gliding like a swan among the pools and fountains of Versailles, and I will drop my best curtsy, and Papa will kiss her hand and . . . Can you imagine!"

Martha Jefferson shook the bare shoulders of her maid gently and affectionately, tossing the mane of bright hair behind her. Sally Hemings nodded to Martha and let her petticoats drop. At any rate, she could walk like a queen, if nothing else.

She fell back into the arms of Martha, pretending to slip, and as she did she let out a whoop: "Her majesty has just glided onto her royal *derrière*. . . ." They all collapsed into new gales of laughter. This brought Madame Dupré to the door of her boarder.

"Girls, ladies, you would think I had a regiment of hussars in my house!"

Madame Dupré was the proprietor of a small rooming house on the rue de Seine. She had been instructed to board the maid of the American minister's daughters while he was away on a trip to Amsterdam and the Rhineland. She had agreed to do this for the sum of twenty-one francs a week plus laundry and dressmaking. The gentle, lovely girl, who had arrived at her door two weeks ago accompanied by the minister himself, had pleased her. As she had not been instructed otherwise, Madame Dupré treated Sally Hemings as she would have treated any maid of an aristocrat: that is, a young girl of a poor family with no dowry who enters the service of a great family as a lady's maid and companion to the daughters of such a family in return for room, board, and protection. Obviously the minister thought enough of her not to leave her alone in the company of his servants when he went abroad. . . .

Madame Dupré had no way of knowing that Sally Hemings was a slave. She had no way of knowing either that a "maid" in Virginia was a polite way of indicating someone who was black. Sally Hemings' complexion told Madame Dupré nothing, except that she was dark. She would even have said swarthy, but a little strange; the particular tint of the young girl's skin was not the same as she had noted in the Italian or Spanish complexion. It was rather an extraordinary shade of buff, without the profusion of down that usually accompanied the ladies of that hue. She was a bit surprised at the meanness of her wardrobe. Certainly if one was poor, one had to know how to sew in order to dress oneself, but then she was to remedy these shortcomings by instructing her in dressmaking and making sure that she had the minimum uniforms of a lady's maid. Certainly her manners and gentleness and soft, charmingly accented French bespoke a certain breeding, and with a little grooming, thought Madame Dupré, she would surely attract a gentleman of property and improve her station in life in the time-honored manner of becoming the mistress or (why not?) the wife of a modest member of the gentry. She, of course, had had no instructions along these lines, but as she liked the child, Madame Dupré decided she would do all she could to improve her while she was in her charge. Besides, through her mistresses, Sally Hemings had access to the Abbaye de Panthémont, where only the finest ladies and young girls retired or were educated. She had only to imitate her betters, she concluded.

When Madame Dupré saw what the girls had been doing, she joined the laughter. The queen's extraordinary walk was renowned throughout the kingdom, and when little *Sallie* showed her version of it, she had to admit it was both seductive and accurate.

"My, that is quite good. Now do me a curtsy, all of you—*comme il faut*. I have come to serve you tea, but you had better put your clothes back on before the servant sees you in the state of nature."

The three girls stood up and Madame Dupré looked at the virginal young bodies pressed close to her. The eldest Mademoiselle Jefferson was so tall she towered over everyone. Some American ladies were immense, and this one certainly took after her father. She had a fine complexion: milk and roses at the same time, except that it was marred by the same freckles that dotted the countenance of the minister. She remarked on Martha's lovely hair. It was hanging down in a mass of thick auburn waves to her waist. Her eyes were without color or lashes and too close together, and her chin, she felt, was impossible: long and jutting, with the promise of unyielding stubbornness so disagreeable to men. Yet the luxurious curls managed to soften the lines of her face and long nose, and her mouth was delicate, firm, and good humored, bespeaking justice if not generosity, and the body was slim, well made, and bursting with good health.

As for the young Mademoiselle Jefferson, she and her maid resembled each other uncannily. Madame Dupré continued her inventory. They were both remarkably beautiful, both dark with hazel eyes, the maid's being a peculiar but fascinating shade of yellow. They both had deep dimples, prized by French ladies, and soft wide mouths with that touch of sullenness found in ardent characters. The maid reflected the promise in body of the mistress, who was still a child; perfect mat skin, long thick dark hair, and fragile yet compact body with a deep bosom and full hips.

Yes, thought Madame Dupré, with a little luck, *Sallie* will make her fortune in Paris . . . if she has the luck to attract a gentleman.

The first time James Hemings came to visit his sister at Madame Dupré's, she fell into his arms with a cry of relief. She had not seen him since she had left the hôtel that March day almost three weeks ago. James Hemings was still reeling from the shock of his sister's seduction, but he determined to show nothing but tenderness and solicitude. He had three or four weeks at the most to convince her that her master had compromised all claims to her love and loyalty by his forcing of her, and that now was the time to claim her rights as a free woman on French soil. Once the demigod was back, his powerful compelling presence would again dominate their lives, and their only chance would be lost, perhaps forever.

He had brought her a letter that had arrived for her from her master.

She had taken the letter from him with trembling hands but had not read it, hiding it in her petticoat pocket. They had then gone out for a walk, as they had so many times before in Paris. Free of uniforms and even the semblance of servanthood, they had roamed the streets and the grand boulevards crammed with new buildings. American Revolutionary ideas were everywhere, and they met them in a form hitherto never encountered by either of them: the newspaper and the broadside.

There were regular newspapers printed every day which, even under the king's Censure Bureau, were wildly critical and full of republican ideas. Anyone with the money to buy or rent or who owned a printing press was free to print and distribute what he liked. These were called broadsides. Anyone doing this was liable, of course, afterward to be arrested by the king's censors for *lèse-majesté*, but no one prevented the broadside from being printed and distributed, even if the author was in the Bastille. It was around the Palais Royal that most of the newspaper vendors congregated and it was usually here, in the magnificent gardens of the palace with its famous meridian cannon fired by the rays of the sun at noon, that brother and sister spent part of their promenade.

The public gardens of the Palais Royal teemed with every manner of man, woman, and beast—from veiled noblewomen on their way to assignations to street prostitutes painted in the gaudy red rouge and white powder in fashion. There were priests and hawkers, lemonade and food vendors, cavaliers and officers of the king's regiment, beggars and pickpockets, raving orators, and all manner of dubious-looking characters. In the center of the gardens was the Duc d'Orléans's new glass-domed circus, the latest wonder of Paris. It was here, amid the pamphlets, engravings, newspapers, broadsides, rumors, and posters, that brother and sister discovered the shadow of things to come.

Each week a letter had come, hand-delivered by James, and each week Sally Hemings had silently hidden it in her petticoats and gone walking in Paris with James. Each week James sought to steal the mind and body of his sister from her master, while she half-listened to his pleas and warnings about her life, too stunned to think of anything except the letter that had arrived.

They were the first letters that anyone had ever addressed to her in all her fifteen years. They had taken on a magic, these letters addressed to "Mademoiselle Sally Hemings." She was unable to explain to James her fascination with the power of these words. Her name had stood independent of herself or her will on the thick white paper. Again and again, she had touched the black letters on the white paper imagining this person "Sally Hemings" to whom they were addressed.

Even not being able to answer these summons, because he was not long enough in each city, seemed right: the magic hold was never broken by the effort it would have taken to answer and thus claim the title by which she was addressed. Instead she had only to wait, to receive, to acquiesce.

The letters themselves, when tremblingly she opened them after James's departure and read the dozen or so lines, were as ordinary as those her master wrote to his daughters, which she also read when they came to visit her. If she expected billets-doux, she got none. Instead, there was a steady stream of fatherly advice, kindly, distant, a little cold, which took on the air of a monologue, since no response was possible. Yet the young girl read and reread her letters. She kept them in a silk envelope she had sewn especially for them. Without knowing why, she showed them to no one, nor did she speak of their existence.

Sally Hemings smiled at her latest geography lessons interspaced with "be a good girl." "Study . . . depend on yourself . . . visit with Patsy and Polly . . . love me. . . ." These fatherly letters disappointed her. How strange these terse letters that arrived from mysterious German cities so remote from her imagination, she thought.

Then, one day, a new letter arrived. It was dutifully brought to her by James to her rooms and dutifully hidden in her petticoats until she returned from their walk to read it alone, and dutifully opened and held toward the light in order to decipher the minuscule, almost illegible writing. When she finished reading it, she sat down weakly, her legs no longer able to support her, and steadied the letter trembling in her hands on her lap. Again she strained over the tiny cramped writing, as if her life had depended on it, and finally she clutched it to her bosom with a cry.

The message was clear. And because it was written, it had for Sally Hemings the binding power of a holy writ.

CHAPTER 15

PARIS, APRIL 1788

THOMAS JEFFERSON woke with the alarm of someone who does not know where he is. The alarm was physical as well as metaphysical. He hadn't remembered for a moment not only where he was but who he was. He had traveled so many miles. . . . He sighed. He was staring at Jean-Simon Berthélemy's painting of "Night" on his own sculptured ceiling over his own bed, in his own room in his own Hôtel de Langeac, and not in some Prussian inn lying in his white-linen envelope among strangers. He raised himself on one elbow and stared at the sleeping girl beside him. He had gone to fetch his slave from her rooms as soon as he had arrived in Paris. She was on her side, turned away from him, her long dark hair fanning out from her body. The white sheets darkened her skin, like a pale sky darkens clouds. He lifted the covers from her and slowly pulled them away from her body. Then he bent his bright head and ran his tongue along the delicate backbone. The taste of honey and pine hit the back of his throat.

"*Mon Dieu . . .*" he murmured, and sank back into his satin pillows. Possessively he drew the girl closer to him and arranged her head on his naked chest. She slept. Without waking her, he caressed the tangled hair. There was a small crescent-shaped scar in the silky down of the beginning of her hairline. A dim recollection made it seem that this scar had something to do with him, but he couldn't remember what. He tenderly rubbed the slightly raised whiteness of it with the tips of his fingers.

Landscape after landscape rushed before him as if he were riding in the jostling coaches and carriages of his Rhine journey.

He had described to the girl again and again the long, lonely voyage through the Low Countries to the north and finally Prussia and the Rhine Valley. His description of the vast, magical Black Forest had transported the young girl into a world of dragons, princesses, and fairy tales. His imaginary carriage slowed now, so that innumerable scenes of rustic beauty floated before his eyes in stately sequence. On the second of April he had arrived at Düsseldorf and had gone straight to the painting gallery. It was there that he had seen the Van der Werff painting that had so moved him: the Biblical story of Sarah giving the slave Hagar to Abraham. That same afternoon he had written to Sally in Paris. Had it really been a sign, he wondered?

He straightened a lock of her hair. He was a rational man. It was unreasonable, he thought, loving for once what he saw and felt without wanting or trying to give a reason, and not caring much if there was one. Sometimes her face took him back to his happiest days. His eyes rested again on the sleeping slave. Her youth, the deepness and serenity of her sleep, stirred him. To be that young . . . Love is never a surprise to the young; but to him! He almost laughed, then remembered she slept. He shifted position carefully and drew her closer to him. After Düsseldorf, he had thought of her often with a growing sense of fatality. Was it not incredible that she was here at all, in Paris, in his arms? Was it not strange and unaccountable the circumstances of her arrival here, of her very birth? That fateful Wayles legacy so intertwined with the past, and now with the future? Future? What possible future except hate and guilt could they possibly have, he reminded himself.

He closed his eyes and drifted back to the Rhine Valley, sailing down the wide flat ribbon of it from Cologne to Hanau and Heidelberg. His return had had a dreamlike and hurried aspect about it after Düsseldorf. By the middle of April he had been in Strasbourg, where he had recrossed the Rhine into France. He had hurried then, remembering for the first time the bitter toil and poverty of the German peasants. Why had he suddenly been so touched by the women—disheveled, worn beyond their years?

His slave stirred and opened her eyes. The low morning sun caught their golden color and flecked green and brown into them. His heart pounded as she reached for him.

His face still held such terror for her. She pulled back from the lips that had brushed hers and looked into the hooded and melancholy eyes with their fair brows, and then at the wide mouth with its slightly upturned corners. Her master's thick, wavy hair fell around his shoulders. There was a mat of reddish hair on his chest. Sally Hemings' eyes took in the mysterious stubble of red beard and the fine age-lines around the eyes and the stern mouth. There were marks of age at his throat, a slight indentation of flesh, and suddenly she felt a piercing flash of pity for him.

CHAPTER 16

SUMMER, 1788

LENT WAS OVER and the promenade of the Champs-Elysées bristled
with multicolored flower borders. Tulips and dahlias, lilies of the valley
and crocuses, spread like Oriental carpets escorting the golden carriages and prancing horses of the Paris gentry come forth to show
themselves and salute spring.

From the upper window of the Hôtel de Langeac I could see the place
Louis XV at the end of the Champs-Elysées and, beyond the place, the
gardens of the Tuileries filled with tiny moving figures. They reminded
me of butterflies swarming among the stone façades and the flower
borders.

The gilt carriages moved down the famous chestnut-tree-shaded
promenade. I trembled at the change in my own small world. From his
daughters' maid I had become the pampered and adored mistress of
Thomas Jefferson. I was one insignificant secret amongst the many
buried under the surface of this spring procession.

It was the summer of my fifteenth year that I saw Marly for the first
time, and like my master who had been transformed by a painting in
Düsseldorf, I was transformed by Marly. I too saw what I wanted to
see. Nothing would ever be the same for me again. Marly had been the
favorite palace of the Sun King, Louis XIV, his retreat and hermitage
from the glories of Versailles. It seemed to float above the earth, in its
own nature, its own sky, its own water, its own sun. More than any of
the other palaces of the kings of France, this was the most magical one.

Imagine a young woman come with her love to Marly, standing beside him, and looking at all this beauty for the first time.

Marly stood planted in the wild blue forest of Saint-Germain-en-Laye. The gardens, canals, terraces, and labyrinths stretched for miles. On each side of the magnificent palace were six summer pavilions connected by walkways embowered with jasmine and honeysuckle. Water fell in cascades from the top of a hill behind the castle, forming a reservoir where swans floated. One fountain sprouted so high, the spray was lost from sight. In the main canal, glistening marble horses mounted by bronze men cavorted; and here and there one could see tiny gems which were ladies moving along the paths and gardens.

The only sound was wind and water; all human sound had been reduced by the vast scale to silence or whispered murmurings. From the top of the hill where the reservoir of Marly's waterworks stood, the day had furnished a rainbow. As the great mechanical wheels raised the water of the river, a pale arc of color hung above it and faded into the colors surrounding us—the silver white of the fountains, the multi-colored flowerbeds, the cream-and-blue shadow of the stone facades, the pearl-gray of the gravel underfoot—pastel colors; pink and lemon, delicate greens and blues, so unlike the harsh, hard colors of Virginia.

That day convinced me that there was no Virginia. No slavehood. There was no destiny, it seemed, that did not include this place, this hour, this Marly.

I looked at the tall figure standing beside me. No. Not tall. Immense. Like some glorious eagle overlooking Marly. I studied the familiar profile. My fifteen-year-old heart burst with pride. I could pale that face with longing. I could part that beautiful mouth with desire. I could fill those eyes with agony or joy.

I thought of Martha and her peers tittering and giggling in their fine watered silks and gauzes, the greedy restlessness and ignorance of them! Prancing by in their convent red; gossiping, silly girls who knew nothing of men. Their feverish fantasies and sickening pride revolted me. I neither despised them nor was jealous of them. I merely pitied them. What did they know about being a woman?

I remembered a scene I had witnessed with Martha at the abbey less than a year before, the mysterious and strangely seductive ceremony of ordination for novices. I watched those girls, most of them my age, their faces and bodies pressed into the cold, humid, unyielding stone: their wedding day, the soft fine wool of their habits spread around them like spilled milk. They married God as one married a man. And if one loved a man as one loved God, was it so different? Did it really matter if it was God or man, as long as it was not both?

I put my hands on my face and pressed my eyes red-gold, as if the image blinded me. I opened them again. Marly was still there. And so was he. Smiling down at me from the vast distance between us.

On the thirteenth of July, 1788, there fell, on the very edge of harvest, the most frightful and abnormal hailstorm ever remembered, completely destroying the crops of the year which had already been much damaged by a long drought. For sixty leagues around Paris, it was said, the ruin was total. The legendary Estates General, that had not met in one hundred and sixty years, would meet again the following May. The king had surrendered. Paris was exultant. Martha and Polly came home from the convent, and an ominous calm fell over the city.

I had had no female companion at the Hôtel de Langeac. And so, although I did not feel that I could confide in her, Martha, when she came home from her convent, became for me a refuge from the masculine world of the ministry, and from my powerful lover. His impulsiveness, his vagueness, interspersed with melancholy silences, his inexplicable bursts of passion overwhelmed and often confused me. Later, I would conquer his moods; but at that time I turned to Martha. She was my link with home, with my mother, perhaps with other women. She returned my affection that summer with a warmth we were never to recapture again. I would accompany Martha on her calls to her school friends before they left for their summer estates. We would stroll along the busy and crowded rue Saint-Honoré, dodging the hackney coaches, or along the chestnut-shaded cobblestones of the quai Pont Neuf, looking. We would walk side by side, arm in arm. A lady and her maid, a slave and her mistress, an aunt and her niece, the virgin and the concubine.

Then, one day, the first shadow of what was to pass fell between us. As in all aristocratic households of the day, hair was dressed daily by professional hairdressers who came to the house. There were more than three thousand of them in Paris alone. The one appointed to the Hôtel de Langeac, after dressing my master's hair, would go to the convent to do Polly and Martha's coiffure. There was a second hairdresser whose duty it was to dress the hair of the servants. There was not a fine household in Paris that did not avail itself of the services of two or three hairdressers every day.

As if in silent recognition, my master's hairdresser began to dress my hair. Martha had no knowledge of this until one day it was whispered to her by a friend that her hairdresser was also her maid's hairdresser, an unheard of breach of etiquette.

"Is it true that Antoine does your hair?" We were out walking. Her clear eyes were puzzled, not angry. I returned her gaze. It was one of the last times we looked into each other's eyes.

"Pierre complained that he had too many heads to do with the increase in staff, and Antoine said he didn't mind doing my hair, since he could not come directly to you anyway." If Martha had thought about it, this would be unthinkable. Hairdressers placed more importance on rank and etiquette than the queen herself.

"I don't think it's fitting," Martha answered.

"Well, it's convenient, Mistress."

"I shall ask Father about it."

"I wouldn't do that if I were you, Mistress. He is so annoyed at Antoine anyway that he will surely fire him, and where to get another as good?"

"I won't do anything if Antoine stops doing your hair."

"What harm is there, Mistress? Besides, he does James's too," I lied. I wanted to keep my hairdresser.

"He does?"

"Yes."

"Oh . . . In that case . . . I guess it's all right. I'm surprised Antoine would . . . If Father says so . . ."

"Master says so," I continued to lie.

It was the first of many lies I would tell to the white women in my life. From that day on, I would lie to her and to others. Poor Antoine became a milestone between me and Martha.

"My dear . . . you mustn't worry if I seem . . . strange sometimes." Thomas Jefferson's voice had the familiar hesitancy of his public speaking. "This is so unexpected and for me, so unbidden. And you are . . . so young and yet so sure. . . . You seem as old as Eve to me, my wise one."

It was part game and part true, he thought. There really didn't seem to be any differences in their ages. Sometimes he wondered who was the child. He felt so young. His naked back was to the silken draperies of his rooms on the street side of the apartments. His huge body was framed in the rectangles of barred, balconied windows.

He reached and cupped the head of his mistress in his giant hands and stared across at her, pressing her tiny skull between them. Her smallness always stirred him. He gave a short harsh laugh.

"I don't know what to do with you!"

"Don't do anything, Master," she replied, "and it will be done."

"Thy will?"

"Thine."

Thomas Jefferson fondled the delicate skin at the back of his slave's neck under the coiled hair. She was indeed his creature. Both in body and in spirit. He had formed and shaped her himself, this wild flower, into something that bordered on the aristocratic—or at least the unique, an exotic hybrid of exquisite beauty and fascination. Her training and tutoring was beginning to show, her musical education as well. Her voice was low, true, with a lilting sweetness that was unforgettable. Her appreciation of beautiful things gratified him. She had even begun to speak her native tongue differently, and her French was perfect. He possessed something he had created from beginning to end, without interference or objections or corrections. In a way, he had birthed her. As much as he had his daughter. He had created her in his own image of womanly perfection, this speck of dust, this handful of clay from Monticello.

"I love you," he said.

"I have always loved you," said his mistress, but he was no longer listening. He had already gone from her, not physically but mentally, as he often did.

Sally Hemings watched secretly the proud, haughty face in a hundred moods for a trace of herself, yet never once had the face she knew as hers—this passionate, hungry, wounded face that had just been so close—ever betrayed him in public. That other face, the public one, was the face of her enemy, her master. But one she owned. . . .

Once, in the privacy of her attic room, she had pulled down her bodice and stared at the smooth skin, expecting somehow to see the branded scar "C" for concubine on her flesh just as the famous La Motte had recently been branded with a "V" for *voleuse* on her shoulder, and her grandmother with the "R" for runaway on her breast. But there had been nothing but smooth skin.

When would he free her? she wondered. What if she asked him now . . . here? . . . She couldn't, she was ashamed. The pallor, the soft eyes, the ribbon undone, the mouth softened by their kisses . . . He was smiling lazily at her. Even now after their moment of passion, there was a violence and a constraint about him that made her tremble. It was then she realized that he liked owning her. She looked back at him. The face that just a short while ago had been hers was now closed. It belonged to the world.

My anxious lover would sometimes touch me or smooth my hair as if I were a touchstone, a relic of Monticello, a living symbol of all the love and happiness that he had invested in his patrimony. Late at night, when the house was silent and Paris slept, he would tell me of his new plans for Monticello, of changes in the Big House, of redesigned gardens and vineyards with German and French grapes, and olive trees not native to Virginia. For him, the Blue Ridge Mountain region was Eden, and even Paris, the most beautiful of all cities, could not replace it.

This I understood even as he spoke of his retirement, of his leave of absence, and our return to Paris. When he spoke of these things, he never made it clear if I was to stay in Paris to wait for him, return to Virginia and be re-enslaved, or be freed at once by his hand. I did not yet ask which of these alternatives he contemplated, but when I brought up my own plans, laid with James and based on freedom in France, he would become silent and morose, or suddenly leave the room.

Just as he willed the revolution that was growing to be a peaceful one, so did he will that my conversion from slave to lover be also without violence. He saw the Revolution through the eyes of a man who had found unexpected happiness and who was determined to avoid unexpected grief at any cost.

"Have you told him I want to speak to him?"

"Yes," I lied. I had begun to lie to James.

"He knows that we are aware that under French law, he cannot hold us against our will?"

We were speaking French. James had an abrupt and excitable manner of speaking in which every other word came out as if underlined.

"Yes." I lied, I didn't know if he knew or not.

"*Did* you *tell* him about the *proposition* of the Prince de Conti's *maître d'hôtel?*"

"Yes."

"*Well*, what did *he* say?"

"He said he would speak to the prince at the first occasion."

"Has he told you, sister, that he has written to ask the Congress for a leave of absence to return to Virginia, and is waiting for an answer?" James had lapsed back into English.

"Yes," I lied. I was shocked; he had not told me anything.

"Don't you *think* it is *time* to claim our *liberty?*" He had reverted to French.

"You mean to ask to be freed? Shouldn't we wait until the date is set for our return?"

"So that *he* can *pack* us up with *his* other *possessions?*"

"You have said that we are not owned. We have gotten wages since last January. He has recognized that this is not Virginia. . . ."

"*You* can *say* that *this* is not *Virginia? Mon Dieu!*"

I blushed, but I kept my head high. "He's given me his word."

"In writing?"

"He's promised."

"And *you* will *leave?*"

"I'm ready when you are."

James turned his hard gray eyes on me. "And you've *told* him you will *leave* him?"

"Yes," I lied.

"He will *never* forgive you. He will *accuse* you of *betraying* him."

"I know." This time I didn't lie. The specter of my master's cold fury, his outraged injury, which I had witnessed once or twice, struck terror in my breast.

"*He* . . . wouldn't *do* you *harm?*"

I thought a moment of my impulsive lover. Yes, I thought, he was capable of hurting me.

"Of course not," I said. "He is the kindest and most gentle of men."

"Why, *why* could he *not* have *taken* a . . . white mistress, if he *must* have *one*, like all *his* friends?"

"I don't know."

Jealousy struck me, unexpected and hot. James and I had never spoken of my concubinage.

"How should I know why he does or doesn't! Do you think he tells me what goes on in his mind? Do you think his secrets concern me?" I stopped short.

I felt sick with this new emotion. The pain of it overwhelmed me, almost carrying me to my knees. He was mine! Mine. So this was jealousy. This is what I would live with from now on.

"Time is running out," James said to me in English. He seemed to be sorry for what he had said.

"You believe that there will be an insurrection . . . a revolution? Our master says not."

"There will be an insurrection. But this was not what I meant," he said gently.

"I'm careful," I whispered.

"Ask Marie-Louise downstairs to help you. She knows what to do and she likes you. . . . There are ways."

I looked at my brother. There was no more boy left in him. He was lean and hard. It was a violent hardness of body. His eyes beneath their long black lashes were disillusioned and bitter. He had been seventeen when he left Virginia. Had it been in Paris that he had known his first woman? And who had she been? A countess whose eye he had caught? A prostitute? Whoever it had been, I was convinced, she had been white.

I lowered my head. I had never thought of such things before. We knew so little of each other—men knew so little of women and women so little of men. I had no idea where he spent his money and free time. Who his friends were. We had barely spoken to each other since I had returned to the ministry, and we had never, until now, spoken of the one important event of my life.

Whoever this man my brother was, he was a man. And no matter what happened to him, he would never be caught like me in the throes of a love which now held me against my will. But, no matter what, I would break that will, I believed. I would reclaim my body, my heart, and I would be careful. . . . I would not be deprived of my one chance in life. I would not fail my brother, I vowed. When the time came, I would run.

CHAPTER 17

PARIS, APRIL 1789

JAMES HEMINGS untied the roasted golden-brown suckling pig and stepped back to avoid the rich dark juices that spluttered out onto the chopping block of his kitchens at the Hôtel de Langeac. He had filled the suckling pig with a mixed stuffing of herbs, walnuts, mushrooms, and ground meat. Around the roast pig, he placed the candied fruits and flowers glazed with sugar. Julien, the French chef, nodded curtly. His apprentice was now a master cook. James stood staring at his dish.

A year had passed since Thomas Jefferson had taken his sister as concubine. Only he saw the dark side of her station: she was still a slave. The master had taken up his political and social life as if nothing had happened, he had simply added Sally Hemings to his bed.

He, James, had become a master cook and his sister had become a master whore, he thought with bitterness. Not that anyone cared, he reminded himself. Her existence, and her romance did not seem to carry any weight in the network of gossip exchanged between the servants, the lackeys, the hairdressers, and coachmen of the great Parisian hôtels in this spring of 1789. This spring there was only news of the political situation. Riots, court intrigues, manifestos that flew from the courtyards to the kitchens and the backstairs of one hotel to another with the efficiency of the Tidewater slave network. An aristocrat's liaison with a lady's maid was after all so common, he thought, so lacking in interest, that it was beneath the notice of even the lowliest scullery maid. For this forlorn silence, James was grateful.

Of course, the servants in the house all knew that the beautiful young

girl, supposedly the maid of one of his daughters, was in fact Jefferson's
mistress. But as far as James could discern, this fact had escaped the
intelligence of the white Americans connected with the household: Mr.
Short, Mr. Humphreys, Jefferson's two daughters. The master was
more than ever a loving father, a sweet-tempered lord, a kind and
compassionate aristocrat, a gallant appreciator of beautiful women. His
many migraines stopped, his melancholy abated, and he seemed to be
unconscious of the undertow of civil discontent which racked France.
"The Revolution is completed," he was fond of saying over and over.

As for most of the visitors who wandered in and out of the ministry,
they had never set eyes on his sister, nor even known of her existence. If
any of the elegant French ladies had remarked her, they certainly would
have dismissed their famous friend's *divertissement* with an amused
shrug. His hope that his master's interest in his sister would be transi-
tory and "in the French fashion" had turned out to be in vain. He might
play at being French, James thought, but his nature was Virginian,
passionate, proud, possessive, tenacious; violent feelings ran under that
polite and remote surface. If anything, he had noted that his master's
obsession with Sally Hemings had grown rather than waned in the past
year. His master, thought James, showed no lessening of the tyrannical
possessiveness and watchful interest in her dependence on him. She
seemed to be a prisoner in this house. And his sister was reveling in it;
she had blossomed under this jealous power. The last childish contours
of her body had dropped away, leving the low-burning smolder of a
woman's maturity far beyond her sixteen years. The final shape of her
face with its high, flat cheekbones and wide-spaced eyes had hardened
and lost some of its innocence. A small, exquisite, heavy-breasted,
slim-waisted body had emerged from the coltish and countrified
adolescent of a year ago. She had honed her natural grace and inborn
elegance on the examples of the most fashionable ladies of Panthémont
and Paris on whom she spied incessantly and indecently, and had
developed a lust for clothes and a taste for finery that went with such
examples.

She had lessons in French, in music, in dressmaking. In her seclusion,
Sally was better read than most ladies. Yet she had resisted all his
pleadings to use her power over the senses of their master to achieve her
freedom and his. She assumed that all would be taken care of in time.
That love would make her free.

James knew better. Men didn't free what they loved. He had surprised Thomas Jefferson more than once looking at Sally Hemings as he

had often seen him contemplating some of his rare objects, those he meant to keep. It was the look of a man who both coveted and had the means to possess what he coveted. How many times had he seen this look as the steady stream of precious objects flowed from the workshops and auction houses of Paris and were set before his master in unending abundance. A look of tender greed would flash cross his face like a bright star, and then his hand would reach out and touch the object presented to him, bringing it under his domination.

He pitied his sister in her enraptured beauty and delusion. She was nubile and Jefferson was virile. It was only a matter of time before her fate as a woman caught up with her.

James Hemings absently gestured to the lackey who had been standing in front of him patiently waiting for the platter to be ready. It was the sixth and last meat dish of the meal and now, along with the other cooks, James hurried to fill the vegetable platters while calculating how much time he had to finish the six desserts that would be served.

It was the third large noisy party of the week. It seemed to him that there had been nothing but an endless round of dinners, teas, suppers, balls, operas, and concerts all season. All of Paris seemed to be in the throes of one long season of pleasure, ignoring the undertow of civil disconent which lapped at the satin and brocade skirts and high-heeled red shoes of his master's aristocratic friends. "The Revolution is completed," his master insisted as each new crumb was thrown by the nobles to the discontented. It must be because of his sister, thought James. He seemed bathed in happiness and determined to ignore the political intelligence all around him. His confidence knew no bounds. His elegant dinners had become famous in Paris thanks to his, James's, cooking. Leonard, the footman, had just delivered the entire list of guests now seated around his master's table devouring the dinner it had taken fourteen hours to prepare.

There was Lafayette, rouged and red-heeled dandy, a hero to both the Americans who had made their Revolution and to the French who were starting theirs. He was surely the guest of honor. He had been the subject of lively debate in all of Paris since his command had been taken away from him by the king. There was Buffon, the famous scientist and hero of the French philosophers; the Baron and Baronne de Staël, arbitrators of style and taste in Paris. There was the Abbé Morellet, who with his friends the Abbés Chalut and Arnaud, was preparing a French edition of his master's *Notes on the State of Virginia*. A famous mathematician, the Marquis de Condorcet—the whitest man James had ever seen—was also there with his wife, Sophie, a celebrated beauty. And, finally, the Duc and Duchesse de la Rochefoucauld completed the table.

James was disappointed. Missing was one of his favorites, Monsieur de la Tude, who dined out on his adventures of having spent thirty-five years on and off in the Bastille and a dungeon of Versailles, and had lived to tell of it. The last time, it had been for making up verses about Madame de Pompadour. He recounted his life as a convict more as a good story than a tragedy, and so ate well and often on his tales.

James Hemings loaded the desserts onto their platters. There were at least four women upstairs in the pale-yellow-and-gold high-ceilinged dining room, he reminded himself, who were having illicit affairs with men who were not their lawful husbands and who were also present. The young wife of the Duc de la Rochefoucauld was having an affair with the pleasant but dull Mr. Short, his master's faithful secretary, Madame de Hunolstein with General Lafayette. The poet Saint Lambert lived with his mistress the Comtesse d'Houdetot and her husband in a happy *ménage à trois*.... At least Madame de Staël's latest lover was not at the table, he thought. He counted the succession on his fingers. The Baronne Germaine Necker de Staël was twenty-three years old and had been married for three years to the Swedish ambassador. Her first lover had been Charles de Talley-rand, now the Bishop of Autun. Her present lover was Comte Louis de Narbonne, who was said to be the illegitimate son of King Louis XV by his own daughter, Madame Adelaïde. And if his own sister, mused James, had entered the room to do some small task—which she often did in order to spy on her master's brilliant gatherings—then there would be five concubines in the same room, he concluded bitterly.

Why didn't he leave this place? What bond held him here in the underworld when above him, rank and privilege and riches consumed his labor? Twenty-three years of servitude.... Why didn't he doff his starched chef's bonnet, take off his apron, walk out, and be gone by one of the forty-seven gates of Paris? Why, why was he unable to do this? Why could he not take his freedom like a man, instead of crouching and waiting to be given it like a slave? No, not like a slave, for James Hemings wanted his master to acknowledge his existence and his debt, instead of simply allowing him to "stroll" away. He wanted him to give back what he had taken. Until then James Hemings knew he could never leave, he would never steal himself.

It was still early April, not long after one of his master's elegant dinner parties. This Sunday night was one of the rare nights Thomas Jefferson had neither a dinner to give nor one to attend. As was the custom, he dined *"en famille"* with his daughters before they returned to the convent.

James Hemings stood behind Martha Jefferson's chair in the small octagonal salon, which served as a dining room for family dinners. There had been much gentle laughter and now, as James Hemings, contrary to French protocol, poured the demi-tasses of strong coffee at the table and offered one to Martha, he discreetly studied the eldest daughter of his master.

It was to Martha that James always directed his services and his sympathy. He saw her rarely now. They had grown up together, Martha and he. He was seven years older than Martha, and more than any of the other Hemings boys, he had been the right age to play the role of elder brother. He had played this role well and lovingly. They had ridden together over the plantation fields and forests, exploring the woods around Monticello, fishing and eating wild berries. It was he who always helped her up after her frequent tumbles off her pony. Whenever she had lost some treasures, it was he who always found them for her. He and his uncle had built her dollhouse, carved its furniture. He had been the one who had driven her pony cart, keeping it spic and span with coats of blue and white paint. When they played, he let himself be tormented, teased, kissed, and generally used, misused, as well as loved by her, as he would in turn do the same to her. Even when she had reached the age of twelve and their relationship would have, according to the mores of the South, come to an end, they had remained in their roles as brother and sister, passing these last four years in the same familiarity of their earlier years.

Martha, like her younger sister, was listening intently to her father.

"My dear Martha, do you not look forward to the tranquil pleasures of America and find them preferable to the empty bustle of Paris?"

Sally Hemings entered the room and stood quietly apart from the group from which she was excluded. Was he going to announce that they were going home? Had the permission finally come to leave?

Thomas Jefferson flashed his frank and charming smile. "For to what does the bustle tend?"

The small group exhaled. This was not the announcement they were all waiting for.

"At eleven o'clock, it is day *chez madame*. The curtains are drawn. Propped on bolsters and pillows and her head scratched into a little order, the bulletins of the sick are read, and *billets* of the well, she writes to some of her acquaintances and receives the visits of others. If the morning is not very thronged, she is able to get out and hobble around the cage of the Palais Royal . . . As for royalty and royal courts, they should be regarded as you would the Tower of London or the menagerie of Versailles with their lions and tigers and other beasts of prey, and standing in the same relation to their fellows—a slight acquaintance with them will suffice to show you that, under the most imposing exterior, they are the weakest and the worst part of mankind. . . . Furthermore, she must hobble quickly, for the *coiffeur*'s turn is come, and a tremendous turn it is! Happy if he does not make her arrive when dinner is half over! The torpitude of digestion is a little past, when she flutters for a half hour through the streets, by way of paying visits, and then to the spectacles. These finished, another half hour is devoted to dodging in and out of doors of her very sincere friends, and away to supper. After supper, cards, bed, rise at noon the next day, and tread, like a millhouse, the same trodden circle over again. Thus the days of life are consumed, one by one, without an object beyond the present moment; ever flying from ennui of that, yet carrying it with us; eternally in pursuit of happiness, which keeps eternally ahead of us."

Martha Jefferson laughed her low melodious laugh, one of her few charms, but she glanced at her father with some apprehension. There was a touch of melancholy to his amusing recital, a wistfulness with an edge; she even detected some bitterness. Was he tiring of Paris life? Homesick? Was he displeased with the kind of education she was receiving at the convent? Did he think, heaven forbid, that she was becoming like those women he described? She frowned. The mere shadow of her father's disapproval sent a wave of misery through her. She stared at him, cup raised, but his face was almost devoid of expression, except for a slight crinkling around the eyes.

He looked up at James as the servant poured another cup of coffee.

"And if death or bankruptcy happens to trip us out of the circle . . . think of poor Monsieur Saint-James—taking asylum in the Bastille as protection against his irate creditors. Well, poor Monsieur Saint-

James's bankruptcy is merely the matter for the buzz of an evening and is completely forgotten the next morning . . . like mine would be."

"Oh, Papa," Martha replied.

Could he really have enough of the glamorous elegant lady friends she so envied? Women who spent their lives in just the manner he described? Not just mistresses like Madame de Pompadour or Du Barry, but women like Madame de Deffand and Madame Geoffrin, ladies of intellect with the most famous salons of the day like . . . Madame de Staël, Madame Sullivan, the Duchesse d'Anville.

She and little Polly stared at him as he continued. Sally Hemings was listening, hoping not to be sent from the room.

"In America, on the other hand, the society of your husband, the cares of children, the arrangements of the house, the improvements of the grounds fill every moment with useful and healthy activity. Every exertion is encouraging, because it also joins the promise of some future good. Leisure is spending time with real friends, whose affections are not thinned to cobwebs by being spread over a thousand objects."

The staid and faithful adolescent that was Martha Jefferson thought of the flighty Maria Cosway and she suppressed a smile. So, she thought, her father was over his infatuation at last with that dangerous and seductive creature.

"This is the picture, in the light it is presented to my mind. Now let me have it in yours. If we do not concur this year, we shall the next or, if not then, in a year or two more. You see I am determined not to suppose myself mistaken. . . ."

Mistaken about what? Martha Jefferson wondered in alarm. What was it he was trying to tell her? He seemed to be almost pleading with her. Didn't he know he could ask anything on earth of her? That her only wish in life was to make him happy? She would agree to any sacrifice he asked of her. If he wanted her to give up her aristocratic friends . . . if he wanted to leave Paris tonight, she was ready.

"Papa! Really! You sound like you want to drop everything and turn into a hermit. Goodness knows, you already go all the time to your hermitage at Valerian . . . you don't want to give up society completely, do you?"

Although her tone was light, Martha's eyes were troubled and she glanced quickly at Polly, who was staring at her father, then she looked at James. What was he asking her to accept, James thought bitterly, sensing rather than seeing the small, silent, discreet figure of his sister.

Martha's face became even paler under the white powder that cov-

ered the freckles James Hemings had known and practically counted
since childhood. She is going to disagree with her father, he thought,
and he held his breath.

"I agree, Papa, that many of the fashionable pursuits of the Parisian
ladies are rather frivolous and become uninteresting to a reflective mind
. . . but the picture you have exhibited, dearest Papa, is surely over-
charged. You have thrown a strong light upon all that is ridiculous in
their characters and you have buried their qualities in the shade. These
women, *your friends*, are not ordinary women. They are a race apart,
with all the dispassion, the irony, the intuitive sense of measure and
moderation of their breed. The state of society in different countries
requires corresponding manners and qualifications. Those of the
French women are by no means calculated for the meridian of America. . . ."

Martha paused. She had been choosing her words carefully. What
did he want to hear? she wondered. Conscious of the silence in the room
and the impervious expression on her father's face, she continued:

"You must admit, Papa, that the Frenchwomen are more accomplished and understand the intercourse of society better than in any
other country. Their education is of a higher caliber. True, the women of
France interfere with the politics of the country and often give a decided
turn to the fate of the empires. . . . They have obtained that rank and
consideration in society which our sex is entitled to and to which they in
vain contend for in other countries . . . including our own! Perhaps,"
Martha said timidly, "I went too far."

At this, her father burst into laughter. "My dear, I've never heard a
better speech in defense of the rights of womanhood. Bravo! Mrs.
Bingham couldn't have put it better!"

Thomas Jefferson almost involuntarily glanced to where Sally
Hemings stood. Although there was no visible agitation on his master's
face, his natural high color, now ruddy in the glow of the candles, James
Hemings knew his master well enough to know that he was not at all
pleased with his daughter's outburst. She, on the other hand, was
visibly frightened.

Martha Jefferson sighed. She was relieved that her father had taken
her inexplicable outburst as he had, but she knew he didn't agree with
her. His displeasure was concealed as usual behind that benign expression she knew so well. Why had she let herself be carried away like that?
Had it been because of the strange urgency in her father's voice? He was
hiding something from her, and even the thought of his secret gave her a

pang of jealousy. If only he would treat her as a woman instead of a child
. . . at least as he treated those frivolous Frenchwomen he was so busy
condemning. She would ask for nothing more. She no longer wished to
be shielded, shut out of his private thoughts.

The handsome trio rose and moved into the small salon. All were in
motion, except for Sally Hemings. She felt at that moment great admiration for Martha. James pulled out Martha's chair and as she turned,
her bewildered eyes met those of her maid. The two young girls held
each other's eyes until the benevolent glance of Thomas Jefferson
flicked between them.

It was a week later that Martha found herself standing in her maid's
room in the attic of the Hôtel de Langeac. Not being able to find Sally
Hemings, she had climbed the steep back stairs to the servants'
quarters with the dozen chemises and bloomers that needed mending.
Now she stood in the center of the small cramped room transfixed, her
elaborate coiffure almost touching the low ceiling and making her stoop
unconsciously. The room was crammed with silk and muslin dresses
and petticoats. There were delicate chiffon shawls and laces piled in one
corner on a chair. The moment before, she had opened a large green
morocco leather trunk at the foot of the narrow bed. In it she had found
dozens of pairs of silk stockings, kid gloves, ribbons, plumes, delicately
embroidered cambric underclothes and petticoats, and pairs upon
pairs of silk and leather shoes.

She turned and fingered the dress nearest her. It was of fine yellow
silk with delicate white stripes and embroidered white roses. She was so
transfixed that she had not noticed her maid's presence behind her as
she stood rooted there, silent in utter consternation. Martha turned,
brushing the skirt of one of the dresses out of the way, and stared at her
maid. She took in the coiffured hair, and the pale-blue silk dress over
green petticoats. This dress too was new. She had never seen it before.

"Where did you get all this?" she asked in something like awe.

Sally Hemings paled but did not answer immediately. Anger had
overwhelmed her at seeing her friend in her room without permission
and without an invitation. Then she realized that Martha was not her
friend, but her mistress and that she had every right to enter at will the
room of her slave—to finger and touch those precious possessions she
found there because by all rights they did belong to her.

"I said, where did you get all this?"

"It . . . it's mine. It belongs to me, Mistress. It doesn't concern you."

"Doesn't concern me! Doesn't concern me! Since when does the fact that my *maid* has the wardrobe of a lady not concern me? I asked you where you got all these things. Did you *steal* them?"

"No."

"No, who?"

"No, Mistress."

"Then someone *gave* you all this?"

"Yes, Mistress."

"Who?"

"I cannot say, Mistress, please . . . don't ask me. . . . Some I bought with my wages. . . ."

"Wages?"

"Yes, Mistress."

"Since when have you been receiving wages?"

"Since last year. . . . Twenty-four francs a month."

"Even a hundred years' salary would not buy these . . . these exquisite things. Tell me"—Martha's mouth set itself in a hard line; the ways of French society were no mystery to her—"it is a lover, is it not?"

"I don't know what you mean, Mistress."

"*You know perfectly well what I mean! I mean you have a man as a lover.* You have attracted the eye of a gentleman and you have . . . become his mistress!"

"I—"

"You think I don't know of such things! After four years at Panthémont. Tell me or I'll beat it out of you!"

"Yes." Sally Hemings' eyes glowed fierce and dry. Her fear had been replaced with outrage. If Martha struck her, she was ready to strike back and her small hands curled into fists of revolt.

"I demand to know who it is."

Martha Jefferson had suddenly taken on all the airs and long-forgotten drawl of a Virginia-plantation mistress. She took her servant's chin and lifted her face so that she could look into her eyes. "I demand to know who the gentleman . . . or rather rascal . . . is!"

"I cannot tell you." She turned her head away from the revolting female hand that touched her.

"Then I will tell Papa."

At this the maid turned her head back toward her mistress and for the last time looked directly into her eyes.

"I wouldn't do that if I were you."

Something in the tone of the young girl's voice stopped Martha Jefferson; she stared at her for a long time.

"*Mon Dieu!* What would your mother say, Sally Hemings!"

"It is not what my mother would say, Mistress, but what yours would say."

Sally Hemings waited for the storm to break over her head. Martha Jefferson was strong. She towered over her slave, and Sally Hemings almost threw up her arms to protect herself. Only pride made her stand and stare up at her owner. Only pride made her still the trembling of her body and cool it with an icy indifference that bordered on hatred. Why, she thought, should I bother to lie to this white woman? Simply because I am expected to calm and soothe her fears? Look how she flounders at the least resistance.

Martha Jefferson waited for the name of her maid's lover, but her maid remained silent.

Once, just this once, let her lie to herself. With this, Sally Hemings turned her back on the intruder who had violated her sanctuary, her only place of privacy. Even this room was not her own. Let her lie to herself, she thought. And she left Martha standing in the midst of her treasures, a pair of white satin slippers clutched in her hand.

April 18, 1789, The Abbaye Royale of Panthémont

My dearest and most adored Papa,

I respectfully and formally request your permission to enter into the Holy Orders of the Abbaye Panthémont as a suppliant and a novice in preparation eventually to take vows as a nun in the Roman Catholic Church and the convent of Panthémont.

I realize this may be a shock to you, but I assure you, dearest Papa, that I have not taken this decision lightly and have been in daily correspondence with the Papal Nuncio, Comte Duganani, and in daily prayers and consultation with the Abbess Madame Mézières as regards this matter. I cannot and will not reconcile what I have learned of the world and its frivolous and disreverent and unchristian attitudes with what I *know* to be the precepts and the Holy Commandments of God and Righteousness. I would rather not *live* in a world where I must be witness to and condone by compliance such transgressions, or *know* and not prevent the punishments for such cruel disregard for His teachings.

I embrace you with an Exultant and Joyful heart and Fervent prayers for your accord in this matter and for the Happiness of my Cherished Papa. . . .

Your loving Daughter

James Hemings knew what had been in the note he had delivered to the mansion on the Champs-Elysées several weeks after Martha's last visit. He had not read the letter, so he could not know if his sister was mentioned by name or by function. He only knew that Martha Jefferson had decided and had told him with passionate tears of joy in her eyes that she wanted to become a nun and enter the convent of the Abbaye de Panthémont. He had listened to her speechlessly as she had told him of her decision.

When James Hemings had entered his master's cabinet he watched Thomas Jefferson casually read the note from his daughter. James waited in silence. But Thomas Jefferson did not betray any emotion; he sat down at his writing table and wrote quickly, and then rang for Petit. The carriage was ordered to be hitched and brought to the front courtyard. He beckoned James to come with him. They rode into Paris together until they reached the rue Royale. They went from shop to shop buying linen for Martha Jefferson. At the end of the morning, James, walking behind his master, was carrying armloads of fine silks, laces, and chiffons. In anticipation of Martha's birthday, he had even bought a sapphire ring. He had also bought a silver locket for Sally Hemings. They had spent two hundred and seventy-four francs that morning.

Two days later, James accompanied his master to the Panthémont Convent, the back of the carriage filled with the purchases. James followed as Jefferson moved quickly into the inner courts of the convent, where he was met by a pale and trembling Martha. James tried to signal some comfort, but she had eyes only for her father. Never had his master's smile been so benevolent, never his manner so tender and charming, never had he shown in public such a fatherly attitude toward his eldest daughter, thought James. Thomas Jefferson kissed her hand and then her cheek, and then turning to the abbess who had entered the somber courts, he disappeared with her into her apartments. Martha and James waited outside the closed oak doors of the abbess's office.

When Jefferson emerged, he was smiling. He told Martha that he had come for her.

Martha Jefferson looked up at the handsome, smiling man who was her father. His auburn hair was flecked with white, giving it a sandy color when it was not powdered, and it was not this day. It was tied in a queue at his neck with a blue ribbon and hung down his back over the Prussian blue of his frock coat fitted perfectly over his broad shoulders. The long powerful legs were encased in pale ivory chamois and he too had on the red-heeled patent leather pumps of the aristocracy. His long chin was set, his eyes clear and guileless as a summer day. His attitude was one of a determined, but attentive suitor. He smiled, showing small white even teeth and without a word, Martha Jefferson took the proffered arm of her father and mounted the double steps into his carriage, the door of which was held open for her by James.

James Hemings closed the door and mounted beside the coachman. The elegant English carriage of lilac and yellow trimmed in dark gray turned and rattled out of the lonely cobbled courtyard onto the rue de Grenelle. Martha settled back behind the white lace curtains into the brimstone-colored silk upholstery. She looked with wonder at the piles of presents and packages on the seat beside her. Never, as long as she lived, would she mention this incident again. She pulled back the silk tassels and took a last look at the white stone façade of the Abbaye de Panthémont drenched in the rosy spring sunlight.

The education of Martha Jefferson was ended.

CHAPTER 18

SUMMER, 1789

THE TWELFTH OF JULY 1789 was a Sunday. There had been riots and food was becoming more and more scarce. The dismissal of the minister, the defiance of the National Assembly, the stubbornness of the king, all conveyed a sense of impending disaster those first weeks of July. Now, the streets were all plastered with enormous-sized *De Par le Roi* inviting peaceable citizens to remain indoors.

From my window, I could look down the length of the Champs-Elysées—eight hundred and twenty double steps according to my master—to the place Louis XV. I could also see, around the bronze statue of Louis XV, the dragoons and hussars assembling in their red-and-white-and-yellow uniforms. All sorts of rumors ran rampant, and James went to the Palais Royal every day to see what he could find out. At twelve, the cannon went off as usual when the sun passed its meridian, but this day, its low thunder struck gloom and disquiet in the hearts of almost everyone.

Through my master's telescope I watched in the distance as a growing crowd, festooned with green cockades, grew and like a flight of locusts filled the place Louis XV. There were some people armed with axes, staves, others with picks and pitchforks. I knew James was somewhere in Paris. Perhaps even in the very mob which was now entering the square. I saw the crowd being charged upon by the German Hussars; I heard noises of shots, sabers flashed clearly, and puffs of smoke from muskets rose like tiny clouds over the heads of the men. Then the crowd exploded along what streets and alleys they could, and suddenly the square was empty with the soldiers pursuing agitators and Sunday strollers alike up the avenues. It was a fascinating spectacle and I sat by the window all day.

When darkness fell, all the roads out of the city, including our own Champs-Elysées, were blocked by pickets and barriers. There were stalled carriages and vehicles of all sorts. Traffic, wheel to wheel, immobile from the tollgate all the way to the place Louis XV.

On Monday, Paris was like a tomb. When James and my master went out to investigate, they found that no one had reported for work; all had joined the rebellion. Everything was closed, except for wine and bread shops. James was sent to prowl the Palais Royal he knew so well and to report back to the mansion. When he returned late that evening, he told us that the people were busily sewing cockades to be worn, not the green of d'Artois, but the red and blue of Paris, on a white background which stood for the constitution. They called it the *"Tricolore."* Our ministry was ecstatic. The people of Paris had chosen the colors of the American Revolution.

Outside our house, the streets were deserted and silent. That evening, by a special new order, every window was lit in every house. I tried to imagine Paris, a maze of winding narrow streets, deserted, crossed by the large boulevards also deserted, except for the shadows of the National Guard patrolling with their torches and flares. All the lights of Paris, no more than a gathering of fireflies compared to the blazing lights of Versailles, where the National Assembly sat through the night. We slept little and by dawn on Tuesday both James and Thomas Jefferson had abandoned the mansion.

While the Hôtel de Langeac was locked and barred, the hot July sun rose and the National Guard prepared to march on the Hôtel des Invalides. By the end of the day, the Bastille, the fortress dungeon which was the very symbol of the king's unlimited power, had been stormed and taken.

James was an eyewitness to that event, which had marked the turning point of the rebellion. Later on, James, like Monsieur de Tude, would often drink and dine out on the tale of the storming of the Bastille. That night, in the oval salon of the hôtel, servants and masters alike were held in thrall to the present. Even James's own highly developed imagination could not embellish the drama of that siege. How much he actually saw and how much he heard about, I would never know, nor would any of his audience, but as he told his tale, we fully sensed the extent of the drama. We sat, Martha, Polly, Mr. Short, Petit, our professors, and all the other servants, spellbound while, in his strangely accented French, he recounted the Fourteenth of July.

He had slipped out of the mansion in the middle of the night and joined his comrades at one of the cafés near the Palais Royal. He had slept on the floor for the rest of the night, rising again at six. Hot rum had been served. Someone had pinned a tricolor cockade on him; the women had stayed up all night sewing. He had taken a butcher's knife from the kitchen as his only arm, and now he joined the milling militia as they surged halfway up the Champs-Elysées and turned toward the Invalides, where someone had said there were arms to be had. James, still in the light-yellow livery of the Hôtel de Langeac, unwashed, already lightheaded on the morning's rum like the rest, became one with the thousands of marching men and women. A strange elation had stolen over him, he said, his heart had beat in rhythm with that of his neighbor, as if everyone were one huge crawling animal of which he felt one particle of skin, one strand of hair.

The mob arrived at the walls of the Invalides, and the garrison did not fire upon them as the walls were scaled and the gates flung open. They had rushed in, spreading through all the rooms and passages of the great building. A roar went up as the place where arms had been was found and seized. Those nearest snatched, struggled, and clutched at them. There was no order, no leaders, no officers as James looked around him and saw thousands of firelocks hoisted onto thousands of shoulders with the cry of "On to the Bastille!" The dreaded prison-tomb with walls nine feet thick which was the Bastille had been battered down, the drawbridge lifted and manned with a cannon since Sunday. Since early morning the cry had been, "On to the Bastille!" and as the cry went up again the whole suburb of Saint-Antoine was marching as one man. The people, now armed, turned as a flock of wild geese, homing toward the eight grim towers that one could see over the rooftops of Paris from almost every point in the city. The new army arrived at the drawbridge of the Bastille at one o'clock. By five o'clock, all the soldiers were covered with blood. The wounded and the dead were being carried into the houses along the rue de la Cerisaie. For four hours the crowd howled before the gates.

Cannon and musket shots from the towers hit at random, crumpling men and women who sank and then were crushed under the weight of others pressing forward. The crowd increased until it spilled down and over the quais of the Pont Neuf. Then, without warning, a cry rumbled back like a wave over the sweating, bleating heads . . . the Bastille had surrendered.

The Bastille was taken. The Bastille had fallen.

James threw up his arms. We were all hanging on to his every word. The forward motion of the mob, like a wave, surged headlong toward its goal, and had not the National Guard wheeled around and leveled its guns against its own, the mob would have plunged suicidally by the thousands into the moat of the prison. The governor of the Bastille tried to kill himself but was taken prisoner. His captors meant to take him to the Hôtel de Ville through the cursing, clutching crowd; only his bloody scalp, held up in a victorious hand, arrived. The head, aloft on a pike, was now traveling through the streets. The rest of him had been torn to pieces.

The evening sun was setting, and James, feverish and exhausted, battered and dirty, fell quiet as did his awed audience. The word of the fall of the Bastille had begun to spread over Paris, and, amid gunfire, we heard the sound of music. The people of Paris were dancing in the streets.

We put James to bed and, despite the bath, the smell of the gunpowder hovered over him. He sat propped up on his pillows grinning. His eyes seemed to say this: This slave from Virginia's made history today. This slave ran with the Revolution! His eyes said to me: I am mine. We are going to take ourselves to freedom. If God let me do this, then He will leave us take our freedom without running. Take ourselves, without stealing. We are going to be free. Everything is changed.

He smiled and I smiled back.

CHAPTER 19

SEPTEMBER 1789

IT WAS AMIDST the ceremonies and processions that followed the fall of the Bastille that I found I was with child.

"*Tu es enceinte,*" said Marie-Louise. She looked at me with kindness and exasperation as I stared at her in disbelief. She had warned me and now she was afraid all her concoctions of parsley, rue, and camphor, or any of her other remedies would be of no avail.

I roamed the streets in a daze, weakened by the cramps in my stomach and the constant nausea. Te Deums filled Notre Dame every day, and procession followed procession, with gay young women in white muslin tied with tricolor sashes moving among the crowds. The processions and the bread lines grew longer. One day I decided never to return to the mansion.

I took refuge with Madame Dupré on the rue de Seine.

She guessed at once what had happened; she took me in her arms, and urged me to return to the safety and comfort of the Hôtel de Langeac.

"Sooner or later," she said, "you will be forced to abandon your child. Paris is notorious for that." She paused. "There are three thousand abandoned children a year in Paris. Surely you don't want to add to that sad number?"

"But you don't understand," I replied, "this is not just a bastard child, it is a slave bastard. It will belong to my master, Monsieur Jefferson."

"But of course it is his!"

"No, Madame, that is not what I mean. I mean it is his not only by blood but by property. It is his property to do with what he likes, just as he can do with me what he likes. I am not free, Madame."

There was a long silence as Madame Dupré tried to assimilate this information.

"You mean you are a slave, like the Africans in Martinique and Santo Domingo?"

"Not like the Africans. I *am* African. I am black."

At this, Madame Dupré seized me and dragged me into the light of the window. She looked searchingly at my face and body, at my hands and nails. At the texture of my hair.

"Then you are a métis?"

"Yes."

"Go back to him. Go back and demand your freedom and that of his child. Demand it in writing and stay here in Paris. You will find a protector. I promise you that. On French soil you are free and you shall stay free. But return to him. Give him the chance to express his instincts as a father and a lover. You may be surprised. He loves you."

"I don't want to be loved. I want to be free."

"Do you really, my child? You love him as well, and there is no freedom in that."

She looked at me with her wise, cynical eyes and shook me gently by the shoulders.

"*Rentre à la maison,*" she said to me. "Go home. *Tu veux rentrer, n'est-ce pas?*"

"*Oui,*" I answered, "I want to go home."

A week after my departure I returned to the mansion. I had stolen myself and now I tried to replace the stolen object quietly, as if it had never been taken from its owner. I entered through the courtyard and servant quarters in trembling expectation of meeting my brother James, but it was Petit that I met in the reception hall. He looked at me without surprise, but with studied annoyance. What havoc I must have wrought in the household to have put any expression, let alone anger, on those cold features . . . as I searched his face, looking for a clue as to what awaited me, a warm expression stole over his face.

"Do not be alarmed, but . . . he is ill. He has been in grips of a migraine headache for almost a week with no relief. . . . James has gone again to fetch Dr. Gem."

I remembered from Monticello the violence of these sudden head-aches that were powerful enough to render my master senseless. I tried to remember what remedies had been used at Monticello to ease him.

"Petit," I said, forgetting my own predicament, "it is possible to get camphor and ice and . . ."

"We've tried everything . . . Mademoiselle . . . except your return. . . . I pray that it will relieve him."

"Why did he not look for me?"

"I do not know."

"And James?"

He ransacked Paris for you."

"But I was at Madame Dupreé's!"

"She swore you were not. She even let him enter and search the rooms."

I smiled. How had she managed to fool James with me installed in her attic?

"Come," he said, not unkindly. "You'll have to face him sometime." Then, turning toward me just as we arrived in front of the apartment, he said, as if in explanation of the state in which I would find my master:

"You dealt him a blow I would not have thought possible." Now he seized my shoulders gently and turned me toward the door.

I entered the apartment. The curtains were tightly shut and my eyes were unaccustomed to the darkness. In the room, there was the same undefinable odor of gunpowder that had stalked the streets of Paris three weeks before. I recoiled as it smote me, and turned to flee. His voice sounded and held me there.

"Why did you do that to me."

The long ashen figure, fully dressed, sat up on the bed, and the face I looked into was one of such desolation my heart almost stopped. The voice was husky and scarred. The fury was barely controlled.

"Why did you do that to me?" he repeated evenly.

"I'm with child. That is why I ran away."

I threw this at him, meaning to convey to him all the despair and loneliness of the past week of rebellion, but instead a fierce joy took hold of me.

"Sally . . ."

"I will not give birth to a slave! I am free now. I will never birth slaves!"

A flush of color came into his deathly-pale face. I stood apart from him—some yards—afraid to approach, stubborn, and poised for flight. It was he who then fell back in pain. I wavered, but held my ground.

"I know . . . that I cannot hold you against your will. Our . . . your child I consider free and will always consider free. You have my word. I recognize that you are free, as free as your heart permits."

I was lost. My heart was his, and he knew it. I faltered, cornered, weak.

"I want him born on French soil. . . ."

"We must go home, Sally, but it is only temporary. We will return."

"That is not enough . . . I want—"

He began to speak very softly to me, drawing me nearer and nearer. Making me strain to hear until I knelt beside him. His voice was low and sweet, as if he were maning a young wild falcon to the block. There were tears streaming down his face and promises on his lips.

His promises mingled along with mine in the sultry darkness. No, I would not leave him again. No, I would not die in childbirth. No, I would not claim my freedom.

Yes, my children would all be free. When? At twenty-one. Twenty-one. Five years more than I had been on this earth.

His voice and his face hovered over me, held me. He touched and pained me with his terrible loneliness. Never would I cause such pain again. My own needs, my own loneliness, seemed nothing compared to his—his needs were so much mightier than my small ones, his space in the world so much more vast and important than any place I could imagine for myself. Slowly, I succumbed to his will.

"Promise me you will not abandon me again."

"I promise, Master."

"I swear to cherish you and never desert you."

"Yes, Master."

"I promise solemnly that your children will be freed," he said.

"As God is your witness?"

"As God is my witness."

"Bolt the door," he said.

We returned once more to Marly, my master and I. We stood side by side on its heights and looked down for the last time, feasting on the panorama. The September landscape was deep and still; I fixed this vision in my mind, vowing to return to it. Here, I still believed, anything was possible. I vowed to keep this dream.

I sensed the same languor invading us both: it was like the rustling of leaves, deep and continuous, barely audible except to the soul; a sweetness that surprised both of us, for I knew he felt it, yet it never occurred to either of us to speak of it. There would always be such silences between us, partly from prudery or because of our temperaments, but also because there were so many things that must remain unsaid. All our lives. I turned toward the immense figure in dark blue standing silently beside me, and between me and the world. I was beginning to understand this strange, impulsive, melancholy man, full of contradictions and secrets, this man who owned me, my family, and my unborn child.

How did it matter that he was master and I slave? That he loved me and risked much for me? That he took more space in the world than most men did, did not concern me, neither his fame nor his power. I cherished him.

My hand was taken in his. I let it lie where it had been placed. The future and our happiness, like Marly, stretched out before me, total and shoreless. The surrounding fragrance drugged me, and made me careless of what awaited me just beyond my view.

CHAPTER 20

THE *WAYWARD*, OCTOBER 1789

THE PASSPORTS with the king's signature had been delivered. Thomas Jefferson, his two daughters, and his two servants were going home. Everything was to leave on Sunday by river diligence for Le Havre.

Petit checked the list again. If he had calculated right, there were eighty-two crates. And his master claimed he was only going back for a visit! Petit shrugged. He was responsible for the safe arrival of the baggage at Le Havre, not Monsieur Jefferson's future plans.

He edged his way toward the south corner of the courtyard, where three carpenters were at work on the packing crates for the great phaeton to be shipped back. The carriage itself, which would be driven to Le Havre, stood in solitary splendor outside the stable door. Poor Trumbull, thought Petit. That carriage had almost driven him to distraction. His master had ordered it from London through his good services.

It had taken more than a year to build, with all the changes and additions that had been made, but it was undoubtedly one of the finest, most original carriages in France; and in Virginia it would, without a doubt, cause an absolute sensation. Petit walked around the carriage, admiring it, and flecked a speck of dust off the shining lilac body. At once the coachman growled to a standing position. Petit only smiled and bowed with great ceremony. He was not supposed to touch the carriage. . . . It was a new crane-neck carriage. How splendid. Petit turned back to supervise, not without pride, the hampers of wine to be taken back to Virginia.

He shuddered at the thought of the long sea voyage. Water, any body of water bigger than the reflecting pools at Versailles, terrified him. Discreetly he crossed himself.

He glanced again at James Hemings, who was busily supervising the closing of the wine crates, making sure that no bottles found their way out of the crates and into the blouses of the workmen. James, who was in his shirtsleeves, sweated over these crates and the trunks, piling up in the noisy courtyard of the Hôtel de Langeac. The Hôtel de Langeac was not the only fashionable hôtel whose courtyard bustled and burst that day with packing crates and trunks. Recent events had been the signal for the first great exodus of aristocrats toward England, Belgium, and Austria.

He shook his head. He was sorry that Jim-mi was returning to Virginia. So much fire and intelligence wasted on servitude. He, Petit, knew himself to be valuable as a second in command, much like an aide-de-camp to a general. He knew his worth. He was an incorruptible, and silent. *Voilà tout;* his entire life. As for James, he was of another race. Like a thoroughbred horse, he would never survive as a servant, as a slave. Besides, he was now a first-class chef and could surely command the best place and the best salary. But James, for reasons Petit could not fathom, had decided to return to Virginia with his sister who was carrying the child of his master, according to Marie-Louise. Petit was sure that James would never again see the shores of France. From one of the upper windows overlooking the courtyard, Petit saw Martha Jefferson. She was calling to James, waving him frantically into the house. Again Petit shook his head. It was only with the return of Sally to the mansion that he had learned the true relationship between the Hemingses and the Jeffersons. James was Martha Jefferson's uncle! The whole Byzantine story of this strange American family had finally been related to him in great detail by Jim-mi. He, who was quite inured to the bizarre nature of French aristocrats, had been profoundly shocked at this odd genealogy.

That blue and black blood would mix was nothing more than the nature of things, but that it would continue into the second and now the third generation seemed to him beyond propriety, even aristocratic propriety!

There was something uncivilized, raw, and brutal about it. On one hand, they hated and despised blacks, and, on the other, they were the objects of the most violent and emotional desires and obsessions. . . .

That the defection of a chambermaid could bring low a man like Thomas Jefferson . . . Adrien Petit pursed his lips in distaste.

He would never understand this American family.

James Hemings felt as if he had been raped. His face held the same blankness of defeat. Men raped men, he thought, as well as women. . . .

He had had his "explanation" with his master and had been left humiliated and outmaneuvered. All his resistance had dissolved in the face of his enemy! His master as a diplomat was as unconventional, imaginative, resourceful, and tough as the best Old World courtiers. His arguments were turned against him, his reasoning inside out. He had become tongue-tied. How could he have been so abject! He had practically thanked Thomas Jefferson when he had said that he, James, would be freed by his grace as soon as he had trained another cook at Monticello to take his place. This, his master had argued, was the least James could do to repay the training and education of these past years. And he had accepted. He would have been a "monster," a "serpent at my breast," a "traitor" if he had refused. James, like his sister, was now locked in a promise of more years of servitude. But he clung obstinately to this one shred of what he considered his essential dignity.

I will never steal myself! he thought. He has no right to force me to do so . . . to make a criminal and an outlaw out of me who has served him for so long and with such loyalty. He must free me legally and openly.

The disappointment of his return burned his chest. Suddenly, tears splashed onto the large leather trunk he was filling with silver. With an uncontrollable sob he flung himself behind the bulk of the crates.

But there were two people who saw him crying: the discreet and ever-watchful Petit, and, from her window, Martha Jefferson.

Neither James nor Sally Hemings could shake a sense of doom as the small party set forth for Le Havre and England. As for their master, he was buoyant and optimistic, giving instructions to William Short about his return to France in a few months. But all four young people stood there in silence, each in his own anguish. Martha, because her father seemed at last willing to separate himself from her and Polly and return alone to France. James, because he, despite all his vows to the contrary, had further servitude to look forward to. If Sally Hemings was apprehensive about returning to Virginia, she was also doubting her lover's promises that they would return together to France.

Even before their arrival in Le Havre two days later there was a bad omen: the axle on the phaeton broke, and they were stranded on the road for hours.

The day after they finally arrived, a vicious storm broke out and continued unabated for six days. Hail and slashing rains and cold sleet, accompanied by unseasonable thunder and lightning—everything the heavens had to offer—came pouring down. The unceasing wind that whistled day and night brought everyone to the edge of endurance. Only Thomas Jefferson remained calm and cheerful, and on the fourth of October, during a lull in the storm, he had their baggage put on the packet for England. But again they were delayed when the storm suddenly returned.

On the eighth of October the gale had dropped and the packet stood out of Le Havre for Cowes, where we would board the ship for home. It was not until the seventeenth that we reached our destination because of contrary winds, and as we approached the Isle of Wight, we encountered a virtual armada of sailing ships, all collected there and unable to sail because of the storm. More than thirty tall ships lay at anchor as our packet approached the shore.

We were met by John Trumbull, who had been waiting for us to arrive for two weeks. He had farewell letters from the master's friends in London and parting gifts for all of us. Together we stood and looked out at all the ships anchored in the somber gray sea. I stood near the slender, black-eyed, black-haired figure of John Trumbull, whose affectation of dressing only in black, but of the richest, most elegant cloth, made him stand out amongst the multicolored, brightly dyed velvets and satins of the large group of waiting passengers on the shore.

As if sensing my inner turmoil, Master Trumbull turned to me, fixing his endearing, slightly amiss gaze upon me. "Are you going home, 'Sallyhemings'?" he asked me. We both smiled. The way he said my name was our own private joke. When he had asked me my name that winter now two years past, I had replied, as my mother had taught me, with my first and last names. Master Trumbull thought it all one name, and had continued even after I had laughingly corrected him to call me "Sallyhemings." Now all the affection he stirred in me turned into a kind of self-pity.

"We will be coming back," I said.

"Indeed?"

"Yes, it is promised. Virginia is only . . . an interval."

"I hope you are right," replied John Trumbull. He frowned, and I knew what he was thinking.

"And you?" I asked.

"Oh, I doubt that I will return to London. I must make my way in my own country." And in his usual wordy fashion he went on: "To earn a living as an artist is no easy matter. If my affairs were as I would wish, I would stay, and accept the offer of your employer to replace Mr. Short as his private secretary. Nothing would make me feel more honored, but, as an artist, I need the patronage of my countrymen—that is, if I am ever to proceed in my work. My future depends on my reception in America and as that shall be cold or cordial, I shall only decide then whether or not to abandon my country, or perhaps my profession. I hope for better things than perpetual though voluntary exile. I do hope that America will encourage me in producing monuments, not only of heroes but of those events on which their title to the gratitude of the nation is founded."

I had great affection for this man. He was a sentimental and dreamy young artist, as bone-proud as my brother James. Both clung to their small eccentricities and obsessions. To stand alone with only a frail sable-hair brush in hand to meet the world took a lot of courage, I thought. I guarded the sketches he had done of me with my life.

"At any rate, Sallyhemings, just in case we don't meet again, I have something for you. I did it these past weeks."

Master Trumbull was looking down at me.

"Mr. Short suggested it would be a gallant thing to make a copy of my portrait of Thomas Jefferson for Martha, which I have done, as I had already done for other . . . London ladies. And for some reason, one afternoon, I did another."

He took something from his pocket and offered it to me. I could not believe my eyes. It was a replica of Martha's new miniature of her father, taken from the portrait made for Master Trumbull's painting of the Declaration of Independence. I did not trust myself to speak.

"Sallyhemings. Don't I even get an 'Ah' or an 'Oh' over the brilliant likeness, the fine shading, the delicate color, the inimitable expression?" He smiled.

"God bless you, John Trumbull."

"I sincerely hope he will, Sallyhemings . . . and you too," he whispered softly. And he was gone.

I clutched the tiny painting to my breast, and looked out over the harbor. Beyond was the sea, rolling and unfathomable. All the great ships in the harbor had their huge sails unfurled like the wings of the sky-darkening flocks of sea gulls that circled overhead, waiting for the wind.

It was a warm and clear twenty-third of November, 1789, when we landed at Norfolk, Virginia. My child stirred, and James let out a string of curses as we stepped off our ship and back into slavehood. The docks were crowded with hustling, sweating bodies of the dockworkers of every hue, from yellow to blue-black. All slaves. The provincially dressed whites who mingled with them seemed pocks on a sea of colored flesh. The low slurred slave dialect reached my ears without meaning and the Virginia accent sounded harsh and uncouth to my ears so long attuned to French.

For some moments I stood bewildered and foreign in my own country. Only my master seemed to comprehend my confusion. He took my arm gently and led me through the melee of orders and shouts that accompanied the unloading of the vessels, toward an inn where I could rest. But before we had gone more than twenty paces, a delegation of Norfolk citizens accosted him, excitedly greeting him as the new secretary of state of the United States of America. Stunned, I was quickly thrust aside. The first promise had been broken.

The looks directed my way were polite and curious until it was discovered I was maid to Master Jefferson's daughters. Then the looks ceased to be those directed at a living person and became the looks one fastens on a crate or a sack of meal. I felt faint with the shock of those looks, so well remembered but also so well forgotten. It was Polly who took my hand and held it tightly until the carriages and horses had been arranged for and we were safe inside. Trembling, I was helped into the rented phaeton by James, who was also energetically supervising the loading of our hand baggage, his own distress lost in the rush of activity. My master was still being held by the press of the anxious, noisy delegation.

In the darkness of the carriage, I pulled my veil over my face, and let Polly sink her head on my shoulder. We both slept, I think, because it was hours before the carriages started up for Monticello.

It took us a month to get home. The slave telegraph, I knew, would communicate not only our arrival but every detail of our journey—our whereabouts, our baggage, clothes, state of health ... including and above all, my impending confinement, which I could no longer conceal. My mother would know long before I reached home.

At Eppington, a more official notice of his appointment, from the United States government, awaited Thomas Jefferson, and finally, at Shadwell, the nearest plantation, four weeks later, the Monticello slaves poured down the mountain to meet us. It was a scene that I would remember forever. The dream of Marly was gone. I knew I would never see Paris again.

The slaves had discovered the approaching carriage as soon as it had reached Shadwell and had come as one body; a flux of undulating black and brown and copper and yellow and white bodies flowing toward us, covered with cheerful ragged clothing. I recognized the unbleached Monticello woven woolen shirts of the field hands, the red-and-blue gingham head rags of the house servants, the brown and black linen dresses of the housemaids with stiff white aprons, the rough, shapeless Mother Hubbards of the female field hands, punctuated now with a red or blue blanket, now with a brightly dyed coat.

Old, shapeless felt hats and beavers were thrown into the air or waved wildly, skirts and petticoats were snatched up, showing bare feet. Most of the men were coatless as the day was warm and bright. The slaves were shouting. Some were singing, waving handkerchiefs and red bandannas; the cries and cheers were a blanket of sounds following us up the mountain. The horses were unhitched and the carriage was opened and we were received into the arms of the singing crowd, my master's servants and my fellow slaves. I sat horrified. Maria and Martha were caught up as well in the pandemonium, lifted out of the carriage, and carried by strong arms into the crowd.

They were happy. This adulation pleased my master, and the veneer of French refinement seemed to be rubbed off by the press of warm flesh.

Only James and I remained untouched by the celebration: James out of shame and bitterness; I out of fear. A wave of nausea overwhelmed me, the nausea of defeat as well as of pregnancy.

I recognized Hemingses among the crowd. And standing in the doorway, rising like a giant accusing finger above the tumult and shouting, was my mother, her hands on her hips, filling the doorway of the mansion like the stone frescoes on the façade of the Hôtel de Langeac.

Suddenly, eager hands reached for me within the carriage; I would have to face the multitude. I put the miniature which hung around my neck on a velvet ribbon, inside my dress, lest it be torn off me in the excitement. The black velvet pressed against my neck with a special softness . . . it seemed to be speaking to me, slowly. If I was ashamed to be home, no one would know it except me. I appeared at the door of the carriage, my veil lifted, a smile on my face, tears rolling down my cheeks. A murmur of "ahs" went out, like the rings of a tossed pebble upon water. "Dashing Sally" had come home! Gently I was lifted from black arms to black arms, my voluminous yellow cloak wrapped tightly around me hid the new life I carried. Joy at seeing Monticello again washed over me.

Then I saw the small figure in the doorway turn her back and walk into the Big House. The wind bit deep into my face as I was handed from slave to slave into the darkness of the now empty doorway.

She would have chosen freedom.

"Mama!" I cried against all the other cries and commotion. But, if she heard me, she did not turn back.

"Mama!" I screamed again and again.

It was years before she answered that call.

Within three months, I had my first child and named him Thomas; my master had gone to New York with James, to take up his post as secretary of state; Martha had married her cousin, Thomas Mann, and left the mansion; Polly had gone to live with her beloved Aunt Eppes, a hundred miles away; and I was left alone, having just passed my seventeenth birthday, the mistress of Monticello.

PART III

1833
The Census
Taker

CHAPTER 21

WASHINGTON CITY, 1833

And what, therefore, is loyalty proper, the life breath of all Society,
but an effluence of Hero-Worship, submissive admiration for the
truly great? Society is founded on Hero-Worship. . . . What we may
call Heroarchy—Government of Heroes.

THOMAS CARLYLE, Lecture on "Heroes and Hero-Worship,"
Albermarle Street, London, 1840

JOHN QUINCY ADAMS took another long look at the tall blond young man
with the clear innocent eyes. *He certainly knows a lot,* he thought, *and
he is out for blood in the name of his lady.* . . . Quincy Adams was
undecided. Jefferson and his father had finally patched up their long
feud, in the face of impending death, but his mother, Abigail, had never
forgiven Jefferson for Sally Hemings, nor for James Callender and
Callender's attacks on her husband. Should he give in to a sudden urge
to voice his true opinions of Jefferson, though he never engaged in
gossiping? He wondered whether this once he should let the chance to
recount a fascinating parable of Jeffersonian duplicity get the better of
his principles.

There was something ironic, almost biblical in Nathan Langdon's
strange addendum to the story of Sally Hemings. *The closing of the
circle, and final contradiction of turning her white for the sake of
history. . . . Sally,* he thought, *probably had a fine sense of the ironic.
The peasant-slave philosophy of her youth would have blended well
with the cynicism of the French education she had received while in
Paris. If he told this young man what he could not find in the Federalist
papers, he would only corroborate what Sally Hemings herself had
already revealed. How extraordinary that she had broken her silence at
all,* he thought.

"Well, I can't say I know the whole story, but our family was closest
to the truth of it. What I do know, however, is confidential, and I should
categorically deny everything if it is repeated." The rugged and pon-

derous Quincy Adams suddenly had the look of a mischievous boy. "The enigma of Sally Hemings and Thomas Jefferson will never be completely solved. My parents were very close to Jefferson. What I know, and I know that what I know is true, I learned from them. Despite their difference with the president at the time, they tried to stay out of the scandal as much as they could. It was a tragic campaign...."

"I know, some of the newspaper articles, and the pamphlets, were inexcusably virulent."

Quincy Adams looked up over his spectacles. Could Nathan be hinting at his own poetic efforts at pornography? His miserable ballad referring to Sally had even bubbled up out of proportion during his own electoral campaign of 1828. Quincy Adams did not immediately take up the conversation. The Sally Hemings scandal had unfolded when he was young, and scrupulous enough to believe that the lives of public men should be led in accordance with their professed opinions ... as his father's had, he thought, thanks in great measure to his mother. He turned in his armchair and gazed out onto the cow pasture that stretched from the unfinished, unpaved Pennsylvania Avenue to the Potomac River. He was thoroughly ashamed of that awful poem.

He would admit that he had greatly admired Jefferson, Adams mused, for his erudition, his interest in science and letters, but that he had always mistrusted his political principles, and disliked many of his personal traits, including much stretching of the truth in favor of the well-turned phrases or the elegant aphorism. Jefferson's affected simplicity irked him, too, when everyone knew his great wealth (if the number of slaves one owned could decently be counted as wealth). Then, too, he continued to think to himself, Jefferson's tendency to live beyond his quite sufficient means offended his Yankee sense of thrift, and he also disdained any man unable to give his ideas a clear synthesis. Jefferson's ideas were scattered in the most voluminous collection of letters of the century, yet nowhere in that morass of words, he thought, did Jefferson state clearly his political or moral principles in a way that corresponded to his political and personal actions.

Quincy Adams' inner voice continued. Why had Thomas Jefferson, a staunch abolitionist up until 1790, suddenly lost all fastidiousness about slavery? Certainly during his presidency, at least the second term, he had had the political and moral power to turn the country around on this subject. Yet, from that time on he had sunk deeper and deeper into compromise with his beliefs, and into a lethargy that couldn't be blamed entirely on the Virginia sun. Sally Hemings? Is that what turned him into a hypocritical gradualist, with no plan for accommodating the second race of America?

Nathan Langdon stirred politely, but Quincy Adams, unconcerned, continued his inner monologue.

That Jefferson had loved Sally Hemings he had no doubt. Whether Sally Hemings had loved Jefferson was less clear, since she had had no choice. That was the tragedy. That such an unnatural love may have changed the course of history, undoubtedly preventing Jefferson from using his power and genius to turn the tide against slavery instead of being an accomplice to all its darkest and most passionate aspects, was tragic indeed. . . . Why had Jefferson revised his stand against slavery when he returned from Paris? What had bound Jefferson to such a deep and lasting contradiction? He had not believed in God; therefore, all his ideas of obligation or retribution were bounded by this world. His duties to his neighbor had been under no stronger guarantee than the laws of the land and the opinions of the world. The tendency of this on a great mind was to produce insincerity and duplicity. Duplicity had ultimately been Thomas Jefferson's besetting weakness.

Nathan Langdon uncrossed his legs and turned his gaze on the silent ex-president. He had come a long way in Washington since his first hesitant steps less than two years before. After his rupture with Sally Hemings he had lost his bearings. The humiliating memory of his broken engagement and his departure from home and family had almost been wiped out by the exhilaration of Washington. All aspects of his life had become resolved and clear, except one: Sally Hemings. Only she remained a haunting obsession. It was only now, after more than a year of working for John Quincy Adams, that he had dared bring up the subject—one that even after all these years had arisen in Quincy Adams' own presidential campaign. He wanted that story, told in a lonely cabin at the foot of a mountain, corroborated. He was determined to do it.

Nathan waited. If there was one thing he had learned in Washington these past eighteen months, it was that when a politician starts off with a disclaimer, you were about to get the unvarnished truth. He faced Quincy Adams, not speaking, using his now perfected technique of never breaking the silence of another man.

"Sally Hemings was indeed in Paris with Jefferson for about two years . . ." John Quincy began.

Nathan Langdon listened, hopeful yet almost afraid of what he was about to hear.

". . . but my mother's worst fears were realized, I'm afraid, since both James and Sally returned with Jefferson to Virginia after their two years in Paris. Her status at Monticello and those of her children were much above his other slaves. When I visited Monticello, I was startled to encounter one or several of them, for they were all house servants and practically advertised their paternity. It was mostly Northerners like myself who noticed. Southerners, especially Southern ladies, seemed to take it for granted. Or, should I say they were so inured to the situation they didn't even blink an eye? I greatly admired their *sang-froid* . . . but then you would know about such things, having been brought up there.

"As for Jefferson, there was absolutely no embarrassment on his part and none evidenced by his daughters or family. All the children seemed to be brought up together. So great were his powers of self-deception that I doubt if he even noticed the stares of his guests—at least those who were not privy to Southern mores—at the resemblance of his slave children to his grandchildren. Yet as you know, so strong are the bonds of silence concerning this Southern taboo, and so ferocious the penalty for acknowledging even *en famille* the concubinal arrangements of Southern gentlemen when the partner is of the dusky race, that it was only when Jefferson sought a second term as president that the scandal broke. Of course, as I said, Virginians had their own private reasons for leaving Jefferson and Sally alone—their *own* dusky partners . . . Jefferson's cousin and enemy, Chief Justice John Marshall, for example. . . ."

Nathan Langdon smiled. John Quincy Adams was warming to his story as it began to touch politics rather than sentiment. Nathan had had no idea about Chief Justice Marshall.

"My mother and father kept their peace, out of embarrassment and loyalty, and in my father's case, a deep love. But my mother could never forgive Jefferson—either privately or publicly—for what she considered a betrayal of Sally, his daughters, and herself. For you must remember, the publicity, when it came, had to be borne not only by Jefferson but by his friends, family, and daughters. It was political suicide. Political suicide," he repeated, shaking his head. Then he went on:

"My father blamed this extraordinary and tragic story on the damnable institution of chattel slavery, and he was right. Nothing is more important to the ultimate survival of this country than the abolishment of slavery. I have introduced in the House a petition for the abolishment of slavery and the slave trade on behalf of the Pennsylvania Quakers . . .

I intend to do it again and again. To force the government to face and discuss this abomination. The end of the slave trade and slavery is inevitable. What is at stake is whether it will come peacefully and legislated, or in a river of blood, in the not too distant future. You, my friend, will doubtless live to see it. So will the children of Sally Hemings. I have an abhorrence of slavery, but just how bad it is no one can imagine without understanding the details."

"I know," said Nathan Langdon softly. All those women's voices he had heard on the day of Turner's trial suddenly filled his head, the room.

"This subject of slavery," continued Quincy Adams, "to my great sorrow and mortification, is absorbing all my faculties!" Adams stared gloomily ahead. He had not meant to speak with such passion. The story he had just told had dredged up the most disturbing emotions and passions. But he was stuck with it. And what did it matter now, thirty years later? One didn't cure the evils of this world by repeating them. He had been president when Jefferson had died. Today Sally Hemings probably wanted to be left alone, to die in peace and anonymity. It was with a certain anxiety that Quincy Adams met the startled, almost childish gaze of Langdon.

"You know, Nathan, you should read Thomas Jefferson's autobiography." Adams spoke again to the young man. "It is regrettable that it ends on the twenty-first of March, 1790, the day he arrived in New York to take up his post as secretary of state. It should have begun there. . . . It seems as if Jefferson made some pact with himself not to speak of himself. Every man, great or small, needs one place where he can explain himself.

"From 1790 to the end of Jefferson's presidency, his ardent passion for the rights of man, his patriotism, the depth of his understanding, the extent and variety of his knowledge, the constant awareness of public opinion, and finally the pliability of principle which he accommodated to his own designs—all these facets of his character emerged during those twenty years. And with them were combined a rare mixture of philosophy and epicurean morals, of burning ambition and stoic self-control, of deep duplicity and generous sensibility, between which qualities, and a treacherous and inventive memory, his conduct appears a tissue of inconsistency."

Adams thought back on the appropriate conclusion he had written in his private diary: "When genius pandered to the will, deceiving others meant one must have begun by deceiving oneself." It was power that was the great deceiver, and those who wielded it were the first to be deceived. How well he knew. It was Jefferson himself who had been the first deceived. He had deceived himself into believing he could love a woman he held in slavery. He had deceived Sally Hemings into believing a man that held her in such servitude could love her. Adams wondered suddenly if she had realized this finally, or had she loved him to the end?

Langdon had gotten what he wanted. But he could not help seeking more.

"But—from what I've read—there must have been a terrible row during his first term about Sally Hemings. Why did Jefferson risk losing the second term?"

A vision of those golden eyes flashed in Langdon's mind, and he dreamed for a second at what he would have done for them. Despite himself he blushed deeply.

"Why did he persist in the face of such humiliation?" asked Nathan Langdon. Quincy Adams smiled.

"It was all in the family, you might say, Nathan, never to be touched by anything from the outside. Washington Irving described it best. 'In a large Virginia estate, the mansion is the seat of government, with its numerous dependencies such as kitchens, smokehouses, workshops and stables. In this mansion, the planter is supreme: his overseer is his prime minister, he has his legion of house Negroes for domestic service, his host of field Negroes, a standing army; a national treasury for the culture of tobacco and cotton. All this forms a kingdom. A plantation produces everything within itself for ordinary use and luxuries, fashion, elegance is carried on with London and Paris, up the Potomac like foreign trade.... Everything, you understand, comes from the plantation.' " Quincy Adams paused. "The absolute power of life and death over other mortals, that was the very air he breathed. It gave him, the great democrat, a magisterial view of the world. Therefore, my dear boy, nothing could humiliate Thomas Jefferson. He was, you might say, Olympian."

> *Let Dusky Sally henceforth bear*
> *The name of Isabella*
> *And let the mountain, all of salt*
> *Be christen'd Monticella*

JOHN QUINCY ADAMS, 1803

CHAPTER 22

NEW YORK CITY, 1834

"THE ONLY THING I know about Sally Hemings is that she was for a time the most famous lady of color in the United States."

Nathan Langdon squinted through the haze of blue smoke surrounding the voice of Aaron Burr. Now that he was here, in the presence of the legendary vice-president with all his messages and letters and introductions, Nathan Langdon was not all sure he really wanted to speak of Sally Hemings to him.

It had been more than a year since he had spoken with John Quincy Adams about her and now he had impulsively sought out her old enemy, Burr. Langdon, now securely ensconced in the inner sanctum of the political machine that ran Washington, was a "Washington lawyer" who would serve whatever politician and party paid him the best.

Aaron Burr, whom he had met several times before, had greeted him like a long lost son: "Why, Nathan, my boy. What brings you to New York City?"

There was something repellent about the tiny old man propped up in his bed, surrounded by his books. Burr was embroiled, as usual, in controversy and notoriety; this time, his own divorce at seventy-eight from his fifty-eight-year-old bride of one year for infidelities and fraud.

"You're not related to her, are you?" Burr asked as he pushed his spectacles down from his forehead onto his sharp nose and peered through them.

Irritated at himself, Nathan Langdon felt a blush coming on. Aaron

Burr always did have the famous knack of smelling out a motive. Now, he was zeroing in for the kill.

"Don't tell me you're a son of Thomas Jefferson!"

"Colonel Burr, sir!"

"How am I to guess," he replied crankily, "when one side of the blanket inevitably resembles the other . . . and I should know."

"I have met . . . two of her sons, and I believe that there is a third somewhere in New York. I would hope to find a trace of him, for his mother's sake."

"For his mother's sake? Then you know Sally Hemings? I had heard that she had been sold on the auction block, along with her daughter, after Jefferson died bankrupt."

"No, she was freed in 1826 and remained in Virginia, where she still resides with two of her sons. I . . . I met the family in my official capacity as census taker of Albemarle County."

"Really? How old is she now?"

"She was fifty-six when I first met her, so that makes her sixty now."

"Is that all?"

"Yes."

"My God! How old would Thomas Jefferson be now?"

"Ninety-three."

"The age I feel today."

"You look very well, sir."

"And you are the worst liar I've met. How do you ever get your clients off?"

"Usually I don't, sir." Langdon laughed. Despite himself, he was beginning to warm to the old man who had an aura, even now, of brimstone and danger.

There was something in the way he had said Sally Hemings' name that made Langdon hesitate to go any further into his relationship with her. Aaron Burr was not, after all, John Quincy Adams. The quick elflike face, the thin wasted body, the still undiminished reputation gave him an indisputable power of intimidation.

Langdon had delivered a packet of letters from Burr's friends in Washington yesterday, and had spent the better part of this afternoon with him as well.

Burr had told Langdon, when the ex-census taker had guided him onto the subject that still obsessed him, that he had only seen Sally Hemings once in Philadelphia at Thomas Jefferson's inauguration as vice-president. He had never been intimate enough with the president (to say the least) to have been invited more than once or twice to Monticello, and there she had not been in evidence.

"But with all the clutter I found upon entering the house, I could have missed her in between the stuffed moose and the statue of Cleopatra. Walking into his entranceway was like walking into the inside of his head. Everything a confusion of relics, of conjecture about things he knew nothing about, loose ends and solid marble. There were Indian relics; bad paintings, including a crucifixion owned by a man who didn't believe Jesus was divine; heads and horns of an elk, of a deer; a map of Missouri drawn by Indians (before he and Meriwether Lewis stole it from them); buffalo hides, bows and arrows, poisoned lances (better than treason trials), peace pipes, wampum belts, several Indian dresses and cooking utensils; and a colossal bust of himself on a truncated column which made him ten feet tall and gave me a good mouse-eye's view. The column, I remember, had the twelve tribes of Israel and the twelve signs of the zodiac upon it; and besides the full-size reclining statue of Cleopatra (after she had applied the asp), there were busts of Voltaire, Turgot, John Paul Jones, George Washington, General Lafayette, and a model of one of the pyramids!

"In the salon, I remember, were busts of Alexander the Great; Napoleon, whom he professed to despise; and, quite aptly, a 'Sleeping Venus' (white, not black). This was, of course, when I was his vice-president. But if I didn't see her at that time, I certainly witnessed several interesting happenings! The guest next to me practically fell off his chair when the spitting image of Thomas Jefferson came in carrying the soup! But this couldn't have been the famous 'Tom,' for he was too old. I think I heard him called James or Jamey. At any rate, the place was crawling with white slaves, literally, since many of them were very young children who seemed to have the complete run of the house. As you know, after that time, the president and I had a slight disagreement. . . ."

Nathan Langdon was shocked even now. To refer to charges of treason as "a slight disagreement. . . ."

"You look shocked, my boy." Aaron Burr loved to shock people and then console them. "If you look at it from my point of view, I was simply twenty years before my time. We must kick the Spanish out, annex half of Mexico, and fight a war to make it stick. All begun by our illustrious President Jackson, twenty years later . . . after *I* planned it. And not a word of credit . . . or thanks!"

Nathan Langdon laughed. He was irresistible, this old man!

"I wouldn't call a trial for treason a 'slight disagreement'!"

"It was a trial, not a conviction, my boy. The jury returned a verdict of 'not guilty because not proven guilty' the first time, and the second trial for the misdemeanor was a straight 'not guilty.' People seem to forget that! The government had no case, and they knew it. Even Hay admitted he couldn't hang me. He sought further treason indictments in Ohio. At any rate, sooner or later Jefferson, with the aid of a complacent and well-rewarded judge, would have gotten his verdict of guilty. After all, John Marshall couldn't follow me through the seventeen states trying me. So, fearing Jefferson's pertinacity in my pursuit, I went into hiding and eventually made my way back to Europe, coming home during the war to resume my law practice. I ran into John Trumbull, the painter, and his poor wife while I was in London."

John Trumbull, Nathan thought. The one man who had made drawings of Sally Hemings as a young girl.

"Is he in New York now?" he asked.

"Oh, yes, you know he became quite a staunch Federalist. He's the president of the American Academy, and he has managed to get his paintings in every federal building in Washington." Aaron Burr pushed his spectacles back up on his high-domed forehead. "Would you like to meet him?"

"Yes, sir," replied Langdon, "if it's not too much trouble."

Aaron Burr would be quite content to give the young man a letter of introduction. The talk about Sally Hemings had brought back his undying hatred of Thomas Jefferson, and had reminded him of the one great mistake of his life: trusting Jefferson to keep his word as a gentleman. What he had always hated about Jefferson was his hypocrisy. It had cost him, Aaron Burr, the presidency, he thought. Jefferson would lie with the whore politics, then rise from her bed, scream that he had been infected with syphilis, and refuse to pay. . . .

"What do you really want to know about Sally Hemings, and why?"

"Everything. Nothing. It is something I stumbled onto, and now—" Nathan Langdon stopped, disconcerted.

"Strange, I had a beloved sister called Sally . . . who protected me from many a beating at the hands of my guardian. When I ran away from home the first time, I was four and she six. She threw herself between me and the rod, a pattern which was to continue all our lives. We had only each other, having lost both our parents and grandparents by then. But, if ever a woman left me cold, and there are not many who did, Sally Hemings was one. Beautiful, yes. I saw her in her prime."

Aaron Burr gazed at Langdon, who was hanging on his every word. "She was possibly the most beautiful woman I'd ever seen, black or white, slave or free, duchess or maid, with the exception of my daughter Theodosia. But there was a cloying self-satisfaction about her that I detested. A hypocrisy that matched her lover's. Leave it to Thomas Jefferson to find the only woman in the South capable of being self-righteous about concubinage. . . ."

"Sir, being an ascetic, Jefferson can't have relished the role of a debauchee."

"My dear sir, scratch an ascetic and you unearth a sensualist! He loved words and used them like an artist; he loved wine, music, food, flowers, beautiful objects, luxurious surroundings, fine books, tapestries, paintings, horses, land. What is eliminated from that classic list of the sensualist? If you count his love affairs with buildings, gardens, scientific instruments, and his own written word, I would say that he, not I, is the profligate. I may go down in history remembered only with the smoking dueling pistol in my hand; but, really, I am a most dispassionate individual. Behind that cold façade he was the passionate one. His hatred for me and all his political enemies was uncontrolled, almost feminine. You could say he was an inconsummate politician, rather than a consummate one. And all this . . . this ardor was consummated, if you like, in the most extraordinary political document of the century: the Declaration of Independence. This, not Sally Hemings, nor any other woman, was his great moment of passion. His pathological hatred for the English and everything English, including the English in himself, impregnated him with a felicity of language he never again achieved. Reread it, Nathan. In the original version, that document grips you like a woman. It is pure passion. That's why it sings, and that's why it moves people. What red-blooded American could resist such a ravishing and virile image of himself?"

"Pure genius, my boy. I rather unimaginatively stuck to women. As for Sally Hemings . . . she came with the plantation."

"Sir, you forget she was a slave. She had no choice."

"Oh, come now, Nathan. This was Virginia, not Mississippi. And this was a Virginian gentleman, not some redneck overseer. Even token resistance would have been enough. If she was her mother's daughter, she probably *seduced* him. Now, *there* was a woman, Elizabeth Hemings. She must have been close to fifty when I saw her, and she looked twenty-five: superb, a Nefertiti with *real* traces of Africa on her brow, and a carriage worthy of a queen. She made you glad you had them, though I would have been trembling in my boots if I had had to prove it to her! No, Sally Hemings was too snobbish, too glacial, too busy playing Joan of Arc and putting on airs to suit me. How old was she in Paris?"

"Fifteen," answered Langdon.

"Then she definitely seduced him. What forty-year-old man in his right mind can resist a healthy fifteen-year-old girl?" Aaron Burr smiled to himself. The profound shock on Nathan Langdon's face told him all he wanted to know. This young man had become involved with Sally Hemings in an emotional way, probably having to do with Thomas Jefferson, maybe as a father figure. He had that hangdog look of a rejected lover. Why? if she had accepted him in the first place. Aaron Burr was intrigued. What would somebody as proud and haughty, as jealous of her prerogatives as Sally Hemings, and as famous, want with a pip-squeak like Nathan Langdon? He decided to try another technique.

"She's in no danger or difficulty because of what happened so many years ago? Surely there is someone to protect her?"

"That's just what I tried to do! Protect her! I was not even sure she was in Virginia legally, and that's why I declared her white . . . you see—"

Aaron Burr didn't see at all, but he intended to. He raised himself up on his pillows in the disordered, book-strewn bed to which he had been confined since his second stroke. How had he managed to get her declared white? Or had he done it himself? To absolve the great man from the "crime" of miscegenation, he assumed. This was fascinating! This cipher had been playing God, and Sally Hemings (knowing a lot about a god, having lived with him for thirty-eight years) had found him out. Fascinating!

Bastards Aaron Burr knew quite a bit about, he thought, having fathered several, but this was a special kind of bastardy. Something deeper than mere illegitimacy. Many great men, including himself, had illegitimate children, yet the special loss of a son or daughter to an entire race had something mythical about it. How fatal and touching this story was, and how ironic that it should be Jefferson, the image-maker, the definer of America, the nation's most articulate voice!

Aaron Burr lay back on his pillows. Nathan Langdon was silent. They sat staring at each other for what seemed like a long time. "Was it Voltaire, dear lad, who said 'There is no history, only fictions of varying degrees of plausibility'?

"Here is a true fable. If only we could unravel the beauty of it from the obscenity and disgrace that has surrounded its revelation. . . . I remember the papers."

"You find it beautiful?"

"Yes," said Aaron Burr. "I can forgive Thomas Jefferson a lot of things because of it."

Nathan Langdon gazed into the large dark eyes which had always been famous for their intensity, and were now, in their twilight, somehow more terrible than ever. Sally Hemings had spoken of them: "What I remember most of him," she had said, "were his eyes, of such size and darkness as to strike terror in the hearts of anyone except the very brave. There was something lewd about their power." Now Burr looked narrowly at the young Washington lawyer.

"Yes," Burr said, "he was lucky in a way. If a man arrives at love, no matter how, when, or why—love beyond convention—then he has already lived well. Does not every man dream of some overwhelming, unfathomable love? But few have the courage to risk it, to keep it, or to honor it. If he did, then Jefferson has once more amazed me."

Nathan Langdon turned from the wistful, smoldering eyes and bowed his head. Lucky. He had never thought of Thomas Jefferson as "lucky." Nathan's own sense of failure oppressed him. He was appraising, not without bitterness, his lack of wealth, his mediocrity as a lawyer, and, yes, as a man as well. Had he not lost the two women he really cared about? Had he not lost all sense of proportion, he thought? For the sake of erasing miscegenation from the crimes of a famous man, he had annihilated his own sense of worth as well. He repeated to himself that Jefferson's biographers were already at work. He would emerge two hundred years from now, spanking clean, shorn of even the few shreds of humanity that had managed to cling to him despite all his efforts to conceal them from the public eye. . . . As for the Hemings family, half of which had already sunk into the unwary arms of white America, no one would ever know how they really felt about their lives. . . .

Nathan promised to pay his host another visit, but Aaron Burr knew he would not. It didn't matter.

"Tell my friends I am in a position to deliver any messages they may have for any of their departed loved ones, as long as they are in the same location that everyone is sure I'll be repairing to quite soon. . . ."

Nathan Langdon smiled.

"As soon as I get there I'll give your best to Thomas Jefferson," he added with a wry smile.

CHAPTER 23

NEW YORK CITY, 1834

"MR. NATHAN LANGDON to see Colonel Trumbull, sir."

Nathan Langdon, fresh from his meeting with Aaron Burr, was introduced into the company of the now famous and fashionable "artist and patriot," John Trumbull. The announcement had been made by a gray-faced, gray-liveried servant, who bowed out as if he were in the presence of royalty.

Nathan almost stood at attention as he introduced himself to the formidable personage that appeared before him. Trumbull was handsome, erect, and slim, with a military bearing, radiating a bitter but unmistakable arrogance and self-confidence. He could better say that he had introduced himself into the company of the Founding Fathers, since flanking John Trumbull were copies of two of his most famous paintings: *The Declaration of Independence* and *The Resignation of Washington*. He found himself staring not only at Sally Hemings' old friend from the Hôtel de Langeac, now himself transformed into a national monument, but at George Washington, John Adams, Thomas Jefferson, Benjamin Franklin, and all the other illustrious names. John Trumbull seemed to blend into and arrange himself as if he were part of the famous assembly of his paintings, and in the glow of the immense skylights that bathed his rooms at the academy, the effect was impressive and not at all coincidental. John Trumbull felt, in fact, that he was well placed in the company of his paintings. He had devoted his long life to painting the glorious deeds and the famous names of the Revolution, he reminded himself every day. Although he had spent only a total of eighteeen months in the Revolutionary Army, and nineteen days as aide-de-camp to General Washington, he had cashed in on his military career since his return to the United States. He had insisted on being addressed, Virginia style, by his military title, a title he had come by belatedly and not without considerable vexation and humiliation, he remembered. Nathan, who had only Sally Hemings' description of Trumbull as a gentle romantic portrait painter, was completely taken aback.

"Colonel, please excuse my staring . . . but I pass the originals of these paintings every day in the Rotunda of the Capitol. They are so familiar to me they seem part of my life. To come across them in New York is quite a shock."

"Well, Mr. Langdon, when one enters the atelier of an artist, one can expect to find the unexpected. Otherwise it is a mediocre artist that you have come in contact with." John Trumbull fixed his dark, peculiarly asymmetrical gaze on his visitor. "I have done several versions of my large painting in the Rotunda. By the way, how are they holding up? I haven't seem them in several years." He went on without waiting for Langdon's reply. "Yes, indeed, I have devoted fifty-five years of my life and my entire artistic career to memorializing our glorious Revolution, and those who took part. I was, of course, in an extraordinarily fortunate position to do so, being General Washington's aide-de-camp. . . ."

Nathan Langdon thought, even at the risk of seeming rude, he had better come quickly to the point, as it was obvious John Trumbull's career as aide-de-camp to General Washington was about to be recounted as part of the tour of his painting studio.

"Colonel, which of the paintings were you working on when you visited Paris in 1788 to do the portrait of Thomas Jefferson?" he asked.

John Trumbull was startled at the sudden turn in what was usually a smooth and well-rehearsed recital.

"Well, I was working on the *Declaration*, of course, but also on the *Surrender of Lord Cornwallis at Yorktown*, and I needed portraits of all the French officers who took part in that event. It was December 1787 when I arrived at the Hôtel de Langeac, President Jefferson's home, and I took with me the prepared canvas of *Yorktown* and painted a dozen portraits of the French officers while I was there. Those that had participated in the battle or were present at the surrender. I remember it was the end of February before I was finished."

Nathan Langdon listened in amazement to the roll call of the French officers trip easily off the tongue of the tall, pompous old man. If he remembered all this, he would surely remember what happened that winter at the Hôtel de Langeac.

"It is, sir, in connection with that visit to Mr. Jefferson's ministry in that particular year that I have come to see you."

"Really? Are you a relative of one of the officers in the painting? And you would like his portrait? I do many miniatures for family and friends from my historical paintings." John Trumbull waited deferentially, and tried to guess, from the manner and clothes of the gentleman, how much he could reasonably ask for a portrait of the young man's uncle, or father, or whatever. He had frightened off many a prospective customer with his high prices. But what did they think? That artists lived on air? He had received only twelve thousand dollars apiece for his Capitol paintings from that tight-fisted Congress, and he had had to completely repair and reinstall the paintings twice. The heartache . . . the trials of those blasted paintings, he thought. The size of them alone, twelve feet high and nineteen feet long, had almost killed him with his one-eyed vision. And then the damp and mildew from the new masonry and the swampy humidity of Washington climate . . . These paintings were supposed to last as long as the Republic! God knows if they will, with all the abuse they get! He turned back to his young visitor. Normally he asked one hundred dollars for a head, one hundred and fifty for a head with hands, two hundred and fifty for half-length, and five hundred whole length. A full fifty percent below his famous competitor . . .

"The topic I had in mind, Colonel Trumbull, was only marginal to your work in Paris and touched you only casually, I think. While you were there, you did, I believe, some pencil sketches and a watercolor of a young girl who was maid to the Jefferson ladies . . . one Sally Hemings."

Nathan Langdon glanced nervously up at the hooded blue eyes of Thomas Jefferson gazing serenely, not at him, thank goodness, but toward the venerable figure of John Hancock.

Then he heard Trumbull saying:

"Sketches? Of a servant? In Paris? At the Hôtel de Langeac? Not of Jefferson?"

Of course he remembered the little maid from Virginia, thought John Trumbull, the exquisite maid with the superb bone structure and the extraordinary complexion, little Sallyhemings. . . . But that didn't mean he should admit it to this young man. So many years ago. She would have to be an old woman now. But still beautiful, if his artist's eye had not deceived him. Yes, she had sailed back to Virginia with Jefferson the very same day he had sailed back to New York. The last time he had seen her was where? In Cowes, when he had given her the miniature of Jefferson. Ah, he had been a romantic young man in those days. Now, how much should he admit to this young man? And who was he anyway? And what did he want with his sketches of Sally Hemings?

"I do remember now. Perfectly. I did several sketches of an exquisite girl at the ministry of Thomas Jefferson, the maid of Polly Jefferson. I gave one of them to her."

John Trumbull gazed at the visitor. Who was this Nathan Langdon and what did he want?

"Let us sit down, Mr. Langdon. I will order tea to be served. You say you would like to commission a miniature. Why?"

"Let us just say I am an agent for a private person who would like a miniature of . . . his mother."

Nathan Langdon held his breath. He had taken a bold step. Either the old gentleman would feign ignorance or the prospect of a commission would bring him around to talk. He had had no intention of commissioning a painting, but he wondered why he hd not thought of it before. He would like very much to have an image of Sally Hemings for himself.

"If you care to, Mr. Langdon, you may tell me what you know, and how you came to know it. But first you must give me your word as a gentleman that you are not of the press."

Again the disclaimer, thought Nathan Langdon, always the disclaimer . . .

"I give you my word."

"And that this discussion will never be repeated to a living soul. You promise this as a gentleman."

"I do."

Nathan Langdon felt much as he had felt that first afternoon in the cabin of Sally Hemings, except that here there were no shadows, no darkness. The surroundings were all light—the bright, elegant studio in the prestigious American Academy, immense, immaculate, filled with portraits of the great and the famous. A subtle and not unpleasant odor of turpentine and paint blended with the steaming English tea served in delicate cups of Sèvres China by the liveried servant. The old man settled into a comfortable English armchair and listened to the young lawyer's extraordinary tale.

When Langdon had finished, John Trumbull sat as still as a great eagle, alert to the slightest gesture. The strange, almost cross-eyed effect came from the fact that the painter had been blind in one eye since childhood.

"You are a Southerner, Mr. Langdon?"

"Yes."

"And an abolitionist, I take it?"

Nathan Langdon flushed. Had he ever really thought in those terms?

"Of course," Nathan Langdon answered.

"You know, of course, my position. It is strange that antislavery has come to be identified with political partisanship and, I might say, with the conservatives of this country. We were the ones who got the slave trading from Africa outlawed, even if the smuggling continues and more Africans still reach our shores. The enslaving of the inhabitants of Africa in the name of Christianity, especially in the name of Christianity, is not only criminal, it is intolerable in our nation. 'Is not the enslaving of these people the most charitable act in the world?' " he intoned, bitterly mimicking the pious tones he had heard on so many lips. " 'With no other end in view than to bring those poor creatures to Christian ground and within hearing of the gospel, we spare no expense of time or money, we send many thousands of miles across the dangerous seas, and think all our toil and pains well rewarded. We endure the greatest fatigues of body and much unavoidable trouble of conscience in carrying on this pious design. We deprive them of their liberty, we force them away from their friends, their country, everything that is dear to them. . . . And are they not bound by all the ties of gratitude to devote their entire lives to our service, as the only reward that can be adequate to our abundant charity?' Ah!" he thundered, "I could forgive anything but doing what we did in the name of Christianity! At least we can't accuse Thomas Jefferson of hypocrisy, can we? He didn't believe in Christianity."

Suddenly, John Trumbull got up and walked to the back of the immense studio. He was gone for a long time, and when he returned he had in his hand four small sheets of paper. In silence, the two men looked at the delicate pencil renderings of a young girl in the dress of forty years before. The sketches were quick, almost futile, with none of the pompousness Nathan Langdon so detested in the large paintings of John Trumbull.

The pose of the first sheet was guileless, the young girl with her hair down, her face cradled in one hand, her elbows supported by the arm of the chair in which she was seated. She looked out of the picture with enormous, wide-spaced, light eyes. The second sketch was a three-

CHAPTER 24

SPRING 1795

I set out on this ground which I suppose to be self-evident that the earth belongs to the living; that the dead have neither powers nor rights over it.

THOMAS JEFFERSON to James Madison,
September 6, 1789

Lord Thomas was a nice young gentleman
He rode a many a town
He courted a girl they called Fair Ellender
And one called Sally Brown.

Is this your wife, Lord Thomas, she cries!
She is most wonderous brown.
When you could have married as fair a young girl
As ever the sun shone on.

They buried the Brown Girl in his arms,
Fair Ellender at his feet.
They laid the Brown Girl in his arms
And let her go to sleep.

Traditional Ballads of Virginia,
Compiled by Arthur Kyle Davis, Jr.

IT WAS A LONG TIME before my mother answered that first call from the carriage that brought me back to Virginia and slavery. And when she did, her words had been: "You got a son, Sally Hemings. A wee darling perfect thing." As she had taken Thomas Jefferson Hemings from my body she had forgiven me at the same time. She focused all her love and hopes on him. "Get that freedom for your children," she repeated like a litany. "And get it for yourself while you're at it," she added. "Don't nothing in life count more than that." She had looked at me with a mixture of pity and exasperation. "Not even love."

That had been five years ago and now it was the spring of 1795, one year since my master had returned from Philadelphia to retirement, since he had come home to me. It had been the happiest year for us both. So happy, it had made up for everything. The return to Virginia and slavery had been a shock to me. I felt isolated at Monticello, and slights and injuries were my daily lot. Even my master seemed helpless against these hurts. His acceptance of the post of secretary of state had been a tragedy for me. We were to have stayed only a short time here, then return to our beloved Paris. In Paris, we had both forgotten what it meant to be white or black, master or slave.

I no longer knew whether to believe him now when he vowed never to engage in politics again. This retirement might not last. The temptations of power were too great. But the hurts and humiliations of the past three years were also deeply etched in his soul. He had "retired" in a sulk from Philadelphia. He was in bad grace with President Washington, who no longer spoke to him; defeated by Hamilton; publicly attacked by the Federalists. Everything had passed: the excise, the Bank, the treaty with Britain. He was back home to lick his wounds.

Our letters these three years had been numerous, and often in French. He had bid me to burn his, but I had not done so. He burned mine, I suspected, yet I took much care in writing them, especially those in French. And the magic of the written word still awed me. Yet for all his letters of love, I was uneasy without his presence. Not just lonely, but unsure of myself. I seemed nothing without him and everything in his eyes. My tutoring and, more than anything else, my music, had continued after my return to Monticello, and so the creature he had begun to create and shape in Paris had finally been ready to receive him when he rode home from his political wars. I rested easier now that he was home, but I still needed to ask.

"Daughter, you ought to know if he loves you or not. If you don't know, then he don't. I know he thinks he loves you, and maybe that's all a woman can expect from a man—that he believes it. . . . A woman knows. A woman knows when a man loves her . . . even a slave woman. It's been six years. . . . A white man don't keep a black concubine for six years without loving her. He loved your sister and he lost her, and now he loves you."

My mother had changed little in the past thirteen years. She had kept her low, compact figure, her slimness, her unlined and perfect skin, her iron constitution. She was now fifty-nine years old and she still ran Monticello, despite my position. Her beautiful, vigorous body still demanded and got the services of lovers of both colors. I knew that I would never take another lover. I loved only my master. A dangerous and stupid thing for a slave. . . . God knows, I knew that.

Five years had passed since the birth of the child I had carried in my womb across the water from France. Five years that had brought me another child. My mother returned my gaze. Had she already guessed it? If I had not been bound to Monticello before, this child fathered on my last birthday was the hostage to the fading memories of Paris and freedom.

"You trapped," she said. "Just like I was before you. But I never had the chance you had. And that will haunt you, daughter, haunt you. Remember, you put yourself in danger when you returned to Virginia. Danger of life and limb, and, God forbid, of being sold. Did you forget about that over there in France? That you returned to the same burden as the blackest, most ignorant field hand? You forgot the first lesson of slavery, your blackness. And you forget the second, loving somebody you ain't got no business loving. . . . The man you got has no business loving, either. He's put himself in danger as well—don't forget that when you start feeling sorry for yourself. In danger from his own white folks, loving somebody, he, with all his money and power, ain't got no right to love."

"Do you think he'll marry again?"

My mother jumped to her feet. "Lord Almighty! You wishing for a white mistress? Your father didn't marry again, did he? I ain't never wished for no white mistress, and thank God I never had one. When there were white mistresses at Poplar Hill, I was in the fields. When I came into the Big House, they were all dead. And you wishing for one? Martha Randolph ain't enough trouble for you? Let me tell you, daughter, white Southern ladies don't seem to mind who sleeps with they husbands, but they mighty touchy 'bout who sleeps with they fathers! I remember my own trials with them Wayleses daughters. Lord! You think a white mistress wouldn't sell you so quick your head would turn? You and your children? Or kill you? Or maim you? Or ruin that beautiful face? You think it's never happened before? You think they don't know what they men doing with their female slaves? You think they believe their slaves gettin' whiter by con-tamination? You think because we're black, they don't feel jealousy? They love the same way. They birth the same way, and they lusts the same way. Why you think they dress themselves up in all those fine, low-cut gowns? They love their men, and they hate us. Don't forget that, daughter. There ain't that much difference between a white and a black female. And," she added, "in case you wonderin', ain't no difference a'tall between white mens and black mens. They all think what they got twixt they legs is Heaven, and what we got twixt ourn is Hell."

My prison was vast and golden. There were his vegetable gardens, his thousands of fruit trees, his forests full of Virginia pine, birch, oak, and linden.

Monticello was five thousand acres in length and width, and across the river were scattered six thousand more divided between his plantations of Tufton, Lego, Shadwell, Broadhurst, Pantops, Beaver Creek, and at Martha's Edgehill. The mountain was enveloped in deep forest, all the way to the clearing at the top, on which the mansion stood, with its lawns and gardens and shade trees. From that point, like the spokes of a wheel, radiated his fields and valleys, his streams and rivers, his tobacco, his cotton, his wheat, his cattle, and his slaves. The forest was threaded as if with silk cords with the forty miles of bridle paths over which my master rode without fail every afternoon. I could see bent backs scattered among the white and green of his lands. He had raced up the mountain to me and now he raced over the hills of Monticello each day always singing. His hands, capable of the most delicate drawings, the most exquisite caresses, now gripped the reins of his thoroughbred horse. He was strong. He was home. He enjoyed his life at Monticello. He read and wrote in the morning, he rode and tended his plantations in the afternoons. His lust for politics had slackened; even his appetite for the newpapers and local gossip had waned.

The great six-foot body had remained the same in leanness and strength through the years. So had his high color. I could now see the beginning of gray in his thick red hair and the lines around his mouth were a little deeper. The heavy-lidded eyes were the same intense sapphire blue I had always known. I wanted to cut off his queue, but he still wore his hair long and tied with a blue ribbon. It fell to his shoulders in loose curls over the fine white cravat I wound every morning around his neck. The only impatience I ever saw him manifest was with his horses. He would subdue them with a whip at the slightest sign of restlessness. He chose his bays for speed and spirit but he mistreated them, making them dangerous animals. I was often frightened. I never really knew if he would come back to me whole or broken to pieces.

Apart from that, my master seemed peaceful and content with his life here.

There were twenty-five house slaves on the mountain, not including the blacksmiths, grooms, carpenters, nailery boys, weavers, and shepherds. First there was my mother, Elizabeth Hemings, housekeeper. Of her "dark" Hemingses, there were Martin the butler, and Bett, Nance, and Mary, who were housemaids. Four more of her dark Hemingses had been inherited by my half sister Tabitha Wayles Skipwell. And then there were her "light" Hemingses, whose father had been John Wayles: Robert, James, Peter, Critta, and myself. Of the white Hemingses, Thenia and her children fathered by Samuel Carr, my master's nephew, were missing, sold to James Monroe. And last year, Robert Hemings had bought his freedom in order to live with his wife in Richmond. Finally there was John Hemings, my mother's last son and my half brother, whose father was a white carpenter called Nelson. Some of us had children so that there were third-generation Hemings on the mountain as well: Critta's son Jamey Hemings, whose father was Samuel Carr's brother, Peter.

And in the hierarchy of slavehood I stood at the pinnacle, even before Elizabeth Hemings, for I was the "favorite," the untouchable. I was far above the station of the other slaves. Accountable to no one except the master.

"I cornered the bastard!"

I smiled at the recollection of James returning triumphantly from Philadelphia and reading to me the written promise: "That if the said James shall go with me to Monticello in the course of the ensuing winter when I shall go to reside there myself and shall there continue until he shall have taught such person as I shall place under him for the purpose to be a good cook, this previous condition being performed, he shall thereupon be made free and I will thereupon execute all proper instruments to make him free. . . ."

Why was he so childishly proud of that piece of paper? Why hadn't he simply stolen himself?

"He would have freed you anyway, James," I said.

"No, he wouldn't. I'm the best cook in these United States. Even now, he would keep me if he could. He's kicking himself already over this piece of paper!"

"What will you do, James?"

"The first thing I've got to do is cook my last meal at Monticello and get out of here!"

"Who have you chosen?"

"Peter, of course."

"Good," I said. "A position as powerful as that shouldn't go out of the family."

He looked at me. "You are your mother's daughter, all right," he said.

"The master will miss you."

"I've already given him six extra years of my life.

"The master," he said. "You always call him that even with me. With that French accent of yours. I call the bastard Jefferson or TJ when we are alone or with other slaves, and half the time I call him that to his face if no strangers are present. But I have never heard you refer to him as anything else except 'the master,' except that you make it sound like an endearment. . . . No wonder he loves you. If you can take the most ruthless word in the English language and turn it into an expression of love . . ."

I turned away. It hadn't been so long ago that he too had called him "master." Did he really believe that that piece of paper erased a word he had mouthed since he was a child? I knew my brother so well. He was so vulnerable. Let him call my lover bastard if it made him feel better. We were all bastards after all, weren't we? We stared at each other.

"He is not God, you know."

"Isn't he, James?"

"Only God deserves to be loved."

"That may be so, but once you have loved a man, it is difficult to love God."

I caught his hand and studied him tenderly.

He was twenty-nine years old now. His beauty had matured. The soft curly hair was denser and thicker. I could no longer remember it with powder. The high-bridged Wayles nose and the perpetual sneer of his perfect mouth gave him a foreign look. His face fascinated women, both black and white, and it was just as well he was leaving this place, I thought. In the years since our return to Monticello, he had made no connection, of this I was sure, although I knew that many overtures had been made to him by women. I wondered, as I already had in Paris, if he had ever loved a woman.

"*Je t'aime*, Sally," he said suddenly.

"Ah, darling James. *Moi aussi.*"

He gave me a kiss, but I felt we were miles apart, countries apart. He will never understand, I thought.

"Help me," he said.

"Yes," I answered.

"I need you."

"I know. If only he didn't need me more . . ."

"Are you sure he does?" he asked.

"I think so," I whispered.

"God help you if you are wrong," he said.

"And God be with you if you are right, James."

We saw little of each other after that.

In my mind, he had already gone from this place.

Adrien Petit came back. He had been persuaded by my master to leave his beloved Champagne country and his mother and make the dangerous journey to America. He brought to Monticello a thread that connected Marly and Virginia, a link to past happiness and a promise that more would come. We slipped back into our old relationship, Petit and I. He was kind to me. Though unshockable, he was nonetheless shocked by Virginia. He could not reconcile himself with slavery and slaves.

Thomas Jefferson began to make drawings for a new house which would rise on the foundations of the old mansion, and we were alive with plans and planting. That year Thomas Jefferson even seeded, plowed, and laid out ten thousand cuttings of weeping willow.

He continued to spend a great deal of time on his horse. He even measured his fields for planting on horseback.

Moses worked in the nailery with Bedford John and Bedford Davy, as did the two brothers James, Phill Hubbard, Bartlet, and Lewis. All were young boys between the ages of ten and twelve. The nailery was on Mulberry Row, not more than sixty feet east of the Southern Breezeway and within shouting distance of the mansion; near there was an avenue of stables, slave dwellings, workshops, forges, and storage houses.

The Hemingses who did not stay in the Big House all lived and worked there, along with the white workmen who now thronged the grounds in preparation for the renovations. Naked children mingled among the blacksmiths and the horses. The clanging forges and the nailery were working all day long next to the steady thump of the weavers' looms where the young girls worked.

In June we began to cut wheat at Shadwell and in early July we cut wheat on this side of the river.

Our reapers were Frank, Martin, Phill, and Tim. Ned, Toby, James, Val, Bagwell, Caesar, and Lewis. The younger boys were George, Peter, and the two Isaacs.

Our gatherers were Isabel, Ned's Jenny, Lewis, Jenny, Doll, Rachel, Mary, Nancy, O, Betty, Molly, and Lucina and her sisters.

Our stakers were great George, Judy, Hix, Jamy, Barnaby, Davy, and Ben, Iris, Thamer, and Lucinda.

Our cradlers were John, Kit, Patty, the two Lucys, Essex, Tom, Squire, and Goliah.

We treaded at Monticello with seven horses, their flanks turning silver with sweat. The spicy, inexpressible fragrance of bruised and trampled chaff rose on the heavy air, impregnating hair and skin. The hoarse cries of the reapers fluttered over the ocean of not yet harvested grain like the mobs of crows which circled in formation as the stocks rose like sentinels in the half-reaped fields. The earth seemed to roll over and sigh with each slash of the scythe, its voice too, woven into the din of the reapers. All seemed to be of one plan and one motion: the burning sun, the earth turning, the wheat slumping under its own weight. Great George constantly mended the cradles and grinded the scythes that were never still. Their steel glint was visible for miles; flecks of silver paper against the high-noon gold. Each day, Nance, Mary, and I distributed the supplies. For every family unit, we gave out four gallons of whiskey, two quarts of molasses, one smoked and one fresh meat with peas.

We worked. My kin, my fellow slaves and I. We worked from sunup to sundown. We worked so that all, according to my master, would move in exact equilibrium. No part of the force could be lessened without it having an effect on the whole, he said. No hand could be stilled without retarding the scheme of things. And nothing could jeopardize his main design or delay it. This was his law: the vast rolling motion of this human machine moved according to the blueprint he had laid down for it. And if a bent back had straightened and a head shaken sweat like a wet dog, and an eye had stared into the sun, and a mind or a heart wondered if this was the way God meant things to be;

my master would have said yes. For wasn't he God at Monticello? And if one loved the man, one could still hate the God.

We stood there on the mountain, silently savoring our last month of solitude before the August company arrived and Martha and Maria came home. The deep clay gave gently underfoot, tender and softened by the constant spring rain. It would be a wet summer, with twice as many wet days as in other years. A burst of fragrance, from a flowering bush, enveloped us with its sweetness.

My lover came around and stood near me.

"Sally," he said, putting his hands on my shoulders, "however far you can see, it is all Monticello. I solemnly promise you there will never be a white mistress here."

I pressed myself into the broad chest behind me. My master might own Monticello and my mother might run it, but Monticello was mine. There had been only one white mistress of Monticello, the first Martha, and she was buried at the foot of the mountain under a pale white stone etched in Latin.

There will never be a white mistress here.

The echo of his voice followed me through the gardens, along Mulberry Row, into the workshops of my brothers. I kept hearing that magic promise over and over in my mind through the noise of construction.

There would be no white mistress at Monticello. He had promised.

CHAPTER 25

JULY 1795

Going out into the open air, in the temperate, and in the warm
months of the year, we often meet with bodies of warm air, which,
passing by us in two or three seconds, do not afford time to the most
sensible thermometer to seize their temperature. Judging from my
feelings only, I think they approach the ordinary heat of the human
body. Some of them perhaps go a little beyond it . . . but whence
taken, where found, or how generated? . . . They are most frequent
about sunset; rare in the middle parts of the day; and I do not
recollect having ever met with them in the morning.

THOMAS JEFFERSON, *Notes on the State of Virginia,* 1790

. . . blind obedience is ever sought for by power: tyrants and sensu-
alists are in the right when they endeavor to keep women in the
dark, because the former want only slaves and the latter a plaything.
The sensualist, indeed, has been the most dangerous of tyrants, and
women have been duped by their lovers, as princes by their minis-
ters. . . .

MARY WOLLSTONECRAFT, *Vindication of the Rights of Women,* 1792

"WHAT DO YOU THINK you're doing?"

I had not expected him back from his ride for hours. He found me
sitting in his room. The only private place in the mansion. I had taken
some of my letters out of my secret place and was reading them.

In two strides Thomas Jefferson was upon me.

"I thought I told you to burn my letters." He was furious. The two
familiar lines of rage etched themselves between his eyes. "I don't want
any letters of mine lying around, do you hear me?"

They were not his letters, they were mine. It said so right there in
black and white. "Sally Hemings." My letters were the only thing that
existed outside him or myself. Sometimes I didn't even bother to read
them as I knew them by heart. I simply stared at my name.

"I always kept your letters in Paris. In a little silk envelo—"

"Sally, this is Virginia, not Paris! It's dangerous keeping letters. I
told you to burn them. I'll never write you another letter if you don't
destroy them."

"I would have to forget you to burn them. I won't do it."

"If you won't, I will."

He picked up a handful of my letters and strode toward the fireplace.

"You burn those letters, Thomas Jefferson, and you'll sleep alone."

He hesitated a moment and then he threw the letters onto the smoldering coals. In a flash I was beside him. I shoved him out of the way. The letters were already going up in flames. I pulled them out with my bare hands.

"Sally! Darling! You'll burn yourself!"

He lifted me up from my knees and his heavy boot came down on the flames, until he had stomped out the fire. He then bent and with his own hands pulled the charred letters from the ashes.

"Here are your letters."

I took them with my good hand.

"At least promise me you'll burn them when I'm dead," he pleaded.

"Or when it is over," I said.

"It will never be over until I'm dead."

I put the letters in my petticoat pocket.

"You've hurt yourself."

"It's nothing. I'll have some blisters tomorrow."

But a sharp pain shot through my right hand and made me feel faint. Before I fell, he picked me up in his arms and carried me to the bed, where he stared at me for a long time, then slowly his head came down toward me. I reached up with my left hand and untied the ribbon which held his thick hair. The eyes above me were dark. I recognized the pinch of suppressed fury, and in them, as always, the inner turmoil.

I felt myself being lifted and borne toward him. He tugged at my knot and it fell undone in his hands. He gathered my hair like a bouquet into a cushion under my head and locked his hands into it. His lips came down on the white scar at my temple.

The letters. They were all of the fragile self I had so painstakingly built in Paris. And he wanted to burn them. He strove as if he wanted to undo the small part of myself I had managed to build these past years. He didn't have to remind me that this was Virginia. Virginia. Virginia. And it would be Virginia forever. Virginia. That's why I clung to my letters. But now we no longer remembered if it was Paris or Virginia.

"What shall we do about your hand?" he asked gently.

"Ask Mama," I said. When he returned, he had a poultice from

Elizabeth Hemings. It smelled of mint and honey. He dressed my hand and let me go to sleep.

Virginia. I knew that what had happened to us could never, never have happened in Virginia.

August brought the girls back. Martha was with child. I was to accompany Maria to her first ball. I looked forward to that evening. As I had not left the confines of Monticello for more than four years, I wanted to see the new fashionable dresses, the carriages, the decorations. I wanted to hear the music, see the latest dance called the *mazurka;* I had been out of touch with even the small world of Tidewater, Virginia, for too long. I sat with the other servants and watched Maria dance.

Dancing was one of the things I most regretted. I had loved it since my first awkward tries with Martha in Paris. I remembered learning how to surrender to that eternity which was the first note of music. I could be anything I wanted for as long as the music played. And tonight the music played and played.

There were as many servants milling around as there were guests. To us all, whites and slaves, the ball was a chance to break the isolation and monotony of living on far-flung plantations all the year; to see new faces, new dresses, new horses, to catch up on Tidewater gossip.

I fingered the bright-yellow bandanna tightly wrapped around my head and savored the soft night breeze in the lavish gardens of Prestonfield Plantation. The dresses were more daring than any I could have imagined. My mother was right. There were new dyes and there was more gauze, more silk, and less satin and velvet. The crinolines were ridiculously large, giving the ladies the appearance of watermelons.

I gazed at everything with new eyes. Through the tall square-paned windows I looked at the swirling figures inside. I contemplated this world of exquisite food and delicate music, of graceful dances, of laces and satin, plumes and powder and perfume, of polished cherrywood floors, and crystal chandeliers.

Why, in the midst of happiness, must I be reminded of Paris? Look at them! I had heard about the Quadroon Balls of New Orleans where the white people were being mimicked, so here these provincial whites were trying to mimic Paris. I sneered at the pretensions of Virginia gentry.

I had known real splendor! What was I doing in this backwater . . . this tomb?

After all these years, John Trumbull was coming to Monticello. I didn't know whether to hide or greet him as a friend. A dinner had been organized for him, and included in the guest list was my master's choice for Maria, Mr. Giles, a senator from Virginia. Thomas Jefferson wanted him as a son-in-law, and he spent his time around Monticello that summer courting Maria; but in the meantime Maria had fallen in love with her cousin Jack, the same Jack who had helped me to lure her on the boat to Paris. Isaac and I commiserated with poor Master Giles as he was kindly but firmly rejected. Maria was too terrified to tell her father her choice, and begged me to do it for her.

The night John Trumbull came, I spied on the dinner. It was not the first time I had spied on my master's dinner guests. I did it constantly. Later, in the privacy of his bedroom, we would discuss the guests, their personalities, and their intrigues. Thus my political education continued despite my isolation. What I didn't learn from spying, I would learn from my mother and the other slaves. They were a constant and reliable source of gossip and funny stories that kept my lover entertained.

The dinner with John Trumbull turned into a veritable disaster. No sooner was the company seated than a lively discussion of the character, conduct, and doctrines of Jesus began. My master sat smiling and nodding as Master Giles, a freethinker, led the argument. I could see discomfiture and then shock on the face of John Trumbull, who defended his faith as best he could. The Massachusetts-accented voice I remembered so well rose in indignation over Master Giles's raillery. Then he addressed my master:

"Sir, this is a strange situation in which I find myself; in a country professing Christianity and at a table with Christians, as I suppose, I find my religion and myself attacked with severe and almost irresistible wit, and not a person to come in my defense but my friend Mr. Franks, who is himself a Jew!"

For just a brief moment his outburst seemed to have some effect on the company. The conversation became subdued. I could hardly hear what was going on. But then Maria's suitor returned to the attack and burst out with as broad and unqualified avowal of atheism as I had ever heard. John Trumbull was almost in tears. He seemed to look directly at me, but I knew he couldn't see me.

"The man who has made the previous statement is perfectly prepared for the commission of every atrocious action by which he can promise himself the advancement of his own interest or the gratification of his impure passions, provided he can commit it secretly and with a reasonable probability of escaping detection by his fellow men."

I froze. No. It was not possible that he saw me. Not even with his artist's eagle eyes. In his fury they seemed more crossed than ever. He rose. Thomas Jefferson remained seated, not saying a word. John Trumbull addressed Master Giles for the last time. He seemed to be addressing me.

"Sir, I would not trust such a man with the honor of a wife, a sister, or a daughter. . . . Our acquaintance, sir, is at an end."

My friend John Trumbull. My hand reached for his miniature. John Trumbull driven from our table. I remembered my last words to him at Cowes. "God bless you," I had said. God. Why had my exquisitely mannered lover allowed such a scene at his own table? I was appalled. Of all things to offend a gentle friend on his religion at one's own table! I clutched my locket. Now people would say Thomas Jefferson was an atheist! Trumbull had left the table. It was a dangerous thing to do, I thought. Humiliate a man in public. In the past years I had learned enough about politics to realize that one never knew when one might need a friend. Enemies were expensive. Politicians could only afford so many. . . .

That night, I asked him why he had allowed John Trumbull, whom he had adored in Paris, to leave his house and his table angry. My master showed no surprise that I had listened in on the dinner.

"I didn't feel like being diplomatic," he said to me. "I'm finished with politics. I have no more need to be polite."

"But why let people think you don't believe in God?"

"I don't care what people think anymore," he said bitterly. This was more than the disappointment of three years in Philadelphia!

"What is it?" I asked in alarm.

He was trembling. "It's nothing. It reminded me of a mistake I once made. Early in my political career, I gave up what I most deeply believed in for the sake of not provoking people. I vowed never to do it again."

He turned toward me. "Why shouldn't Giles have said what he thought? At least he had the courage to say what he means, which is more than most people in the world do. . . ." He looked at me. "What is it?" His pale sapphire eyes had turned their strange night-blue color.

"You. You were three years old then. Your brother Robert was with me in Philadelphia."

I turned toward him instinctively.

"They had given me the Declaration of Independence to draft. At thirty-three! I was very young and very passionate," he said slowly. "I poured my soul onto sheet after sheet. I wanted to place before mankind the common sense of the subject, in terms so plain and so firm as to be undeniable. After all, I was fighting for our lives and those of our family, and the families of all the other rebels—because that's what we were then, rebels, insurrectionists. We all stood to be hung and quartered and it was up to me to explain ourselves to the world. . . . I set to work on it in a little brick house at the southwest corner of Market Street and Seventh. After a week or so of work, I copied off a rough draft and took it to Dr. Franklin and John Adams. John Adams liked it. Dr. Franklin had more than forty corrections, but he softened it with his story about the hatter. . . ." My master smiled. "That was mild compared to what happened in the Continental Congress. It was the third of July. My declaration was ready for a hearing by the gentlemen in Congress. The secretary, Mr. Thompson, began to read my draft aloud. At first everything went well. Several of the members nodded. I was congratulated on my felicity of language. They got to the end of page one. Some delegates were deeply moved. Franklin leaned over and said, 'I wish I had written it myself!' Then the secretary began to read the facts, the nearly thirty accusations against George III. Thompson came to the last charge. I had left it to climax the list of grievances. . . . The delegates had criticized certain phrases. . . . 'King' was used in place of 'Tyrant,' and so on. Every change hurt." He smiled. "I was young. I sat in the back of the room with my thermometer on the windowsill outside. I was next to Dr. Franklin, who dozed off every now and then. There was little time to lose. We had to sign the Declaration. The revolution was already in motion. Your brother Robert waited for me outside. I was much worried about my own standing at the Virginia Convention. I feared to be knifed out of Congress. Martha was expecting our child, and I had not heard from her in three weeks. My mother had gone to her grave only three months before. I sent Robert twice a day for the mail, but there was never anything. Not a word since I had left Virginia. . . . The secretary read the last charge against the king, which was that he had waged a cruel war against human nature . . . the enslavement of the Negro people."

I held my breath.

SALLY HEMINGS

"With the exception of South Carolina and Georgia, everyone was in principle opposed to slavery. Benjamin Franklin was the president of the Pennsylvania Society for the Abolition of Slavery." His voice broke then and took on that charred husky tone of real defense.

" 'I think it too passionate,' somebody said.

" 'Turgid.'

" 'Irrational.'

" 'A tirade.'

" 'Completely irrelevant.'

" 'Too strong for such a dignified document,' said another. 'It's a philippic,' said somebody else. The Reverend Witherspoon questioned its accuracy. 'After all,' he said, 'the traffic existed long before George the Third was born.' Then Edward Rutledge of South Carolina said that the question of slavery should be determined by the states themselves. The Virginia delegate said, 'It concerns not only the importing states, it concerns the whole union.' 'What enriches a part enriches the whole,' said Rutledge.

"At that all bedlam broke loose.

" 'It is dishonorable,' put in the Maryland delegate.

" 'Honor has nothing to do with it,' said the South Carolina delegate.

" 'In time,' said Lynch, the delegate from Georgia, 'it will disappear of its own accord.'

" 'Neither morality nor wisdom have anything to do with this,' Rutledge declared. 'Interest and interest alone is the governing principle of nations. If the gentlemen from New England will consult their own interest, they will not oppose the importation of slaves. New England is the chief carrier! Who builds the ships? Who sails them?'

"John Adams was mortified, because he knew this was true. So did Samuel Adams. The arguments ran back and forth. Robert was waiting outside with the package of new gloves I had bought for Martha. I had bought her seven pairs. The two Adamses descended on me.

" 'The whole passage will have to be cut or South Carolina will never agree to the declaration,' they said.

"Benjamin Franklin opened his eyes long enough to agree with them, and to say the passage would destroy our still precarious unity.

"I was so young. I listened to the debate swirl around this resolution in silence. I never once defended it. I didn't think it was proper for me to defend my own declaration. I was upset. I had submitted my draft. . . if the Congress chose to mutilate it . . .

"I had taken no part in the debate and had tried to keep calm. I

192

prayed the passage would not be cut. The temperature at three o'clock was seventy-six degrees." He brushed his hand across his face. "To preoccupy myself, I took my new thermometer out of its box for another reading, but my hands were shaking so, I dropped it. It fell and broke on the floor. I covered the fragments with my handkerchief. Dr. Franklin had been observing me under his half-closed eyelids. I suppose he took pity on me. 'Come to my house tonight,' he said. 'Sally's making a wonderful dinner.'

"Those were his last words I remember. Sally was his daughter.

"You were three years old . . .

"The next day I took my seat again in the last row. I kept my eye on the Southern delegation: Rutledge, Middleton, Lynch, Gwinnett, Hall. . . . Washington was named commander-in-chief of the American armies that morning. Dr. Franklin kept pressing upon me the need for an agreement on the declaration. I wished mightily for George Wythe . . . any ally—but he had been detained in Williamsburg. He would arrive when it was all over," he said bitterly.

"The Congress skipped over the passage on slavery and read the closing portions. I sat and marked the mutilations on my own copy. After the final paragraph had been read and revised, they took up the passage on slavery again. I listened in silence to the appeal to God, to reason, to humanity, to future generations.

" 'National sins will be punished by national calamities,' somebody said.

"All through the afternoon they droned on. Everybody was restless. The flies from the stables across the street tormented us. The declaration could not be postponed. The news from New York was bad. Washington was in trouble. Staten Island was taken. The declaration was vital. Nothing should jeopardize the main design or delay it further. If the passage in question blocked the road to unity, it would have to be cut.

"The honorable gentlemen from the North were confused. 'Compromise,' 'Yield,' 'Hope for the best,' 'Concencus,' 'Delay,' 'Fight the war first,' 'Time,' 'Shipping interest.'

"Where was majority rule? I thought. But I was silent. Franklin was silent. Sherman was silent. Adams was silent. And Rutledge held the trump card: secession from the not even formed union. . . . John Adams looked at his watch. I looked around me. Everything in the room, the smell of sweat and tobacco, the heat, the flies, the Northerners, the Southerners, Adams, Hancock, Franklin, said, 'Let's worry about slavery another day . . . let's get out of here." He smiled.

"I remember everything hurt. My eyes. My neck, my head, my stomach hurt." He paused. "The clause reprobating the enslaving of the inhabitants of Africa was struck out in complaisance to South Carolina and Georgia," he said quietly, but his voice shook. He passed his hand in front of his face again, as if to wipe out the last weary arguments.

"What an incomprehensible machine is man! Here we were, rebels, all of us, depriving one-sixth of our population of the same liberty we were fighting and risking our heads for!"

"But you think black and white can never live in peace and equality here."

"I would have sent them home."

I sat stunned. I tried to embrace the immensity of what he had just told me. I grasped at the easiest thing to understand: that three years after I was born, he had tried to rescue me. He had truly tried.

"I have often thought," he whispered, "if my declaration had been adopted as I had written it . . . you would not be here, for there would be no slavery in America, no slaves."

In the terrible silence that followed, how I loved him.

Then I did look at him. He had turned on his side. His voice was muffled.

"From that day I vowed never never to put myself in that jeopardy again. I vowed never to raise my voice in defense of myself or my principles—especially about *that*. I washed my hands of it! I vowed to let the Almighty, if there is one, do his own work!"

There was only silence in the room. His brow, his cheeks, his lips were relaxed. He had fallen asleep.

I snuffed out the candle.

We would never speak of Philadelphia again.

CHAPTER 26

CHRISTMAS 1795

On what consists the greatness of a despot? In his own intrinsic merits? No, in the degradation of the multitude who surround him. What feeds the vanity of a patrician? The consciousness of any virtue that he inherits with his blood? The list of his senseless progenitors would probably soon cease to command his respect if it did not enable him to command that of his fellow creatures.

FRANCES WRIGHT, *Views of Society and Manners in America*, 1821

Perhaps the condition of women affords, in all countries, the best criterion by which to judge the character of man. Where we find the weaker sex burdened with hard labour, we may ascribe to the stronger something of the savage, and where we see the former deprived of free agency, we shall find in the latter much of the sensualist.

FRANCES WRIGHT, *Views of Society and Manners in America*, 1821

HOLDING THE GREAT iron ring which housed all the Monticello keys, Elizabeth Hemings hurried down the whitewashed breezeway between the kitchen and the main house. The keys, her badge of authority, jangled in rhythm with her brisk step. The cooking odors of her domain followed her halfway down the main hall. There was only one thought in her mind: her son James was to be set free the next day, Christmas 1795, more than five years since his return from France. He had served his master while he had been President Washington's secretary of state, she thought. And that Thomas Jefferson was at last living up to that piece of paper James had made him sign . . . now that his young brother Peter knew all about the art of French cooking.

Elizabeth Hemings nodded in satisfaction. Two freed, she thought, and five to go. . . . Five only because she knew her daughter had surrendered to her love for Thomas Jefferson with such abandon. But he was as faithful to her daughter as a bridegroom, thought Elizabeth Hemings. Martha Wayles Jefferson had been dead thirteen years now and the master gave no indication of replacing her with another white wife. Thank the Lord. Not that they weren't after him, poor man.

As she hurried along the passage and came into the dining room of the mansion, the sounds of hammering and sawing assaulted her. After everything he had promised, Thomas Jefferson was tearing up the house again, one day before Christmas! And Sally Hemings was no help at all, egging him on in all those ideas.

Elizabeth Hemings' face softened at the thought of the new baby; a girl child, Harriet, more beautiful than Sally, more beautiful than anything she could have imagined. . . . There was another new baby over at Edgehill, too. Martha Jefferson Randolph had delivered promptly every year since she had fled Monticello into the arms of her cousin Thomas Mann.

She liked Martha and wished her well, but her departure from Monticello had been a great relief. It left Sally Hemings mistress and, through her, she, Elizabeth Hemings, continued to rule. Elizabeth Hemings bumped into Big George.

"How's ol' Jimmy holdin' up?" He smiled at her. "You'd think this here's a daughter's weddin' the way Masta Jefferson a carryin' on."

"It ain't every day that the masta goes around freeing people, Big George. He ain't been none too generous with this here freedom you might say." Elizabeth Hemings smiled wickedly. Her son Robert was the only other slave she knew of that Thomas Jefferson had ever freed, and he had bought his freedom with borrowed money.

"Bett and Queenie out there, Big George," she called after him. "You get them to help you get out all that heavy silver, you hear? Get it all out. Sally tends to dress a table tonight you ain't never seen the likes of!"

When Elizabeth Hemings entered the hall of the west portico, she found her daughter on her hands and knees, arranging the velvet drapery and the presents at the foot of the Christmas tree. With characteristic quickness of movement, Sally Hemings spun on her heels and was on her feet by the time her mother reached her side. She was now twenty-two years old, and twice a mother.

"Everything is ready for tomorrow, Maman."

Elizabeth Hemings nodded at her beautiful daughter and winced at her "Maman." She had affected it ever since her return from France, and Elizabeth Hemings didn't like it. She had never dared tell her daughter this, however, so she continued to sprinkle her conversation with French expressions. Elizabeth looked up at the immense tree.

It was the tallest Virginia pine they could find on the slopes of Monticello, and it almost toppled over with the weight of the decorations, many of which her master had brought back from France. The French had taken up the Anglo-Saxon habit of decorating Christmas trees with a fervor and imagination that had outshone the often modest homemade decorations that were traditional in the United States. The French decorations gleamed like jewels and were the special joy of her daughter, who had taken it upon herself every year to trim the tree. The delicate silk balls with their silver pom-poms, the crystal snowdrops and lace snowflakes and the spun sugar James had spent a whole day creating, mingled with the cloved oranges and the pine cones. The top of the tree touched the ceiling of the entrance hall where tomorrow the white family and all the house servants would gather around after dinner for the distribution of presents.

"Tomorrow is going to be one happy day, daughter."

"Oh, Maman, James will be free at last! If it hadn't been for me, he would have been free years ago. I . . . I was so sure that things were going to turn out differently."

And what about you? Elizabeth Hemings wanted to say, but she held her tongue.

"How's little Harriet?"

"She's fine, Maman. I just left Suzy's cabin. She had finished nursing." Her daughter's dimples flashed in a quick smile of excuse. Elizabeth Hemings was silent. She loathed the fact that her daughter would not nurse Harriet. Her daughter knew this. She had given her to a newly delivered young slave who worked in the cotton mill to wet-nurse while she bound up her breasts in the French fashion to get rid of the milk.

"Bring her into the house, daughter. She can sleep with me. I'll get John to bring in her cradle. Suzy can come in to nurse hers and yours together."

"But I enjoy . . ." Sally Hemings began.

"Now, daughter, it's decided." Elizabeth Hemings had spoken.

Sally Hemings dropped to her knees to straighten a fold of velvet drapery at the foot of the tree. She had no intentions of giving up Suzy's nursing.

"Let Big George do that, Sally," Thomas Jefferson's musical voice rang out behind them as he strode into the hall from his study.

"I much prefer to do it myself, Master. The crystal snowflakes from Paris are so delicate, and we can't get any more. I found some we didn't use last year. Martha will be so surprised. . . ."

"And how is Harriet?"

"Harriet is fine, Master. I've just come from her."

Elizabeth Hemings turned away. The look she caught between the two people embarrassed her. She didn't understand it. She never would.

Christmas Day that year of 1795 was warm and sunny. It was almost four o'clock when Big George and Martin slipped away from the dining room, where the white people were lingering over the last meal James would cook at Monticello. He had helped me light the hundred Christmas tree candles. James, Ursula, Peter, and my mother were in the kitchens laboring over and admiring this last triumph of James: the rich turtle soup. James had made one of his specialties: a roast pork, fragrant with fresh herbs, garnished with its own deep-fried chitterlings, walnuts, and mushrooms. The meal continued with pigeons and pheasant baked in a pastry. An endless succession of vegetable platters followed. James had outdone himself. All kinds of pies ended the feast, along with profiteroles and the fashionable new French dessert: ice cream. Toasts of fine Burgundy and clarets, more groans, cries for the "Chef," and the meal ended.

There had been eighteen white people at the table with as many servants, one behind each chair for this special dinner. When the banquet was over, the company filed in from the dining room, flushed and happy. Big George gathered all the servants and the increasingly homesick Petit for the celebrations that were to follow. The children of the house, both black and white, were holding on to their mothers or their nurses. Although part of the house was already being torn down, the central hallway was still intact; its pale-blue damask gleamed in the reflected candles we had just finished lighting. The late-afternoon sun and the glow of the Christmas-tree candles imparted a golden haze to the entire company. The sculptured busts of Voltaire, Lafayette, and Washington seemed to be staring down from their pedestals.

I stood to the left of the master, with the other slaves in a semicircle. Martha stood to the right of her father, the white people curving in an arc to her right completing the circle.

Outside the sun was setting. The plantation slaves were gathering two hundred strong. Their good-natured conversations wafted through the glass doors of the vestibule toward the circle around the pile of packages. The black half of the circle faced the other half, the white half that was in turn closed by Martin and the ten-year-old Michael Brown, son of George Wythe and his freed mulatto mistress, Lydia Broadnax. His father had acknowledged him publicly as his freed slave, son of his housekeeper. All of Albemarle County, however, knew the truth, for he did nothing to hide either his pride or his love for his only son. Michael had been brought so that he could enjoy the celebrations and stuff himself with Christmas dinner with the other slave children in the kitchens.

As I stood, the two-month-old Harriet in my arms, the five-year-old Thomas Hemings clutching my skirts, I became only one in the web of blood ties that weaved itself in and across and around the two parts of the circle, binding one half to the other in arabesques as twisted and complicated as the hanging strands of silver cord on the tree above us. My mother had gathered nine of her fourteen children; facing her were two of Master Wayles's daughters. Elizabeth Hemings was either mother, stepmother, grandmother, aunt, or great-aunt to practically everyone present. To those she was not actually related to by blood, she was related to by bonds of property. This kingdom was hers, and she ruled as queen mother, a force of life to be revered and reckoned with by both black and white. She had loved, reared, nursed, birthed, served each person in this room.

There were no secrets for her here, neither heart nor body that she did not hold the key to—just as her iron ring held the key to every room and closet in Monticello. In her arms was one of Martha Jefferson's children.

My eyes went now to the white side of the circle and my two half sisters, Tabitha Wayles Skipwell and Elizabeth Wayles Eppes. It was Elizabeth who had sent me to Paris with Polly Jefferson so long ago. I caught the eye of Martha, standing next to her husband, Thomas Mann, whom she had loved for such a short time and who was now sinking into the melancholy which would lead him to insanity. Had she rushed into marriage, two months after we arrived from Paris, in order to escape me and her father's connection with me? I wondered. If so, she had been mistaken in her father's hold upon her, for though she lived at Edgehill, forty miles away, she clung to Monticello. Pity rose in me as I surveyed Thomas Mann Randolph. His bulk was growing with each year, along with his violent temper that had become legend in Virginia. His drinking sometimes sent his desperate wife and children scurrying to safety at Monticello. He was now looking at his wife with that same baffled, expectant expression with which my brother had sometimes looked at me. They both knew no other man would ever supplant

Thomas Jefferson in either her heart or mine. And it was driving Martha's husband crazy.

Next to Thomas Mann stood James Madison, small, round, birdlike, timid, and insignificant—a schoolteacher dressed for a funeral, Elizabeth Hemings once said. He gazed in silent adoration at his unexpected prize, his bride the widow Dolley Todd. It was said that Madison—to his great surprise—had captured his new bride from the attentions of Aaron Burr. She stood beside him, resplendent in rose satin trimmed in silver, a gray chiffon scarf was tucked into the low-cut bodice that revealed a splendid bosom, and her eyes roamed restlessly over the assembly, not liking very much what she saw.

James Madison, I thought, was a real politician. He would succeed where my master—fastidious, uncompromising, stubborn, proud— never would. Politicians, I had long decided, should not be very bright, or at least should not think very much. And, I thought, if I were free . . . I gazed at the glorious Dolley Madison. She reminded me of certain French ladies I had observed. There was the same cynicism hidden under the soft feminine manner, the same ability to manipulate, even this rustic company, to shine, and put herself in the best light. There was a sharp mind behind her pretty appearance. She had, I sensed, the ambition to succeed. Dolley Madison would succeed because she had no competition. And envy, mingled with the constant ache of my own deprivation, invaded me.

My dress. It was four years old, the last of the dresses from Madame Dupré. I gazed at the emeralds glistening in the earlobes of James Madison's wife and at the matching bracelet on her plump arm. A wife, I thought. A real wife. Recognition. Nothing delineated me from the other servants except my position of honor next to the master, the tiny ruby earrings fastened in my ears, and the heavy silver locket around my neck. I lifted my chin.

George Wythe looked proudly at his mulatto son, who had the same round face, the same soft intelligent eyes as his father. Michael Brown was splendidly dressed, in the Quaker fashion, his shorts in buff with white stockings. His long brown uncut curls reached his shoulders and hung loose, giving him an angelic, princely look. My mother adored him and envied his education. He excelled in Latin and Greek, mathematics and astronomy taught him by George Wythe, who was determined to prove him brilliant not only beyond his color and station but beyond his age as well, and there was the wanness of overwork about his face.

Next to Master Wythe stood Polly, and next to her our cousin Jack Eppes. From the frightened child I had escorted to Paris and the uncertain adolescent that had returned with me, Maria had become the serious and remote beauty who stood timidly beside the man she deeply loved, and had been afraid to tell her father she wished to marry.

All last year, after her return from Philadelphia, I had nursed her through illness after illness. She had inherited the health of her mother, and her delicacy. Her mother had loved and accepted my mother and her children as part of her inheritance. For Maria, too, the Hemingses had always been a part of her life, and she had long ago acknowledged that still another Hemings, the one she loved best, held a permanent place in the affections of her father.

It was Petit who now joined the circle between Martin and George Wythe, unwittingly attaching the white half of the circle with the black. Our eyes met. Affection? Pity? Horror at this Monticellian "family"? He shrugged and with a wry smile looked at Martin, his black equivalent.

Thomas Hemings tugged at my skirt and his father's hand came down on his head in a caress.

My brother moved next to me. I shifted two-month-old Harriet, whom I held in my arms and reached down for his hand. It was cold. He was trembling violently. I increased the pressure of my hand in his, hoping to quiet him while the distribution of the presents went on. Then I registered the movement the other side of me. My master began to speak. He began to announce what I couldn't, yet must, believe: the emancipation of my brother. James had won. He was being given at last what he had vowed never to steal. But the speech was ringing with phrases which under the circumstances were self-righteous and pompous. I felt humiliation for James and embarrassment for my master.

James's mouth twitched downward as he whispered to me, "I should have blackmailed him years ago . . . I notice he doesn't mention anything about back pay." James's salary had stopped the moment he set foot in Virginia. "This morning he gave me thirty dollars and a horse."

". . . with a flare of genius for the culinary arts and the temperament—or I should say the temper—that goes with it . . ." Thomas Jefferson was finishing his speech, "he has served me faithfully, devotedly, and unselfishly in his craft and art, and I am loath to part with him. He shall ever have in my heart and my affections a special place, just as his brother Robert does for all of us here, and I am sure there is not a person present that does not wish him every happiness in his new and justly deserved . . . *freedom!*"

I looked up at my brother, who was almost as tall as my master. This ceremony, I had been shaken to find, not only released him from his long bondage as a slave but from the bonds of a vow which had kept him in chastity all these years. It had been last summer when I had finally gotten the courage to ask him about a wife. He had laughed in my face. "Since when do slaves marry?"

"A wife is a wife whether she is married or not."

"You think I would spill my seed as a slave! To father other slaves! You think I would enrich some white master by breeding more slaves for him. If I spill it, it will be as a free man who can father free children. This I vowed long ago. In Paris. I vowed I would never touch a woman as a slave. My life has been celibate, sister," he had said. "I have never known a woman."

I looked now into those clear eyes. They looked over my head to hold those of his ex-master, in a gaze of such love and hatred that Martha and I, the only persons present whose eyes had not strayed from James Hemings, lowered our heads over our respective babes in arms.

Thomas Jefferson was thoroughly moved by his own speech. He blinked back his tears and turned away from James. Petit, to Thomas Jefferson's surprise, was crying. He felt a small hand on his sleeve.

"They are waiting for you, Master," a voice said softly just as the excited drone from outside swelled into a babble of cries: "Presents! Presents! Master. Master . . ." He gave the signal for the company to pass through the glass doors of the hall onto the west portico and stand facing the multitude gathering in front, as a cry—half-cheer, half-plea—went out from the throng of slaves, now jumping up and down in anticipation and cold.

Sally Hemings and Martha started to distribute the Christmas bundles. Martha handed out the clothes. His slave wife handed out the presents, the sweets, the cider, and whisky.

The lines seemed never ending, yet Thomas Jefferson knew that his Farm Book was mightily depleted of the names of many of his slaves. Secretly, he had had to sell more than a hundred slaves to cover outstanding debts that went back twenty years, and still the end was not in sight. He had been forced to sell Elk Hill—the estate he had wanted to give to Maria as a wedding present—for ready cash. The debts he had undertaken had mounted, with accumulated interest, to an unbearable load. In desperation, he had sold slave upon slave to meet the claims upon him. His son-in-law had attended to the details, so that nowhere did his name appear on the sale of his property. Yet the results had been disappointing. He had averaged only about forty pounds a slave; there had been a time when a good Negro had brought upward of two hundred. He had even been compelled to break up one family, something he hated to do, simply because the male was too valuable and essential. He had asked his brother Randolph to buy the wife and children or, failing that, to sell them to some good master in the vicinity, so that they might remain near their husband and father. No others, he had instructed, were to be sold under any circumstances, in the immediate neighborhood.

Thomas Jefferson looked out with emotion over the heads of his slaves. There would soon be a mortgage on all of them in order to finance the rebuilding of Monticello.

> I always had a fancy for a closet with a window I could more peculiarly call my own.
>
> ABIGAIL ADAMS, 1776

CHAPTER 27

SPRING 1796

I BENT OVER the fine-lined drawings on the blue-squared French archi-
tectural paper of my master's new plans for Monticello. I leaned over
his shoulder as he explained to me how he was to change my house.
Now was my chance to ask for what I wanted. The demolition had
already begun, with his workmen prying loose three to four thousand
bricks a day; the noise, the confusion, and even the danger at times
resulted in achieving what war and revolution had never been able
to produce in my mother. She would cry every day. Most of the household was camping out. Only his bedroom and study had any semblance
of order, and it was here, before his drawing table, that he was seated
while I stood behind him, my arms about his neck on a fine spring
day. He had made great plans for his house. He had in mind to remove
the second-story attic and spread all the rooms on a single floor. In
place of the attic, he wanted an octagonal dome, like the one on the
Hôtel de Salem in Paris that we had visited so many times. Around
the interior of this dome would be a mezzanine balcony, thus providing
privacy for the bedrooms intended for his white family. In his own
apartments on the ground floor, he envisioned a double-height ceiling
with a skylight and a bed alcove between the bedchamber and the study
accessible to both, and with a passage between them. To do this,
he must demolish the fireplaces that stood where his bed would
stand.

I had never asked him for anything before. Even now, with a new life in my womb, pressing into the solid warmth of his back, his hands encompassing mine, my lips on his hair, I hesitated, but the closeness and his excitement at the new changes gave me courage. He shifted his good hand to hide his infirm hand, as he was wont to do.

"What is it?" he asked, as if he sensed my agitation.

"I should like you to design ... to build a room for me." I went on quickly, before he had time to respond. "A secret room adjoining yours where I may pass to and from without crossing the public hall where anyone who happens to be about may see me," I said. There was not a servant or member of the household who did not know that only I had access to the apartments of the master. I was mistress of his bedchamber and his wardrobe. His premises were forbidden to all, including his daughter. Yet I felt naked every time I had to enter by the public hall, always full of people: visitors, work-men, servants, relatives. It would be so easy to find me a little space of my own somewhere. I longed for the shadowed recesses and the vast apartments of the Hôtel de Langeac with its endless attic rooms, secret corridors, unused apartments. Here, every space was occupied by slave or master. Twenty servants ran in and out of the main house, not counting all the other people, and even once a horse. . . . I recounted all this without stopping, as if I would run out of courage before I ran out of breath. Only the ticktock of the French clock broke the sound of my breathing. Outside a whippoorwill trilled.

"You shall have your room," he said.

I waited for him to tell me where and how, but he said no more. There was a mischievous look on my master's face, as if he had had in mind to build me a room all along. I raised him from his seat, put my arms about his waist, and kissed him.

That same spring Thomas Mann Randolph and Martha went to Warm Springs, leaving their children at Monticello. The servants of Edgehill were whispering that ever since the birth of Thomas Jefferson Randolph, their master was losing his mind, driven by the dark forces that seemed to overtake all the Randolphs in their prime. He and Martha had traveled as far away as New York seeking relief, and Martha had turned more and more to Monticello and her father for solace and comfort. Polly, who was now at home, my mother, and I would care for them. There had been many a time when Martha would take refuge in Monticello, having run away from her husband.

"What are you going to do about Martha coming here so often?" said Elizabeth Hemings.

"What can I do? She's her father's daughter, and Monticello will be hers and Polly's one day. It is her right. Besides, she's lonely, I think, and unhappy."

"Poor man, he can't help his sickness. First thing, she won't have a husband."

"I think that would suit her just fine," I answered.

"Would it suit her father as well?"

A throb of jealousy sounded deep in me. Elizabeth Hemings always knew where to probe for her answers.

"I think it would. He needs her. He dotes on her and he loves her." I didn't add, "more than he loves me," but I thought it. "He doesn't like his son-in-law," I added.

"Well," my mother said, "he is not the first hard-riding, hard-drinking, evil-tempered bad Masta Randolph these parts have seen. Think on his cousin John Randolph of Roanoke. Rumor has it he don't have no head for business. Thomas Jefferson be well to put this plantation in other hands than his. Seems he's practically ruined."

"It's Martha's dowry they are living on."

"That's so, now."

I sighed. "As if you didn't know, Maman!"

"Well," chuckled my mother, "we got to keep our white folks informed and—"

"And spied upon twenty-four hours a day," I said.

"Don't we belong to them twenty-four hours a day?" replied Elizabeth Hemings. "When they give us a few hours' freedom every day, we'll give them a few hours' peace."

"You'll never forgive me for coming back, will you? Or dragging James back here for all those wasted years. . . ."

"Daughter, all that's history now. What's left is between you and Thomas Jefferson. James is free. He's over there in France, cooking for them nobles like he dreamed."

"I forgot, Maman."

Elizabeth Hemings looked at me without understanding.

"It's harder, maman, to forget freedom than slavery. Over there, I had forgotten what it was like, if I ever knew. You raised me as free as any white child in the Big House. I came back to that, not to my real condition."

"You came back because of that child."

"No, Maman, I came back because I didn't remember who I was."

"You remember now, don't you."

"Yes."

"And the masta didn't do much reminding, did he?"

"I don't think he truly remembered, either. We were like children. He with his illusions, and I with mine."

"You were a child, then, true; but he had no excuse except his own selfishness."

"It wasn't true selfishness, Maman. White people are different from us."

"They ain't different, daughter, they simply expect to get what they want or what they need in life, that's all. It never occurs to them—as it *always* occurs to us—that they won't get what they need, nor what they want. You want to stroll away? Nothing stopping you."

"Nothing?"

"He wouldn't pursue you. There's enough gossip already."

"I think he would."

"Never, daughter, no matter how much he wanted to. His pride would stop him."

"His pride is great, Maman, but not as great as his passion for owning things. I belong to him. I'm his, and no other man's. And he'll keep me. He's given up too many things he's loved in life."

"Got to let you go if the Lord claims you."

I got up and walked toward the warmth of the smoldering kitchen chimney. I had come for company, as my master was out in his fields. I hadn't wanted this conversation. For years, I had been avoiding this conversation. . . .

"Being free isn't so important I'd die for it," I said, and turned to face her.

"Don't tell me freedom ain't worth dying for! Black people dying left and right, in the fields and on the ships, being beaten to death for not yielding, being hunted like dogs for strollin', being killed for standin' up like men and women instead of grovelin' like dogs! Don't give me any of your lip about 'not worth dying for'! They's even white folks— abolitionists who's risking their lives—their white lives for black people, helping them run. And you, you with your pride! Thinkin' that slavehood would never touch your precious body, or your precious spirit, that it would not hurt you and damage you and change you. . . ." My mother's face had darkened. It always changed colors when she was in a rage. "Pride has given you a worst burden than any field hand out there, because theirs can be lifted, but yours never will. Thomas Jefferson playing father to you, me spoiling you like I didn't know your color. If you had stayed here, you would have learned. . . . Oh, Lord Almighty, how I wish I had never put you on that boat!"

My mother had grasped my wrist with her strong rough hands and had drawn me toward her. I looked at her without expression. I had long ago abandoned myself to that particular joy of not being responsible for oneself. I had struggled against everything that surrounded my master and was hostile to me. I had overcome the fearful disgust which his situation as master and mine as slave inspired in me.

"If you don't want it for yourself, at least get it for your children!"

"I have, Maman. I have the promise."

At that moment, I didn't care about that. I still had not accepted the great ring of household keys, which was my badge of authority, from my mother. I let her cling to it. The warmth of the fire stole under my skirts and up the back of my legs and spine. He would be coming home soon. I looked at my mother with impatience, as she continued to hold on to me.

"What if he grows tired of you?" my mother asked.

"Then," I answered, "I just might think about dying for freedom." I smiled, and my mother released me. I looked down at my wrist and saw the rosy mark left on my skin by her fingertips.

"Sally?"

I had been reading a letter from James. I turned toward him. He was almost shouting, the demolition of our walls making it virtually impossible to be heard.

"I want to transplant all the rhododendron along the south hedge. I was going to tell Giovanni to do it, but I wanted to ask you what you thought."

"What does Petit think?" I asked.

"He said to ask you."

"I liked them where they were," I said. "And what will you do with all the babies in the nursery, then?"

"Find a new place for them. I thought to make an alley at the end of the formal garden."

"Oh, no." I hesitated, then called him by his name. He seemed pleased, and laughed out loud. I had pronounced his name as it was said in French, dropping the "s." *To-mah.*

"Always call me thus," he whispered.

He held out his arms. I looked up at him.

It was more than a year before I had the room I could call my own. But true to his word, he built it. A tiny winding stairway led from the foot of his bed to a narrow passageway over the top of his bed alcove which ran the length of it and was lit by three round windows giving onto his rooms. The shape of the windows had been inspired by the painting of Abraham and Hagar he liked so much, as well as those for my room. My room was octagonal, hidden under the eaves, and looked westward over the mountains. There I waited, accumulating my account of hours. My small treasures from Paris filled the room: the onyx-and-bronze clock, my Paris sofa and bedstead, the copper bathing tub that Joe Fosset had copied for me, my chests full of dresses I never wore, my linens, my bolts of fine silks and cambrics, my books, my guitar. There I was free, solitary, away from the multitude of the mansion. I savored entering his inner sanctum by my own stairway. Only in my official capacity as slave and mistress of his wardrobe did I enter by the public hall on the ground floor.

Only after he had built the miniature stairway to my room did he discover to his dismay that the two new wings of his mansion had no stairs at all! He quickly ordered my brother John to add a stairwell to each wing. It was barely wider than my own—a mere two feet across—and had to accommodate not only the bulk of his masculine company but the hoopskirts of his females. I thought of the great stairway at the Hôtel de Langeac, that monument of rose marble I had fled down that March morning eight years ago. Only my secret room, with its passage-way and tiny staircase, resembled the great houses of Paris, and it linked us to the past. Soon our private existence would give way once again to the demands of the public and of power but, for a while at least, I was safe, happy, hidden, and loved.

CHAPTER 28

PHILADELPHIA, MARCH 1797

"THERE IS NOTHING I so anxiously hope as that my name may come out either second or third—the last would leave me home the whole of the year, and the other two-thirds of it. . . ."

With these words, our happiness in retirement came to an end. On Christmas Day 1796.

My master was now the second vice-president of the United States. So loath was he to leave home that he considered having himself sworn in at home in Virginia. As for me, I was in mourning. My third child, Edy, had not survived her first months, and now came the blow that I would lose my master again to his old mistress, politics. Neither Martha nor Maria were to go with him to Philadelphia for the inauguration. To cheer me, he offered to take me with him for the ceremonies.

I looked forward to the eleven long days of journeying; anything to rouse me out of my deep depression. Perhaps I would have news of James, from whom I hadn't heard in over a year.

We departed. Day after day, new landscapes sped by as we traveled farther north. We passed Ravensworth, and Montpelier, Dumfries, Elkridge, and Georgetown. We had taken the Paris phaeton, and Isaac and Israel as outriders were charged with the extra horses. We were drawn by the six beautiful bays of Monticello. On the second of March, after leaving Chester, my master tried to obtain a public carriage to carry us to Philadelphia, but none was to be had. We delayed until evening, with the intention of entering the city in secret, but the yellow-and-lilac carriage with the Monticello coachman had been recognized and our arrival had been reported by messenger. As we entered the city, we were greeted by a large, roaring crowd carrying a banner proclaiming: "Jefferson, Friend of the People," and by a company of artillery that fired sixteen rounds of ammunition in salute. A cold dread seized me, and I clutched at my master's sleeve and buried my face in his shoulder. It had been almost eight years since I had come down off the mountain that was Monticello. I was once again out into the world. That mountain on which I had spent almost all my existence had rolled away like a great stone covering a tomb and let in the light and air of the world, and this world was pounding on the sides of the carriage and screaming slogans and love as my master laughed and disengaged his arm from my clutches, the better to lean forward toward the window and show himself. Burwell, who was inside the carriage, stuck his head out the other side and watched Davey and Jupiter soothing the frightened horses, smiling, and waving at the crowd as if they had been born to do it. I peered out nervously behind the bulk of Burwell onto a sea of white faces cut into by the booted and spurred legs of our outriders. I had not seen so many white people at once since Paris. I remembered James's description of the Bastille mob and the crowds, and I saw myself in the Paris streets. That memory became one as I glimpsed these friendly Americans come to acclaim their vice-president. Had I forgotten, on my mountain, that the world was made up of white people? This howling, laughing, unruly crowd was the white world. I uttered a small cry and clutched at Burwell as I had at my master, but he, like his master, was only interested in those faces swarming around us. He shrugged off my hand and ignored me.

The next day I roamed the streets of Philadelphia, a city that seemed to be made up of only one color and one material: red brick. The streets as well as the houses were made of it. The wetness made the bricks slippery underfoot and, several times, Burwell kept me from falling. We strolled down Market Street looking into the shop windows, at the street vendors and the newspaper sellers. I looked for my master's little house at Seventh Street, noisy and filled with young boys, both black and white, selling broadsides and pamphlets and newspapers, all proclaiming to have the story on the first succession to the presidency of the United States. Burwell bought several of them for the plantation.

In the course of our walk, Burwell would point out the freed men as they crossed our path, and I couldn't help but stare at them. They were all wearing neat clothes, and conveyed the feeling of self-confidence. I knew, of course, that in Charlottesville there were many freed people of color, but this was the first time that I had looked into the faces of Negroes who had never been slaves. Some seemed rich, the women with long elegant skirts trailing the sidewalks, accompanied by dignified men in dark broadcloth and snowy linen. I had put on my best dress, and although it was years out of fashion in Paris, it was not noticeable here. I was looking forward to seeing the elegant ladies tomorrow in their fine gowns, cloaks, hats, and gloves.

The day dawned clear and sunny. We followed our master, walking to the Senate building, where the swearing-in ceremony was to take place. I strained my hearing to the utmost, but was still unable to make out one word, either of the speech or of the prayer he offered for the country. It was the first time I had ever heard my master speak in public, and after the first few words his voice lost all its musical resonance, and became little more than a husky whisper. In order to learn what he had said in a public speech, one had to have recourse to the printed speech in the newspapers. After giving his prayers for the happiness, peace, and prosperity of our country, he led the senators and the crowd to the House of Representatives, where Master Adams was sworn in. It had been almost ten years since I had last seen John Adams from the back window of the phaeton taking Polly and me to Paris. He had not grown slimmer with age, and where he had been square and stout, he was now round and fat. With his prim countenance, long, pinched nose, and tiny piercing blue eyes, he resembled nothing so much as a Virginia hare in his pearl-gray frockcoat, waistcoat, and breeches. I felt an old surge of affection for him, wondering what my life would have been if he had sent me back to Virginia that summer long ago. Abigail Adams was nowhere to be seen. Had she not come to honor her husband on this day?

As I looked around, I realized that there were practically no women at all. All the fine ladies I had hoped to see had stayed home and this gathering looked as if there were only men in this United States.

At the side of George Washington was his slave Samuel, as old and stony as his master. President Washington was dressed all in black: a tall old man with an old-fashioned powdered wig with rolled curls at the sides, and with cold, small blue eyes set in a face so white it seemed blue. The nose was large and his lips were so thin they were invisible until he drew them back in what was meant to be a smile showing his large, black false teeth, which were famous. Now and again he waved stiffly at the crowd, and as he did so, exhibiting his black smile in a pure white face, the slave at his side would also smile, exhibiting his pure-white smile in a black face. The crowd cheered the outgoing president and tears began to slide down the face of the president and that of his slave shadow Samuel. John Adams made a fine speech in his harsh Massachusetts accent. He too was greatly cheered. To this day, I wonder why Abigail Adams did not come to see her husband made president of the United States.

Standing outside the Senate House after the ceremony, Burwell and Jupiter at my side, I looked over the now dispersing assembly, trying to recognize friends of my master whom I had seen at one time or another at Monticello. Suddenly I noticed a short, handsome man. He was magnificently dressed, wearing buff, with yellow lace showing at the neck and wrists.

His curly black hair was pulled back from an abnormally high forehead, the pallor of his skin contrasting with the jet-black hair and eyebrows that were arched in a quizzical expression over deep brown eyes. He headed directly toward us, stopping once or twice to greet people who hailed him, turning swiftly from one side to the other on the balls of his feet in a dancing motion that was most graceful. Finally, he was upon us.

"Davey Bowles! Jupiter! The imperturbable and good Jupiter! Miss? . . ."

"Masta Burr, suh. A glorious day for the Republic, suh. You looking for Masta Jefferson, suh? He went with a group of gentlemen over to the Representative House . . . suh."

Jupiter stepped protectively in front of me as he made his speech. Jupiter was the same commanding height, as well as the same age, as his master. He towered over this Master Burr, who came up to his chest.

"Why isn't Bob Hemings here, Jupiter? Where's that boy?"

"Robert Hemings, he freed, Masta Burr, suh, like James. He done bought his freedom from Masta Jefferson so's he could join his wife and his daughter in Richmond, who's slaves of Master Strauss there. Masta Jefferson, he signed his manumission papers on Christmas Day '94. He regretted thoroughly leavin' Masta Jefferson, Masta Burr, but he jus' couldn't prevail upon hisself to give up his wife and his daughter."

"Well, I wish him well, Jupiter."

"Yassuh."

Aaron Burr didn't take his eyes off me. He waited patiently, apparently used to Jupiter's evasions, and said nothing.

Finally, Jupiter, after more rambling conversation that astounded me by its servility, gave in.

"This here child, she's a servant of Masta Jefferson, too. She's a Hemings, and Burwell here is her nephew. She's called Sally Hemings of Monticello," Jupiter added unnecessarily. It was the longest speech about me that I had ever heard Jupiter make.

"Another Hemings of Monticello! Good God, how many of you are there in this family? And how is James, by the way? I heard he went back to France. Mr. Jefferson's dinner parties haven't been the same since. As a matter of fact, he has spent the last year trying to steal other people's cooks! And this girl, surely she's not a field hand now, is she?"

"She's mistress of Masta Jefferson's wardrobe, suh," Jupiter replied grandly.

This man called Aaron Burr turned his black and burning gaze on me as if I were standing before him naked.

"The . . . mistress . . . of . . . Thomas . . . Jefferson's wardrobe . . . Jupiter?" he uttered slowly.

His eyebrows arched almost up to the hairline of his wide high forehead and gave him the appearance of Satan himself. His eyes raked me with such a mixture of contempt and lewdness that my blood turned cold. Never had a man looked at me thus. I was trembling. When I met his gaze he insolently held it. He threw back his head and laughed—a high, tinkling, peculiar laugh that was most unpleasant. I decided then and there that I detested Master Aaron Burr.

"From the way he dresses, Jupiter, I didn't think he had a wardrobe, let alone a mistress of it. Except for today," he added, "as he is looking most elegant in French blue, possibly because he has his mistress here to dress him . . ."

I felt Jupiter tense.

"*Je vous en prie, Monsieur. Je suis la femme de chambre de Mademoiselle Maria Jefferson,*" I interrupted coldly in French. I don't know why I did it. I was flushed with anger and I was glad my face was half-hidden by my hat. Master Burr was as astonished as if a dog had started to speak Latin.

"*Ah! Que je fus inspirée. . . .*"

"*Quand je vous reçus dans ma cour,*" I replied.

It was the first lines from an aria that Piccinni, the singing tutor to Marie-Antoinette, had written. Marie-Antoinette was rumored to have sung it in public to her lover, the Count Fersen, at one of the famous parties at Trianon. It had been made into a limerick by the Parisian populace. Everyone who had been in Paris just before the Revolution knew it by heart. I couldn't help smiling at his astonishment, and he smiled back at me; a wide, handsome wicked grin. I blushed, sorry that I had smiled at him despite myself.

"*Vous parlez très bien le français,*" he said with his heavy American accent. "*Vous avez bien dit, une servante de Maître Jefferson? C'est a dire, une esclave?*"

"*Oui, Monsieur,*" I replied.

He looked questioningly at Jupiter, then at Burwell, neither of whom answered since they had not understood what we had said. Burwell too had put his "don't-ask-me-I-just-a-poor-darky" expression on his smooth golden-brown face.

"*Eh bien, ton maître a tant de choses à célébrer en plus de son poste comme vice-président . . .*"

"*Que Dieu le protège dans sa tâche,*" I replied, curtsying low and in the French manner.

"*Bien dit*—well said, indeed. That God protect him. From his enemies and his friends."

So this was my master's rival, I thought, the rich and famous lawyer from New York, Aaron Burr. I loathed him.

"Burwell, take your aunt out of this mob. Jupiter ... Davey, Mademoiselle Hemings of Monticello ..." Again he drew out the words sarcastically.

Outrage filled my breast. If I had been white, he would not have dared address me so, servant or no servant. Despite my rage, I curtsied low, and to my surprise, he bowed expertly. He spun on his heels in a curious dancing movement and walked jauntily away. He spoiled the effect, however, by looking over his shoulder at me, and promptly bumped into a tall handsome man who, Jupiter whispered, was Alexander Hamilton. The comic effect of the formidable Master Burr falling over himself in his attempt to get a last look at me didn't dispel my hatred, nor the sense of dread the crowd had evoked in me. "Enemies"? I had thought that in all this great crowd there were only friends and followers of my master. Who could be an enemy of Thomas Jefferson and why? Who could wish him any harm? Certainly my master had complained at times about the envy and the malice of political life, but mortal enemies seemed impossible to conceive. Master Jefferson, the absolute ruler of Monticello, was so gentle, so serene. He was surrounded by love. Could he be surrounded here by people and forces he could not control? People that could thwart his will as easily as he could that of his servants? I thought of the newspaper articles I had read in the past few days. Yes, there were people here he could not rule, could not order, could not even fight or convince, who were as intelligent, as rich, as powerful as he. There were friends whose support he would need to seek. Mysterious enemies from whom he had to defend or protect himself. And, above all, there was the "public": that dangerous and volatile mass that one could call neither friend nor enemy, for it could change from one day to the next. And this "public" had been given the name "The People" by their government, thereby making it one body, one will, the sole source of power that the great sought with such tenacity. "The People" now stood milling around the blood-red courtyard; "The People" brushed up against Jupiter, Burwell, and me as we stood to one side of our carriage. "The People" could destroy my master. And if my master was destroyed, what would become of me? It was then that I understood that my master's enemies were mine as well. That, in this white world, I had nothing but enemies.

"Jupiter, I'm going into the carriage. I feel faint."

As Jupiter helped me into the carriage, he said, "I expect that Thomas Jefferson don't want you out here minglin' with this mob, being scrutinized. I don't think he'd like the idea of you being exposed to this riffraff. He expected you to go home after the ceremony. You can see there ain't no ladies here." With that he slammed the door of the carriage.

". . . and, I told him, my inclination would never permit me to cross the Atlantic again."

I stared at him. With one willful declaration, the spoken and unspoken promises of the last eight years were broken. All my dreams of ever returning to France had vanished. Even now, with James gone without me, and with two children to raise, buried deep, I had always hoped to return to Marly. Now that subject was closed forever.

Three days after the inauguration, my master, accompanied by Jupiter, went to a dinner given by Master Washington. Despite hopes by everybody of a reconciliation between him and the new president, Adams, it had been evident at the dinner that their relations were so cold and so singular as to foment gossip even among the servants in the kitchens. Servants industriously discussed every aspect of the political situation. They sometimes seemed to have more information than the actual participants in the feuds and intrigues that evolved. Jupiter was not surprised, therefore, when his master returned from the dinner in a rare rage that only he and I were ever permitted to witness.

His face was flushed way beyond its usually high color, and he tore at his cravat so brutally that he practically strangled himself. His long legs paced the floor of the tiny room, shaking the floorboards, and his voice trembled with anger.

"The first and only thing John Adams proposed to me was that I return to France!"

He then let out a stream of imprecations against his old friend Adams; against Hamilton, Knox, Pickering, Burr, and the others. They were all against him. I memorized the names. So, I thought, these were my master's "enemies." In great agitation, he called for Jupiter to get a horse saddled, then changed his mind. He sat down long enough for me to pull off his boots. He stood up in his stocking feet and let loose another string of insults.

"If John Adams and his inherited Federalist cabinet think they can shut me out of the government, they had best think again!"

His huge fist came down on a small table beside the bed, smashing it to pieces.

My brief excursion into white America was over.

When we returned up the mountain, from Philadelphia, the mountain was in bloom.

He stayed home for almost the whole year.

At the end of the following summer, Maria Jefferson married her cousin Eppes in a small ceremony, amidst the demolition work going on over our very heads at Monticello. The couple would reside at Bermuda Hundred, more than a hundred miles away. For her wedding, her father gave Maria twenty-six slaves, seventy-eight horses, pigs, and cows, as well as eight hundred acres. Our good-byes were tender, for Polly had always treated me as a friend. We had managed to forge an unwritten truce that placed our love for her father as security against our love for each other. There were no secrets between us. When I showed her the room connected with that of her father's, her sigh of relief was as great as mine.

"Oh, Sally, how very nice!"

"He changed his apartments last year to accommodate it, and Joe and John are building the staircase."

"It means you no longer have to cross the public hall to enter and leave."

We never mentioned why this new arrangement would be better for all concerned. Nor would she ever mention this new arrangement to her father or ever allude to it.

"Remember, in Paris," I said, "all the secret stairways and rooms in the mansion? How we would imagine romantic stories about them?"

"We were so young in Paris," Polly said.

"You still are, Mistress. Seventeen is a wonderful age. . . ."

I had a safe harbor at last. But a mother is never safe. My master had been home for almost five months, Polly was still on her honeymoon, when rumors of an epidemic spreading up from Charlottesville struck terror in the heart of every mother, black or white. Both Tom and Harriet fell ill. Martha's daughters were sick at Edgehill, as well as half a dozen slave children. During the next weeks, we worked without sleep, nursing the children, Martha traveling back and forth between Edgehill and Monticello. Dulled by exhaustion, shedding bitter tears, Martha and I watched my little Harriet, only two summers old, slowly suffocate to death.

I laid her next to Edy, in the slave cemetery. Four of his white children lay under their stones in the white cemetery. The dividing line did not even stop at the grave. But what did it change? They were all his children, and they were all dead.

Harriet's death brought me low, undermining the fragile movements of still another new life in my womb. The winter reminded me of Paris in '88, long and cold and nothing like normal Virginia winters, with candles burning in the afternoon, keeping everyone, slave and white, indoors. My first-born, Tom, survived, and I clung to him with all the desolation I felt that winter.

Martha, who had lost a daughter at the same time I had lost Edy, raced back to Edgehill and her children in mortal fear, leaving me alone.

Only one living child left, except the one in my body. I kept Tom indoors the whole winter, never letting his sturdy red-headed figure out of my sight. My heart pounded at every cough, stopped at every complaint.

At the end of March, I sent word that my time was approaching. A few days later, a sofa came made of fine mahogany with carved legs and back in the Jacobean style; a feather mattress and down coverlet of silk arrived as well. He had not forgotten me. When I wrote that I was safely delivered of a boy, the reply came back, "Name him Beverly," and I did.

Not long afterward, a harpsichord arrived from Philadelphia. Martha came up from Edgehill to see it almost immediately. I looked with envy on her four healthy children. I too would have had four . . .

"It is for Maria, you know."

"Yes, so I understand."

Martha didn't mention the fact that Maria no longer lived at Monticello, but away at Bermuda Hundred. I was delighted with the harpsichord.

"It is a charming one, I think," she said, "but certainly inferior to mine."

She was looking not at the harpsichord, but at the white, blond, blue-eyed slave child I held in my arms . . . her half brother.

CHAPTER 29

MONTICELLO, OCTOBER 1800

What security for domestic purity and peace there can be where every man has had two connections, one of which must be concealed; and two families. . . .

HARRIET MARTINEAU, *Society in America*, 1837

The organ of justice, is the couple considered as a personal duality, forming by the contrast of attributes a complex being, the social embryo. . . . Nature in man and woman is not by consequence, the same. Moreover, it is through him that the conscience of both of them opens onto justice, each one becomes for the other at the same time witness, judge and a second self. Being in two personages, this couple is the real human subject.

PROUDHON, *Pornocracy or Women in Modern Time* [published in 1875]

The Richmond Jail, Sept. 13, 1800

SIR,

Nothing is talked of here but the recent conspiracy of the Negroes. One Nicholas Prosser, a young man who had fallen heir, sometime ago, to a plantation within six miles of the city, had behaved with great barbarity to his slaves. One of them, named Gabriel, a fellow of courage and intellect above his rank in life, laid a plan of revenge. Immense numbers immediately entered into it, and it has been kept with incredible secrecy for several months. A number of swords were made in a clumsy enough manner out of rough iron; others by breaking the blade of a scythe in the middle, which thus made two swords of a most formidable kind. They were well fastened in proper handles, and would have cut off a man's limb at a single blow. The conspirators were to have met in a wood near Prosser's house, upon Saturday before last, after it was dark. Upon that day, or some very short time before it, notice was received by a fellow, who being invited, somewhat unguardedly, to go to the rendezvous, refused, and immediately informed his master's overseer. No ostensible preparations were, however, made until the afternoon preceding the night of the rendezvous, and as the militia are in a state of the most contemptible disorganization, as the blacks are numerous, robust, and desperate, there must have been bloody work. But upon that very evening, just about sunset, there came on the most terrible thunderstorm, accompanied with an enormous rain, that I ever witnessed in this state. Between Prosser's and Richmond, there is a place called Brook Swamp, which runs across the high road and over which there was a bridge. By this the Africans were of need to pass, and the rain had made the passage impracticable. Besides they were deprived of the junction and assistance of their good friends in the city, who could not go out to join them. They were to have attacked the Capital and the penitentiary. They could hardly have failed of success, for after all, we only could muster four or five hundred men of whom not more than thirty had muskets. This was our state of preparation while several thousand stands of arms were piled up in the Capital and penitentiary. I do not pretend to blame the executive council, for I really am not sufficiently master of the circumstances to form an opinion. Five fellows were hung this day and many more will share the same fate. This plan was to massacre all the whites, of all ages and sexes, and all the blacks who would not join them; and then march off to the mountains with the plunder of the city. Those wives who should refuse to accompany their husbands were to have been butchered along with the rest, an idea truly worthy of any African heart. It convicts with my knowledge that many of the wretches, who were, or would have been, partners in the plot, have been treated with the utmost tenderness by their owners and more like children than slaves. . . .

I read through the rest of the letter, which dealt with general political opinions, and to the name of the sender: Thomas T. Callender. I fixed the name in my mind, then handed the letter my master had asked me to read back to him.

"I suppose you already know all about it," the familiar voice added with something like sadness.

Indeed, the slave intelligence had brought the news long before now, and the story of Gabriel Prosser was already legend.

Davey Bowles had brought the first news and told me of the uprising. Gabriel Prosser and Jack Bowler had been the leaders of the insurrections. Gabriel, a handsome, twenty-four-year-old giant of six-foot-three and his comrade Jack, three inches taller and four years older, had organized more than a thousand men in Henrico County. Brilliant and literate, he had carefully planned his rebellion. Gabriel's wife, Nanny, had been active as well, as were his brothers Solomon and Martin. They had all been betrayed by a fellow servant called Ben Wolfolk, who had heard of the conspiracy through two loose-mouthed slaves, George Smith and Samuel Bird. The insurrection was to have taken place on the first of September; the rendezvous for the rebels had been a brook six miles from Richmond. Eleven hundred men were to have assembled there and were to have been divided into three columns. All were to have marched to Richmond under the cover of night.

The rebels had counted heavily on the French, whom they had understood to be at war with the United States, for the money that was due them, and that a warship, which would help them, had landed at South Key. If successful in this first stage, the penitentiary in Richmond had enough arms, the powderhouse was well stocked, the capital contained the state treasury, the mills would give them bread, the control of the bridge across the James River would keep off enemies from beyond. Thus secured, they had planned to issue a proclamation summoning to their standard of red silk, with the words "Liberty or Death" printed on it, their fellow slaves and humanitarian whites. In a week, they had estimated they would have had fifty thousand rebels and could have taken other towns. In case of failure, they were to retreat into the mountains, as the rebellious slaves of Santo Domingo had done.

There had been intimations all summer of insurrection in Richmond, and the white table talk had been ominous with it. Yet the attack itself had surprised and shaken them. Why? I wondered, when they all lived, black and white, with this threat every day of every year. The whites had been surprised and unprepared. Only treachery had prevented success—treachery and God, for the appointed day had been prey to the most furious storm ever known to Virginia's memory. Why? I asked myself again and again. A tempest had burst upon the land instead of insurrection. The governor of Virginia, Master Monroe, had called in the United States Cavalry and the hangings had begun. I looked at the date on the letter. It was already outdated. Gabriel Prosser was already dead. Captured by treachery on a schooner in Norfolk, he had been brought back to Richmond in chains. There he had manifested the utmost composure and taking all the responsibility onto himself, had conducted himself as a hero, and had made no confession. Now, I looked at a fourth letter. Master Monroe was writing to Thomas Jefferson for advice. How to stop the hangings? More than thirty-five had gone to the gallows, and the Richmond jails were groaning with prisoners. They had suspended the trials. If they hanged everybody, they would annihilate the blacks in that part of the country.

"I think there has been enough hanging."

Why, when he kept so many things from me, did he want to share this particular burden? Did I not already have enough to bear? He knew that I could never come down on his side in this.

My lover looked at me with surprise.

"You know about the hangings?"

"Yes."

"You know how many?"

"Rumor has it forty or fifty, with hundreds waiting to be tried."

"Governor Monroe doesn't know what to do. Here, look at this."

I read Master Monroe's letter.

"All I can say is," I said, "you can't kill every slave in Virginia."

He got up from his desk and came toward me. "No," he said slowly, "you can't kill every one." He took the letter from my hands and went back to his desk. "When to stay the hand of the executioner is an important question. Those who have escaped from immediate danger must have feelings which dispose them to extend the executions. . . ."

"I still say there's been hanging enough. You can't kill everyone."

I thought of the new seed planted in my womb. A new slave.

"You must understand," I began, "they are not felons or common malefactors, but persons guilty of what our society obliges us to treat as a crime, and which their feelings represent in a far different shape—"

"I know this," he interrupted. He was turned away from me, the frightened, imploring letter of Master Monroe still in his hand.

He turned toward me but did not approach. He was afraid of me. He could forget in private, but he could never forget in public.

More to himself than to me, he said, "It is certain that the world at large will forever condemn us if we indulge or go one step beyond necessity."

At the word "necessity," I looked into his eyes but said nothing.

"Our situation is indeed a difficult one," he continued, "for I doubt if those people can ever be permitted to go at large among us with safety."

"Then exile them! The French and British do so," I begged. "Those people" were my people! Even as we spoke, he forgot. Banishment. Was that not James's choice? I pressed my palms to my womb. If I could save one . . . just one of them.

"I have thought of it," he said. "Surely the legislature would pass a law for their exportation, the proper measure as you have pointed out on this, and . . . all similar occasions."

I thought again of Gabriel Prosser. He had died on the gallows with ten of his men and with hundreds in the Richmond jail waiting to be tried and hanged, but they, the slaves, didn't believe it. Already there was a song that had started somewhere on some plantation, and was now winging from slave quarter to slave quarter. Prosser, the song went, didn't die on the gallows, but escaped with the help of a young slave boy named Billy. He lived to rise again. We were not about to let Gabriel Prosser die. He would rise again. Another black man would rise to take his place just as he had at Santo Domingo. My master looked down into my eyes.

"Exile them," I whispered.

Relief broke over his face. "Thank you," he said, and his eyes were filled with an ineffable tenderness. He, for the first time in his life, had a glimpse of the terror of slavehood and loving me he had acknowledged this terror. On this mountain, his eyes seemed to say, we can hold everything at bay, even this.

Shyly he reached out and touched me. He still seemed afraid of me. "Let me work now," he said.

I suffered his touch, but my mind was ablaze. There were so many things I wanted to say.

I turned and left him to his letters. I climbed the miniature stairs at the foot of his bed to my room. It was not until my master had left for Philadelphia, the balloting for the presidency still in doubt, that I heard that the last of Gabriel's condemned rebels had been reprieved and banished from Virginia by James Monroe.

I had not pleaded in vain.

CHAPTER 30

OCTOBER 1800

JAMES CAME HOME. He had arrived from France more than a year ago, and we dreamed to hold him at Monticello until the summer. He had seen his ex-master in Philadelphia.

"Thomas Jefferson says my journeys will end up on the moon! If only it could be so, for I am tired of this earth and its inhabitants!"

"When did you see him? How is he?"

My brother looked at me in disgust.

"He is fine. Embroiled in politics, as usual, and complaining about it, as usual. Burwell sends his love. Your master has no stomach to govern men. He says, 'I leave to others the sublime delight of riding the storm, better pleased with sound sleep and a warm berth below, with the society of neighbors, friends, and fellow laborers of the earth, than of spies and sycophants. . . .' So, I guess he misses you, sister. He can't decide whether he wants to be vice-president or not. Certainly, according to the newspapers and the backstairs, they are giving him a hard time. He looked so worried and despondent, I proposed that he join me on my next voyage to Spain to forget his troubles."

"Spain!"

Both Elizabeth Hemings and I exclaimed at the same time. We were sitting in one of the cellars next to the kitchens where it was cool. We had stuffed James with everything good we could find to eat in the pantries. He was wearing the latest French fashions and looked splendid. Men no longer wore breeches, but long pants, slender, and tight, and tucked in tall boots. The colors had changed as well—no more rose satin or pale-blue silk. Frock coats were shorter, fuller, in dark colors with high collars and white linen swathed the chest and neck up to the ears. James no longer wore his hair long; it was cropped short in a mass of curls.

"But why Spain?" we asked.

"And why not Spain? As I told your master, it is the only country not fighting, or getting ready to fight, with France! Don't think that France is any party since the Revolution; we had only the beginnings of it that October of eighty-nine, and the stories we've heard here are nothing compared to the reality. When I arrived in France, I had hoped to find work with one of the great houses I had known when we were there. Only I learned that most of the great houses were closed, or gutted and burned, their owners and occupants either in exile or gone to the guillotine, like the poor king and his queen. And the 'citizens,' as they call everyone now, were looking askance at the servant class as well. Many cooks' and valets' heads came off along with their masters'. Petit knew what he was doing to leave when he did.

"Once Robespierre was dead, it was thought that the bloodletting would be finished, but it goes on even now. There is civil and foreign war. Everyone is attacking France or getting ready to attack her. Because of the upheaval, there had no been no planting and therefore no harvest. There is no bread and no money. People pray only for a deliverer. The Estates General is paralyzed. Everything—everything is chaos, yet your Jefferson still hopes for victory for the Revolution. Nothing but a miracle will save France now. Never did I think the fine house of the old Comtesse de Noailles on the Ile Saint-Louis would be gutted and burned to the ground; as well as the Hermitage, and the Tuileries Palace. There was no trace of the Bastille, but think on this: they destroyed Marly as well. Nothing is left."

Marly. So it too was gone.

"And all of Master Jefferson's friends?" I asked.

"How changed their fortunes are now! Lafayette is in a prison at Magdeburg. Madame de Corny is a widow and has retired to Rouen with a pittance she salvaged from her jewels. Mrs. Cosway has gone into a convent at Genoa. Monsieur de Condorcet escaped from a hanging indictment, and is a fugitive. The Duc de la Rochefoucauld was torn to pieces by a mob before the eyes of his mother and wife. Those who have not been separated from their heads are either in exile or in prison. The Directory could well use the Bastille we tore down!" James licked his lips.

The recital of murder and trials went on long into the night. We listened at first with horror and interest; then numbness set in as the litany went on and on. James took delight in the demise of one great aristocrat after another. His hard eyes glinted when he told the tales of the Terror and Jacobins and finally Robespierre's death. Now there was the chaos and civil war of the Directory.

"We Americans didn't have a revolution worth talking about," James continued. "We're just as much slaves now as in 1776! We're just as much slaves under a vice-president and a president as we were under a British governor. They still import as many slaves into this so-called Republic. If the French could make an insurrection with stones and pitchforks, why can't we?"

"James, hush your mouth!" Elizabeth Hemings cried.

But there was no master here to overhear what we said. I was the mistress of Monticello.

"I'm trying to say, Mama, that there are thirty thousand slaves in the state of Virginia alone. In South Carolina, we outnumber the whites. . . . Thirty thousand Virginia slaves . . . that's an army. You realize that? An army!"

My mother rose as if to block the very words out of James's mouth. But who was listening?

We moved outside and I watched the mountains turn gold, red and silver as the sun dipped. James's eyes glowed, feverish as ever. The low-hanging smoke from the slave fires dimmed the pink of the sky, and the buzz of night creatures mingled with the droning of James's familiar voice.

What did I really feel? Horror, vengeance, delight, sorrow, indifference . . . yes, indifference was the closest to this tight stony feeling that pushed itself up into my heart.

"Lord, you know that sounds like some slave revolt!"

"That's what I mean, Mama, if you could see what the Revolution—theirs, not ours—brought down as we saw it, then you would know that anything is possible!"

"But them aristocrats," my mother said slowly, "was weak."

"And our masters are strong? Those white people were just like us; militia and passes, and lynchings . . . Just like us, Mama! Can you understand a little of what I'm trying to say to you?"

"I understand more than you think, James Hemings. I understand when you talk about revolution and how many slaves there is in Virginia and how our masters with all they privileges ain't no stronger than that King Louis. I understand you just like anybody got two cents' worth of brains understands you. But I know what we *ain't* got, and what we ain't got is a leader to lead us. A Moses. We ain't got him. He ain't come and unless he do, we ain't going nowhere. You talking about people who followed because they was *led.* I'm ready to follow, but who's going to lead? All the white folks get together even if the poor trash can't stand the rich white folks. They get together from all the plantations to put it down. Make an example of the leaders, put the fear of the Lord into everybody. France got some troubles on its hands, and I don't think what they be needing is a pastry cook. What they need is somebody, one body to pull their coals out of the fire, not their petit fours. . . ."

"I don't intend to go anywhere near an aristocrat or a citizen, for that matter," James said, "but where there's war, there's money. That I learned from our politicians and bankers up in Philadelphia. And I intend to make a fortune. I came back for just one reason—to get my sister. You coming, Sally Hemings?" James's voice cracked onto the still air like thunder in my ears and I sat up struck by it.

"Come with you?" I whispered.

"Nothing stopping you," he said.

"Nothing . . . except two children."

"Leave them with Mama and come back and get them, or take them with you. I don't care which."

"You don't know what you're saying, James. I couldn't—"

Without warning, James's face contorted with rage. "Mama, listen to her. You hear her! Mama!" It was a scream. "Eight years and she hasn't learned anything! After all the promises in Paris, it took him seven years to free me, and I got thirty dollars and a horse. I traded freedom for promises, because I thought he loved me: a few cooking lessons in Virginia, and I ended up giving him seven years of my life for thirty dollars and a horse, and I even said *'Merci, Monsieur.'* He promised her her children would be free at twenty-one, pokes out her stomach with his bastards, says he loves her, and she says, *'Merci, Monsieur.'* Fool!"

"Coward!" I screamed. "Afraid to steal yourself! Why didn't you run? Why? What stopped you? And now, look at you! More than five years of freedom and what do you have to show for it? Nothing!"

"And you do? I suppose. You could have made more in a bordello!"

"What do men make of the world for women except a bordello!"

"And you revel in it!"

"Men revel in it! Lovers and husbands, brothers and uncles—you all revel in it! My whoredom is yours and you know it!"

"I know it," he cried, "and it never leaves me, even in sleep. I want only to forget it! To leave you to it, if you want it!"

"Then leave me to it. Leave me, leave me!" I screamed.

"I'll never leave you to it as long as I have breath in my body, as long as I dream at night."

"We all have dreams," I said deliberately. "You think yours are special, but they are not. I've had enough of chasing eleven-year-old dreams of Paris."

"You sound just like him.'Enough of chasing rainbows...' Stay where you are. Lay up money. Be a good ex-slave. Make something of yourself. And I look at him. I look at those cold blue eyes and I say, 'You've already made something of me...' and the bastard doesn't even understand what I'm talking about."

"James, you got to stop hating yourself." This was Elizabeth Hemings speaking. Her voice trembled in a way I had never heard before. My brother's violence had undone her. I realized she was afraid of her son. She who was afraid of nothing.

"Mama, you ain't got no idea what hate is," James said.

"I guess I ain't," replied my mother.

"Women! Somebody cover you with dung and you wipe it off, wrap it up and start crooning a lullaby over it."

"You better go on back over there across the water, son."

"I'm going, Mama. I just want to know, for the last time, if she's coming with me." He turned to me and his eyes were dark burning holes and the look in them was the same he had turned on my master that Christmas Day five years ago.

"You coming, Sally Hemings?"

"No," I said.

"I'm never coming back here for you again. Save yourself, sister."

"No, James."

This time I could not keep the pride out of my voice. Was I not the legatee of my half sister? I had love. Did I not have a room of my own? I had privacy. Did I have a white mistress? No, I did run this place. Had I not saved ten black men from certain death? I had power. How could my brother speak of saving myself. I had no need to.

James looked out. The sense of desolation he had carried all these years enveloped him with the familiarity of an old friend. Loneliness. Dislocation. Thomas Jefferson's pompous proclamation had no more freed him than his own impotent declarations in Paris so long ago, he thought to himself. No piece of paper ever would, he had finally realized. Happiness had dissolved before him. The future no longer stretched before him full of hope, but swerved back onto itself and his past. He was not free. Only if he took Sally away . . . freed *her*, would he feel truly emancipated. Why, James wondered to himself, did he need the freedom of Sally Hemings? He looked at his sister. Suppose she never left Thomas Jefferson? Never left Monticello? What would become of him, James, who needed her freedom more than he needed his own?

James left Virginia for Spain on an English ship out of Norfolk sailing for Gibraltar. At the end of December, his letters began to arrive. Sometimes his "You coming, Sally Hemings?" would echo like a heartbeat on the page after page of fine script full of adventures and descriptions, plans, hopes, and dreams . . . always dreams, and the culmination of those dreams, always just one more letter away.

Many times that winter I thought of Richmond and Gabriel Prosser. The state capital was guarded these days by armed and uniformed sentinels and a permanent cordon of bayonets. This was the lasting memorial to Gabriel's defeat. The insurrection hung over the valley and all that was in it which was his.

I thought about what my master had said:

"An insurrection is easily quelled in its first effects, but far from being local, it will become general and whenever it does, it will rise more formidable after every defeat until one will be forced after dreadful scenes and sufferings to release them in their own way. . . ."

"And how?" I had asked.

"I don't know, but if something is not done, and done soon, we shall be the murderers of our own children. . . ."

Had he known what he was saying? I felt a numbness come over me.

"You must be chilled, my dear," he had said with a concerned voice. "Shall I ask Jupiter to come and light a fire for you?"

He could speak of murder and his children, and then his slave Jupiter . . .

The summer of 1800 that had just passed so quietly at home was also the summer that was, ballot by ballot, crowning my lover president of the United States. The scent of power had seeped into the mansion. The house had been abuzz with messengers, letters, newspapers, and visitors.

It seemed to me an omen that the duel for power between Thomas Jefferson and Aaron Burr came to an end while Jupiter lay dying. The faithful Jupiter was fifty-seven years old and he shared his birth year with his master, whom he had served since the age of fourteen. The handsome black face, gray now with illness and impending death, flooded with joy as I bent over his still bulky and powerful form to whisper the news of his master's presidency.

"I knowed from de beginnin' at Willam' an' Mary dat Masta Jefferson was gon' be first in de lan'. . . ."

The words in their soft slur escaped me at first, and I bent closer to the pain-racked body in order to hear.

"Uncle Jupiter, I have greetings for you from Master Jefferson. He says you get well and he bring you up to Washington City to the president's house. . . ." I slipped into the slave dialect: "He say you younger than him by four months and you ain't got no business gettin' all sick without his permission. And you shore ain't got no permission to lay out and die on him. . . . He says ol' Davey Bowles, he can't drive his bays like you. Say he tearin' up dem bays, dat young pip . . ." My eyes filled with tears as I soothed the old man, the soft Virginia drawl falling as easily from my lips as the French I sometimes spoke with Polly. "Full-blooded bays, Masta Eppes bought fo' Masta Jefferson's carriage in Washington. You'll be seated behin' dem, Uncle Jupiter. . . . They's de mos' spirited, de mos' showy, de mos' beautiful. . . . They cost de masta sixteen hundred dollars. Best horses in Washington . . . first in de lan' . . ."

We had called the black doctor from Milton and the white doctor from Charlottesville. My mother had strained her knowledge of herb remedies to the limit, but nothing had helped.

"Uncle Jupiter," I said softly, "you wan' som' milk bread? Try a little, Mama made it jus' fo' you. . . ." But he could not hear my words; my mother closed his eyes, and, on either side of him, Martha and I knelt. I was going to have to write my master that his beloved Jupiter was dead.

The news of Jupiter's death spread throughout the household, and then out toward the slave quarters and outlying plantations. The slaves began to gather for the wake, a low moan lapping up the mountain from the underside of Monticello.

It was at the funeral of Jupiter that most of the slave population learned that they were now the property of the president of the United States.

CHAPTER 31

MONTICELLO, 1801

HE CAME HOME for the first time as president. Except for Maria, who was too ill to come to Monticello, everything on his mountain was safe and at peace.

He was proud. He was loved, not only in his own domains but by the whole nation.

We watched a rainstorm break over Shadwell, far in the distance. From the north terrace, we could see the gray mists resting on the range that stretched for forty miles to the Chesapeake Bay. In the distance, we could see the low-hanging clouds of a spring storm, which looked like a theater set to the two of us standing in the weak April afternoon sun.

He had built not only power last summer but his mansion, which had taken its final shape. I could feel its space, every foot of its masonry, every inch of its brick and mortar, behind me like a fortress. He had overlooked no detail, had underplayed no effort toward perfection. He had goaded his master builders, John and Joe, into a sublimity of effort. His long-accumulated books, paintings, sculptures, and instruments—some of them in their cases since our return—had at last found their proper places. His curtains and draperies, china, silver, Persian rugs, linens, clocks had also been incorporated. His plants, his trees, his roses stretched in gigantic patterns on the west and south sides of the mansion. The house stood, a one-story brick building facing west, surmounted by an octagonal dome that camouflaged its second story, while the terracing and sloping of the mountain camouflaged the understory. The beautiful and perfectly proportioned façade, with its Doric columns and heavy cornice and balustrades, looked over the vast lawns and gardens down onto the valley, and out onto the world. Behind that façade, which had taken so long to build, his slave and white families lived with his other possessions.

He looked down at me. "Look at the rain clouds," he said. "It rains, it storms, and yet we feel not one drop."

"It thunders, too," I said, as the first rumblings of the spring storm's fury was carried over the distance of the mountain.

"And it lightens as well," he laughed as the sky beyond us burst white. "Yes, we are not lit by it."

"And thank God," I said.

We stood watching the shower. The servants would be lighting the candles in a little while and setting the table for eight places, even for his solitary dinner, in the rosewood-paneled dining room off the center hall.

I knew what he was thinking.

His Eden was complete.

In another month, there would be a new addition to our family. He wanted a girl, so I prayed for one, for him. A president's daughter.

"If it is a girl, name her Harriet, after our Harriet," he had said.

"And if it is a boy?"

"Then name him James."

I knew he was happy. I begged him to await the birth. He had never been present at the birth of any of my children. Again, he left me to the final weeks of waiting.

On the eighth of May, the very anniversary of the birth of his last child by my half sister Martha, whose death had begun the journey to my destiny, I gave birth to my fifth child.

I named her Harriet, as I had promised.

My mother was not pleased. "Martha Jefferson did the same thing," she said, "and she lost both of them Lucy Elizabeths. Don't name this daughter Harriet, Sally."

"Her father wants her named Harriet. He's lost one Harriet, and he wants another. This one will survive."

"Not for you or him to say if she gonna live or die. God has still got some rights, even in Virginia. Masta may be president, but he aint' got that last power—life and death, and well he should know it!"

"You're just superstitious, Maman, it doesn't make any difference what her name is. You sound like one of those Indian squaws who dress their son up like a girl so that God won't know he's a male."

Yet, even as I argued with Elizabeth Hemings, the sense of doom that had plagued me since Gabriel's insurrection took hold of me. I looked down on the ivory-skinned, auburn-haired infant sleeping in my arms, another Harriet, and pressed her to my breast. She would survive. And she would survive to live free.

"My Martha named that second Lucy Elizabeth after the dead one, when I told her—"

"I don't care what you told your precious Martha Wayles. I don't care what Martha Jefferson did or didn't do. I'm not Martha Wayles. I am me! Martha Wayles Jefferson is nothing to me, nor do I want her to be."

"She's your sister, if you like it or not, and I told her—"

"Mama! I don't care if she was my sister or not! She has nothing, *nothing* to do with me or my children. This is my Harriet. Mine and Thomas Jefferson's."

"This is the first time in my life, daughter, I ever heard you call him by his name." There was amazement in her voice. "Lord, child, what's the matter? I know who you are, I know you not your half sister. I'm your mother, not hers, though it's true I loved her. But you can't ever say I loved her more than I love you."

"You did, Mama. Admit it. You've said it a million times. Your white daughters. Your sweethearts."

Anger now hung like a cloud between us. I had hurt her. But I had not been able to stop myself.

"No, child," she said, "it's not like you say. I guess I am like that Indian squaw. I pretend I love you less so that God won't punish me by bringing hurt on you. I'm only afraid for you. You won't fight for yourself. You won't protect yourself. I only want that. That you fight for yourself and your children, that's all. I didn't mean no offense."

We looked at each other. She didn't understand. I was fighting. I was fighting him. I was fighting love, slavery, and Virginia.

"No, Mama, you never mean any offense," I said.

"But, daughter, you might suckle her yourself and not give her over to a wet-nurse like you did the others."

I tightened my hold on Harriet. Martha Randolph was pregnant and ready to bear. My mother always made it a point to remind me that Martha nursed all her babies.

"Now don't go getting resentful about nursing," she said, as if she had read my mind. "You careful, it won't hurt your bosom any. Martha Randolph done suckled all her children, and she still got a beautiful bosom. Pretty enough for any man to lay his head on."

I don't know why, but I started to cry. Sobs of rage and scalding resentment shook me. What did I want? He loved me. What did I want? He listened to me. What was it then I wanted?

My mother took me in her arms. Her face next to mine was dark and cloudy.

The summer meant the return to Monticello of my master's white family. Thomas and Beverly were swept up in the ever-increasing swarm of children, slave and white, that mingled in total freedom all the summer months. My Thomas, red-headed and gray-eyed, romped on the west lawn with Thomas Jefferson Randolph, red-headed and blue-eyed; and the Randolph girls, all dark like their father with his Indian blood. Anne and Ellen found in blue-eyed Beverly the perfect doll. Martha Randolph had proudly announced to my mother, much to her vexation, that she was again "expecting." My mother had wanted only me to give birth this year.

A test of power at Monticello between Martha and me had been postponed by the simple expedient of letting my mother keep the huge iron ring of house keys that hung at her waist. My mother, now sixty-six, knew her position as dowager queen could not last much longer. Nevertheless, while she ruled, she ruled, and it was to her that all the children, Martha's and mine, turned to as ultimate arbitrator and bounty-giver. I knew my mother secretly feared that I would never have the will to fight for Monticello. She had often said that once she let the reins of power go, it would be Martha, not me, who would take her place. But she didn't know that Monticello had been promised to me by my master.

It was bad enough that I could not take my place at the head of the table at Monticello. But that Martha should wear the keys . . . never!

The summer was hot and humid. The heavy perfume of jasmine, honeysuckle, and peach blossoms exuded a sweet, deep, dangerous sensuality. It was the heat, I suppose, and some mysterious chemistry that seemed to combine into a volatile mixture of sullen arrogance and irritability. The mountain reeked of that climate that bred fevers and sudden violence.

Both Maria and Martha were coming home to give birth. Maria arrived first. She was enduring her second difficult confinement, still a semi-invalid, suffering the complications of her first child's birth. She brought, as usual, her own servants. They were Monticello slaves that had been given to her on her marriage and who found their friends and family again. They included her personal maid, her coachman, her cook, her outriders, her nurse, and several of their children.

Next came Martha Randolph, heavy with her sixth child, along with all her children, Anne, Thomas Jefferson, Ellen Wayles, and Virginia. Both her husband and Maria's were in Washington City and would arrive in August with their body servants, coachmen, horses, and luggage.

I greeted my nieces with my babe in arms. We were genuinely glad to see one another. The winter had been long and lonely. Maria, ill all of the time, isolated at Bermuda Hundred, enjoyed the added attention, the music, the conversation, and her father's triumphal presence. After only five years of marriage, her bright beauty had washed away to the almost transparent delicacy of a much older woman. As for Martha, her big-boned and robust body had already settled into middle age. Her face had hardened with the bitter struggle against her husband's erratic and increasingly uncontrollable behavior. After several years of relative lucidity, Thomas Mann Randolph was again slipping back into the melancholy and depression which were the harbingers of his insanity. All the weary travels from doctor to doctor, from cure to cure, had not helped him. More and more Martha looked forward to summers at Monticello with her father. Like him, she too suffered from violent migraines that disappeared only on the mountain.

There were now thirty-two servants for six white people, including the children. Before the summer was over, there would be as many sleeping guests.

We settled into our positions, re-establishing the old accommodation and bonds among ourselves. We girded for the arrival of the men, who must at all cost be recaptured, comforted, redomesticated, and spoiled after their long absences. The air, as always, again became heavy with jealousies and unrealized dreams.

All this would focus itself on Thomas Jefferson. All the loves and hates and jealousies of Monticello would gravitate toward its center, my master. Calm and possessed, he would ride above the often stormy, half-smothered passions that struggled around him, both at home and in Washington; and by his fierce will, would repress any open violence. He would turn a deaf ear to the problems of all of the women on the mountain. And we dared not intrude upon him. He wanted peace. And he wanted his façade of perfection. He would not tolerate less. And I, I tolerated Martha and Maria on their summer visits, but they were not the mistresses of Monticello. I was. That was our covenant. He had promised.

Even before the men's arrival, the first bad news of the summer had filtered into Monticello. Danby Carr, the youngest of the hot-tempered Carr brothers, had been involved in a duel. He had severely wounded his opponent and had been arrested. Danby had rowed across the James River in the early dawn, cocked his pistols at a friend, and half-killed him, then had gone bragging all over Milton and Charlottesville on the quality of his pistols and the cowardliness of his target. Peace? If Thomas Jefferson thinks he is going to have peace, I thought, he had better think again. Depressed, I began trying to keep order among the slaves, to find rooms for the ever-increasing white family, which now included the Carrs and Jefferson's sister, a poor relative. I suppressed the dark foreboding of the months to come and lifted my own burdened and disappointed heart to my task.

The August sun beat down on his back and bared head. It was the second time he was riding up his mountain as president. He had taken his saddled horse and mounted up at Shadwell, leaving the phaeton with Davey Bowles and Burwell, and had gone galloping ahead, his still reddish hair brushed back by the wind. Thomas Jefferson returned depressed and convinced that his robust constitution had finally failed him, stricken with a dysentery that had not left him since he had taken office. He had also begun to keep track of the deaths of the signers of the Declaration of Independence with the same precision as he noted the singing of Dick, his mockingbird.

The death of Jupiter had struck fear into his own heart. . . . Not without bitterness, he remembered that neither Martha nor Maria had written to congratulate him on his election as president. He had won by a hairbreadth over Burr, and now he would have to crush his power as well as the lingering residue of Federalist influence.

Thomas Jefferson looked up at the tall Virginia pines. He was haunted with death. The bursting mountainside underlined the tragedy of that other summer, so many years ago, when his great love had let life go, after giving birth to a girl child, now also dead. It was the nineteenth anniversary of Martha Jefferson's death. And now, in fear, he clung to the image of his slave wife who gave birth easily.

He reined in his bay Wildair, and sat slumped under the arched green vaults of his own forest, the bridle paths leading up the west slope, etched by the years of riding his own favorites. The dappled sunlight played about his broad shoulders, and the flanks of his horse.

He had left Washington City in a state of weariness. His illness, the unfinished president's house, the strain of political life had taken a toll on his state of health. His migraines, which had not tormented him since he had left France more than ten years before, were plaguing him again. His estates were slipping, and the Wayles legacy of debt was still not resolved. Yet, he thought, raising his head, the mountain was still there; a young mother waited for him at the top; his two daughters, and his grandchildren were within his embrace. He dug his spurs into the sweating flank of Wildair, urging him faster and faster up the mountain.

My master returned with the news that James was back on these shores. James had written to me all last year, wild incoherent letters filled with impossible dreams of fame and fortune, as he wandered from one European capital to another in the wake of refugees fleeing the wars of Napoleon. He still begged me to leave Monticello. Like some flying eagle, he had dipped and swooped above my head, rattling my nest with the beating of his wings, always with his lure and song of freedom. But I had known he would be back. James had turned his back on his former master, and had refused to come to Monticello, or even send greetings to me, his own sister.

The master ensconced himself in his private apartments, reading and writing in the morning, appearing for dinner, then riding out for hours in the afternoon. Only I was allowed entrance into his chambers where he worked, often morose and depressed. Yet, he appeared without fail at the supper table, cheerful and serene.

All the children, black and white, competed for the attention and love of the master; all fought for their places in the sun.

In August, Martha went into labor. The double-faced clock on the east patio rang hour after hour, as the birth, despite the ease of the previous ones, proved to be a long and difficult one. My mother and I sat on either side of Martha's plank as the midwife, Ursula, struggled silently to bring forth the new life. Martha's labor had begun the night before, and now, well into the end of the day, her eyes were glazed with pain and exhaustion. Our dresses clung to us in the August heat, but we could not throw open the windows that were sealed shut, nor douse the fire that burned in the hearth. Martha moaned, filling me with dread. I thought of Maria, no more than a month away from her travail. I had so begged Maria to attempt no more children, just as my mother had begged Maria's mother before her; but now there was no time to think of Maria. There were only Martha's moans, and finally only her screams; almost eighteen hours after the first pains, the girl child came at last.

Downstairs, the white family waited as I descended to announce the birth of a girl, who would be named Virginia. During the long hours of labor I had a premonition of the awaited test of power. Two days after Virginia's birth, when Martha's milk had not come, it happened.

"You will wet-nurse Virginia, Sally. You have plenty of milk." Before I could answer my mother answered for me.

"There's no need for that, Mistress. There's two newly delivered slave women. I'll send for Sulky for you."

"I don't want Sulky, Mammy Hemings, I want Sally. She will be the one to nurse Virginia. After all, she doesn't have anything else to do!"

"But, honey, your milk will come, it always do, and meanwhile Sulky, she much better, she's—"

"I said I want Sally to do it."

My mother shrugged and turned away. This was between Martha and me. She watched with horror as I took the white infant, and with tears of rage streaming down my cheeks, pressed her to my breast.

Virginia's birth was celebrated for two days. The school bell rang, the slaves were issued whisky and the children candy; the white family celebrated with French champagne in a state of happy relief.

It was in this festive atmosphere that Danby Carr attempted to seduce my sister Critta. Critta belonged to Peter Carr, who was the father of her children, and neither of the other Carr brothers had ever dared to coerce my haughty and beautiful sister.

I was sorting linen with Elizabeth Hemings when Critta, pale and distraught, burst in on us.

"Mama, Masta Carr messing with me!"

My mother didn't look up from her sorting.

"Which Masta Carr?" she asked.

"Danby!"

We both knew the danger. Danby had always been jealous of Peter over Critta. Now he was bloodied, he had decided to challenge him, and Samuel, the eldest brother, was probably egging him on. Danby had just fought one duel. . . . Trouble. They were spoiling for trouble.

"He put his hands on you?" Elizabeth Hemings asked.

"Not yet."

"He going to?"

"He got a mind to. You know what Masta Peter do to me, he find out?"

"Did you tell him yourself?"

"Tell him?"

"Tell, tell on Danby? Tell Masta Peter he messing with you?" Elizabeth Hemings looked into my sister's hazel eyes. She was beautiful, but not too bright. Disgust drew down the corners of Elizabeth Hemings' mouth.

"It's the only way, Critta, 'less you want real trouble."

"I ain't looking for no trouble," Critta said. "I just want to be left alone."

"Well, you ain't going to be left alone with them boys around. Just try to stay out of their way. Don't get into any close quarters with him. Stick close to Masta Peter."

"But Peter's going to Richmond tomorrow."

"Then come stay with me. You can stay in my room. Don't sleep alone."

"He set on it," Critta said.

"Well, he can get set off it. Them nephews got enough slaves in trouble around here, including you."

"Why you suppose all a sudden? . . ."

"Jealous of Peter, feeling his oats with his dueling, showing off to Samuel—how should I know what goes on in white men's heads?" The helplessness of the situation caused a tremor in the hand Elizabeth Hemings placed on my sister's shoulder.

"If worse come to worse, I'll tell Masta Jefferson. There ain't nothing else I can do to protect you from a white man. Best you tell Peter first, then, if that don't work, I'll tell Masta."

"They'll fight," Critta said.

"Better they beat on each other than you! Let them kill each other." Anger shook my mother's voice.

"But what old Masta going to say he find out Danby and Peter fightin' over me?"

"There's going to be hell to pay," Elizabeth Hemings said grimly.

I could see Critta hesitate.

"I'll tell him," Critta finally said. "I'll tell him he come messing with me, I'll tell his brother."

"They'll all get thrown off here they make a ruckus. . . ."

Elizabeth Hemings looked at me after Critta had left. I could tell what she was thinking. Bad blood. Bad blood between brothers. Bad blood between Martha and me; all the pauper relatives feeding off the larder. . . . She began to count up the supplies the household had gone through this summer, then stopped. She started to laugh. She sat down hard and laughed until the tears poured down her face.

"White workers running rampant like a herd of goats through the slave quarters, relatives eating me out of house and home, and everybody come to me . . . the head slave in the harem! I hope . . . I hope Peter Carr beats the tar out of his brother!"

Elizabeth Hemings looked up at me. I didn't know if she was laughing or crying.

The fight between Danby Carr and his brother over Critta started in the ice cellar, where Critta had been cornered by Danby. Her son Jamey, who had gone to fetch his father, witnessed the fight of his father and his uncle over his mother. Critta was hurt in the fracas, having been pushed against a wall. Her wrist was broken and she had begged Martin to take Jamey off to Pantops after Jamey had tried to attack his father. Critta took shelter with me, and Maria promised she could go back to Bermuda Hundred with her when she returned. Critta went back to Peter Carr, and Danby left for his plantation.

Maria's baby came at the end of September, and, as feared, the birth was long and difficult and the child feeble. I didn't think there was that much blood in a human body, as we fought to stem its flow with teas and herbs. Finally, a doctor was called, and he recommended more bleeding to "rid" Maria of poisons that might lead to infection. On this murderous note, he left, after conferring with a distraught husband and father, who declined to follow his advice.

Little by little Maria fought her way back, willed to live by my mother and me, but the child continued to suffer convulsions. I took the infant Francis to my own breast as well.

No sooner had we suffered through Maria's recovery, as if God's own vengeance was sweeping down, a plague of the dreaded whooping cough swept through the children on the hill. Once again all of the women on the mountain were waging the fight against death to the children. All grudges were forgotten then as we joined in the struggle to preserve the fragile lives.

This time no child perished.

Exhausted, we parted, Martha and Maria returning to their plantations, Critta gratefully going along with Maria, leaving Elizabeth
Hemings and me alone on the hill to face the winter. Anything the
winter would bring, I thought, would be better than the summer just
past. But I was wrong.

The preparations for Christmas were under way; my chests of decorations had been taken down from the attic, the housecleaning and
baking already started. I was sitting, playing the new harpsichord,
when I heard the strangled cry of my mother and the heavy spurred
boots of Davey Bowles, who had ridden two days without stopping from
Washington City to arrive before the letter.

I had seen Davey Bowles lips moving, but it seemed to have taken
forever for the words to reach me.

It was the fourth day of December 1801. Davey had come to bring the
news of James's death.

He had been found dead under mysterious circumstances in Philadelphia, shot, perhaps by his own hand, although the weapon was
nowhere to be found. He was already buried in unconsecrated ground
up North. There had been no belongings, no letter, no message. Only
John Trumbull's silver-framed portrait of me and a small silver dagger
were found near his bedside. Davey handed them to me in silence as I
stood screaming James's name over and over again.

James's death seemed to herald the final calamity that was to befall
us.

From this day on, I would live like a perfect slave, in perfect love, and
this slavery and this love would be my strength and my fortress; never
would he forgive himself or his world for it, and never would he escape
from it. It would be the master who would be branded and bonded to
me forever. I would turn love against the possessor and daze him into
the everlasting hell of guilt! I vowed Thomas Jefferson would see only
what he wanted to in the silver-and-gilt mirror of my love and, with that
reflecting force, I would strike him down, blind him, commit arson
against him. And what arm would he have against it? If I could not hate
him, I would kill him with love. And if I could not kill him, I would
maim him forever, cripple and paralyze him, so that he would have no
possibility to walk away from me, no voice to deny me. A ruthless joy
took hold of me. I fled from the room and from the mansion out of doors.

I would free his sons.

CHAPTER 32

NOVEMBER 1802

If there is any country on earth where the course of true love may be
expected to run smooth, it is America.

HARRIET MARTINEAU, *Society in America*, 1837

THE RECORDER
Richmond
September 1st, 1802

It is well known that the man, *whom it delighteth the people to honor,*
keeps, and for many years past has kept, as his concubine, one of
his slaves. Her name is SALLY. The name of her eldest son is Tom.
His features are said to bear a striking though sable resemblance to
those of the President himself. The boy is ten or twelve years of age.
His mother went to France in the same vessel with Mr. Jefferson
and his two daughters. The delicacy of this arrangement must
strike every portion of common sensibility. What a sublime pattern
for an American ambassador to place before the eyes of two young
ladies!

If the reader does not feel himself disposed to pause we beg leave
to proceed. Some years ago, the story had once or twice been
hinted at in *Rind's Federalist*. At that time, we believed the surmise
to be an absolute calumny. One reason for thinking so was this: A
vast body of people wished to debar Mr. Jefferson from the presidency. . . .

By this wench Sally, our president has had several children.
There is not an individual in the neighbourhood of Charlottesville
who does not believe the story; and not a few who know it. . . .

'Tis supposed that, at the time when Mr. Jefferson wrote so
smartly concerning negroes, when he endeavoured so much to
belittle the African race, he had no expectation that the chief magistrate of the United States was to be the ringleader in shewing that

his opinion was erroneous; or, that he should choose an African stock whereupon he was to engraft his own descendants. . . .

Mute! Mute! Mute! Yes very Mute! will all those republican printers of political biographical information be upon this point. Whether they stir or not, they must feel themselves like a horse in a quick-sand. They will plunge deeper and deeper, until no assistance can save them.

If the friends of Mr. Jefferson are convinced of his innocence *they* will make an appeal of the same sort. If they rest in silence, or if they content themselves with resting upon a general denial, they cannot hope for credit. The allegation is of a nature too *black* to be suffered to remain in suspense. We should be glad to hear of its refutation. We give it to the world under the firmest belief that such a refutation *never can be made*. The AFRICAN VENUS is said to officiate as housekeeper at Monticello. When Mr. Jefferson has read this article, he will find leisure to estimate how much has been lost or gained by so many unprovoked attacks upon

J. T. CALLENDER.

"James T. Callender." I repeated that familiar name once again. "James T. Callender."

My mother burst into tears.

"Sweet Jesus! You mean that's printed in the newspaper for everyone to see?"

"Not only *The Recorder*, Mama, everywhere in Virginia, by the *Examiner*, in the *Virginia Gazette* in Lynchburg, in Fredericksburg, in Philadelphia, in Washington City, in New York." I had left out the parts she couldn't understand.

"But what does it mean, daughter?" For once, my mother didn't know what to say.

"It means, Mama, that they are attacking the master through me, to hurt him. They accuse him of many more dreadful things than miscegenation. They accuse him of being a coward, of trying to seduce another man's wife, of being an infidel. . . ."

My voice had broken. In truth, I knew so little, entombed here at Monticello. Maria and Martha certainly knew more, but refused to speak. Even Maria. So we remained in our cocoons of silence, not able to comfort one another. For once, the slave intelligence had been silent. Yet the plantations all knew. My shame was the common knowledge of every field hand in Virginia. The intelligence passed from those who could read to the multitudes who could not.

"And Thomas Jefferson, up in Washington City? What does he say?" my mother wanted to know.

"He doesn't say anything, Mama. He doesn't even know that I know about the newspaper articles."

"He ain't said *nothing* to you?"

"No."

"And to his friends? . . ."

"He has kept his silence. He has said nothing to no one."

"But it can't go on like this! He will sell you and the children . . . out of Virginia. O God, have mercy on us!"

"God," I said, "has nothing to do with this."

My mother looked up. "And Martha?"

"She knows as much as I, or perhaps more, but she is as silent as her father."

"And Maria?"

"Maria, too, is silent."

"All are silent?" my mother asked. Her voice was small in the empty, white-draped room where we sat facing each other, mother and daughter, two generations of white men's concubines.

"Oh, no. His friends are rallying around him, denying everything. Denying that I exist. Calling Callender the most foul and blasphemous slanderer ever to be born. Meriwether Jones, the editor of the *Richmond Enquirer*, has wished Callender in Hell by means of the James River. He's the one who wrote: 'Is it strange, therefore, that a servant of Mr. Jefferson's at a house where so many strangers resort, who is daily engaged in the ordinary vocations of the family life, like *thousands* of others, should have a mulatto child? Certainly not. . . .' "

My mouth twitched. *Certainly not.* I thought of my sister Critta, my half sister Mary, my mother's daughters, Nance and Betty. I thought of my mother, Elizabeth, and of her mother, the African. I thought of all black bondswomen everywhere in the South at God's and Fate's mercy. Thousands.

"But he, the masta, says nothing?"

"Nothing, Mama. Even this summer, when we were all ignorant of the danger, there were hints in the newspapers, but it is this one, Callender's story, that has caused all the furor."

There had been others, more serious because they had been closer to home, I thought. Callender was a foreigner, a Northerner, an enemy. These other men were friends and neighbors. The editor of the *Frederick-Town Herald*, for example, had been seen in Charlottesville, by Burwell and Davey Bowles, asking questions of servants and neighbors and townspeople and of the small outlying farmers who got their wood from Monticello. All those who had known my master from birth knew who I was. They knew who my mother was. There was one calumnious article after another, the most recent from the *Virginia Gazette*, whose article had asked the same questions and got the same answers. *"Why have you not married some worthy of your own complexion?"* one had written in an editorial.

My eyes filled with tears. I heard my master's voice: "Tell me who die . . . who marry, who hang themselves because they cannot marry. . . ."

I stared at the white back of one of the draped pale damask armchairs from the hotel in Paris, and fondled the richly carved wood.

"I believe he will never say anything to anyone about me."

"Daughter, you don't understand white men. They loves you. Sometimes all they lives. But when you go up against they real life, they white life, white friends, white children, white power, you got to lose. You got to be cut down. You got to be put away. Thomas Jefferson's real mistress is his politics. It was that way with Martha and it's that way with you. Nothing will stand in the way of that. No woman will ever keep him from that. Even a white wife would not have been as bad as this. . . . He will send you away. He has got to do it. His white folks will destroy him if he don't. At least he has got to say what is true is not true. . . ."

"He will not lie, and he cannot avow, so there is nothing left except silence," I said.

"Silence," Elizabeth Hemings spat out into the white room, "or sale."

For one moment my heart seemed to stop as she uttered the dreaded words. Sale! Had I lived too long in Monticello, hidden, petted, spoiled, and loved? Had I forgotten it was love that ceded, and not the white world? Then I said:

"He will not sell me, Mama. And he will not abandon me or send me or the children away. Not for me, not for his daughters, not for his friends, not for his enemies, not even for the presidency."

"And why, pray, daughter?"

"Because he cannot live without me."

It was true. I had made it so. This had been what I had wanted. There was no triumph, no smugness, no pride; there was not even joy in my voice. Only the reality of how it was between us.

"He cannot live without me." The words fell like pebbles in the room. They seemed to take a long time to reach my mother, as if they had been thrown down a deep well. But the words struck the sides of my being like flint against flint, and, like flint, struck fire in me. We had won.

"I'll have the keys to the mansion now, Mama."

After a moment, my mother unfastened the great iron ring with its score of keys. The dull glint of forged iron struck the light. Their metallic music was the only sound in the room except for the tick of the clock. I knew she would never understand. Why now? Why at a time when we had been betrayed by servants and neighbors, why, when everything was lost, when I should be fleeing for my life and those of my children, when I should be paralyzed with fear, why had I decided to stand, when I had never stood before? She would never understand. Yet I knew I was right. This was the line. This was the battle. This was the test that Thomas Jefferson would have to pass. If he passed this trial, it meant victory for us. A feeling almost of elation filled me. We had the power of love on our side. We were stronger and better than the monstrous iniquity we had sprung from. I held out my hands. My mother placed the mass of iron into them. I took the keys and weighed them, and then, without a word, attached them to the black ribbon at the waist of my black-and-white calico dress. The keys hung low and nestled into the folds of my skirt. Elizabeth Hemings recognized the orderly transition of power just as my master did; that day, Monticello had passed from one ruler to the next. Her reign was over.

"We wait, Mama," I said a moment later, "in silence. We wait and we let them rant and rave. But, if they really want to hear about Southern gentlemen and Negro mistresses, we have some stories to tell, no, Mama? We can start with John Marshall, the chief justice of the United States. Virginians talk in their sleep, you once said, Mama. And who hears them? Their servants."

Elizabeth Hemings looked at me with dawning respect. I hadn't spent three years in France for nothing.

"Now you know why Martha and Maria have left for Washington, when they have always refused until now," I said.

"To dampen the scandal by their presence."

"Yes. And to keep Dolley Madison from the head of the presidential table."

"I never could figure why they both left."

"Now you can. And now, I want the word spread among the slave population. My name is never again to be mentioned. Nor those of my children. To anyone black or white. I do not exist anymore, nor do my children. My name on our people's lips is forbidden. Forbidden! Spread it among our people, black and white, on pain of being fired or sold. And tell Jim I want to see him."

I dismissed my mother.

It was only when Fanny and Edy returned from Washington that I learned the amplitude and the viciousness of the campaign which had raged about us. It was from Fanny that I heard the part of a poem by the famous Irish poet Thomas Moore that referred to me, and that was making the rounds of the kitchens and salons in Washington and Virginia, in New York and Baltimore, in Boston and Philadelphia.

Fanny, who could write, had copied it out on the back of a sheet of butcher's paper in her large childish scrawl:

> The patriot, fresh from Freedom's council come,
> Now pleased retires to lash his slaves at home;
> Or woo, perhaps some black Aspasia's charms,
> And dream of freedom in his bondsmaid's arms.

I stared at the large printed letters. Freedom. What had I won? I had bound him to me as surely as I was bound to him. Nothing could change that. Not poems or ballads, not slander or insults, not the crudeness of mankind. My tears fell on the oiled paper and rolled off, making no mark, just as I made no mark on the surface of the world; except for these lewd cries of indignation, crude obscene scrawls, smirking winks of slander and perfidy.

Fanny's excited voice dented my thoughts.

"You is the most famous black lady in the whole United States! I tells you, you is famous! I saw a letter about you in a Philadelphia newspaper, but it was too long and hard for me to copy it. And in Washington—you is the talk of the town! But we servants don't say nothing about what we knows, or don't know. And poor Masta Jefferson—as if every Virginia gentleman that holds the title ain't messed with a black mistress. Why they family gives them one at sixteen or seventeen. How can they expect that they don't cherish them later? I do declare, white people are one strange breed of humanity. They do everything they want and then cry distress when they *do* gets around to people who don't do it, because they ain't got it to *do* it with! I do declare, I'm glad I got me a black husband. A good black man. And don't have to be sniffing after no white masta who is hell on earth!"

My mother looked at the bisquit-colored Fanny.

"Yo Mammy," she muttered.

"Yourn," replied Fanny, evenly, without blinking.

She was a match for my mother, and she knew it. Not only did she have the estimable advantage of being cook at the president's house, she could read and write as well. Fanny held Elizabeth Hemings' eye, but, before the onslaught came, I stepped between them.

"Enough, Fanny," I said. "I know you and Davey so tried Master Jefferson's patience with your squabbling that he sent for Mister Bacon to sell you both in Alexandria." I looked at her. "I trust you begged your way back into his good graces, since you are standing here and not on an auction block."

"I hear it's mostly died down," Fanny said contritely. "I expect it's finished, Sally. But Lord knows, it sure made a stir! You can't imagine. . . . Them white folks is outraged."

"Then let it be finished. Lord God. 'Cause we is sick of it at Monticello," Elizabeth Hemings said as she took Fanny by the shoulders, and with a slight push, propelled her toward the door of her kitchens.

He still would sell a slave in pique or to assure his domestic tranquillity. He was still white. He was still the master. And he was not the same in his white world. My master amongst white Americans was not the man I knew. I wished he would come home. I wished he would come home where he was safe and loved. People, I thought wearily, like horses, tire; and the uses of silence born and bred into every slave, would serve me well.

CHAPTER 33

MARCH 1803

Love is, in a great degree, an arbitrary passion, and will reign, like some other stalking mischiefs, by its own authority, without designing to reason.

MARY WOLLSTONECRAFT, *Vindication of the Rights of Women,* 1794

Duty's a slave that keeps the keys,
But love, the Master goes in and out
Of his goodly chambers with a song and shout
Just as he please—just as he please.

DINAH MARIA MULOCK CRAIK (date unknown)

IT WAS MARCH before Thomas Jefferson arrived again on his mountain. His slave family rushed to greet him. Thomas, Beverly, and Harriet. He seemed to hesitate in greeting them, then he saw her. She approached timidly.

"Thomas," she said softly.

"Thine own," he replied, adding his harsh short laugh.

"Thomas. Thomas. We . . . you cannot. The risk . . ." But the risk has already been taken. And pride had sealed it. They had won.

"The thermometer at sunrise today, my darling, was thirty-four degrees. I have marked it in my book. I have taken it every day for the past four months and I didn't drop the thermometer once."

His voice was husky and scarred as it was that day in Paris. She began to cry. She knew he would listen to no one, accept no advice, no opinions, nor have this passion discussed, revoked, diluted, appended, crossed out, objected to, or any part of it destroyed. She would not be excised. She would not be censored. She would not be discarded. She would remain at Monticello.

There was irony and love in his voice:

"Hold, little one," he said. "The peach trees begin to blossom and I see the well has plenty of water in it after having been dry for eighteen months."

She pressed her head into his chest, and his great hands came up and cupped her skull. Her tears wet his vest and shirt. Here was her victory, written in his haggard and loving face. They were like the lone survivors of an earthquake. It had shaken the mountain, but the mountain was still there.

Thomas Jefferson sat making delicate sketches of the plan for his new pleasure ground: a grove of the largest trees, shaded with poplar, oak, maple, linden, and his beloved ash trees. A green labyrinth, which had at its center a small temple: a safe place.

His troubles were far from over.

This trip was to try to avoid the possibility of a duel with his old friend John Walker over his wife. Callender had not stopped his pen. With the aid of the Northern papers he had enlarged its scope to include the Langhorne letter to George Washington involving his nephew Peter Carr. Then there was the everlasting charge of atheism, of Jacobinism, and now the threat of publishing his letters to John Walker over something that had happened thirty-three years ago! It was insane.

"Why have you not married some woman of your own complexion?" The *Virginia Gazette.*

He ground his teeth. Why? "Tell me who die," he thought, "who marry, who hang themselves because they cannot marry. . . ." He prayed that Sally had not seen most of what had been written about them. He came home feeling defeated. Everything reminded him of his two families and the problems they faced. The presence of Maria and Martha in Washington last winter had dampened all but the most infamous gossipmongers. They had not deserted him. He had had his explanation with them and now he must arrange a meeting with his injured friend and avoid a duel at all cost. He had already talked his son-in-law Thomas Mann out of a duel with his cousin John Randolph for the sake of Martha; now Madison must do the same for him. He could not leave either his white family or his slave family unprotected by his death.

Thomas Jefferson looked up at his slave wife as she entered his rooms. She appeared terribly small to him and fragile.

She wouldn't know the worst!

The following day James Madison arrived at Monticello. He was bringing good news. He had interceded in Thomas Jefferson's favor, and there would be no duel.

"I can't tell you how relieved I am, Mr. Madison, with the outcome of this unfortunate affair . . . and how I thank you."

"Mr. President, I don't think Mr. John Walker was any more anxious for a duel than you."

"My dear Mr. Madison, I've never even held a pistol in my hand. The very idea of one man murdering another in the name of injury is insanity. We already have enough ways of men killing men without inventing an etiquette for it."

"The law of Virginia 'honor' is a rather crude one, sir."

"Mostly the law of vanity, dear sir. I am a simple man. I accept with relief your intervention in this senseless affair and am quite satisfied that Mr. Walker has accepted my apology."

James Madison noted a slight hesitation. Thomas Jefferson was anything except a "modest" man and "insanity" or not, he was a Virginian brought up in its codes and mores. The Walker affair had distressed him much more than he was willing to admit. And his vanity had indeed been touched. There was yet one more thing.

"As for the other calumny . . ." began James Madison, "I believe Mr. Monroe would be happy to take her."

Madison couldn't bring himself to say Sally Hemings.

"Take her?"

Thomas Jefferson swayed slightly and the blood rushed from his face.

"Temporarily, of course," added James Madison, alarmed at the sudden pallor of the man standing before him.

"Take her where?"

"Why doesn't she . . . I believe . . . she has a sister Thenia at Mr. Monroe's. She could . . . retire there with her children until the time when—"

James Madison raised his eyes from the silver buttons on Thomas Jefferson's waistcoat and looked directly into his eyes. How could Thomas Jefferson not know in what political danger he was? He, James Madison, simply had the duty to warn him that Virginia would not tolerate, even from Thomas Jefferson, certain unpardonable things. He had to understand.

James Madison involuntarily stepped back. The cold blue eyes had now turned a deep aquamarine.

"The Hemingses are mine," said Jefferson. "All of them. I will deal with them personally."

"I didn't mean to presume . . ." began Madison. He concentrated on controlling the tremor in his voice. He brought his handkerchief out of his waistcoat and mopped his brow. He had gone too far. Too far for his own good. Relieved, he realized that Thomas Jefferson had already

façade he cherished almost as much as he cherished the façade of Monticello.

He had paid. There was something he could do: remain silent. And this silence would be payment. Payment for my servitude, which he would not change. Payment for our children, whom he did not recognize. He had paid with a kind of helpless, bewildered pride, for I was Monticello.

CHAPTER 34

MONTICELLO, 1803–1805

"Familia" did not (originally) signify the composite ideal of senti-
mentality and domestic strife in the present day philistine mind.
Among the Romans, it did not even apply in the beginning to the
leading couple and its children, but to the slaves alone. Famulus
means domestic slave and familia is the aggregate number of slaves
belonging to one man. . . . The expression (familia) was invented by
the Romans in order to designate a new social organism that head of
which had a wife, children and a number of slaves under his paternal
authority and according to Roman law, the right of life and death
over all of them.

FRIEDRICH ENGELS, *The Origin of the Family,
Private Property, and the State,* 1884

God forgive us, but ours is a monstrous system, a wrong and an
iniquity! Like the patriarchs of old, our men live all in one house
with their wives and concubines: the mulattos one sees in every
family partly resemble the white children. Any lady is ready to tell
you who is the father of all the mulatto children in everybody's
household but her own. Those, she seems to think, drop from the
sky.

MARY BOYKIN CHESTNUT, *A Diary from Dixie,* 1840–76

*Oh, how can you think of slaves and motherhood!
Look into my eyes, Marianne, and think of love.*
KATE CHOPIN, "The Maid of Saint Phillippe," 1891–92

THE NEWS of the Louisiana Purchase came like a bolt of thunder at the
beginning of the summer. The guns were fired in Richmond, the bells
rang, and there was great rejoicing. The news of Master Monroe's
success in Paris caused a sensation all over the nation and made him the
hero that would someday make him president. My master had doubled
the territory of the United States, purchasing the whole expanse of
Louisiana and the Floridas for fifteen million dollars.

256

"Typical of Thomas Jefferson," Elizabeth Hemings declared, not without pride, from the vastness of her kitchens. "He sets out to buy four acres and a mule, and ends up with a plantation and a herd of cattle!"

"No, Mama. He set out to buy New Orleans and he has ended up buying an empire."

Now that we had weathered the worst of Callender and the Federalist newspapers, it seemed we had reason enough to celebrate. On the sixteenth of July, the cabinet agreed to the purchase of Louisiana, and on the seventeenth, Meriwether Jones danced a jig on the west lawn of Monticello. It was not to celebrate the Louisiana Purchase but to celebrate the death of James T. Callender. He had been found, dead that morning, in the James River, drowned in three feet of water.

A year passed. A year free of scandal, although *Monticellian Sally* still rose now and again in the press.

My master won his re-election by a landslide, losing only four electoral votes out of one hundred and seventy-six, and not one for Aaron Burr. It was his moment of greatest triumph, for he knew, if he ever was to know, that the whole nation loved him. I felt keenly the pleasure of his triumph. Gone were his protests of disdain, his abhorrence of public office, his flight from using power. Truly, this outpouring of love and gratitude was enough to turn the head of a man who, more than anything else, loved to be loved.

His sixty-one years lay lightly on his shoulders. His hair was now gray. His troubles of five years ago were gone with the daily horseback riding in which he indulged. His skin was clear and high in color. His thick neck and wrists gave an impression of great physical force, even though his frame was slender, long and shackling. His feelings ran strong and deep, buried under the surface of a seemingly sunny and even-tempered disposition, but I knew him as he was: passionate to the point of cruelty, sensitive to the edge of brutality, eager for approbation to the limits of honesty, constant in love, lonely behind his facade of perfection, and imperfect in his fear of loneliness. Our fate had been tested by scandal, our love tempered by it. And our family grew like a many-rooted oak on our mountain. We were safe. Or so I believed.

In the spring they brought Maria up the mountain on a litter made out of rope and wood borne tenderly by Burwell, John, Davey, and Israel. She was dying from the complications of childbirth.

"Things change, only to remain the same," he said, standing framed in the doorway of her room. And it was true that it was now I rather than my mother who nursed and fed and washed and tended Maria, and it was my son Thomas who stood with Maria's son, Francis, wide-eyed in the hall.

The horrible ulcerating breast was surely gangrenous by now. The pain so intense that even laudanum gave no ease. In the afternoon, when the pain seemed the worst, I would sit for hours holding Maria in my arms, and thus her father would find us when he came to the door of her room to stare silently. He had withdrawn in a solitude with his books and his horses, as if they could nullify the fact of Maria's agony. But her agony was not to be nullified, neither by him nor me nor Maria.

I would brush her long auburn hair that fell to her waist, still lush and luxurious, until it began to come out by the handful. This I tried to hide from her, saving all the long strands, as the hairdressers in Paris used to do, to supplement the natural hair of their mistresses with chignons and poufs.

A nauseating sweetish smell clung to this exquisite woman not yet twenty-six, and I desperately changed her three or four times a day. She who had never been overly fond of dress or ornament was calling for her jewels. She who was always vexed by allusions to her beauty now required them from me, her sister, her husband, her father.

After her husband's visit, for which she would endure hours of toilette, she would turn her face to the wall and cry. As for her son, she would not let him enter her room. My own anguish lay buried deep within me. I was only waiting.

The day was fine and hazy, with a mist that hung low, even in the afternoon. On the mountains, with their tops bright with sunlight, every blossom and bush pushed its way toward the warmth of the sun. Suddenly, there was only the sound of my own breathing in the room. It was so still that I looked at the sealed window to make sure that the sun, the sky, and the unfolding nature were still there. And then I knew why it was so silent.

She had died. Without a word, her hand in mine. I too made no sound. No sound the human voice could make could express the pain I felt. I stayed beside her a long time before I finally rushed from the room to inform the small group that was still at supper: her husband, her son, her father, her sister. Then I returned to the room to wash and bathe her for the last time. Like my mother before me, I wept, for now I could weep as I wrapped her in white linen and then covered everything in the room. I descended into the garden, and with Wormley, I cut every spring flower there was, leaving not one remaining in all the vast gardens to insult her death with its life. I filled her room with them, scattering them on the beds, and blocking the light with them.

Only then did I allow her white family into the room.

We stood staring at each other over the fresh grave of Maria and that of her child, who had succumbed to convulsions.

Maria's death settled between us like a hungering beast, separating us from each other, ugly and terrible. Fear descended upon us, and over her grave we clutched at life. We clung to each other in our despair and our grief and we hurried back up the mountain as if the Reaper himself were pursuing us.

A new life was made that day, for my third son, Madison, would be born nine months afterward to the very hour. . . .

The second four years of my master's mandate began. For the second time, he had walked to the Capitol flanked by excited crowds and popular acclaim. For the second time, he delivered an inaudible speech to the gathered crowds, and again it was only the next day when they were able to read it in the newspapers that they knew what he had said.

Aaron Burr killed Alexander Hamilton in a duel at Weehawken in New Jersey, a misty July dawn 1804, but my master's country was at peace except with one nation.

An irresistible current moving west was making it a white man's country. The white man was crushing the Indian as he crushed the slave under the heel of the boot he placed on every inch of soil he could tread. The land which now stretched from the Carolinas to Vermont, and from the Atlantic shore to the Appalachian Mountains contained, according to the new census, five million whites, two million slaves, one million mulattoes, and an undetermined number of native Americans.

In the past four years, my master, as president, by fair means and foul, had transferred fifty million acres of Indian land from their sovereignty to the United States, paying a total of one hundred and forty-two thousand dollars; one-tenth of a penny an acre, or as he said, the equivalent of one hundred and forty-three prime male Negro slaves.

For another four years, he would be lost to me and Monticello. I was barred from the President's House. But I determined one day to set my foot on its planks. Davey Bowles brought me secretly, at my stubborn request, to Washington that winter. I traveled by night in a curtained carriage, and slipped into the mansion by the servants' entrance. It was more than ten years since I had ventured from Monticello.

Shielded by the Monticello servants there, hidden during the day by Burwell, I roamed at night the unfinished cavernous rooms that I knew I would never see again. I noted the fixtures, the hangings, the paintings, and the stiff old-fashioned furniture that had been installed by the Adamses. After the elegance of the Hôtel de Langeac, the President's House seemed crude, barnlike, cold, and dismal. The roof leaked, there was no heat, the stairway sagged, gloom and dust were everywhere. Even Thomas Jefferson had an unkempt, run-down appearance.

The large kitchens, where Edy and Fanny worked with Peter, were the only cheerful rooms in the whole house. I visited Petit, who was installed in Georgetown, a gentleman farmer, and Davey Bowles managed to take me out driving in one of the carriages to see Washington City.

It was a place of incredible distances, interspersed with a few scattered buildings; a quagmire of mud when the sun shone, and a sea of frozen ruts during the winter nights. The gaunt wooden skeleton of the Capitol building rose like a gallows on the hill, while swarms of workmen and slaves struggled in the soft earth with the enormous white stone that had begun to sheathe it. Surrounding the Capitol was the Federal City, which consisted of seven or eight boardinghouses, the best being Conrad and McMunn, and all of them brimming over with senators and representatives. There was a tailor shop, a shoemaker, a printer, a washerwoman, a grocer, a stationer, a dry-goods establishment, and an oysterhouse.

This, then, was the new capital of the United States. The swamps on all sides emitted the putrid odors of decay and a rancid fog hung over the city half the time, as the inhabitants fled at the first hint of the malarial fevers that periodically swept the city.

I inspected the half-finished Capitol, where John Trumbull's paintings would hang; the mansions surrounded by wastelands stretching down Pennsylvania Avenue to Georgetown reminded me of those that had been constructed back when I was in Paris on the Champs-Elysées.

The Champs-Elysées. It stretched dimly now, its perspective fifteen years behind me. The fashionable golden and white buildings that had been so "modern" then must have already settled into old-fashioned respectability. Respectability! I laughed to think what the Federalists now dead. He had been here for James's Christmas emancipation. I picked up eighteen-month-old Madison. There were now two Madisons. Martha had named her last son Madison to cancel out mine in the affections of his father. White vengeance had many faces.

"And what are they saying in the Richmond kitchens, Mama?"

"Well, Masta Wythe's nephew George Sweney been charged with murder and the white folks is up in arms and having a fit. You know how scared they is of poison with all us cooks. . . . Ain't nothing caused such a sensation in Richmond since the British. You know old Masta Wythe considered a saint in Virginia. You know how well loved he was, how mild and kind and how he done served on the Continental Congress and signed the Declaration of Independence, and served on the High Court and all. . . . Well, he done wrote a will giving his house to Lyddy Broadnax and his property and half his bank stocks to his son Michael Brown. The rest of his money he left to his nephew George Sweney, with the regulation that if Michael died before Sweney, Sweney would get Michael's part, too. Lyddy says Sweney found out about the will the night before Whitsunday, the twenty-fifth. Masta Sweney came as he sometimes did when Masta Wythe was at court, and went to his room and found his keys of his private desk. He opened the desk, and when Lyddy went in she found him reading a paper that her masta had told her was his will. She done tied it herself with a blue ribbon.

"Well, in the morning, when breakfast was nearly ready, Masta Sweney came into the kitchen. Lyddy said he went to the fire and took the coffee pot to the table while she was toasting the bread. He poured a cupful for himself and then set the pot down. She saw him throw a little white paper in the fire. He then drank the coffee he had poured for hisself and ate the toast with some fresh butter. He told her good-bye and went about his business. She didn't think there was anything wrong then. In a little while, she heard old Masta Wythe's bell. 'Lyddy, did I leave my keys in my desk yesterday, for I found them there last night?' he said to her. And she said, 'I suppose so, Masta, cause I saw Masta George at the desk reading that paper you gave me to put there. Masta George said you had sent him to read it, and to tell you what he thought of it.' Old Masta Wythe said, 'I fear I am getting old, Lyddy, for I am becoming more and more forgetful every day. Take these things away, and give Michael his breakfast, and get your own, Lyddy.' She gave poor little Michael his breakfast and as much coffee as he wanted, and then drank a cup herself. After that, with the hot water in the kettle, she washed the plates, emptied out the coffee grounds, and scrubbed the coffee pot bright. By that time she was so sick with cramps she could hardly see, and Lord, she was poisoned and her son and her master as well. And now they're both dead and Lyddy Broadnax wish she was. Her son—her only son—dead. And they had had such hopes for him. Wasn't no boy in Richmond educated like Michael. Masta Wythe didn't spare nothing for his education. And freed him too, from the beginning, and Lyddy as well. He had the finest books...."

For the first time I saw fear in my mother's eyes.

"Who did she tell all this to, Mama?"

"Well, first to the doctor, Foushee, then to the other doctors who opened up poor Masta Wythe and found the same inflammation as in Michael. Then she had to tell it to the Court of Examination. This was after Michael died. Before then she was suffering something terrible and Michael was suffering worse than either her or Masta Wythe. She was so sick that she didn't even know when her son died. It was the Sunday after the poisoning that Masta Wythe, dying himself, found out his son had just died. He cried out, drew a long breath, and said pathetic-like, 'Poor boy.' Well, it seems that Masta Wythe immediately called for his will to change it, since he knew by then he was murdered. 'I am murdered,' he said, and he struck George Sweney from his will. 'Let me die righteous,' were his last words."

The cords on my mother's neck stood out. Her eyes seemed to be on some horrible object far in the distance coming toward her. Her hair was a silvery white, her skin darkened by age, but hardly wrinkled. Rather it seemed solidified. It was neither flesh nor stone, but a thin, fragile, paperlike substance hardly covering her bone and muscle. Her eyesight was intact and she had all of her teeth.

"But that George Sweney, he'll hang for it, won't he?"

"I think not, Mama. Black people and mulattoes can't testify against white people. Lydia Broadnax can't accuse her son's murderer."

"No! It ain't true!"

"Thomas Jefferson made the law himself. He and George Wythe."

"No! Lord God. Lyddy. Lyddy."

"There's no sense calling on God. He only takes white men's testimony," I said with bitterness.

"Oh, Lord Jesus Sweet Saviour have mercy on us black women," she moaned.

My heart burst. Mama, after seventy-three years of slavery still believed in justice. She rose, her body quivering with age and fury; I looked at her helplessly. I could do nothing for her. Just as I could do nothing for myself. Thomas. Michael. Beverly. Madison. What protection did we have from white vengeance?

"Darling," Elizabeth Hemings whispered suddenly, her face gray with fright, "you think they'se trying to kill us all?"

The deaths of Lydia Broadnax's son and lover destroyed my mother. Her spirit broke. She who had always been envious of Lydia's freedom and privilege and her son's education, she who had made freedom and recognition for herself and her children the supreme goal in her life, now saw that being free did not lead one from the dangers of blackness.

All her life, she had urged me to get freedom for the children; to strive for that magic circle which she thought was safety, only to find that there was no safety for us anywhere. There was only one escape from white will and white justice. And she decided to take it.

"Think I'm going to die now," she said simply one day, and she folded her apron and took to her bed. She refused her food. "They" were trying to poison her and she decided to die before she was murdered.

Martha and I spent the days of the summer watching and listening as she strained toward death, her life running out in rivers of words. And, to the end, she clung to the idea that somebody was trying to poison her. We did everything. We ate her food in front of her. Both of us. Martha. Me. We fed the children out of her refused plate. But she opened her mouth only to speak.

"Put your hand on my chest and push down," she had finally whispered. "My heart won't stop beating."

By the end of August, Mama finally won her battle to die. She was buried in the slave cemetery. I was now all alone and the second legacy of blood and kin fell upon me: not only to love but to survive.

I did not know how my master had taken the death of his well-loved friend and benefactor until he came home for the summer after the murders. He had not written from Washington City of the death of his professor, and it was only upon his arrival that I fathomed his grief and his shock.

I learned that he had been mentioned in Wythe's will. He paced the floor as he told me:

"Such an instance of depravity as has been hitherto known to us only in the fables of poets."

I said nothing. George Wythe had flaunted Michael's intelligence, his education, his beauty, had freed him and, by making him his heir, had advertised his parentage for all to know. Against the most sacred law of the South . . . he had gone against the rules and he had paid with what he had loved most: his only son had died before his eyes.

"When I think that we all gathered at the Washington Tavern in the capital in March, less than a year and a half ago to celebrate my second inauguration, and John Page asked George to retire and then proposed a toast to him, praising his wisdom and integrity as a magistrate, his zeal and disinterestedness as a patriot!" My master shook his head. "The hall resounded to nine cheers . . . as many as were given to me—" His voice broke. "He had left me his library, his scientific instruments, his silver cups and walking stick—" He paused. "And he had made me a guardian of Michael Brown. . . ."

Oh, God, I thought, not only had the quiet, mild-mannered George Wythe advertised his miscegenation by leaving an inheritance to his yellow son, he had advertised the plight of Thomas Jefferson by placing a yellow boy under his guardianship.

By the time the trial began in September, it was famous throughout Virginia. Edmund Randolph, Martha Randolph's cousin by marriage, defended George Sweney. The outcome was as I had predicted. For the murder of George Wythe, signer of the Declaration of Independence, codifier of the Virginia laws, judge in the High Court of the state, George Sweney was acquitted for lack of evidence, despite forged checks in his uncle's name, despite the arsenic found in his room, despite the eyewitness account of Lydia Broadnax, who was never allowed to testify. If it took only a few minutes for the jury to return a verdict of not guilty of the indictment of murder of George Wythe; the indictment for the murder of Michael Brown was dismissed without a trial. For the forged checks in his uncle's name, George Sweney was convicted and sentenced to six months' imprisonment and one hour's exposure on the pillory in the marketplace in Richmond, but he never served even this sentence.

George Sweney was free. Mama, Wythe, and Michael were dead, still freshly in their graves that September day when I stood posed to mount the staircase to my room. I still remember his voice.

"How painful and melancholy to reflect that a man so pure, so upright, so virtuous, and so beloved should have met an unnatural death."

A flash of disbelief went through me. I turned and almost stumbled. He was lying to himself! He was going to lie to himself even about this! Oh God, when would we stop the lies.

"Unnatural death!" I screamed. "It was murder. *Murder!* Don't you understand? Oh, Thomas, can't you face your white race this one time?" He looked up. There was actually surprise in his eyes.

Remember Callender! Remember, Goddamn you, Thomas Jefferson! Remember the hate, remember the filth, remember Callender dead in the mud of the James River! This is what you can expect from your white world. Death and hatred and damnation for you, for me, for the children!

"Free us! Free us! Free us, Thomas!"

"I would have to banish you from me . . . by law, and I cannot. . . ."

"Oh God, how can you keep me . . . us, in such an abomination?" I stood, my back to the staircase as he came toward me.

"By loving you," he said quietly.

"Why do you do it?"

"Because I love you."

Love me and remain a slave.

"And what do you wish me to do about that?" I whispered.

"Love me."

"You think love pardons everything."

"Does it not?" he replied gently, reaching for me.

"Have I not loved you since I was a girl of fifteen, Thomas?"

Love me and remain a slave.

"This is the only way I have to love. This is the only way I have to love and protect you. This is the only way I have to keep you safe."

"The only way?" I whispered. "But you are the President of the United States!"

He said not a word. He had turned stone-white. I reached up and brought his face down to mine, searching his eyes for hope. But I found none. There was no safe place for us. He could no more protect me than my mother could! He thought my safety was in slavery. She had thought it was in freedom. Now I knew that both of them were wrong. His country hated me and my race enough to do murder. His friends had sanctioned the killing of the man Thomas Jefferson had loved liked a father. And his son. If they had done this to their own . . .

What would they do to me?

And my children?

White America meant to destroy me, my lover, and my children. These people meant murder. Lydia had known it. Mama had known it, and now it would be my turn. I was alone. I could expect no help from Thomas Jefferson. He had been warned, and he had chosen to disdain this warning; but I vowed never to forget it. Never. There would be no freedom, no recognition, no emancipation, no flight, only stubborn silence would rule our lives from this day hence. If I had ever hoped that somehow, someday, my lover, who stood before me like a monument, would avow his yellow children, I laid that hope to rest in the graves of Michael Brown and Elizabeth Hemings. As for me, I could no longer afford his grief, his misery, his plea for forgiveness. Their deaths had unearthed the long forgotten specter of emancipation and his abnegation had sealed it.

I would not be destroyed, I would survive. I would survive Marly, mother and master.

He began to cry in rage and I took him in my arms. So he too had thought we had a safe place.

That winter, he unleashed the Embargo of 1807 upon the country after the frigate *Chesapeake* was attacked by the British.

"Now they have touched a cord which vibrates in every heart," he said. "Now is the time to settle the old and the new."

The embargo lasted two years and ruined Virginia.

Once more he stubbornly proposed to a stubborn Congress the prohibition of the African slave trade. He welcomed home with joy Meriwether Lewis, returned safely from his expedition in Louisiana. And he tried Aaron Burr for treason.

The bitterness and resentment I felt against my lover, against my fate, I turned against Aaron Burr. When there were so many white men to hate, why did I choose Aaron Burr? Was it because of that one frank stare of lewdness that day in Philadelphia? Was it because he was the first man, black or white, who with one look of contempt had insinuated that my whoredom was of my own asking?

I hated him. I badgered my master for news as he sought affidavits against Aaron Burr from New Orleans to Maine, from Indiana to New Jersey. I wrote to him constantly, always stressing the danger of assassination from this man, of the duel with Hamilton, of his hatred, of his threat to my master's power. And he wrote meticulous letters home describing his progress in gathering evidence. He commanded me to burn the letters. But these letters, like all the others, I vowed to keep until my dying day.

Aaron Burr was brought to Richmond for his trial, which had the air of a country fair. People swarmed into the city. Balls and dinners were given in his honor. He strode the streets with his daughter Theodosia on his arm, the immaculate dandy. Besides himself, his defense lawyers were Edmund Randolph and George Wickham, the defenders of George Sweney. The trial opened with a hundred government witnesses, and my master's arch enemy John Marshall presiding. I followed the trial passionately, but like the trial of George Sweney, the outcome had been predetermined by Chief Justice John Marshall. The jury returned a verdict of "not guilty because, not proven guilty."

The great treason trial was over. And by the end of that trial, in January 1808, the African slave trade was abolished. I was again with child. My seventh. The next May I gave birth to a son, whom I called Eston, my only child born in the presence of his father, who celebrated his birth as if he were white.

CHAPTER 36

MARCH–OCTOBER 1809

> Here arise questions of value, tact, and tolerance. . . . For what, one must ask at last, would these Southern ladies and domestic slaves have known and felt about their being relatives? And what would it have meant for Jefferson whose only son died unnamed at the age of three weeks, to send into safe oblivion, a mulatto son who is said to have looked very much like him?
>
> ERIK H. ERICKSON, "Dimensions of a New Identity," Jefferson Lectures, 1973

> There is love-making and love-making in this world. What a time the sweethearts of that wretch, young Shakespeare, must have had. . . . The poor creature that he left his second best bedstead to, came in second best all the time, . . . Fancy people wondering that Shakespeare and his kind leave no progeny like themselves! Shakespeare's children would have been half his only; the other half only the second best bedstead's. What would you expect of that co-mingling of materials?
>
> MARY BOYKIN CHESTNUT, *A Diary from Dixie*, 1840–76

THOMAS JEFFERSON HEMINGS and Thomas Jefferson Randolph raced each other down the mountain to greet their father and grandfather. My master's second term as president was over.

Bareheaded, their identical red curls flying in the March wind, the cold and speed raking their already high color, the two boys made for Shadwell, four miles away, as fast as they could without crippling their horses.

I was thirty-six; Thomas, nineteen; Beverly, almost eleven; Madison, four; Eston, one; and their sister Harriet, almost eight. Martha was also thirty-six; Jeff, seventeen; Anne, eighteen; Cornelia, ten; Ellen, thirteen; Virginia, eight; Mary, six; her Madison, three; and Benjamin, one. Maria's only child, Francis, was eight. Nineteen years of childbearing.

The children were scattered on the steps of the mansion, Randolphs and Hemingses mixed together, as always. The boys were fair, their bright, red-blond and auburn heads like wild poppies among the dark heads of the girls, who took after Thomas Mann, except for Harriet, who had the thick red hair of her father.

Both Thomas Jeffersons had fled out of the schoolroom when Jim, the overseer, brought the news that the master had already arrived on horseback at Shadwell, and was riding hard through the March snow-storm for home. The boys, blinking back the glare of swirling snow-flakes which lay on their shoulders and their horses' flanks like powdered sugar, raced to meet the returning ex-president halfway down the mountain. With shouts of joy we could hear all the way to the mansion, they had accompanied him the rest of the way to Monticello, riding on either side of him, pressing jealously as close to him as their horses would allow.

In a mist of fine snow, the whole household of Monticello stood on the west portico waiting. Besides myself, Martha, and our families, there were the household slaves and their children. Everything had been ready for weeks. Wormley had been working by torchlight in the gardens to get all the tree planting done. Five hundred peach stones had been put in and as many pecans, new English turf planted for seedlings, every blade of winter grass manicured, every hedge, every bush, every flower bed in the vast gardens dug, raked, nourished, and attended to. A week had been spent hog-killing, the butcher planks running red, the house resounding with the high-pitched cries of the black-and-white Calcutta hogs, each weighing between three and four hundred pounds. Peter had sweated over the mincemeats, sausages, bacons, hams, pickled ears and skin, scrapple, and hog fat for soap and candles. In the house, Critta, Mary, and Edy had shined floors and polished silver for a month. There had been a great deal of sewing, too. I had wanted a new dress as had Martha, Anne, and Ellen, and all the other children. Six seamstresses had been kept busy for a month. Ursula had sorted, mended, rewashed, and used up seven kegs of starch on the household linen. I had left nothing to chance, the house sparkled, candles burned, and I stood watching the young men and their famous father and grandfather ride toward me. It had been eight years. Thomas Jefferson was coming home forever.

Shouts, cries, and kisses greeted the master of Monticello as he dismounted.

"How you all." He laughed. "Peter, what have you got good?"

"Masta, I got guinea hens and *carré* of lamb. I got rabbit in mustard, the way you like it, and Masta Meriwether Lewis's mother done sent over three of her hams for you!"

Everybody burst into laughter as he grabbed Eston, tottering on unsteady legs, and swung him around, sweeping him off the steps, and into his arms.

After that, there was bedlam as the children, black and white, tumbled down the stairs of the portico to greet the riders. Thomas Hemings beat Thomas Randolph to the reins of his father's horse. He was half an inch taller than his father, with the same luxurious red-auburn hair, blue eyes, rangy loose body, which was still awkward and uncoordinated from the growth of the past year.

Every summer for the past seven years, when the hordes of visitors descended on the estate, Thomas had been sent away to a neighboring farm almost fifty miles away, returning again only for the winter. This year would be the same, and the precious months before June would be the only ones in which he would see us until Christmas. But then, this Christmas would be different, I thought. This Christmas Thomas Jefferson would be home with his sons.

James Madison was now president. Dolley Todd Madison was finally mistress of the President's House, I thought, smiling. My master had been forced to borrow eight thousand dollars from Mrs. Tabb in order to pay his overdue bills before leaving the capital, according to Burwell. His inheritance of debts over eight years in the President's House was horrendous and his embargo against England and France had ruined him. It had hit the Southern states even worse than the mercantile states. His friends, the Virginia plantation-owners who had counted themselves rich, found themselves, like him, with useless assets on their hands, and a pile of debts. My master's tobacco was worthless; wheat had fallen from two dollars a bushel to seven cents; land values had been completely swept away. The only wealth that remained were slaves. The only industry that seemed destined to survive in Virginia and reap sickening profits was the breeding of slaves for inland trade to the deep South. He had returned home penniless and depressed. The Louisiana Purchase was the only thing he could take real pleasure in.

Meriwether Lewis's mission, in the beginning, had been a secret one. Under the guise of exploring the Territory for "literary" reasons, Meriwether and William Clark were to open up British territory for private traders, since they had been forced out of business by government traders on this side of the Mississippi and had been resentfully inciting discontent among the Indians. Why not, Thomas Jefferson had asked himself, divert their hopes of profit in the direction of the Missouri River? He could kill two birds with one stone: the government traders would be left in undisputed possession on this side of the Mississippi, with the aim of bringing the Indians into debt and forcing them to sell their lands; while the dispossessed private traders could open up new land for trade which now went to Great Britain. If traders went, settlers would not be far behind, and the Territory would become white instead of red.

He had needed someone he could trust for the expedition, someone who could combine daring, prudence, woodsmanship, surveying, familiarity of the Indian character, with a good knowledge of botany, natural history, mineralogy, and astronomy. What better choice than his brilliant secretary Meriwether?

My son Thomas had dreamed day and night of that expedition, had begged his father to let him go, although he was much too young. Meriwether Lewis had chosen William Clark and his slave York to go with him. For two years and four months, they had toiled and marched the uncharted wilderness. Of this my master was proud. But even this happiness, we were to discover, was mortgaged.

It was at the end of summer, the September golds and oranges already turning into October's reds and browns. As if in a dream, repeating itself, I heard the heavy tread of Davey Bowles in the hall, the strangled anguished cry, only this time it was a male cry. I had time only to turn to see Thomas Jefferson burst into his study, his face contorted with grief and incomprehension.

Meriwether Lewis had committed suicide in Tennessee. He was dead at exactly the same age as James. The cold terror of that self-murder ran through me as I stared in fearful apprehension at his wild grief.

James gone. And Maria. Jamey. And Michael. And Mama. And now Meriwether. Death lay around our feet, like the neat piles of raked leaves Wormley had left scattered on our lawn. Thomas Jefferson had turned away from me.

I knew how much my master had liked Meriwether Lewis. He had taught him surveying, as my master's father had taught him. He had taken him on as private secretary, and it had been Meriwether who had assuaged the loneliness of the sinister President's House in Washington City. He had introduced Meriwether into the circles of power, and when he had needed a leader of the expedition to the Pacific, who had he chosen out of his "family" but Meriwether? He had thought of the danger, I knew, but had refused to shield a "son" from becoming the first to explore it simply because of his own fears for safety. And Meriwether had done him proud. He had become a hero and my master had covered him with honors, made him governor of Louisiana. And now Meriwether Lewis was dead by his own hand: Accused by James Madison, another "son," of mismanaging Louisiana. As dead as James, and for reasons perhaps as unknown.

"All my hopes were in Meriwether. He was the last. Why must I always lose what I love? Why can I never hold what I cherish? Why have I no sons of my own?"

His words stunned me. What about the census of his family? I had seen it with my own eyes..

I said quietly, "But you have four sons."

Could not Thomas or Beverly be instructed in botany, in astronomy, in surveying; could not Madison or Eston learn natural history, mineralogy, Indian affairs? I wanted to scream.

He took a long time to answer me. "I don't have four sons. You have four sons."

Silence.

I had burned for him and I had birthed for him. Seven times I had descended into that valley from which neither his wife nor one of his daughters had returned. And my sons stood as testament and hostage to a body I could never call my own. I felt an explosion of insulted motherhood, all red and brown, like the leaves scattered on the lawn outside the window.

His back was turned to me. My eyes sought the iron poker lying within my reach near the chimney. I wanted to strike that broad blue-sheathed back. I wanted to strike and strike again, with all my strength, to smash him. Oh God, I wanted to kill him, for now, after all these years, I understood what he had understood from the beginning, but had not had the courage to tell me. He had renounced his sons from the day of their birth!

The red and brown were swimming now in patches of blackness, like a flickering candle. Snatches of darkness overtook the colors. I reached for Joe Fosset's iron poker. The master had no sons, the slave had sons. The white man had no sons, the black woman had sons. It was she who had lusted, not he. She who had seduced, not he. No, Beverly or Thomas or Madison or Eston could not be instructed in mineralogy or botany, in Greek or Latin, in music, in architecture, in natural history, in astronomy. They would never count as real sons.

Never.

Then why had he clung to us all these years. Why had he bound us soul and flesh to him? Why had he not relinquished and freed us? And why, why had I stayed?

Love me and remain a slave.

Now the colors had darkened.

The iron poker appeared dull and lethal. His back was still turned to me. In my mind's eye I struck and struck and struck. I wanted to see the look of surprise as he turned to defend himself. I wanted to see terror and disbelief in those innocent eyes. Then I wanted the poker to smash that high-arched nose, to see that expression of mild benevolence disappear under blood. I wanted him dead. Dead as Meriwether. Finally, all the colors became that almighty color: black.

I felt horror for us all. Master. Concubine. Bastards. I no longer had the strength to lift Joe Fosset's poker over my head.

I didn't—would never—have the courage to kill Thomas Jefferson.

But I would free his sons.

I swung around, my back against the deep, many-hued valleys with its army of black pines, and faced the impeccable whiteness of Monticello.

I put my mind to it methodically, as if making up a household inventory. When would Thomas Jefferson Hemings "stroll" away? How much money did he need? How much did I have? Could I sell my sapphire bracelet secretly in Richmond through Burwell? Would he or would he not say good-bye to his father? Where would he go? Who could I trust to help him? Did it really matter that he was nineteen and not the "promised" twenty-one? He was white enough to pass for white, as his father had said of Jamey. Would he leave Monticello a white man? Could he do it to save himself?

No, Thomas Hemings would not say good-bye to his father, to be charmed or willed or loved out of going away. Yes, he would leave Monticello a white man. At the top of my stairs, I stared into the mirror, just as I had one day twenty years before in Paris. The long Calvary of the renouncement of one child after another was beginning.

But the departure of my eldest son did not go as I had planned. I had not planned that he would meet his father unexpectedly on his stolen horse, with all the money I had in the world on the Fourth of July.

The father and son met on the wide front lawn of the west facade of the mansion, under my window, each on horseback. Thomas Jefferson was hatless as usual, his fine sandy-gray hair lifted in the breeze, wet from the summer dawn; my son's deep auburn hair as wild and thick as his father's. They seemed almost a double image, the same long, pale faces, stubborn chins, and pale hooded eyes.

They faced each other for a long moment, their horses stock-still under their expert hands. So still that they resembled two equestrian statues in the pink morning; sculpture erected to commemorate some long-ago and forgotten heroic deed. A slight movement of the horses, nervous and ready to run, shattered the illusion. They rose in their saddles as one and drew together in an embrace that lasted a long time. It was Thomas who broke the hold of his father, who then spun his horse and sped away at a reckless gallop on sloping terrain, taking a nearby hedge in a jump that would have unseated anyone except him.

My son reined in his horse, frightened by the sudden movement, and sat a long time looking after the vanishing horseman.

I gazed at my own reflection distorted in the thick glass. I placed my hands in front of me, between myself and the windowpane. They were soft, strong, and steady. On my left hand, I wore a wide yellow band of gold. Wife. My hand came down upon the window hard, but it would not shatter.

Thomas Jefferson Hemings turned and looked back at the columned facade. In something like a salute, he raised his arm as he turned and rode away down the mountain.

PART V

1834

Albemarle
County

CHAPTER 37

DECEMBER 1834

The female slave, however fair she may have become by various comminglings of her progenitors, or whatever her mental and moral acquirements may be, knows that she is a slave, and, as such powerless. . . . She has parents, brothers, sisters, a lover, perhaps, who all suffer through her and with her.

MARGARET DOUGLASS (from prison), 1853

Though the effects of black be painful originally, we must not think they always continue so. Custom reconciles us to everything. After we have been used to the sight of black objects, the terror abates, and the smoothness and glossiness, or some agreeable accident of bodies so coloured, softens in some measure the horror and sternness of their original nature; yet the nature of their original impression still continues. Black will always have something melancholy in it. . . .

EDMUND BURKE, "On the Sublime and Beautiful," 1756

SALLY HEMINGS closed her eyes and remembered. The smooth eyelids slid over the dark openings set like caves in a clay mountain, leaving the pale oval countenance flattened and glowing like a polished bone in the dark of an unearthed grave. In the cabin, the fine French clock of onyx and bronze struck the hour, then ticked over a new minute of silence. In her mind she saw her son ride away.

She rose from where she was sitting and went over to the light. Carefully, she untied the black velvet ribbon she wore around her neck, and opened her locket. She took out the lock of red-auburn hair and brushed it with her lips. Then she stared at the painted image in the locket for a long time. Tomorrow was another son's wedding day.

Scrupulously, with the edge of her muslin scarf, she wiped the tears that had fallen onto the portrait. Then she replaced the bright lock within and closed the case, the fine mechanism of the lock giving her a moment's satisfaction.

She stared out of the window, remembering another December more than twenty years before. Another kind of "black death." The December of the murder at Rocky Hill, in 1811.

"T.J.'s dead sister, Lucy's boys, Lilburn and Isham," her sister Critta began, "been condemned for killing, and dismemberin' Lilburn's body servant, George, out there in west Kentucky. The news is just reachin' Virginia."

Critta had sat in the darkness of her secret room at the top of the staircase and told her the bad news from Kentucky. That was the reason why her master had snatched her up, along with Fanny and Burwell, and fled to their newly finished house at Poplar Forest. Away from the mansion.

"Last December, on the night of the fifteenth, Lilburn decided to chastise his slave George and ordered a bonfire built in the meat house of the plantation, and ordered all his slaves present. There, Lilburn and his brother Isham had two slaves tie up that poor boy, not two years older than Beverly, and then laid him on the meat block. First people thought Lilburn was only going to whip George. 'Hand me that ax,' Lilburn told his brother. Then the people thought Lilburn only going to chop off a finger or an ear, or maybe a whole hand or foot. But Lilburn first cut off the boy's two hands and flung them into the fire and then cut off his feet. Then the people knew Lilburn's goin' to kill his slave. Lilburn started chopping and the people started groaning. Lilburn continued on with the slaughter and the people fell silent. Some say Lilburn chopped the head from the body, others say he threw George into the fire and burned what was left of his slave alive. All this because George broke a favorite milk pitcher of his dead mother. All this because Lucy Jefferson Lewis's linen kept gettin' ripped and her aprons kept disappearin', and her dishes broken."

Critta had paused. Sally Hemings stared at the trickle of saliva that had formed at the corner of her sister's mouth. Wasn't it James's dream that Critta was telling her? James's dream that she'd known in her bones for twenty-four years. Was she mad, her sister?

"And then people wailed into the night, and of course, according to them superstitious slaves, they done stirred up nature itself because an earthquake, they call it the New Madrid, an earthquake now rocked the Mississippi and it flowed backward, turned red, and overrun the banks, and all the ground shook and trembled, and windstorms came, and lightning, and all sorts of strange occurrences came on that night; and Lilburn's wife went mad with the knowledge of what he done, and fled to her brother's, and her ravings brought Lilburn and Isham to their ruin. . . . The slaves buried what was left of George, and Lilburn locked up his raving wife in the house. But the sheriff of the county came around asking questions, and when Lilburn's hound dog dug up a jawbone, and the sheriff seen it was a human jawbone, he got the Lewis slaves and made them tell where they had buried George, then he made them dig up the rest of George's charred bones. Lilburn and Isham were arrested for murder and taken to Salem and indicted."

There had been a small sigh of exhaustion, and Critta had stared out the window for a long time saying nothing. Winter still lay on the land. The Blue Mountains were shrouded.

"The sheriff released them two brothers," Critta had continued, "on bail of five thousand dollars to await their trial, but Lilburn made a suicide pact with his brother to shoot each other over the grave of their mother. Isham fired and Lilburn he fell dead. Isham fled, but he was captured after a few days. He was tried for his brother's murder and sentenced to be hanged. But before they could hang him, he escaped and is still not found."

"And this is true, Critta?"

"As true as death, sister."

"And how . . . how do you know?"

"How could I not know?" Critta said in disgust. "White people knows. So it follows that anything they know, we know."

"But how?"

"Lilburn and Isham's father was in Virginia at the time. The Lewis slaves, they all knew. Then it come in from the West on the slave intelligence, the trial in the newspapers. Only reason you ain't read it is that Masta Thomas hid the newspapers. White people don't know how many slaves can read. White people going around tiptoeing and whispering and slamming doors in their servants' faces and locking them, and shutting their mouths in front of the servants. As if we wouldn't know of it! They sat around here with blank faces with you and Masta Jefferson gone. He high-tailed it out there to Poplar Forest with you, like he could get away from it. Silence when you entered a room. Looks. They really think we don't know what's going on."

She had stared at Critta. Her master had said nothing to her all those days. Had Burwell known? Fanny? Had he really thought she would not find out? Or had he simply decided to let someone else tell her? He had not had the courage to tell me, Sally Hemings thought. But then she had never had the courage to tell him of James's nightmare either.

"For weeks," Critta had continued, "when any of the house servants entered a room, the conversation stopped. I swear I will never under-stand white people. Do they really think their lies fool the people who serve them? They go around whispering 'Not in front of the servants,' yet they done butchered a poor boy in front of the servants! They commit their crimes in front of the servants. They commit murder in front of the servants!"

Sally Hemings stood up, trembling, blocking the light, drawing in the room with her breath. She stood against the window as she had stood in the doorway of her cabin the day the census taker had come up her road. Except that now the violet was outside. The deep shadows of a sunless afternoon. The clock ticked over another moment of silence.

"You! You don't know *nothing* about slavehood," her sister had said. "You brush your silk skirts against it, that's all. Petted and pampered and hidden and lied to. . . . Buried alive by your lover! You ain't never puked from the smell of whiteness . . . begged God to take this cup from you. . . ."

"Critta," she had said, "you are crying. . . ."

"Aw God, have mercy on us! Lord Jesus Christ in Heaven, have mercy!"

"Critta. . . ."

Sally Hemings' face was seamed with rivulets of tears. They fanned out like delicate transparent lace on ivory satin.

Critta had accused her of not knowing anything about slavery. But she had known everything there was to know. Critta had been ill-used. She had been raped and scorned. But Critta was she and she was Critta. They were and always had been one and the same, and they in turn had been one with every black field hand bent over the tobacco and cotton that had kept their white family in *servants*. Yet what had they known about their *servants*? She knew everything there was to know.

The *servants* surprised the master at stool and fornication, childbirth and menses, in every secret intimacy. They knew if he was clean or filthy. Everything that was spotted, soiled, unwashed, creased, rum-pled, worn and discarded, they picked up, and washed, folded and mended, and laid out anew for him. They knew if their master slept alone or not, and with whom. They recognized his waste and his possessions. They knew the true color of his hair and the true age of his sorrows. They saw him in fear and pain, jealousy and anger, lust and happiness. They knew his bastards, because most times they were their own children. Their master's footsteps were as familiar as their own, his voice recognized in the midst of company.

They saw him fight vice or honor it, swallow truth or pronounce it, flatter for power, gossip for amusement, wife-beat for amusement, flog out of viciousness.

They knew if he destroyed out of envy or built out of pride. They knew his station in life and how he came to it. They knew if he hoarded his money or spent it, honored his debts, believed in his God. They smiled at his follies, laughed at his jokes, defended his reputation, nursed his children, despised or respected him as they pleased, obeyed him if they were compelled, ignored him when they had a mind to. They brought his children into the world, laid out his dead, buried his forgotten, hid his sins from the world, even from God—if they could. But not even they could always do that. And still the master thought he could speak the truth only out of their earshot, *never in front of the servants.* . . .

Sally Hemings drew in her breath just as the hour struck. The jerking shadows of the firelight etched into the shadows of her face. The horror of the murder had lost the allure of memory and stood exposed before her there on the cabin floor—the dreadful amputated stump of slavery itself.

She and Critta had stood that day, servant to servant, concubine to concubine, and had been one with their mother and their mother's mother and *her* mother. One long line: The African and the beast hunter Hemings, the housekeeper and the slave master Wayles, the slave mistress and the American Jefferson. . . .

He had not told her. His hands had been bloodied with his kin's crime, and not only had he pretended not to know it, he had pretended that she would not know it. Those hands that had drawn her and had known her in all the secret places had not revealed his white secrets. And hers? Had her hands revealed her black secrets? James's nightmare? Her hands that had soothed and caressed, had they been any less bloody? Didn't she have James's blood on her hands? On those immaculate hands she had kept so soft for him. And Critta, had her hands been free of blood? Had they not served the same murderers? And the slave boy George, hadn't he lain down on the meat block for his masters; and his fellow slaves, hadn't they tied him up and looked on and kept silent?

How many had they been to witness murder? How many of them had been grown men? How many of those grown men would it have taken to overwhelm two white men and their guns? How many had thought only about their own flesh, their own sons; their precious flesh opening under a steel ax, their blood spraying like mist onto the heated air; their heart carved out on the butcher's table.

They were all bloodied, thought Sally Hemings. The whole race was bloodied. Not only with the real blood of suffering, the real blood of chains and whips and hatchets, but the blood of race, polluted, displaced, and disappearing in rape and miscegenation, and cross-ties of kin—that fine lace of bastardy that stretched across the two races like the web of a spider filled with love and hate—claiming cousins and nephews, daughters and sons, half sisters and half brothers. . . . The whole race was bloodied, the whole race had served with bloodied hands and had wiped them on their masters.

They had washed and scrubbed and polished and glazed, but how could they, bloodied as they were, have cleaned anything? How? Sally Hemings' mouth formed the word, but there was only silence, and a lonely woman in a cabin on the boundary of Monticello.

She had never revealed to Thomas Jefferson that she had known about Lilburn and Isham. But she had turned away from his hands that day. From his touch. From his "darling." And if she had told him, what would he have said? *That it had had nothing to do with them.* He would have spoken about "the insanity of mankind." He had always taken things out of the specific, out of reality and made an abstraction of them. But men were real. Blood was red. George and Lilburn and Isham and James and Meriwether were not merely "mankind." They had been his blood. If he hadn't been responsible for his own blood, for his own issue, for his own race, then who had been responsible? So she had left it unsaid. She had forgiven him for so many things. Why not one more?

And the years had passed like seeping water from a drying well. Silence between them. A whole kingdom of silence.

The peeling gray mansion of Monticello stood bleak and deserted on its mountaintop while the wind howled and snow swirled around it.

Sally Hemings sat until she could no longer see her hand before her face, and then she rose and went out into the snowstorm, hugging her shawl, her skirts dragging in the white satin layer of crystals beneath her feet.

She went to her henhouse to gather some eggs, and on her way back she saw him again ahead of her, breaking pane after pane of silvery light, and then she knew that the circle was closed. It had been twenty-four years since Thomas Jefferson Hemings had strolled away, thirty-

one since James had died, and forty-four since she had last seen Marly.
Should she hurry to catch up with him, she thought, stay twenty paces
behind, or return to the mansion?

In the white mist, breathing softly, Sally Hemings listened to the
coursing of her blood. She pressed her hands against her womb, and
whispered, more to herself than to the dark figure, who, after all these
years, still strode his Elysian fields:

"Tell me it is not true, love, that I was never happy. . . ." But she
knew then, she had made her pact with the infernals. The number of
kisses it might take to redeem her now was beyond even the power of
Thomas Jefferson.

"Martha gone and sold Monticello, Mama."

Mama?

"Mama, Monticello's sold! To tradespeople in Charlottesville!"

Madison Hemings was desperately trying to pull his mother back
from her reveries. She was standing in the December evening. It was six
o'clock. She was chilled yet she would not move. He tugged at her,
shaking the delicate snowflakes that had settled on both of them.

He had helped pull a drowned man out of the Ravina once. He
remembered the incredible weight of that waterlogged body—it
seemed a hundred times the weight of a normal man. He remembered
the pull of his muscles, the strain, the ache to drag the broken body up
on the bank, and how he had stood there breathless, staring at the
bloated shape, heavier than lead and no longer human.

"Mama?"

Sally Hemings felt herself being wrenched upward by an incessant
humming in her ear, like a dying fly at the onset of winter. It was her son
Madison.

"What did you say, Madison, honey?"

"Mama! I said Martha done sold Monticello to the druggist named
Barkley in Charlottesville for his business and two thousand five hun-
dred dollars. The price of three slaves! Ain't the Randolphs' no more.
Ain't Papa's no more!"

Madison was shocked. For the past five years, only the mansion itself
and grounds surrounding it had remained: empty, deserted, decaying,
but still theirs, a link to the past. In the spring, they would have been
going up to the cemeteries to clean and weed and replant. . . .

"Mama, you be careful going up there to the cemetery, 'cause you'll be trespassing now. . . . Every time you pass the boundary line, you'll be trespassing. . . ."

Sally Hemings stared up at her gray-eyed son. So much like James . . . the same cat eyes. He had filled out in the past year. The ranginess and some of the violence was gone. Mary McCoy, she guessed. Madison and his black freeborn Mary McCoy. They would marry tomorrow. She stared up at him, but she didn't have to ask if it was true about Monticello. She knew it was. The mansion. Houses died or were killed, just like people. She felt neither pain nor sorrow. The last link with the world was gone. She could drift now, she felt light. As light as snow-flakes drifting.

The weight of that house, which had been on her shoulders since she was seventeen, slipped off.

PART VI

1812
Monticello

CHAPTER 38

SUMMER 1812

Love songs are scarce and fall into two categories—the frivolous and light and the sad. Of deep successful love, there is ominous silence.

W. E. B. DU BOIS, *The Souls of Black Folks*, 1953

SALLY HEMINGS stood in the middle of Mulberry Row. Her hands were on her hips, her face protected from the sun by a wide-brimmed hat. Around her, children, dogs, chickens, horses, and slaves swarmed and threatened to capsize her not more than a hundred yards from the Big House. She surveyed what the summer of 1812 had wrought. Her body was tensed and leaned slightly forward.

Along Mulberry Row, there continued the incessant thump of the nailery, the weaving cottage, the blacksmiths' and the carpentry shop. From the stables came the sound of snorting, restless animals. The stables held stalls for thirty-six horses, and they were full, with the rest tethered on the pasture land behind. Bacon, the overseer, had given up trying to feed the forty carriage horses of the guests. He had begun to cut down on the feed, but the master had reprimanded him severely for it. Edmund Bacon had just arrived in the kitchens with a wagonload of his wife's mattresses to supplement the depleted resources of Monticello. Every bed was full and in the upper rooms and attic, mattresses were strewn everywhere; servants slept on the floor on straw pallets in the hallways and corridors, which were so narrow Sally Hemings had to step over sleeping bodies every morning to get to her smokehouses and larder.

Larder, she thought. Edmund Bacon had killed a whole beef day before yesterday and it was completely gone! Like hordes of boll weevils, the summer company had gone through their supplies like a field of cotton, leaving nothing in its wake. They had come from everywhere: Richmond, Charlottesville, Louisville, Alexandria, and a dozen other places farther away.

About the middle of June, the travel would commence from the lower part of the state to the Springs, and there would begin a perfect throng of visitors. Whole families came with carriages, riding horses, and servants, sometimes like now, three or four gangs at the same time. Their carriages and buckboards lined the mile-long road to the house, and they stayed and stayed, from overnight to all summer: not only family but friends, neighbors, sightseers, and even total strangers. A dog yelped around her skirts and she gave him a hard kick. The table would be set for forty tonight, and the children, white and black, would eat in the kitchens.

She saw three housemaids coming from the washhouse farther down the road, their arms full of snowy, newly washed and ironed linen. A footman was following with two mattresses on his head.

Sally Hemings yelled at him. How many times had she told him not to carry mattresses on his nappy head! To tie it with a clean rag! He turned, stuck his tongue out, and continued on his way. Two other housemaids came by her carrying slop jars, a small child, who was crying, trailing one of them. Around her wafted the cooking odors of the midday meal, savory and pungent in the torpid air; farther down Roundabout Row, in one of the slave cabins, somebody was cooking chitterlings from the freshly killed hogs.

After Thomas Jefferson's return from Washington City, she had stood under the shade trees on the east lawn and watched Martha Randolph, with her wagon train of household goods, and all her children, make her way up the mountain for good. She had finally come to stay, she with her brood of children and her mad husband. Not that her family had had any place else to go. They had become penniless, with debts so overwhelming they could barely pay the interest on them. Thomas Mann had excelled his father-in-law in spending money and raising debts. She wondered if Martha were pregnant again. Thomas Jefferson had pleaded with her. What was he to do? Let them starve? Leave Martha, his only living child, at the mercy of her husband? His only living white child? And since then there had been no mistake about who was now mistress of Monticello. Thomas Jefferson had broken his vow. He had brought a white mistress back to Monticello: his own daughter.

"But you promised me!"

"Martha isn't a 'white mistress,' for heaven sakes, she's my daughter . . . your niece, our family!"

"And who runs Monticello?"

"Martha does."

He had said it. And he would not be moved on this; she knew him too well. There was an air of indifference about him now, a calm produced by the gratification of every wish. Beneath the suave manners, the glacial serenity, the almost deferential politeness, remained that special Virginian brutality that came from the habit of despotism and privilege, of never being crossed, of handling blooded horses, controlling ambitious men, ruling your own small kingdom, and contemplating your own place in history. He had forgiven himself everything, and he didn't care if she forgave him or not. He was letting the Almighty do His own work. But she had kept the keys.

"Sally Hemings, what on earth are you doing standing out there in the hot sun with your hat on when you know I need you right this minute, you hear me?"

I hear you, Martha. I barely hear you over all this racket; this noise and heat and running back and forth and hammering and yelling and screaming and crying and playing children, and horses and cows and chickens; but I hear you, thought Sally Hemings, and I'm coming. Just don't rush me, not today.

It was the anniversary of her mother's death five years before. She would never forget her. An image seared her and then dissolved. What was a black woman's life? What was a woman's life? Sally Hemings decided to ignore Martha's summons for the moment. She let the waves of noise and smells ride roughshod over her, hardly caring, because in a few days she and her master would escape from the crowds to their unfinished hideaway, Poplar Forest, leaving Martha to cope with feeding, housing, and entertaining almost fifty people.

When, she thought, were people going to stop persecuting Thomas Jefferson with their "most felicitous and cordial and heartfelt thanks for your hospitality"?

They were officeseekers, relations, friends, artists, biographers, young Daniel Webster, Madison, Monroe, foreigners, natives, the famous, the near great, nonentities, and total strangers. They pretended to come out of respect and regard for him, but she thought that the fact they saved a tavern bill had a good deal to do with it. She was tired of seeing them come and she was tired of waiting on them, and, most of all, Monticello just couldn't stand the drain much longer!

There were several ladies, parasols in hand, strolling along the edge of the west lawn not fifty yards from her, and on it, a dozen children, mostly Randolphs and Hemingses, were playing blindman's bluff. She looked up. At night the very floorboards of the house seemed to sag under the weight of humanity housed within. Maids and footmen and butlers, many of them promoted only for the summer crowd, broke the dishes, scorched the linen, mislaid the supplies, dropped the platters, and were slow as molasses to obey. This summer had seemed worse than any other. Her master seemed more withdrawn than ever, Martha more present.

Let Martha lead the table at Monticello and preside over this madhouse, she thought. They would go to their hermitage for half the summer and all the fall, in their new octagonal brick house, and laugh and talk and tell old tales. She smiled.

"You know how many names they got for Papa's chamber pot?"

"Beverly!"

"Well, Mama, it's true. I heard Mammy Ursula talking to Fanny the other day 'cause little Ned had an accident, 'cause he fell asleep."

"What?"

"Papa's *State of the Union* came out and spilled all over Ned's head!"

Beverly had begun to laugh. He had a laugh like his father's, she thought, short and abrupt, and likely to bring tears to his eyes if prolonged. Sally Hemings had laughed as well. Her lover had built an inside toilet, which was the object of much mirth among the household slaves. He had invented a way to move his chamber pot by a system of ropes and pulleys and wheels along a tunnel leading from the house to an opening in the ground about twenty-five feet away. It had been christened "The Underground Railway," over which traveled his "runaways." She and the other household slaves had elaborated on the theme until now there were "inaugural addresses" pronounced "in-all-urine-ass-dresses," "states of the union," "cabinet meeting," "Federal Reserves," "Treasury bonds," "ultimatums," "levees," and "Indian Treaties."

"Aunt Bett found a new name," Beverly had continued. "She said they were his "manumission papers." But in that case, he ain't *shat* in a long time!"

"Beverly!"

"I named it his *Declaration of Indepen—*"

"Beverly!"

"Now, Beverly, you want a good switching," she had said to his grinning face. But she had been laughing too hard for him to believe her. Blasphemy! She had tried to explain to her sisters how the mansion on the Champs-Elysées had been of the most modern construction, and had had as well as bathrooms, *lieux anglais*, or indoor water closets.

"That may be very well and good in Paris, France, honey, but trouble is, sister," Bett Hemings had said, "once this thing gets out there, there is still got to be a slave standing there ready to catch it, and empty it! Typical that Thomas Jefferson can't invent nothing that don't have a slave on the receiving end of it. . . ."

She saw him now in the distance saddling up one of the bays he loved so much. First thing he had done when he came back from Washington City was to build a new carriage. John had built the body, Joe Fosset had done all the ironwork, and Burwell had painted every bit of it. Only the plating had been done in Richmond, and a finer carriage there was not in Albemarle. That carriage, with its four bays, Diomede, Brimmer, Tecumseh, and Dromedary, each pair guided by a slave, with Burwell outriding on Eagle, was some pretty sight, almost outshining in splendor his cousin John Randolph's, with his blooded horses and his slaves following with perhaps a dozen more.

The Randolphs.

They were the bane of her existence.

The Randolph blood.

It was the tragedy of her life.

Without it, Martha might never have returned to Monticello and Thomas Jefferson.

Without it, she and Martha might have lived out their lives apart.

The Randolphs, and God knows there were enough of them, were strange people. John Randolph was one of the most eccentric men who ever lived, and Thomas Mann Randolph was well nigh his equal. Like two identical steers. Having Thomas Mann on the mountain permanently didn't make her sleep any easier. Thomas Mann didn't like it any better—living with his father-in-law and watching his wife worship the ground her father trod on, any more than Thomas Jefferson liked his son-in-law drinking and acting crazier and crazier. But Martha was in such bliss to be back up here, she didn't seem to notice that her husband was crazy. Jim, the overseer at Legos, had told her the other day that

Thomas Mann had driven Dromedary over to Edgehill and right into a row of haystacks, just like that. Scattering them in all directions and covering himself with straw. When he had reached the overseer and finished his business, he had calmly declared that he thought an old bull must have gotten into the wheat field, 'cause he had seen a good many shocks overthrown and scattered on his way over. As serene as you please, when he had done it himself, she thought. The overseer had laughed, because he knew Thomas Mann Randolph was crazy as a loon! Burwell said he had seen him take Dromedary's tail and run him up the mountain as fast as he could. And he was in money trouble too. Bad. Selling his slaves for cash.

Then there was Anne Cary, Thomas Mann's sister. She had been brought to trial for infanticide with her cousin and lover Richard Randolph. That had rocked the gentry!

Her thoughts were interrupted by the screams of the half-naked children who came racing by her; Ceres, the bull terrier, on their heels. Sally Hemings looked up into the lacy greenness of the immense ash trees that shrouded the Big House in shadow—trees planted by her lover before she was born. She loved these trees. Encompassing her in their soft violet shade, they seemed to stand between her and the world. Protecting that strange love which was her secret and her burden.

A dull pain struck her temple. She was almost forty years old. If she lived as long as her mother, there was as much of her life behind her as in front of her. And in those forty years she had had to learn slowly, like her mother before her, like every female before her, the uses of love.

And Martha. Everything would be all right, she thought, if only there were not two mistresses at Monticello, as if there could really be two mistresses of anything.

CHAPTER 39

SUMMER 1812

THOMAS JEFFERSON was happy. He had deeply missed the pleasures of Monticello. He had missed his slave wife. How many times when he had been away from her had he imagined his hands riding over that beautiful body, seizing it as if it were handfuls of his own buff clay Monticello earth; the fragile woman's landscape of her turning, twisting, rising, and falling under his hands; the long black hair winding like a tributary of his own Ravina River; the golden eyes which turned dark amber in heat, shining upon him like his own Virginia sun, steady and enervating. Those eyes, this mountain, his friends, his neighbors. They were the only places he really felt safe. The mansion, his mansion, was finally finished. His burden of state, his presidency, was over. Only his university remained to be built now, and his family to care for: slave and white. He thought of Anne, soon to be married, and dismissed Sally's son Thomas, who had deserted him. He turned and beckoned to Beverly. Often, for the last year or so, he had seen Beverly waiting, as he was now, saddled up, hoping to be invited. And sometimes, when he really didn't feel like being alone, he would take Beverly along with him. Isaac, who held his horse, looked up at him and then over to Beverly, who sped to join his father.

As young as he was—thirteen and a half—Beverly was a splendid horseman, thought Thomas Jefferson. He rode almost as well as Burwell, and certainly better than anyone near his age at Monticello. Sometimes, when they raced, he would rein in Brimmer and let Beverly win. Sometimes. Beverly had grown so much in the past year, the boy's height would equal his own.

The two bright heads met in the light, Beverly's hair brighter and blonder than the fading, graying mane of his father. The two bodies were cast from the same mold with their heavy, awkward necks and wrists, their huge hands, and their long legs. Beverly flushed with pleasure and adoration as they rode off silently together. He had taken to riding the fields, asking questions, demanding—yes, demanding— instructions, begging to be taught, calculating, planning, counting, pleading for more knowledge. His father had been surprised at the astuteness of his questions, his quick mind, his grasp of trade, banking, interest, exports, tariffs, yields, crop rotation, loans . . . everything seemed to fascinate him.

His mother had begged that he be allowed to go to school with the Randolph boys in Charlottesville, if only as a body servant. She had not succeeded in this, but he had finally agreed that Beverly could be tutored secretly after classes by the instructor there, Mr. Oglesby. He was proud of Mr. Oglesby's reports on Beverly's progress. Beverly was the only boy he allowed the freedom of his library. Even his grandson Jefferson had to ask first. What power there was in teaching, he thought. His dream now was a university in Charlottesville and he was determined to build it.

Yes, thought Thomas Jefferson, his slave wife would forgive him in time for Martha. He had had no choice, and he had wanted his daughter with him. Peace. He was home. He had returned to the scenes of his birth and early life, to the society of those with whom he was raised and who had always been dear to him. The long absences, the pomp, the turmoil, the bustle, the splendor of office had drawn but deeper sighs for this place; he longed for private life, friends, and family. He had laid down his burden of power and hoped only that he had obtained for himself the approbation of his country. He mused.

He reined in his bay and waited for Beverly.

Thomas Jefferson's knees and thighs increased the pressure on his mount as Beverly reached him. Then, as they moved together, he cast a sidelong glance at his slave son. The clear, handsome profile was a replica of his own, even to his color. Love. God knows, he loved the boy's mother. Cherished her. He was bonded to her. She owned him just as surely as he owned her, the only difference being that her possession of him was a gift while his was a theft.

He was stirred as always by the thought of her fragility . . . her smallness, her smooth round skull he could cup in one great hand, the voice, that lovely voice. . . . He never ceased to be amazed at her beauty that seemed to deepen year by year. She was more beautiful now than at twenty, he thought. As for his own age, he wore it lightly, despite his attacks of rheumatism, his constantly aching right wrist, his bouts of dysentery. His wife had been dead for twenty-nine years, and this woman, whose image was before him in her plain blue gown, he had loved faithfully, with a mixture of guilt and passion, for more than twenty-three years.

Beverly, he thought, would soon be a man. He stared at his second son. A wave of love and bad conscience overwhelmed him.

"And how are your studies coming with Mr. Oglesby?"

"Fine, Master, sir."

"He's treating you well?"

"Oh, yes! He's very kind, Master. He's . . . wonderful to me, Master, sir."

Thomas Jefferson felt a pang of jealousy. It was the Charlottesville schoolmaster Beverly adored, not he. This Scottish schoolmaster was opening the door of the world to him, leading him, not he. . . .

"Come to my study this afternoon, Beverly. I have some books for you."

"Thank you, Master, sir. Shall I come before my classes?"

"Yes. You can show them to Master Oglesby."

He took a deep breath but the pain remained. Why didn't this son, whom he had never called son, and who had never called him father, love him?

Martha Jefferson Randolph was four weeks into her twelfth pregnancy. Twenty years of childbearing, and her eldest about to marry. She sat at the downstairs window of the salon and watched her father ride away with Beverly Hemings.

She wondered where Jeff was. Of course he was in school, she remembered. How stupid. Jefferson was eighteen now, a gentle boy, but not a Jefferson. Simply a Virginia gentleman without any special talent. Soon he would carry on his fragile shoulders the responsibility of the whole estate. Not only his father's affairs, which were in a dreadful state, but his grandfather's as well. Martha shuddered. How would he hold up under such a burden? If only Thomas Mann . . . But Thomas Mann was lost to her, to everyone. He had turned on his family. His delusions of persecution had cast her out. He accused her and the whole family of the most detestable crimes. Yet, he slept in her bed every night, got her with child every year, and made her life hell. She only hoped that Anne would do better. She didn't trust the handsome, rich, well-born Bankhead. She prayed that Anne would never live to regret her choice.

Why did she feel so old? She smoothed back a strand of hair, already turning gray, into the indifferent coiffure of the morning. She was only months older than Sally. Yet Sally's face was unlined, and her body seemed as fresh as it had been in her eighteenth year. Her own body felt used and abused, and she knew she had a slovenly air about her. Even her father had said so in so many polite words. Since then she had made a special effort to appear not only neat but with some style, especially at dinner.

Martha felt a burst of loneliness. She tried to conjure up the image of her mother, dead now for twenty-nine years. The unclear face of her mother flickered briefly before her. After Martha Jefferson's death, her father had gone on a rampage of destruction. There remained no vestige of her portraits, letters, journals, accounts, diaries . . . everything went. He had never forgiven her for dying and leaving him. But she, Martha, had forgiven her. She strained to remember the face of this woman before the time when, sick and wasted, she had bound her father to a vow which had kept him wifeless and her motherless.

Then, Martha Randolph realized, she did look into the face of her dead mother every day. When she looked into the face of her slave, her aunt Sally Hemings. She had realized it even in Paris, although she didn't know how long it had been evident to her. There were differences, but there were the same eyes, the same small stature—so different from her own—the same dreamy look, the same steely submission that masked the same taste for luxury and powerful men, except that her slave had more of a taste for politics than her mother had ever had. And if this is what she saw when she looked at Sally Hemings, what might her father see? She would give all of Monticello to be as adored as that. Or would she?

Martha Randolph shifted the weight of her awkward body. She picked up her sewing. Two things Sally Hemings, for all her resemblance to her mother, could never be: she was not white and she was not free. She, Martha, was mistress of Monticello now, and she would rule here, she vowed, until the day she died. Her father could have his pleasure. She would have Monticello, and her children after her, and her children's children. Monticello would descend upon her children unto the third and fourth generations, she thought proudly.

Sally Hemings held her straw hat in one hand and shaded her eyes with the other. She watched Beverly Hemings ride down the mountain with his father. The small head glistened in the slanting sun, the smooth brow furrowed with the effort of following father and son as far as she could see. Sally Hemings was in the summer of her life. There was a voluptuous richness about her. The yellow eyes had darkened to gold with a glint of steel, and the ivory skin to a delicate amber. The soft, pointed chin and dimpled mouth had the set now, not only of authority but of confidence. Her children were all born. Each birth had been difficult, but she had always recovered quickly. She had inherited the robust constitution of her mother and the vicious will of her father, so that pain had never stopped her from anything.

Thomas Jefferson was sixty-nine years old. Their passion, she knew, would diminish. She would not regret it. He had been an amazingly virile and passionate man, and their life together had been rich and full. But the body tired. The body simply refused. She would never take another lover. She had been one man's only. His. And if they were now like father and daughter, their contours, she thought, would always blend into that entity which was the human couple.

The summers seemed to pass more quickly. Europe was at war. Her beloved France was at war. The United States and its territories were at war with England. James Madison had been re-elected. Her master had reconciled with John, but not Abigail Adams. And now there was a fourth generation of Hemingses on the mountain. Little Sally Hemings and Maria Hemings, as well as her Harriet, had been sent to the weaver's cottage to learn to spin this summer.

She looked out over the land. They plowed in terraces now, following the contours of the hilly land instead of the straight rows up and down which had allowed the precious soil to run down into the river. Black hands plowed horizontally, following the curvatures of the hills and hollows on dead level; each furrow acting as a reservoir to receive and retain the rainfall. At least, thought Sally Hemings, in point of beauty, nothing could exceed that of these lines and rows winding and unwinding along the landscape. She stood contemplating it all for one more moment, and then, with that quickness of motion her lover had always remarked, she swung around, the heavy iron ring of keys at her waist jangling like a tambourine, and entered the mansion.

CHAPTER 40

WINTER 1819

BEVERLY HEMINGS' eyes roamed the hilly, hard-to-work farmland that stretched to the east. It had once been worth fifty to a hundred dollars an acre, but now with the Panic, it was worth barely twenty. His father was in money trouble. It had dawned on him more than three years ago, the day they had packed up his library and shipped it up to Washington City, the library that had been Beverly's only real education, aside from Mr. Oglesby.

My father needs money, he had suddenly thought. That realization had brought terror with it. Money troubles for the master meant only one thing for the slave—the auction block. His hands had trembled as he, along with Burwell, Harriet, and his mother, had carefully wrapped and packed the books into the cases that had been prepared by his Uncle John and Dinsmore, the master carpenter. The Randolph girls— Virginia, Cornelia, and Ellen—had helped as well. When they had finished all the packing, there had been sixteen wagonloads of books— three thousand pounds each—forty-eight thousand pounds of his father's life. Each book had been handled, read, and touched by him.

No, Beverly was sure, he would never have sold his library, even to the United States government, if he hadn't needed the money desperately. The British had burned the Library of Congress when they had burned the Capitol during the war. He remembered with what horror and rage his father had received the news, and now all his books were leaving. . . . Beverly had burst into tears; his grief was not only caused by the sudden loss of "his" books but the meaning behind it all. His father had let him take out his favorites from the lots, but had made him promise never to reveal this to a soul.

"If everyone were allowed to take out their favorite books, me included, I would have nothing to sell to the Congress. . . . You understand, Beverly, I have made a promise. I can't except anyone from the rule, even you. . . ."

From that day on, Beverly had had only one thought: how to keep his father, and thus himself and his family, safe from the threat of financial ruin that seemed to hang like a pall over Monticello. He had studied and looked and listened and planned and prayed as he saw the net drawing tighter and tighter around them all. And now the Panic had made everything ten times worse. There was real fear in the air.

Beverly Hemings stood watching the cavalier tear across the furrowed field just below the slope where he had set off his balloon. He laughed. He knew well who it was by the checkered black-and-white gingham coat with the huge metal buttons on it, the size of a dollar. The pantaloons were of the same material. The rider, mounted on a bay— Eagle, he guessed—was going at great speed. He was hatless as usual, his very head seemed on fire as his white hair caught the golden light, and he had a lady's parasol, probably Mama's, thought Beverly, stuck in his coat behind him and spread over his head to protect him from the sun. Beverly's heart filled with a kind of ironic tenderness. For his father.

It was now ten years since he had ridden home from the presidency. The time it had taken Beverly to grow up. His mother had not so much grown older as lighter, Beverly thought. Not so much in color; as a matter of fact, her beautiful face had grown darker—and not so much in authority either, for her presence was still as formidable as ever. Rather, there was about her a gradual disappearance . . . a seeping invisibility, so that even as he heard her voice, as sweet and thrilling as ever, with its soft lilt and slight foreign sound, it was as if it were coming to him disembodied.

If his mother was as transparent as a looking glass, his father glowed like the sun in it. He, Harriet, Thomas, and the younger boys seemed not even to have been created by this golden monster on his blooded, dangerous horse, and his mother, as still and deep as a reflecting pool. He didn't understand either of them. They were beyond mortality. They were like stones or trees. One couldn't rile against stones, could one? One couldn't curse trees. Beverly flung his fair hair out of his eyes.

They were the strangest couple he had ever encountered, his mother and father. His tragic, terrifying parents.

Perhaps she is a miracle, he thought, to have loved him and to have survived this long. But now Monticello needed another miracle—no disembodied voices, no guardian angels, no supernatural beings were going to resurrect this place or save it.

Jeff Randolph was fighting mightily to keep Monticello from bankruptcy, but he was fighting a losing battle. The unprofitable condition of Virginia estates in general, and his father's in particular, had left it next to impossible to avoid ruin, especially with the failure of the banks. It was he who helped Thomas Jefferson Randolph run the plantations, now that his father had put his affairs in the hands of his grandson.

All the planters had been in bondage to the banks, which held tons of paper on every plantation in Virginia, and this would continue unless some change took place in the mode of working them. What the estates needed was a complete reorganization, away from agriculture and slave-breeding. The unprofitable land should be sold and the money invested in the developing cities of Richmond and Fredericksville. Lumber should be their staple crop, not slaves; they should be supplying the fast-growing cities with lumber, and making investments that would make possible the exploitation of the thousands of acres of forests that belonged to them. Beverly was certain they had the means to save Monticello and make a fortune to boot. But no one would listen to him. It seemed so simple to him. His father didn't want to be a slave-breeder, didn't want to live off the labor of slaves. Instead of slaves working in wheat, tobacco, and cotton fields, whose crops were at the mercy of Northern bankers and boll weevils, they should have freed men, each with their family, housed in community housing, working for wages in Monticello lumber yards, nail factories, iron works. . . . Goodness knows, they had labor!

With the rendezvous of the boats from western Virginia only a few miles away at Milton, they could ship thousands of tons of nails, thousands of cubic yards of good Virginia pine to the newly building cities, the settlements of the Louisiana Territory, not to mention the rebuilding of Washington City. And what about wagon wheels?—with the iron, the lumber and the manpower available, they could make millions of wagon wheels for the West. It just took a little business sense, something his Viriginia aristocrat cousins knew nothing about. The nail factory, for example, was ludicrous. Run by an illiterate slave and a dozen children. It should be twenty times bigger, run by a foreman, white or black, it didn't matter, with men and the latest tools and forges. They had the land to build a real factory, not those miserable cabins they called a factory. White people were settling the Territories, and white people needed nails, iron pots, wagon wheels, farm tools, ax heads. And why not? Iron parts for the new steam engines, rails for the new steam carriages.

Beverly stopped abruptly. This was a good way to go crazy, he thought bitterly. He was nothing. A slave chattel. Why was he standing here watching his eccentric father ride, dreaming of a fortune in nails and lumber?

Yes, he would leave him in the end, this man whom he hated. Whom he wanted to adore. He had no choice. He was outlawed from him by his mothers's blood.

His father dismounted next to him. It always amazed Beverly that he was taller than his master, as broad, and now, with the years piled on Thomas Jefferson, stronger, much stronger.

"Thank you, Beverly. You, Isaac, be sure to wipe off Eagle. Wipe him down and rub him good. He's as tired as I am."

"Yessa, Masta."

Beverly had waited almost an hour for his father to return. He had wanted to talk to him about his ideas for the nailery and the south forests. But now his courage faltered. He knew that the only thing his father really wanted to talk about was his university. The university that he, Beverly, would never see the inside of, except as a carpenter or a floor polisher.

Last year he had ridden out with his master, his Uncle John, and the white workmen and slaves to commence the building of the university. Bacon had fetched a ball of twine from Davey Isaacs' store in Charlottesville, and his uncle had found some shingles and made some pegs; and they had all gone out into the fields that had belonged to Master Perry, now the grounds of the University of Virginia, and struck out the foundations of the building.

His father thought he could build a university that would take his mind off his decaying fortune, his mortgaged estates, his terrifying debts. His father would go on talking about his university in his presence without the least acknowledgment that every word was like an arrow in his breast: the new professors, the new buildings, the library,

Francis, when he came of age. In this way, Beverly's cousin, Mat, thirteen, was to become the property of his white cousin Francis, also thirteen years old.

Then, over at Edgehill, Thomas Mann sold Fennel's four-year-old Ely to Edmund Bacon for two hundred dollars. One day Fennel came home from the fields and his daughter wasn't there anymore. His wife lay in a faint; their baby girl had been sold away from them. Fennel had come riding from Edgehill to Monticello to recover his daughter from Edmund Bacon. When Bacon had heard Fennel was coming, he pleaded with her to calm him, as "he didn't want to harm him."

She had heard Fennel come howling down Mulberry Row as door after door closed upon his terrible face—the face of a man already dead, for wasn't he here to kill the white man who had bought his daughter or the one who had sold her? He had been pursued all the way from Shadwell by the black overseer, Jim, who had caught up with him almost in front of Elizabeth Hemings' former cabin. He had clubbed Fennel to the ground, and then had taken him tenderly in his arms. A ring of black men stood watch while Fennel had howled his grief into the night, within hearing distance of the Big House, howled like an animal, like the wild wolves that sometimes came up to the very doors of the slave cabins. His cries had washed over Monticello, over her and her children, safe within the mansion. Finally, dazed and beaten, Fennel had been lifted gently and flung over Jim's horse, and Jim had taken him back to his plantation.

That was when Beverly had left.

"Where is he?"

Sally Hemings was too tired to be frightened by the tone of her lover's voice. The violence of it was like a taste in her mouth. What could he do to her that he hadn't already done? She waited while her lover struggled to bring himself under control. She waited as she always had, supple and coiled and ready to spring to the left or the right, or fling herself down the center of his fury, depending on how it struck.

"I won't tell you," she said evenly, "because he doesn't want you to know where he is. He doesn't want any help from you. He's gone. North . . . as a white man. Of all your sons, he is the only one who hates you."

Thomas Jefferson stared at the woman who had been his mistress for thirty-five years. He would never completely understand her. She had raised these slave children, and if this son hated him it was because he had been taught to hate.

His long, gaunt figure moved quickly as he raised his slave wife from her chair. He knew now why this sensation, this chill, this sense of jeopardy was so familiar to him. He had never known, all these years, if one day he might not wake up, or come home, and find this woman gone. He drew her to him and looked into the eyes, which burned back at him like the sun.

I will free his sons.

Then she broke.

"Oh God, another gone!"

"And thank God for it," said Thomas Jefferson.

He felt his own throat go dry as he watched her strain away from him, watched her tremble once more above the abyss of contradiction which was their life together, peering over the edge into that moment he knew would come one day; when he would no longer be able to hold her, when she would choose to follow Beverly.

The woman looked up at the man.

Thomas Jefferson braced himself, as the small body he held against him crumbled, the tiny hands raking and clutching the material of his frock coat.

"Sally. Mother. Don't cry. Please don't cry." He was disconsolate. His face was a mask of helplessness, bewilderment, and rage that resembled nothing so much as that of the slave father Fennel.

CHAPTER 41

SPRING 1822

THE SPRING cut through her like the memory of a lover's quarrel. The May sun was high in the sky as she wandered down toward the sheep pastures, taking the shortcut through the sparse woods on the east slope. The moss had turned from silvery gray to emerald green and the ground under her feet was covered with white clover that looked like new-fallen snow, except that the earth was warm, not cold, and it was May, not December. New life was reaching out, claiming its inheritance. The earth, in its eagerness, was warm enough to walk barefoot. She stood among the black pines and inhaled the spring silence, opening her mouth wide in a soundless scream.

Thomas Hemings had given his father a grandchild, a white grandchild. Her son had secretly announced the birth of a little girl to her. A little white girl.

God, stand up for bastards, she thought. She shook her head. Martha had finally abandoned her husband. Thomas Mann Randolph had been elected to the governorship of Virginia, to everyone's surprise, and Martha had refused to accompany him to the governor's mansion in Richmond, preferring to remain with her father at Monticello. She had finally made her choice between husband and father.

Also, to everyone's surprise, Thomas Mann had proposed a plan for the emancipation of all slaves in Virginia and their deportation out of the state. Crazy Thomas Mann Randolph had had the courage to do something that his father-in-law had never dared. The proposition was defeated in the House of Burgesses. Thomas Jefferson had remained silent on the issue. Her sons had been beside themselves. The enormous prestige of their father could have saved the bill, they were sure. But he had said nothing to help his son-in-law.

It was the last thing he could have done for his slave children. It was the last thing he could have done for his precious Harriet, his only other daughter.

Harriet. Didn't he know he would lose her, too? More, even than his sons, she was lost to him. His darling little girl.

Sally Hemings came out of the woods. She saw her daughter converging on her from the direction of the house. The daughter had seen the mother and now she hurried. She didn't want to face her. Not now. But it was too late to escape back into the green. She stood and watched.

She could almost imagine that it was Maria who came running, so light and young and fragile and like her, except in height, was the young girl who approached. Harriet was now nineteen. She ran with her sunbonnet in her hand, and the light struck her auburn hair, which her mother had never cut and which was drawn back in a long braid reaching to her waist. As she ran, she held her head down under the weight of it. When the young girl stopped before her, there was only the slightest blush of pink under her cheeks.

"Mama . . ."

Sally Hemings looked into the emerald-green eyes of her daughter. She was out of breath and very beautiful. And she, the mother knew, was next.

Her twenty-first birthday.

Beverly had been gone for almost six months.

This would be her last ball as a slave. But Harriet Hemings expected to attend others on her own. The music of the slave orchestra wafted out over the expanses of lawn and jasmine bushes, the banks of roses and flowering magnolias of the Prestonfield Plantation. In the light from the tall windows of the ballrom sat an assembly of maids, carriage boys, valets, body servants, drivers, outriders, lackeys, footmen, and mammies: every shape, age, condition, and color of slavehood. Slavehood. She would peel it off like a dirty petticoat. She had been raised like a lady by her parents, educated with her cousins, and then, to her shock, had seen her adored playmates turn into masters overnight. Nothing would ever erase that pain. But then her mother had explained to her who she was and what would eventually happen to her.

The magic of her twenty-first year, when she would be freed. Free, as her father had promised her mother long ago in Paris.

And so she had played the game, but always in her mind was the knowledge of her reward, the breaking of the evil spell cast on her by . . . by whom? Whose fault was it that she was a slave? Her father's? Her country's? God's? Her mother had never been able to explain this to her satisfactorily, and she had never dared ask her father.

Hope had been her birthday. Now she was slave about to be free, black about to be white; girl about to become woman; without a past, about to be given a future; all for her birthday. She looked up at the sky. The moon was no more than a white sliver in the immensity of blackness. And what if the sky were white and the moon black? she thought.

Harriet had come into the circle of light from the ballroom windows, where she stood with the rest of the servants, entranced with the scene unfolding inside. The slave orchestra broke into a sprightly quadrille. Without the knowledge of the dancing white people it was playing Gabriel Prosser's song. Harriet shook her head and laughed with the rest of the servants while the whites continued to dance. Wasn't it typical, she thought, of white people to dance to a tune they didn't even know the words of. The whole South was dancing to a tune they didn't know the words of. The ladies and their escorts swung and looped, turned, skipped, grouped, and regrouped, forming circles and breaking like water on a creek bed.

Harriet's slender foot tapped to the music; her hips began to move. Suddenly, someone caught her from behind and swung her around. The maids and the lackeys had begun to dance in the circle of white light. They would continue to dance as long as their masters, far into the night, laughing and flirting, cooler outside than their sweating masters inside. They would outlast them, and then have to drive them home, undress them if they were drunk, wash them if they puked, pick up their clothes where they had dropped them, and put them to bed.

Harriet's skirts bobbed and swayed as her feet kept time and she sang the words of Gabriel Prosser's song:

> *There was two a-guarding Gabriel's cell*
> *And then more in the jail about;*
> *And two a-standing at the hangman's tree*
> *And Billy was there to get Gabriel out.*
>
> *There was musket shot and musket balls*
> *Between his neckbone and his knee,*

But Billy took Gabriel up in his arms
And he carried him away right manfully.

They mounted a horse and away they went,
Ten miles off from that hanging tree,
Until they stopped where the river bent
And there they rested happily.

And then they called for a victory dance,
And the crowd they all danced merrily:
The best dancer amongst them all
Was Gabriel Prosser who was just set free!

Harriet Hemings carried a razor-sharp stiletto deep in her petticoat pocket. It had been her Uncle James's. She would kill the man, black or white, who tried to force her. As her Uncle John had explained how difficult it was to kill, she had decided if she could not kill, then she would maim. She would die, but there would be one slave, or one master, who would never rape again.

She was going to be free. She was going to choose her husband. She was going to be married in a church. And she was going to her husband a virgin. She picked up her skirts and whirled in familiar black arms.

Everything was ready, and soon she would leave. It was November, already six months past her birthday. It was as good a time as any. Her mother had been working on her trunks for over a year. She had sweated and sewn until her hands were raw and swollen. Not only her mother, but her Aunt Critta, Aunt Bett, Cousin Betsy, Aunt Nance, Mammy Dolly, Cousin Ursula. Her Uncle John had made her three wooden trunks of the finest rosewood, with leather and copper fittings, lined in scarlet linen. Little by little, the trunks had been filled with dresses, linens of all sorts, petticoats, underwear, sheets.

Her mother had cut up everything she owned, either for the material or the trimmings. Even her yellow cloak had been torn apart, cleaned and recut into the most elegant yellow-and-black-velvet redingote she had ever seen. Her mother didn't dare let any of the white women of the house see it, for fear it would be confiscated. It was her strolling trousseau.

Her mother.

A slave inherited the condition of the mother. Was it her mother's fault that she was a slave? But why was her mother a slave? Wasn't that her father's fault?

More than any of her brothers, she had endured her temporary evil spell, her temporary slavehood, if not happily, then without rancor, and without suffering, grooming herself for the moment she would shed it, as her father had promised.

What no one had told her, and what she had had to fathom for herself, was that there was no freedom without whiteness; that to shed her slavehood was also to shed her color. If she were to escape the dangerous, persecuted, and harassed life of a freed slave, she would have to pass from one race to the other, from black to white.

Her mother.

Her mother still lived on memories of France while sitting in her secret room at the top of the mansion at Monticello, year after year, unable even to call her body her own!

Harriet Hemings had seen that room. It was filled with private treasure: silk dresses and petticoats, satin and kid shoes, and gloves, muslin and lawn dressing gowns, books, sheet music, a beautiful onyx pendulum clock, a green morocco leather chest, tooled in intricate designs and filled with linens, silk, and lace. There was also a delicate French writing table, a *coiffeuse*, bolts of velvet, and, most extraordinary of all, a hammered copper bathing tub called a *baignoire*. Her father had made a drawing of the *baignoire* her mother had used in France and Joe Fosset had built her one. All jammed into this one room: a whole secret life, full of beautiful treasures.

Most of it would be hers, her mother had told her. It was, she had reminded her daughter, her only dowry. She didn't need to indulge in her passion for beautiful clothes and beautiful things any longer.

Harriet Hemings was young and she was selfish. She would not throw away the gift of freedom as had her mother. She would grab it and run. Harriet's heart was heavy as she thought about the stagecoach that would take her away from everything she loved. But unlike her brothers, she would say good-bye to her father.

Adrien Petit had already arrived from Washington City to escort his former master's daughter to Philadelphia. He had left Monticello long before she was born, but Harriet had heard all about the indomitable Petit in Paris, in Philadelphia, at Monticello. Now her father had asked him to come and get her, and as a last service to his former master, he had arrived: a prosperous gentleman farmer and caterer, and, if the truth be known, richer than his former employer by many thousands of dollars.

Petit had prospered and bought land cheap around Washington and watched it double, then quadruple in value as the city thrived. He had tried, in the beginning, to persuade James Hemings to join him as a partner and chef, but James had had other ideas and had finally left for Spain, saying he would never live in a slave country again. Petit had wondered why James ever returned. But when he learned of James's death, he forbade himself to ever wonder again.

Petit sat now with his former master, receiving instructions about his daughter's settling in Philadelphia.

"You 'strolling,' Harriet?"

Madison Hemings was seventeen years old, tall and rangy with the bitter, suppressed violence of his uncle. He was trembling with rage.

"Yes, Madison. I'm leaving at nightfall."

"You going to pass for white?"

"Yes, Mad, I'm going to pass."

"Father knows you strolling?"

"Yes, Mad. He's arranged everything. He sent for Monsieur Petit to come and fetch me to Philadelphia."

"Who's that? A friend of Papa's? You got any money?"

"Papa, he gave me fifty dollars, and Petit, he's seeing to the rest."

"You know how much you worth on the slave block, Harriet?"

"Oh, Madison, don't. Mad. Mad."

"You worth a pile of money, sweetheart. I tell you. You a *fancy*!"

"Madison . . ."

"I tell you Father could get five thousand dollars for you on the block! Five thousand dollars in New Orleans . . . at one of those Quadroon Balls . . ."

"Oh, Madison. Don't cry. I love you so. I'll always love you. Do you think it's easy to leave you? If I don't take this chance, what other chance do I have? What future if I don't?"

"You'll be alone with no family, Harriet . . . the end of Mama. You're deserting her."

"I know, Madison, but I'll always be a part of you. I'm *you*; *you*. I'm your sister. I'm your flesh and blood, and I'll always be, no matter what happens. No matter how far away I go. I'll never forget you."

difficult not to stare at her. She had her father's incredible hair and his creamy complexion, unvexed by Thomas Jefferson's freckles. Her eyes were a perfect combination of the yellow of her mother and the blue of her father. She had his pride, his stubbornness, and his vanity. This one was hard. And she was superb. She would never cry, and she would never bend. She would die first. How could his former master bear to lose her?

He understood that she would now pass for white. She would have to change her name, he supposed. What would she call herself? Harriet Petit, perhaps. . . . He flushed as if he had said it out loud.

He was leaving America for good—rich, old, and still a bachelor. He would return to the Champagne region and live out the few years remaining to him. He would not mind at all leaving his name behind.

Harriet Hemings lifted her head and looked at her father for the last time. She wanted to tell him that she was his. His daughter. She would always be his daughter. But she said nothing. Then she turned her gaze, hard and candid and green, on Petit, imploring him to take her away from this place forever.

He straightened instinctively under the command of those eyes, then bowed and helped her into his carriage. His last service to Thomas Jefferson.

Darkness was descending as they drove down the mountain.

Adrien Petit and Harriet Hemings rode away and never knew that within hours of their departure, Thomas Jefferson slipped on a decayed step of one of his terraces at Monticello, breaking his forearm and dislocating the bones of his right wrist for the second time.

Harriet would not have known its significance, and even Sally Hemings, rushing to the aid of her injured master, could not have savored the special irony of this fall. Only Petit, opposite a violently trembling, but dry-eyed young orphan, would have remembered his master's original fall from grace, in the Paris of Maria Cosway, the year of Our Lord, 1787.

CHAPTER 42

OCTOBER 1825

"SALLY!"

It was Martha's voice, sharp with anxiety. I didn't know why I had come down the east stairs from my room as if I had been summoned, but I was in the hallway when she called. I saw her leading her father from the dining room, where he had—as usual—been entertaining a group of young students from the University of Virginia.

The door had been left ajar, and I could see the assembled young men, several of whom I didn't recognize.

As was his custom, Thomas Jefferson's place had been set separately, at a small table which was now empty, the chair pushed back. The young men were all on their feet, and several were peering anxiously through the opening of the doorway.

"Sally, he's been taken with a malaise," Martha said.

"No, Martha, I'm perfectly all right now."

"Here, let me help you."

He leaned heavily on me. I felt the tremor of his hand on my shoulder. How fragile and weak it was. Those hands that had had so much strength, that had guided, shaped, designed, and caressed. Now they rested, palsied and without weight, on my shoulder. I turned my back to open the door, and slowly we made for his room across the hall.

"Get Burwell," he murmured.

Burwell's gone to Charlottesville, I thought in panic as I looked over

my shoulders beyond the open door into the glare of the candle-lit
dining room.

Then I thought without surprise, He is dying.

From Harriet's departure on, misfortune had plagued us. No sooner
had my master recovered from his fall from the terrace than he had
ridden and had been thrown again by Brimmer. Stubbornly, he had
ridden once again, and this time it had been Eagle that had slipped
while fording a river and my master, entangled in the reins with his
crippled wrists, had almost drowned. Next had come a fever that had
confined him to his bed for three weeks. Then a flash flood had swept
away the dam he had been building for over a year. He began to sink
under the weight of his debts, which seemed to have no end. He had had
to borrow from his son-in-law Jack Eppes and had pledged Varina,
Martha's estate. Then his eldest and favorite granddaughter, the lovely
and gentle Anne, whom we called Nancy, died, believed by everyone to
have been killed by the brutality of her husband. Charles Bankhead, a
young, handsome aristocrat, had turned out to be a drunkard, a bully, a
coward, and a wife-beater. Many a time one of the overseers, or Burwell
himself, had saved her from a beating by her husband.

Six years earlier, Jefferson Randolph had accosted Bankhead on the
courthouse steps in Charlottesville and accused him of abusing his
sister. Bankhead had responded by stabbing Jeff several times with a
long knife. When Thomas Jefferson had heard the news, at nightfall, he
had mounted his horse and galloped down the mountain the several
miles to Charlottesville. Then, before I could stop Beverly, he, too, had
saddled up and ridden out to find his father. "He'll kill himself in this
weather," he had said. Fear in his face, he had taken Brimmer and sped.
When Beverly arrived at the store where Jeff had been taken, he saw his
father kneeling by the head of his wounded grandson, weeping. Jefferson Randolph had been conscious and when he saw his grandfather
crying, he too had started to cry. Burwell and Beverly had watched in
silence. Jeff, unlike his sister, had survived.

It was Eston who rode out after Thomas Jefferson now, fearful that
he would come to some harm. He would ride down to his university
that Eston and Madison had seen the inside of only as carpenters. . . .

In one way or another, all my master's "sons" had forsaken him.
Thomas Mann in insanity, Bankhead in brutality, Jack Eppes in pre-

mature death, Madison and Monroe in ingratitude, Meriwether Lewis in suicide, Thomas Hemings in flight, Beverly in whiteness. There was only Eston who remained a son. And in his hurt and melancholy and loneliness, he had shown more affection and tenderness to Eston than to any of our other children. He had given Eston Maria's pianoforte, encouraged his music, paid for his lessons; given him and Madison a plot of land of their own to earn money. Madison had become a fine fiddler, but even this tired and tardy recognition left me unmoved. I was like a piece of ground too long soaked with water which remains damp and cold even when the sun appears.

In the end, it was the master who sought his sons and their love, their attention, who wanted more from them than was his due; for if he had loved them, had he trained them as sons, a fierce and loyal love would have been his. His white grandchildren would never be able to give him the special kind of desperate love his yellow children would have laid at his feet. His grandsons were, after all, one generation removed from his flesh. Madison, Thomas, Eston, and Beverly were the sons of his passion.

At the end of 1824, one man who could remind him of our beginnings arrived at Monticello.

Resplendent, Lafayette returned again in February to Monticello, at the end of his triumphal tour of America, where he was laden with honors and voted by Congress two hundred thousand dollars and a township of land in appreciation for his services to the country during the Revolution. For my master, it must have been a bitter mockery of our own desperate situation.

General Lafayette's first visit to Monticello had had the aura of an official visit. There had been more than three hundred people present to witness the two old men shuffle into each other's arms, tears flowing.

The crowds had gathered outside on the west lawn that day to see with their own eyes the meeting of the two heroes of the Revolution. The fastidious and luxury-loving Lafayette had not changed his tastes, nor his mode of living, I saw, French Revolution or no French Revolution. As the elegant carriage rolled onto the flattened clay and sand, a dapper, finely dressed Lafayette had descended amidst cheers.

The last visit was quiet and more intimate, the true closing of a circle begun so long ago, the rendering of accounts, toting up of long-lost memories.

It was during this second visit that I made the acquaintance of

Lafayette's companion, the mysterious Frances Wright. She sought me out, eager to speak. Frances Wright, a rich, well-born orphan of Scottish descent, was rumored to be General Lafayette's mistress and had been his constant companion for several years.

She was twenty-nine-years old and Lafayette sixty-seven. The thirty-two years difference between her and her general was three years more than the difference between me and my president. She too had to fight Lafayette's daughters for a part of his affection, and if she had begged him either to marry her or adopt her, as was rumored, it was in the same futile hope of legitimate protection for her love as I had dreamed of for mine, and with the same despair.

Frances Wright was as tall as Martha Jefferson. Her hair was magnificent, but she was not especially pretty. Her fortune, her education, her unmarried state had given her a freedom and an independence unheard of for a woman. There was about her carriage, something of the radiance of a young man unafraid of whatever fate had in store, and confident that she would overcome whatever it was.

She did not seem in the least affected or aware of my position, or my color. I sat and listened as she outlined her ideas on emancipation, not only of slaves but of women. She was the first abolitionist I had ever met. I longed to speak to her of Thomas, of Beverly, of Harriet, but they were no longer Thomas, Beverly, or Harriet. They no longer existed in my world. They existed in the white world now, and I had no right to speak of that world to anyone, white or black.

One day, Frances took my hand and spoke to me passionately.

"Merely freeing and enfranchising the Negroes is not enough for them to participate in a free society. Only after they have been given some education and trained to support themselves can their freedom be meaningful."

She spoke with fervor of the communities set up by two men in Pennsylvania, Robert Owens and George Rapp. She spoke of helping slaves and whites alike live on a basis of equality, somewhere in the West or South, paying with her own fortune, where the slaves would be not only freed but educated. Blacks and whites would go to school together, people would be free to love and marry whom they chose. She also spoke to me about a woman called Mary Wollstonecraft, an Englishwoman, who had written a book on the emancipation of women called the *Vindication of the Rights of Women*.

"More than ever, it must be proved that black and white can and must live together," she lectured. "Since the Missouri Compromise, we have a country that is divided between slave and free societies. It cannot and will not endure thus. . . ."

It was the first real courage I had ever encountered in a woman. Frances Wright evoked a vision of life I did not recognize, and it seemed just as well that my life's illusion was near its end.

"Oh, Sally Hemings, let's understand what knowledge is . . . let's clearly perceive that accurate knowledge regards all equally. Truth is the same for all humankind; there are not truths for the rich and truths for the poor, truths for men and truths for women, truths for blacks and truths for whites, there are simply TRUTHS. . . . At least this much I have learned. While you are bound can any American woman say she's free? Can any American woman say she has *nothing to do with slavery?* And can you, Sally Hemings, say you have nothing to do with us? With me? We are all you and you are we . . . and THAT'S the truth.

"Nowhere outside my investigations of the rights of slaves could I have acquired a better understanding of my own rights . . . woman-hood's own rights. The anti-slavery cause is the high school of morals in this land. The school in which human rights are more fully investigated and better understood and taught than in any other. Is this country a *Republic* when but one drop of colored blood shall stamp a fellow creature for a slave? . . . Is this a *Republic* while one half of the whole population is left in civil bondage . . . sentenced to mental imbecility?"

I smiled. Oh, if only Harriet could hear her, I thought.

"You don't count the bonds of love and passion as one more bondage? You, a modern woman?"

Frances Wright smiled back at me. It made her face beautiful.

"Love and civics unfortunately don't necessarily go together," she sighed.

Later that year, she purchased two thousand acres of land for her new settlement of Nashoba, fourteen miles from Memphis, Tennessee, and there she put her ideas on women and Negroes and education into practice. When her experiment failed, her name would become, as mine had once been for the public, equal to every vice, and she would be denounced as "The Great Red Harlot of Infidelity," just as I had been denounced as "Black Sal." Her name, as mine had been, would be coupled with the unspeakable crime of miscegenation.

At the same time that Lafayette left America and Frances Wright left Virginia, Jeff Randolph tried to organize a lottery of our estates to satisfy my master's creditors. Timidly, he had showed me his letter to the Virginia Legislature for permission for the lottery, carefully enumerating his services to the nation.

Thomas Jefferson begging! I wept. "Why not ask John Adams?" I asked. But he shook his head slowly. The nation and Virginia had forgotten him. He was too proud to ask Adams. His son, John Quincy, was now president of the United States, and who knew how John Quincy Adams felt about Thomas Jefferson?

Thomas Jefferson would die thinking his lottery was going to save Monticello. And he died hard, just like Elizabeth Hemings.

He had persisted in riding to the very end. Isaac and Eston would lift him up on Eagle, aged like him, and he would ride out alone, with Eston or Burwell or Isaac following at a safe distance to watch over him. He would be out for hours, his white hair whipped by the wind, his coattails flying. When he no longer could ride because of the terrible pain, he semireclined on his couch, unable to either sit, lie, walk or stand.

"The doctors are trying to keep the old man alive until the Fourth," Burwell said on the third of July. "I don't think he's going to make it."

"I swear he will," I replied.

On that day, it was Burwell who had understood and lowered his head. When Burwell left the room, I realized I would soon have to give my master up to his white family, which was gathering. Martha, who was at Varina, would never make it up the mountain in time.

He was mine alone.

"The letters," he murmered.

So he had not burned them all.

I went to his desk and opened the drawers one by one. Mementos, locks of hair, a ribbon of mine, secret things I had never dreamed of, faced me as each drawer opened and closed. I spied a soft lock of fine blond hair. Which dead baby was it? I fell upon a packet of my letters.

"You found them?"

"Yes."

"You know . . . what you must do . . . Please?"

It was the first time he had ever addressed that word to me.

"Ask Burwell to do it," I whispered, "for I cannot." I backed away from the desk.

He reached out his right hand and clutched at my skirt. The twice-broken wrist was doubly twisted with arthritis, the hand atrophied. I slipped to my knees to come closer to him and looked into his eyes. They were the eyes of a young man; the same sapphire blue as always. One dies with the eyes one had as a child, people say. Even when the body is unrecognizable with illness and age, eyes are the eyes of childhood.

"Did you love me?" he asked.

After thirty-eight years he still had to ask.

"Lord, keep me from sinking down. . . .

"Lord, keep me from sinking down.

"Lord, keep me from sinking down," I repeated over and over again into that silence. A whole kingdom of silence. A whole world of silence.

When Burwell entered the draped study, there were tears streaming down his face.

"He left everything to Jeff Randolph. Madison and Eston are freed by his will. They are left under the guardianship of John, who is also freed. Joe Fosset is freed . . . so am I."

I stared at Burwell, waiting, but he stood there, his face contorted, his hands hanging loosely at his side, a look of grief on his face which resembled nothing if not stupidity. Still I waited. Waiting was my natural condition.

"He didn't free no . . . women."

I smiled. So he held me even in death. I had guessed as much when I had not been summoned to the dining room. I sat smiling. My smile must have been as stupid to see as Burwell's.

The death of a master, good or bad, is always a catastrophe for the slave. Sometimes he grieves out of real affection for the dead master, but mostly he grieves for the state of his future, which from that moment on is as vague and dangerous as his first journey out of his mother's womb.

Death of the master meant sale, separation from the land, from friends, and, if there were any, from wife and husband. And most of all, from children. The white family always took these outpourings of grief as proof that they were beloved, or of how much the dead master had been.

The Randolph family assumed as much, though here there was true grief as well. My master had been a "good master." The Randolphs were genuinely moved by the sorrow and mourning of the Monticello slaves. What they did not know, however, was that the slaves knew very well that Thomas Jefferson had died penniless, bankrupt, with a lottery on his land and his creditors hounding him to his very last breath. And they knew, too, that sooner or later Monticello, as had his other plantations, would fall.

It came sooner rather than later.

At Christmas I found Martha alone, standing in the threadbare blue salon, her heavy silhouette against the light, her white hair making an angry halo around her head. To my surprise, this day she had on gray silk, not black, an old dress, let out and pieced to accommodate her bulk. As I stood waiting for her to speak, I thought of our lives. We were only nine months apart, and I looked into the fifty-five-year-old face, so familiar to me, even more than in youth—a female replica of her father's face.

Age had marked it as it had not my own. The fair and fragile skin was etched with a thousand lines around the mouth and eyes, the skin crumpled like linen, the mouth drawn down in unhapppiness. Tiny red veins, broken under the skin, gave it a flushed appearance. Her blue eyes had been burned gray by some internal fire. I could hardly see the eyes, so pale were they behind the spectacles she was now forced to wear.

My mistress. Had her life been so much different from mine? Or as happy, for that matter? Slave or free, white or black, women were women and they were indentured to husbands, fathers, brothers, children, in sickness and in health, in death and life, to pain and pregnancy, work exhaustion, grinding solitude, and waiting. Ah, God, above all, waiting. It was all in Martha's face.

I waited. I knew what she had to say to me. I was to go on the block. The rumors were no longer rumors. In less than a month, Monticello and the remaining plantations would be auctioned off and everything on them, including the seventy-odd slaves. The inventory had already been taken by Jeff. I was listed as worth fifty dollars. And Martha? Was she worth any more than I? The domain we had struggled for in an undeclared war that had lasted thirty-eight years was no more to be fought over. It lay under our feet and hung over our heads, a decaying, awful parody of its master and builder.

This, then, was the last battle.

If the power had been hers, I thought, the endurance was mine. My face, I knew, was without line or crease; my complexion clear; my hair still black and abundant; my figure, except for a thickening at the waist and ankles, the same.

Martha took off her spectacles, which left scarlet bruises on her nose and brow.

"Ah, Sally."

"Martha."

We stood facing each other, sentinels to four decades of lies.

"I have something to tell you . . . such terrible news. . . . I don't know just how to . . ."

I waited for her to finish speaking. The words droned on without meaning. I then found myself staring at Martha in disbelief as she continued.

". . . and as he instructed me, you were to be freed within two years of his death, as soon as Eston was of age and could act as head of the family. I thought . . . forgive . . . that this day . . . that today was a good day. . . . Eston will be twenty-one in a few months. . . until then you may stay here, at least until July, as the house will not be sold, but you must know, since you people know everything, that the auction is the beginning of the year."

The date of the auction! Her voice suddenly reached me, clear and fraught with meaning.

"We cannot hold out any longer, Sally, and I dare not wait any longer to give you your papers. I hereby free you as my father wished, but could not acknowledge for . . . reasons of his own. He asked me to tell you this. He petitioned me, begged me, to free you. And for his sake I do so."

Here she paused, waiting for me to make the proper gesture. But what gesture was there to make? I knew of none.

"You have nothing to say?" she asked.

"Nothing."

"Nothing?"

"Nothing," I repeated.

I thought of my mother and her mother. It would have been slavish to have said anything. And I was not her slave.

"I think you could at least express your thanks. He petitioned me, but only I have the power to make you free. I could have allowed you to be sold on the block with all the rest!"

I stared at Martha. Did she really think she had the power to free *me*? Free *me* with a piece of paper, when I couldn't free myself with all the total yearning of a whole lifetime?

"Martha, I have no thanks to give. You cannot free me. Even *he* could not free me. He couldn't free me living, he couldn't free me dying, and he can't free me dead. He did what he had to do, as have you and I. I am an old woman, Martha, worth fifty dollars, and you are as worthless. Our lives haven't been all that much different, and death has us both by the hair. Can we not at least explain ourselves one to the other before it's too late?"

"You think I'd ever *explain* myself to you? I would rather die." Martha's voice was strangled with anger.

"Recognize that—" I began.

"Recognize! Do you think I'd ever recognize you? Recognition for the harm and slander you caused an innocent and great man?"

She would lie to herself to the end. She waved the white envelope in the air above my head like a child's gift.

"A thank you from the family?" It was our family she spoke of. "Recompense from the family? A souvenir from this house? A silver watch, perhaps?"

"Everything I'll ever need in recognition I've had, and souvenirs I have more than enough, even to silver."

What I did then, I don't regret, but it was a gesture as futile as our lifelong lies. I did it in cold anger and hatred of that white power she waved over my head. I pulled out the locket with the miniature John Trumbull had given me at Cowes and showed her his face: the same face in miniature that Martha always carried with her, the image she thought was hers and hers alone, I had carried for thirty-seven years around my neck.

The lock of his hair, blood-red, slipped from its place and fluttered to the floor. She made a gesture as if to stoop and catch it, then straightened with a sob, almost touching me. I fell back. Lie, I thought, lie to yourself, for it is your only hope. Deny me if you wish. Deny me with your last breath, your last cent, for in time, in this land, it will come to that.

"He loved me more than you! He loved *me*! You are nothing, you black slut! You slave whore! You know your children are not his! Never! They'll never be his!"

"Perhaps, but I was his. He loved me, Martha. It is not out of vanity or pride that I say it, but that was how it was between us. We loved. It was all that mattered."

"How can you speak of love between a master and a slave . . . between a hero and chattel?"

"We had no need to speak of it. . . ."

"You were nothing to him! A convenient slave paramour, a . . . receptacle!"

The evil words clattered like iron nails in the coffin of silence. There was nothing but pure hatred between us now. Martha's face pressed into mine and I looked into its decay as if in a mirror. Those eyes would not leave mine. She would not leave me in peace. The breath. The feverish face. We were like two bitches worrying over a rotting and long-dead carcass. Didn't she understand that it was over?

Then she drew back. Dread seized me by the throat like some wild animal. She was going to tell me something.

"Didn't you ever love me?" she whispered.

It was the same thing her father had asked. A wild, uncontrollable desolation bore down upon me. A howl like that of a wild animal caught in my throat. When . . . when would they understand this farce and this tragedy? I knew that only the one who stopped loving, who stopped needing love, would survive. And hate seemed to drop over me like a veil. Love had left me, and hate had filled that space. The grief and loneliness without him; the empty meaningless days and nights dissolved like dry straw. Hate lifted me up in a kind of exaltation. The white envelope which said I was free but which I knew would never really free me remained in her hand.

I didn't need anything anymore. I didn't need Martha. Martha needed me to free, but I didn't need Martha to free me.

I, like my mother and her mother before her, had survived love.

CHAPTER 43

NOVEMBER 1826

Notice from Richmond *Enquirer,* 7 Nov. 1826
EXECUTOR'S SALE

On the fifteenth of January, at Monticello, in the county of Albemarle, the whole of the residue of the personal property of Thomas Jefferson, dec., consisting of valuable negroes, stock, crops, etc., household and kitchen furniture. The attention of the public is earnestly invited to this property. The negroes are believed to be the most valuable for their number ever offered in the state of Virginia. The household furniture, many valuable historical and portrait paintings, busts of marble and plaster of distinguished individuals, one of marble of Thomas Jefferson Ceracci with the pedestal and truncated column on which it stands, a polygraph or copying instrument used by Thomas Jefferson for the last twenty-five years, with various other articles useful to men of business and private faculties. The terms of the sale will be accommodating and made known previous to the day. The sale will be continued from day to day until completed. The sale being inevitable is a sufficient guarantee to the public that they will take place at the times and places appointed.

[signed] THOMAS JEFFERSON RANDOLPH
Executor of Th. Jefferson dec'd.

It has long been known that the best blood of Virginia may now be found in the slave markets. . . .

FREDERICK DOUGLASS, 1850

THOMAS JEFFERSON RANDOLPH, better known as Jeff, sat in his grandfather's study, his long legs stretched out under the old man's writing table. He was the image of Thomas Jefferson.

He stared at the laboriously written inventory. It was pitiful, he thought. Not more than five years ago, these people would have brought four or five or even ten times these amounts. Of course, the most valuable slaves were not at Monticello, but at Poplar Forest, where they were about seventy odd who would bring in money as prime laborers. The Monticellian slaves were all more or less fancies, high-

331

yellow or white slaves, highly trained, but they were too old. He had never known Monticello without them.

He had lined them all up on the west lawn, practically in front of the window he was now gazing out of, and had gone around from one to the other making the inventory with Mr. Matter, the auctioneer. His nurses, his playmates were all there. He had taken out his own slaves— Indridge, Bonny Castle, and Maria—and those of Aunt Marck's, which were the most valuable, except for Davey Bowles. Damn! Davey Bowles should have been able to bring at least two thousand. . . . He had passed each familiar face, some so dear to him, that tears had welled in his eyes. When he had stood before Fanny, he had wanted to throw himself in her arms bawling.

Mr. Matter had kept apologizing for the low estimates, explaining that the bottom had fallen out of the market in the past year and that prices had plummeted almost eighty percent! At least they would keep the house with one miserable acre. That was all.

His eyes roved to the miniature staircase at the foot of his grandfather's bed. The passageway would be sealed at the request of his mother. Only the tiny staircase would remain. No one had taken the trouble to explain the relationship between the Hemingses and the Randolphs, but children had a way of finding out what they wanted to know, thought Jeff. Like the day of the inventory when he had looked into the eyes of Sally Hemings. He had heard Mr. Matter's automatic whisper:

"Age?"

"I reckon between fifty and sixty," he had answered.

"Fifty dollars," Mr. Matter had said.

And Sally Hemings had said, "Oh my husband," looking straight at him.

She had said it, damn it. Clear as a bell. Only once, but he had heard it. When he had told his mother of it, she had shrugged and said that Sally's mind was probably wandering with the shock of the sale. She had never had a husband. Then his mother had announced that she was freeing Sally Hemings because his grandfather wanted it that way. It meant they would have to petition the Virginia legislature for her to remain in the state—dangerous.

Of course, Sally Hemings hadn't said those words to him, for her eyes had been fixed on the Blue Ridge Mountains, and they had had the most unearthly yellow glow. God damn! . . .

Barnaby	$400	Davy	$500
Hannard	450	Zachariah	350
Betty old woman	no value	Nace	500
Critta	50	Nance an old woman	no value
Davy senior (worth nothing)	~~250~~	Ned	50
Davy junior	250	Jenny (of no value)	
Fanny		Moses	500
Ellen	300	Peter Hemmings	100
Jenny	200	Polly (Charles' daughter)	300
Indridge (the younger)		Sally Hemmings	50
Bonny Castle		Shepherd	200
Doll (of no value)	—	Indridge the elder	250
Gill	375	Thrimston	250
Isaac an old man	0	Wormsley	200
Israel	350	Ursula	
		and her young child	300
James	500	Anne & child Esau	350
Jersy	200	Dolly ~~22~~ 19	300
Jupiter	350	Cornelius ~~18~~ 17	350
Amy	150	Thomas 14	200
Joe to be free in July next	400	Louisa 12	150
Edy & her child Damie	200	Caroline 10	125
Maria 20		Critta 8	100
Patsy 17 or 18	300	George 5	100
Betsy 15	275	Robert 2	75
Peter 10	200	Infant valued with Ursula	
		its mother	60
Isabella between 8 and 9	150	I have omitted Aunt	
		Marck's and mine, also the 5	
William 5	125	freed ones	
Daniel 1½ Lucy's child	—	The ages are set down as	
		near as I can come at them	
Good John, no value	—	without the book	
Amy same	—	Johnny to be emancipated	
Jenny Lewis (of no value)	—	July next	300
Mary (Bet's) young woman	50	Madison same	400
		Eston same	400

11,505

[signed] THOMAS JEFFERSON RANDOLPH

CHAPTER 44

JANUARY 1827

THE DISMANTLING of Monticello by the slave auction of 1827, the abomination of the sale of my kin, the ticketing and labeling and pricing of every stick of furniture, every sheet, every curtain, every dish, every book, painting, sculpture, each clock, vase, bed, table, horse, mule, hog, and slave that had been Thomas Jefferson's; that had been he, himself; all his parts and pieces, his choices, his favorites, his ears, his hands, his eyes, was the sorrow and pity of my life. His life had been parceled and lotted and priced by the auctioneers who thronged through the house. His life's bits and pieces probed and handled, weighed, inspected, and priced. Everything, animal and human, including my own flesh.

I despised the steaming crowd that had gathered round the west portico of Monticello that January day, come to bid like vultures on the carcass that had been a man and his house. If only he had not loved everything so much! If everything had not been love and memory as well as collection!

People arrived by the wagonloads. A county-fair atmosphere reigned as the prospective buyers strolled in and out of the barns that held the slaves, and the house that held the objects, their flyers in hand, inspecting: objects tenderly accumulated in Paris; a house of brick and wood assembled by my kin; the brilliant English gardens, now brown and colorless; and the orchards, now leafless and barren; and beyond, the rolling fertile fields, woods, cascades, and rivers. Already the deep black lands of Pantops and Tuffton, Lego, Poplar Forest, Bear Creek, Tomahawk, and Shadwell were gone, now the humans attached to them were going. One thousand four hundred and fifty lots had been auctioned off that day, forty-two hogs, fifty sheep, seventy cattle, fifteen horses, eight mules, and fifty-five humans from Monticello—more than half of the slaves were my sisters, brothers, cousins, nieces, nephews. And one hundred and twenty from Bedford.

The crowds had begun to assemble early that day. They had come from as far away as Kentucky for a chance to buy prime black flesh, livestock, or an object that had been, as I had been, a possession of Thomas Jefferson. There had been that same lewdness in the air, that same miasma of death and contempt and titillation that always accompanies the trial, judgment, and condemnation of a man's life. Around me festered the curiosity about the great, the aura that sets some men above others and brings out that predatory hatred of the common for the extraordinary.

My master had left debts of one hundred and seven thousand dollars. Martha and Jeff had struggled valiantly to save Monticello, selling off all the other lands and plantations; the lots in Richmond and Charlottesville, everything. But everything had not been enough. The gods had demanded and got all but the mansion of Monticello.

Strangers had roamed his precious gardens, treaded his polished floors, inspected his linen, looked into his barns and the mouths of his slaves, pinched velvet and flesh, sniffed tobacco and the smell of human sweat, hefted samples of cotton and the private parts of male field hands, rubbed their hands over the woolly rumps of Marina sheep and the heads of pickaninnies, discussed the qualities of Monticello blooded bays and Monticello pure-bred bodies.

Hatted and veiled, my identity hidden behind my color and the name of "Frances Wright" of Tennessee, I had roamed the crowds that day as a freedwoman, despite the danger, willing myself to engrave every moment in my memory, hoping to save one or two of the children, and vowing never to forget the sale of Thomas Jefferson.

"If you don't be good, I'll tell Master, and he'll sell you to Georgia, he'll sell you so fast . . ."

How often had those words struck terror in a slave child's heart? How long, how much longer, would they continue to? He had been good, but he would be sold anyway.

"What do I have, whatdo I have, whatdoihave for this lot number thirty-four, three prime male field hands, twenty-six to twenty-nine,

335

broken here at Monticello, in perfect health, no scars, bruises, defects *of any kind*; never been whipped, docile, strong, perfect for breeding. What am I bid, whatamibid, three hundred, four, four fifty. Do I hear five? Five, five twenty-five, six, six, six. Do I hear seven? Yes seven, seven twenty-five, seven fifty; only seven fifty for this prime lot, three . . . ladies and gentlemen, three prime Monticello slaves, three for the price of one. Ladies and gentlemen, I ask you, is this the best you can do? Eight, eight fifty. Do I hear nine? Nine, do I hear nine, nine, nine, nine—going once, nine going twice, nine going three times—sold, sold to the lady for nine hundred dollars. Prime, male house slave, thirty-two years old, Israel, father of seven in the next lot, locksmith and metalworker. Prime, housebroken pickaninnies, a lot of seven. Just a few years and they'll be prime field hands or house servants, healthy stock, no blemishes, light-skinned. Do I hear five hundred? Five hundred once, five hundred twice, five hundred three times. Sold! Sold! Sold! A female, twenty-nine years old, breeder, light-skinned, seamstress and cook, perfect for a housekeeper for a young gentleman; may I start at four hundred? Four hundred fifty? Elizabeth, Israel's wife. Do I hear four? Four, four fifty, five . . . female slave, fifteen, guaranteed virgin, healthy, bright, best stock of Monticello, trained as a house servant. Priscilla, Israel's daughter.

"Do I hear three hundred? Three hundred. The best stock at Monticello. Docile, perfect for a lady's maid. Only five hundred dollars. Ladies and gentlemen, Christmas was a week ago! I cannot let this prime female go for less than three fifty. Do I hear three fifty? Yes, three seventy-five. Do I hear four? Four. Four. Do I hear four? Sold to the gentleman for four seventy-five. Dolly.

"Prime first-class female. Cook. Thirty-six years old; served at the President's House in Washington City. Pastry and all-around cook. Do I hear one hundred dollars? Two? Do I hear three? Three for this treasure trained in French *cuisine*. Of impeccable stock, guaranteed fertile, mother of three. Three fifty, do I hear four? Four fifty, do I hear five? Five fifty once, five fifty twice, five fifty three times. Sold to the lady for five hundred and fifty dollars. Fanny. One big black healthy mammy trained as washerwoman, midwife, and pastry cook. Weighs in at two fifty [laughter]. House servant for twenty years. Sixty-two years old, ladies and gentlemen, I won't lie to you, but she still has some good years in her. Loves children, mother of eight herself. All them children in lot fifty-six hers! Loyal, honest, clean house mammy. Do I hear thirty

what mere Time will do . . . : how if a man was great while living, he became tenfold greater when dead. How a thing grows in the human imagination when love, worship and all that lies in the human heart is there to encourage it. . . . Enough for us to discern far in the uttermost distance, some gleam . . . in the center of that enormous camera-obscura image to discern that at the center of it all was not a madness and a nothing, but a sanity and a something.

He watched her as she stood, her arms wrapped around herself. And as he watched her, Nathan Langdon felt the gulf between them. It had grown, he realized, with the years. Even as he stood there unknowing, the distance separating them was a canyon, a bottomless crater, a fissure in the earth, uncrossable, unbridgeable, unfathomable, unforgivable. The sound of summer thunder rolled over the Blue Ridge Mountains, a distant prediction of turbulence to come. What Nathan Langdon did not know is that the turbulence to come, which he would witness in sickness and despair, would claim the lives of three of Sally Hemings' grandsons. A bitter struggle that would cost five hundred thousand lives. One life lost for every slave freed.

Sally Hemings stood in the violet rectangle of her cabin, her arms outstretched, her palms pressed against the oak doorframe, the dark shadows framing the still lovely face. She contemplated the cherished and familiar landscape. It calmed her. The lush Southernness soothed her nerve ends, the colors washed over her flesh so long contorted and deep with memory. Memory had no shame. All were equal before it. Then she stepped outside. Her body dove into the languid summer landscape like a swimmer, and her head lifted as if she sensed a presence. She looked toward the Blue Ridge. But all she saw was the dark-green forest and luminous sky and all she heard were the sounds that summer makes.

She had never reached out beyond her triple bondage. She had clung stubbornly to the only thing she had ever found of her own in life: love, and love had been more real to her than slavehood. And she had survived both. This was the truth of her life.

Sally Hemings closed her eyes against the sunlight and against the blinding pain in her head. She stood in her own embrace, triumphant; beyond love, beyond passion, beyond History.

And surrounding the two solitary figures, lost in the vast intractable

343

wilderness of the American landscape, was the infinite chiaroscuro of silence, where all biographies become one.

She picked up her skirts and started up the mountain toward the safety of her beloved shade trees, just as, with a kind of violence, the census taker turned away and headed back down her road.

AFTERWORD

FIFTEEN years ago, when I first published *Sally Hemings*, many factors differed greatly from what they are today. My first book of poetry had just been exquisitely and lovingly edited by Toni Morrison, who was not yet the Nobel laureate. Black studies were in their infancy in American universities and the name Sally Hemings was totally unknown to the general public. Everyone involved with publishing *Sally Hemings*, including the author, underestimated the emotion and controversy that would swirl about a novel that gave flesh, blood, and sinew to a long-held and much discussed conviction that Thomas Jefferson had a slave family by the half-sister of his dead wife. This conviction was long held by his contemporaries, from John Adams, who received Sally Hemings and Jefferson's daughter at the American Embassy in London, to Gouverneur Morris, a New York Congressman who was with Jefferson in Paris in 1789, and long, long denied by others.

I had wanted to illuminate our overweening and irrational obsession with race and color in this country. I would do it through the man who almost single-handedly invented our national identity—and through the woman who was the emblematic incarnation of the forbidden, the outcast; who was the rejection of that identity. I would use the form of the nineteenth-century American Gothic novel, whose very essence is embedded in the American psyche.

But I was a poet, a sprinter in literature, not the long-distance runner that the novelist is. Timidly, I began *Sally Hemings* as an epic poem.

Then I discarded that and wrote an outline of something I called *Diary of a Slavegirl, Paris 1788*. Discouraged, I begged Toni Morrison to write this story. Had that happened, the rest would have been history; but she was busy with her own work. I tried to convince every writer I knew to take up my task. They all had their own lives and Sally Hemings wouldn't let me alone, nor I her. Finally, Morrison advised me that the only solution was the historical novel. When I protested, she smiled the most incisive and irreducible smile in American letters and said, "Stop talking about it. Just do it, Barbara."

I do believe that if this story had not begun in France, where I have lived since the early sixties, I would never have attempted to unravel the morass of legend, disinformation, evasion, hostility, symbolism, and false perceptions of almost mythical dimension that it encompasses. I don't know that I myself would have believed the story of Thomas Jefferson and Sally Hemings if it had begun in a field at Monticello, as many have chosen to imply, rather than in the revolutionary Paris of 1787. And never knowingly would I have taken on the old-guard Jeffersonians, powerful, southern white men with an agenda: to protect the good name of Jefferson, by any means and at all cost, from their greatest fear—the accusation of race-mixing, or as it was misnamed around 1864, miscegenation, a term that originally had nothing to do with race, but referred to the intermixing of heathen and Christian motifs.

But what makes the story believable is precisely that these two personages were taken completely out of their racial and social context and redefined in a France fermenting with ideas of social and personal liberty. Sally Hemings, described in the memoirs of Isaac, a Monticellian slave, as "mighty near white" with long black hair hanging down her back and known as dashing Sally, was white enough to pass as white in Paris and most probably did so. Otherwise, Jefferson's circle in that city would have remarked that in his household he had a blackamoor, a coveted and fashionable status symbol among the European aristocracy at the time, who cultivated the exotic "Moorish" style. Jefferson's friend Maria Cosway had such a blackamoor in her residence in London. On the other hand, Thomas Jefferson had, for the first time, ventured beyond the provincial and racist slave-holding plutocracy he had been born and raised in. He could perceive Sally Hemings for what she truly was. In France, both of them were free. And then consider the astounding blood ties between them that reached back through three generations of slave mistresses and made Sally Hemings the half-sister of

Thomas Jefferson's wife, aunt to his legitimate daughter, and sister-in-law to Jefferson.

Moreover, I had to find a way to elevate a member of the most despised caste in America to the level of the most exalted. I had to do that in order to make believable Sally Heming's liaison with America's most famous historical name: Thomas Jefferson. Linguistically, I solved the problem by always referring to Sally Hemings by her full name. I felt that neither the author nor the reader had the right to call Hemings "Sally," much as Hemings dare not call Jefferson "Thomas" until they were equal in love. This subtlety was sometimes lost on my copy editor, who wanted to know what difference it would make if a few "Sally's" slipped in. But as far as I know, over fifteen years (and counting), no one has commented on this styling and its efficiency—apparently, and gratifyingly, because the supposed artifice seems natural to readers. It simply lifts Sally Hemings well out of her role as a slave and helps make a minor historical figure the equal, as a genuine archetype, of Thomas Jefferson.

Perhaps that was one reason the novel was railed against from the pulpit, from CBS "Sunday Morning" and from Monticello itself. Three months after the publication of *Sally Hemings*, on the night of July 3, 1979, the stairway at the foot of Thomas Jefferson's bed was removed, leaving a huge, gaping hole to greet the dawning of the Fourth of July. I was not told why the stairway was removed; I was only ardently assured that it had *not* been removed because it was mentioned in *Sally Hemings* and tourists were asking to see it.

The book itself had gotten the Jeffersonian scholars and enthusiasts up in arms; now they were roiled by news that God forbid, *Sally Hemings* was going to be a movie. And, in fact, my eyewitness to the removal of the stairway had been a screenwriter working on his movie adaptation of my book. On the third of July, when the screenwriter had been at Monticello, the staircase had existed; and when he returned on the fifth, it had disappeared.

Two months later I discovered the unplastered, uncamouflaged hole where the stairway had been. When I stormed into the curator's office, he rather shakenly assured me that the removal of the stairway and its demolition had nothing to do with me or Sally Hemings. I was being "paranoiac," I was assured. "The staircase was not authentic," he explained; I asked what was authentic and received the answer "steps." That man's present, excellent successor as research director explained that indeed, the staircase had been removed in seventy-nine and that they had been proved "right" in their presumption that it was false because they had found Victorian nails and a discarded Victorian tool under the stairs.

The original analysis may have been proven correct, but on the basis of the act that followed it, one might soon hear the experts say: "Next let's break all the Victorian windowpanes at Monticello and never replace them, because they are not authentic." As of this writing, the staircase has never been replaced, by "steps" or anything else. Nothing has been placed in the stairwell because any structure there, I was told, would be "misleading to the public." One would have to believe that America's greatest architect built a stairwell not meant for a staircase from the foot of his bed to nowhere for no earthly reason.

But now all the old-guard Jeffersonians of our century, including the most illustrious, Dumas Malone, have disappeared. In his last interview with *The New York Times*, Malone admitted (as, I suppose, a kind of testament) that he could accept that "it" (a clandestine liaison between Thomas Jefferson and Sally Hemings) had taken place "once or twice." I am not sure if he meant one or two *children*, or if this most fervent admirer and greatest biographer of Jefferson preferred to accept the idea of Jefferson as a casual seducer or rapist of slave women, rather than to consider the possibility of a long-standing human relationship between "his" president and Sally Hemings. He also never addresses Jefferson's sexual life between the ages of 39, when his wife died (he was 43 when Sally Hemings arrived in Paris) and 81, when his life ceased.

Now the Jeffersonians have a different stratagem from the pained silence of old: categorical, sound-bite denial; in certain cases, fudging of dates and of historical evidence; and disinformation. These Jeffersonians also contend that Jefferson never changed his mind about race. They cite his *Notes on the State of Virginia* ad nauseam to prove his racism, and incidentally, to reinforce their assertion that an intimate human relationship between a slaveholder and a "black" slave was impossible.

Yet, as the "strident," "enraged," and "blasphemous" detractor of Jefferson, I think otherwise. The *Notes on the State of Virginia* were not written for publication; they were letters to a Frenchman in 1784 when Jefferson lived in a backwater, oppressive, slaveholding Virginia society, and had never ventured outside this closed environment. Twenty years later, Jefferson wrote to another Frenchman, Condorcet, concerning the black mathematician Benjamin Banneker, whom he had hired along with L'Enfant to lay out the city of Washington, D.C.

> ... I procured him to be employed under one of our chief directors in laying out the new Federal city on the Potomac, and in the intervals of his leisure, while on that work, he made an almanac for the next year, which he sent to me in his own handwriting ... I have seen very elegant solutions of geometrical problems by him. Add to this that he is a very worthy and respectable member of society. He is a free man. I shall be delighted to see these instances of moral eminence so multiplied as to prove that the want of talents, observed in them, is merely the effect of their degraded condition, and not proceeding from any difference in the structure of the parts on which intellect depends.

Could he have been any clearer? Are we to believe the provincial Thomas Jefferson of 1784 or the President of 1804? The Jefferson before his only voyage outside America, or the Jefferson after? That notable absence of one indispensable American from the newly independent United States lasted for five years. Yet even today there exists not one serious volume dedicated to Jefferson's activities or thoughts during those years he spent in France.

Whom would we elect the true Thomas Jefferson? The man on record before Sally Hemings came into his life, or the one that spoke and wrote after she had produced her third daughter, Harriet, the subject of my 1994 book *The President's Daughter*?

The debate between the new Jeffersonians and me abides, and not without incident. A fitting, ironic piece of evidence came to light in February 1993, the 250th anniversary of Thomas Jefferson's birth. The Monticello research department discovered in their own archives a letter dated December 19, 1799, in Jefferson's own hand, addressed to his son-in-law, Francis Eppes, in which he announces the birth of still another child of Sally Hemings, born December 7, 1799—nine months after Jefferson returned to Monticello from Philadelphia. Indeed, we know he was present in the life of Sally Hemings nine months before the births of all the children now known to have been born to her. But, for me, the true, heart-stopping, hair-raising shock came when I asked for the name of the child and was told that it was Thenia, and that she had lived just beyond her second birthday. In my novel *The President's Daughter*, which had already been delivered to the printer's, I had *invented* a Thenia, who is rescued by Harriet Hemings from the Monticello slave auction and taken north with her, into her new life and oblivion. (To this day, I do not know why I called her Thenia.)

So there is a real Thenia, one who really existed and was Sally Heming's daughter; and there is the Thenia of my imagination, Harriet Hemings's alter ego. Where is "truth" and where is "fiction"? Who is real and who is unreal; who false and who genuine? What is history and what is romance?

In *Romancing the Shadow*, Toni Morrison writes:

> It has been suggested that romance is an evasion of history (and thus perhaps attractive to a people trying to evade the recent past). But I am more persuaded by arguments that find in it the head-on encounter with very real, pressing historical forces and the contradictions inherent in them ... Romance, an exploration of anxiety imported from the shadows of European culture, made possible the sometimes safe and other times risky embrace of quite specific, understandably human, fears: Americans' fear of being outcast, of failing, of powerlessness ... In short, the terror of human freedom—the thing they coveted most of all. Romance offered writers not less but more; not a narrow ahistorical canvas, but a wide historical one; not escape but entanglement ... It offered platforms for moralizing and fabulation, and for the imaginative entertainment of violence ... and terror's most significant, overweening ingredient: darkness, with all the connotative value it awakened.

> There is no romance free of what Herman Melville called "the power of blackness," especially not in a country in which there was a resident population, already black, upon which the imagination could play. . . .

In other words, nineteenth-century Romance has always served in America for what I would call the metaphysics of race.

If Thomas Jefferson offers himself up as a surrogate for meditation on the problem of human freedom, then Sally Hemings is available for meditation on terror, darkness, invisibility, dread of failure, guilt, and powerlessness. Even her "whiteness" is perceived as blackness.

It is this *perception* of race and blackness that is at the hidden core of early American literature and early American history. It is as if we were desperately trying to tear out this heart of darkness that is an integral part of the American identity—a part that cannot be excised, but must be absorbed, reconciled, and above all, recognized.

AFTERWORD

Sally Hemings and Thomas Jefferson are a most poignant, tragic, and irreducible addendum to the enigma at the very heart of our history and our literature; that of the races and the sexes in our country.

Barbara Chase-Riboud
Paris, April 1994

AUTHOR'S NOTE

When I first published *Sally Hemings* in 1979, I introduced as a character the French majordome Petit, who served Jefferson in Paris and later at Monticello, where he was employed as a registrar for over two years before following Jefferson to Washington.

Until then, historians, if they referred to Petit at all, referred to him by last name only. No one knew his first name. So, for the purposes of *Sally Hemings*, my assistant and I invented a first name for him—Adrian. Then, in an obscure list of Monticellian registrars, I found his real name—Hugues Petit.

But Hugues Petit didn't ring "true" to me, and it didn't sound "French" to me. Moreover, as certain historians are fond of saying, "It wasn't in character." So, because I could, in a novel, invent a character in all innocence, I kept the name Adrian Petit. Little did I dream that he would become my own private experiment in the writing and interpretation of history.

As Voltaire so aptly noted, *"There is no History, only fictions of various degrees of plausibility."* If I had wanted to find out how a plausible invention becomes part of the march of history, I succeeded. No one bothered to check whether "Adrian" Petit was real, because he "sounded" real, he "sounded" French, he "sounded" in character. By assuming "Adrian" Petit was the actual name of the majordome and not an invention, many historians did, in fact, follow me down the road of fiction into history, from an imaginary character (or at least as imaginary as Charles Franklin, Dexter Madison, or Serge Monroe) to what passes for and is served up as reality. Since 1979, when *Sally Hemings* was first published, every historical publication, biography, and novel, if they mention him at all, misnames the real Hugues Petit as "Adrian" Petit, the fictional Adrian I created in *Sally Hemings*. "Adrian" Petit has become historic, so much so that I have been admonished not to confuse Hugues Petit with Adrian Petit.

Who is "Adrian" Petit? Who did this or thought that, according to "history"? Whose "Adrian" Petit is this? Mine? Theirs? History's? Certainly not history's. And, more important, what about the reverse of this process, what about when a piece of unwelcome reality is metamorphosed into fiction because it doesn't "fit"? We can be sure that this occurs as well—take the case of Sally Hemings.

Yet, because of the sanctity of the "science" of history, Adrian Petit is more "real" to us than Hugues Petit will ever be because Adrian Petit is listed in the indexes of various history books. And so, in a backhanded homage to Voltaire (Francois Marie Arouet de), the new Jeffersonians have unknowingly taken a fictional footnote and venerated it into reality as they see it, just as they accept the uncollaborated statement of a six-year-old (Ellen Randolph was six years old in 1802 when the Sally Hemings/Thomas Jefferson scandal occurred) as historical "proof" that Jefferson's nephew, and not Jefferson himself, was the father of Sally Hemings's children.

I have no particular reason or desire to embarrass anyone except those who indulge in taking their desires for reality at all costs and their "scientific" arrogance for a license to obfuscate, eliminate, suppress, fudge dates, and indulge in unsubstantiated sweeping statements in their own or the "public's" interest.

For if my little experiment with Adrian Petit proves anything, it proves that in a free nation, History should be revered, not the people who make or write it. And this history should be revered, warts and all, with all the dangerous passions, secrets, contradictions, anachronic interpretations, dark undersides, and self-preserving lies that go with the mythology of a nation, and should be revised often.

For history is nothing more than the human adventure as told by fallible humans, with all their prejudices and psychoses and visions, to the society which they serve. The result is sometimes, even most often, "scientific" truth, but not always. So, it is well to remind ourselves of Voltaire's words that there "is no History, only fictions . . ." when we encounter the name Adrian Petit in the index of a Jefferson biography, and to note that only a free, vigilant, and uncensored society can afford truth and only truth affords a free, vigilant, and uncensored society.

My editors and I have kept the name Adrian Petit in this edition of *Sally Hemings* for, as you may well smile, "historical" reasons. Although Adrian Petit never existed in "real life," the reader would not recognize a character called Hugues Petit.

We have done this as a lesson to all in historical humility and respect for the unending and ever-fascinating secret history of the world.

Dedicated to the memory of Fawn Brodie

ACKNOWLEDGMENTS

ALTHOUGH a bibliography would be long and out of place here, I must acknowledge certain published and scholarly works not previously mentioned and without which this book could not have been written. They are not, of course, responsible for any errors, interpretations, or misinterpretations I have made.

First, Fawn Brodie's book, *Thomas Jefferson, An Intimate History*, and her two articles published in *American Heritage*, "The Great Jefferson and Taboo" and "Thomas Jefferson's Unknown Grandchildren."

Second, the memoirs of Madison Hemings, of Edmund Bacon, of the ex-slaves Israel Jefferson and Isaac Jefferson, as well as the diaries of Aaron Burr and John Quincy Adams.

Third, the letters of John and Abigail Adams and the Family Letters of Thomas Jefferson, his Farm Book and his Account Book.

An unpublished paper at the University of Virginia Library by Jean Hanvey Hazelton, "The Hemings Family of Monticello," must be mentioned, as well as the Jefferson Lectures of Eric Erickson at Princeton University; Cornel Lengyel's *Four Days in July: The Autobiography of John Trumbull*, and the Nathan Schachner biographies of Thomas Jefferson and Aaron Burr.

Last to be mentioned: *The Jefferson Papers* of Julian Boyd and his article "The Murder of George Wythe," published in the *William and Mary Quarterly*; *Thomas Jefferson, The Darker Side*, by Leonard W. Levy; the catalog and the exhibition, "The Eye of Thomas Jefferson," organized by The National Gallery, Washington, D.C.; and Michael Durey's *With the*

ACKNOWLEDGMENTS

Hammer of Truth: James Callender and America's Early National Heroes, published in 1991.

I would like to thank the Schomburg Collection of Black Culture and its former director, Ruth-Ann Stewart Lewis, my researcher Rother Owens, my secretary and editorial assistant Carolyn Wilson, my editors, Richard and Janette Seaver, and especially Victoria Moreheim, Mary McCarthy, Lynn Nesbit, Mitch Douglas, my new editor, Cheryl Woodruff, who so elegantly and brilliantly brought *Sally Hemings* back into print, and my family and friends.

I would like to acknowledge with tenderness and friendship, Jacqueline Kennedy Onassis, who was the original editor on this book and acquired it for Viking Publishers in 1978. Her hospitality, her iron-clad determination that I should write this book, our conversations on love, power, sacrifice, and the presidency were both morally and intellectually essential to my taking on, in a first novel, the first American.

My final acknowledgment is to a nineteenth-century novel *Clotel, or the President's Daughter*, published in England in 1853 by William Wells Brown, a runaway slave, considered the father of the African American novel. Although I read the original version only after I wrote this book, I was touched to the quick by the recognition of cadences, themes, and wellsprings of feeling that are the roots of African American writing. That the theme of this novel, the first black novel published outside the United States, is the same and was written by an expatriate in the true sense of the word, only brings the circle full round.

SOURCE DOCUMENTS

Census Entry, Albemarle County, 1830 *(Courtesy of the Microfilm Division, The University of Virginia)*

Letter from Thomas Jefferson to Francis C. Gray, 1815 *(Writings, Thomas Jefferson [Monticello Edition], Lipscomb and Bergh, Volume XIV, pp. 267–71)*

Passport issued by Louis XVI for Thomas Jefferson, Maria and Martha Jefferson, James and Sally Hemings, 1789 *(Manuscript Division, The Library of Congress)*

Description of harvest at Monticello, List of Slave Workers *(Thomas Jefferson Garden Book [1795–96])*

Promise of Emancipation of James Hemings, 1793 *(Writings, Thomas Jefferson, Philadelphia, September 15, 1793, Boyd, 18 vols., Princeton)*

Two letters from James T. Callender to Thomas Jefferson, 1800 *(Manuscript Division, The Library of Congress)*

"The President Again," by James T. Callender, *The Richmond Recorder,* 1802 *(September 1, 1802, Archives, The Virginia State Library)*

The Census of My Family, Farm Book, Thomas Jefferson, 1807 *(Thomas Jefferson, Farm Book, 1807, Massachusetts Historical Society)*

SOURCE DOCUMENTS

The Slave Inventory and Advertisement of Slave Auction, Monticello, 1826 *(Courtesy of Jefferson Papers, University of Virginia Library, Manuscript Department. Notice from* Richmond Enquirer, *November 7, 1826, courtesy of Jefferson Memorial Foundation, Monticello)*

Excised portion of the Declaration of Independence, 1776 *(Manuscript Department, The Library of Congress)*

About the Author

BARBARA CHASE-RIBOUD was established as one of America's most passionate and distinguished historical novelists with her first book, *Sally Hemings*, which won the 1979 Janet Heidinger Kafka Prize as the best novel written by an American woman. She was awarded the 1988 Carl Sandburg Prize as best American poet for her second collection of poems, a melalogue, *Portrait of a Nude Woman as Cleopatra*.

Chase-Riboud is also the author of *Validé* and *Echo of Lions*. She is a graduate of Yale University and holds several honorary degrees. She has been the recipient of John Hay Whitney and National Endowment for the Arts Fellowships and was the first American woman to visit China after the revolution. The author divides her time between Paris and Rome, where she lives with her husband and two sons. She is currently at work on the third volume of The Sally Hemings Chronicles, *Liberty*.

THE PRESIDENT'S DAUGHTER

by

Barbara Chase-Riboud

A CROWN PUBLISHERS, INC., BOOK.

Now available in
THE LITERARY GUILD

Read on for the opening pages of
the extraordinary sequel to **SALLY HEMINGS...**

CHAPTER I

God, from the beginning, elected certain individuals to be saved
and certain others to be damned: and no crimes of the former can
damn them, nor virtue of the latter save them.

THOMAS JEFFERSON

THE DAY I ran away from Monticello as a white girl, I left my mother
standing in a tobacco field filled with moths and white blossoms, a good
way beyond the peach orchard and the mansion. My one thought was
that her only daughter was leaving her forever, and all she did was
stand there facing east, leaning into the wind as I had seen her do so
many times, as I imagined explorers did, her skirts whipping around
her, staring toward the Chesapeake Bay as if she could actually see the
ships, in this year of 1822, quitting the harbor, leaving port.

My mother was famous in Albemarle County, and had been ever
since I was born. People as far away as Richmond knew her as my father's concubine, mistress of his wardrobe, mother of his children. I was
one of those children, and my father, a celebrated and powerful man,
had hidden us away here for twenty years because of a scandal they
called "the troubles with Callender." I was never told any more about
it then, except that it made my mother the most famous bondswoman
in America and put me in double jeopardy. For despite my green eyes
and red hair and white skin, I was black. And despite my rich and brilliant father, I was a bastard.

As I approached, my mother remained as quiet and immobile as a
monument. I walked around her as if she were one. She was the most
silent woman I had ever known. Only her famous yellow eyes spoke
and they spoke volumes. Her eyes had always given her face the illusion
of transparency, as if one were gazing into a lighthouse beam. Those
eyes were gold leaf in an ivory mask, windows onto mysterious fires that
consumed everything and returned nothing to the surface. She was caring and kind to us children, but she surrounded herself in a shell of se-

crecy and disappointment that we were never able to penetrate, try as we might. We loved her, adored her, but we often wondered if she loved us.

"*Maman?*"

"*Laisse-moi.*" My mother spoke in the French she had taught me and which we used between ourselves all our lives.

"Maman, the carriage is waiting."

"I know. *Laisse-moi*, please leave me."

"*Au revoir, Maman.*"

My mother remained staring toward the bay.

"*Je t'écrirai, Maman . . .*"

"*Oui. Ecris-moi, ma fille.*"

"*Tu ne viens pas?*"

My mother looked at me as if I were mad. The yellow light of her eyes struck me like a blow.

"*Non, je ne viens pas.* I'm not coming," my mother said.

Last night, my mother had closed my trunks readied for Philadelphia, filled with my "strolling" trousseau.

"Promise me," she said, "that if you ever reveal your true identity to your future family, never tell your own children. Choose a female of your second generation, a granddaughter. Grandchildren are easier to talk to than your own children, and any secret is safer with your own sex."

"Why is that, *Maman?*"

"Women carry their secrets in their womb," she said, "hidden and nourished by their vital fluids and blood, while men," she continued, "carry their secrets like they carry their genitals, attached by a thin morsel of mortal flesh unable to resist either a caress or a good kick."

I'm not sure what passing for white meant to me in those days, except fleeing slavery and leaving home. In reality I was doing it for other people. For Maman. For Grandma. For Papa. I had no yearning for freedom because I had no specific definition of it. I hadn't even known I was a slave until I found out I couldn't do what I wanted to. And freedom was a vague and indiscriminate thing: neither animal nor mineral, neither real nor phantom. It wasn't solid like a field or a tree or a snap of cotton. I only knew what I'd seen and what my grandmother had said: "Get that freedom . . ." It became a possibility, or rather an enticing and kind of limitless labyrinth of possibilities, all of which I intended to explore, precisely to see what would happen . . .